# SKIN
# OF THEIR
# TEETH

## MICHELLE KIDD

JOFFE BOOKS

Joffe Books, London
www.joffebooks.com

First published in Great Britain in 2025

Cover art by Nebojša Zorić

ISBN: 978-1-80573-309-6

# Skin of their Teeth

## ALSO BY MICHELLE KIDD

### DI NICKI HARDCASTLE SERIES
Book 1: Missing Boy
Book 2: The Trophy Killer
Book 3: The Hardwick Heath Killer
Book 4: Skin of their Teeth

### DI JACK MCINTOSH SERIES
Book 1: Seven Days to Die
Book 2: Fifteen Reasons to Kill
Book 3: Sixteen Carved Pieces
Book 4: Twenty Years Buried
Book 5: Three Broken Bodies
Book 6: The Twelfth Floor
Book 7: No Red Lines

# PROLOGUE

*Crown Street, Bury St Edmunds*
*Wednesday 22 May 2019*

Jacob Towers raised his head towards the sky. With the night as clear as it was, all he could see was a carpet of winking stars. It was truly a beautiful sight. And it was while standing some forty feet above the ground that he came to realise he didn't know any of the stars' names, not a single one.

*Why don't I know what they're called? They've looked down on me every night of my forty years on this planet, and I don't even know their names.*

His brain careering into overdrive, Jacob felt a shudder travel the length of his spine. Blood thudded in his ears, while his stomach clenched with an ever-sickening squeeze.

*Was tonight a good night to die?*

It was a question he'd asked himself repeatedly that evening, and in the weeks leading up to it. Dragging in as deep a breath as his lungs could manage, he shuffled closer to the edge.

*Shit.*

How had it come to this?

Eyes still trained on the dark skies above, he started to wonder what would happen if he took that extra step and did the deed. Would his life flash before him like so many said it would? Jacob wasn't sure he particularly relished that thought. Acidic bile bubbled as memory after memory tumbled through his head. He would welcome one last look at his beautiful wife, Denise, and one last chance to gaze at his children. But there were other, more troubling parts of his life that he didn't wish to revisit, memories he'd done his utmost to forget, burying them deeper and deeper so he could convince himself they hadn't happened at all.

But, of course, he couldn't.

Memories, especially the ones you desperately wanted to hide, always managed to find their way out. Shit always floated to the top, wasn't that the saying?

And the very reason Jacob was standing here tonight was down to one such memory.

He glanced down at his feet as the temptation to edge forward surged again; one more step and it would all be over. He wouldn't have to deal with the guilt anymore. As he balanced on the edge, a curious thought entered his head.

*I wish I'd worn better shoes.*

He knew his underwear was clean, his clothes recently ironed — but his shoes were scuffed and tatty looking. Would that be how people remembered him? For having crappy shoes?

Dark humour twitched at his mouth. He could feel the dried blood encrusting his lips as his head pounded in rhythm with his rapidly increasing heart rate. His face throbbed. The pain had been partly tempered by the pills he'd swallowed, but it hadn't gone away completely. Pain never did — not true pain, anyway.

And he should know — he'd spent the last fourteen years trying to do just that.

*Wesley Barton.*

It was inevitable that Jacob would think of the man as he teetered on the edge. Some people might call it karma, the past finally catching up with him and giving him his long-overdue punishment — and maybe that was exactly what this was. Retribution. Revenge. Call it what you will, he was being made to pay for his past.

Barton may not have deserved to die the way he had, but as Jacob stood on the brink of his own mortality, he knew that jumping off the top of a tall building in Bury St Edmunds wasn't going to change that one bit.

# CHAPTER ONE

*Crown Street, Bury St Edmunds*

Detective Inspector Nicki Hardcastle ducked beneath the crime scene tape and made her way towards the huddle of bodies gathered up ahead. She'd heard the sirens earlier in the evening but had paid little attention to them. She was enjoying a few long-overdue days off and had embarked on a redecorating spree at her one-bedroom townhouse, the place being in desperate need of a freshen up.

Finding her younger brother Deano again after all this time had shocked her to the core. The way he'd been ripped from their lives so brutally almost twenty-three years ago had carved painful fissures deep into the Webster family, and such cracks would take time to heal, if they ever did. But what it had done was leave her craving a fresh start, a new beginning, which had led to the purchase of a variety of new shades of emulsion paint from the local DIY store.

She'd spent the day in a pair of baggy denim dungarees that had managed to catch most, but not necessarily all, of the wayward drips as she'd wielded her paintbrush, and had planned to spend the evening finishing off the front room.

But then the phone had rung.

*"You might want to see this one, boss."*

So, annual leave or no annual leave, Nicki had rushed out of the door minutes later, only stopping to put the lid back on the paint and dispose of her paintbrush.

Already dressed in a protective forensic suit, DS Graham Fox was waiting for her just outside the inner cordon at the junction of Crown Street and Honey Hill, beside St Mary's Church, the road itself now sealed off to traffic.

"What have we got, Graham?"

Fox gestured towards the white tent erected behind them, a flurry of activity from white-suited crime scene investigators already surrounding it. "Call came in at 10.19 this evening, the caller reported a person falling from the top of that house behind us."

Nicki instinctively looked skywards as they ducked under the tape. That would explain the emergency sirens she'd heard earlier, just as she was applying the final coat of French Grey to the walls surrounding the fireplace. She noted the building stretched over four floors, with an estate agents' FOR SALE sign fixed to the outside. "Does anyone live here?" From the dark recesses of her memory, she thought she could recall one of the houses in this stretch of road having scaffolding up recently, as if under renovation.

Fox soon confirmed her thoughts. "Currently uninhabited. The owners live in Portsmouth. Place has been undergoing redevelopment for the last few months and was put on the market three weeks ago. Initial reports say that the man was seen to jump from the roof."

*"Seen* to jump?" Nicki's eyebrows shot up. "We have an eyewitness?"

The detective sergeant nodded. "Of sorts, yes. A taxi driver was parked up back there, just outside the Dog and Partridge."

"So, it's definitely a jumper?" Just a few minutes' walk from her house on College Lane, the scene was chillingly close to home. Nicki tore her gaze away from the house. As she did so, she noticed the look on Fox's face and immediately knew there was more to come.

The detective sergeant grimaced in response. "So he says, but . . ." Fox nodded towards the white tent. "Best go and see for yourself, I think."

Nicki accepted the white protective suit and pulled it on over her paint-splattered dungarees. She caught an enquiring look from Fox as she snapped on a pair of gloves. "Don't ask," she sighed. "Long story."

The pair made their way over to the tent, the flaps held back for them as they approached. Nicki recognised Faye Armstrong, crime scene manager, standing a few feet away in conversation with a member of her forensic team. They exchanged a nod.

"I'm told Dr Mitchell is on her way — stuck in traffic, apparently. Town seems to be gridlocked tonight." Fox let Nicki enter the tent ahead of him, a tent which enclosed the whole front entrance of the house, including the steps — and Nicki soon saw why.

The body was lying face down, impaled on a thick black metal spike, the end of which protruded from the man's back. Blood had soaked through the front of his clothing, collecting on the pavement below. She'd witnessed the aftermath of someone impaled on a railing before, and it was never pretty. Depending which organs the spike hit on its way through, blood loss could be significant and death prolonged.

Nicki caught Fox's eye. "Nasty. What makes us think this isn't just some tragic accident or suicide? Because I'm assuming that's where this is going?"

"We've already managed to ascertain a few facts about the deceased, and the time immediately leading up to the fall, but things don't quite seem to add up."

Nicki's eyebrows hitched. "Don't quite add up how?"

Without further word, Fox slowly bent down to retrieve a plastic evidence bag. "His mobile phone survived the impact, and the screen was locked to a parking reminder — informing him that his parking session in Ram Meadow car park ran out at eight p.m."

Nicki's brow creased as she cast her eyes towards the phone sealed in the transparent bag, her brain starting to connect the dots. "You're wondering why our victim bothered to pay for parking if he intended to jump off the top of this building."

Fox made a face. "Well, yes, there's that."

"What time do we think he jumped?"

"According to the taxi driver, just before he made the call, so 10.19 or thereabouts. But that's not all — we also have a name."

Nicki watched the detective sergeant swap the evidence bag for another identical one. "The officers first on scene checked for an ID and found a wallet in his back pocket. Inside, we have a driving licence in the name of Jacob Towers — a local man, judging by the address. The photo is a good likeness, and we also have bank cards with the same name, so it looks to me like we have our ID. There was one other thing — another patrol car was on its way to the scene when they got caught up in traffic behind a Tesco van making a delivery." Fox straightened up and caught Nicki's eye. "You'll never guess whose house they were delivering to."

Nicki let her gaze travel back down to the body still impaled on the spike, and then the wallet encased in the plastic bag still in Fox's hand. "I'm guessing that would be our Mr Towers."

Fox nodded. "Order placed at ten o'clock yesterday morning."

Nicki bit her lip as she followed the detective sergeant out from the tent and back towards the crime scene tape. "I see what you mean. Yesterday our deceased places a supermarket food shop, then today drives into town and pays for parking." She half turned to look back over her shoulder and once again let her eyes drift skywards. "Before jumping to his death off the top of a four-storey house."

"That's about the size of it. There's just something about it that niggles me, and it must have struck some kind of chord with those first on scene, too, because they called it in."

All thoughts of finishing the final coat of French Grey now sidelined, Nicki hovered on the other side of the inner cordon. "Let's keep the scene preserved — treat it as suspicious until we know otherwise. You mentioned Caz was on her way?"

Fox nodded. "Caught up in the same traffic jam as the patrol car, I think. But things have eased now. She shouldn't be much longer."

Sensing a long night ahead, Nicki pulled her phone from her pocket and extracted a twenty-pound note from its casing. "I'll wait here for her to arrive — how do you fancy trying to persuade someone nearby to give us some decent coffee?"

\* \* \*

*Maynewater Lane, Bury St Edmunds*

The overwhelming temptation was to stay, to stop and watch the circus as it began to unfold. But it would be a risk far beyond the one he was willing to take. And he'd stayed long enough as it was. He wasn't stupid. There was too much to lose, and still so much he needed to do.

Sliding back into the shadows, he made his way along the deserted street to where he'd left the car — far enough away not to attract suspicion, but close enough for a discreet getaway. He'd skulked in the shadows long enough to hear the sirens, their sound momentarily causing his heart to skip a beat. Knowing what they would be heading towards, and what they would find when they got there, gave him a dark thrill. But his presence was no longer required or indeed advised.

Another fluttering filled his heart as he pulled the cap more firmly down onto his head and masked his emerging smile. The plan was working, another step completed.

Although the sirens were now silent, the urge to turn back and witness the aftermath of his handiwork continued to build. With his footsteps only faltering for a moment or two, he instead continued on his way. The end was so close now; he couldn't afford to make a silly error like returning to the scene. They did that in the movies, and it never ended well.

Besides, he still had four more to go.

\* \* \*

*4 Old Railway Cottages, Dullingham, Nr Newmarket*

The cold sweat clung to his skin, making him shiver. How sweat could be cold had always baffled him. Sitting bolt upright in bed, he wiped his brow and pushed the damp duvet away. Waking up in the middle of the night, heart pounding, was nothing new to Dean Webster — but it was no less disturbing when it happened.

The nightmares hadn't come straight away; it had taken several years for them to fully develop. As a child, he would have vivid dreams of knights and dragons, spacecraft and aliens, witches and wizards — looking forward to bedtime, wondering what magical land he would be transported to next.

But as he grew older the dreams started to change.

And then they weren't dreams anymore — they were nightmares.

Glancing at the bedside clock, he noted it was only one thirty in the morning and reached for the glass of water he was now accustomed to bringing to bed. As the cool liquid quenched the dry fire in his throat, he felt his heart rate at last begin to settle. Pushing the rest of the duvet onto the floor, he leaned back against the damp pillows and closed his eyes. If he was lucky, he might drift off again for a few more hours before the day began.

The nightmare that had ripped him from sleep was always the same, yet always somehow different, too. It would begin the same way — with the same sense of adventure and excitement building. Five-year-old Dean Webster would be alone on the caterpillar ride, but being alone didn't scare him.

Being alone meant he was a big boy now — riding the caterpillar *all by himself.*

Although it was a dream, Dean could still feel the frosty night air whipping past his cheeks as the ride gathered momentum, feel the lurch of his stomach as the caterpillar negotiated the dips and bends. In hindsight, and with the wisdom of his advancing years, Dean knew the ride hadn't really been going all that fast — but five-year-old Dean Webster had thought it to be as fast as the wind, maybe even as fast as a space rocket. Despite wearing the woolly bobble hat his mother always insisted he put on to ward off the cold, he still felt the chill as the caterpillar went around for the second time.

When the ride was over and the safety barriers raised, Dean climbed out of his seat, grinning and eager for more. He was sure his sister would let him ride it again, so he ran to the end of the walkway to search for her. But as all the other children melted away into the night, he was left with nothing.

And no one.

It hadn't worried him to begin with — still feeling so exhilarated from the ride — but it didn't take long for trepidation to sneak in, pushing his excitement aside.

*Where's Nicki?*

Pulling his bobble hat further down over his ears, the cold now starting to chill his exposed skin, the euphoria from the ride was quickly wearing off.

*Where is she?*

At some point, a hand had extended towards him — a kind hand, a soft hand. A hand that would take care of him.

Eyes snapping open, Dean took another gulp of water. Since discovering the truth about his past, the dreams — or nightmares as he now reluctantly called them — were coming much more frequently. Before, he could go months without thinking back to that fateful night, but over the past few weeks they were coming almost daily.

As he lay back in the dark, he let the memories continue to tumble, knowing it was better that way. If he tried to close them down, tried to ignore them, they would only haunt him for the rest of the night. Best to let nature take its course — the past would sort itself out, given time.

Inevitably, his thoughts turned to his sister. Did she experience similar dreams about that night? Did their parents? And what about the Brownings? Or was he the only one?

As the cold sweat subsided, he grabbed the duvet back up from the floor and reached for the sketch pad and pencil box he always kept on the bedside table. Knowing a return to sleep was unlikely, he decided to make use of the time and selected a charcoal pencil.

# CHAPTER TWO

*Bury St Edmunds Police Station*
*Thursday 23 May 2019*

Nicki had returned home to change out of her paint-splattered dungarees in the early hours but hadn't really slept. She'd tried, but it just wouldn't come. Instead, she headed out at seven thirty to pick up a round of pastries before making her way into the station. There was a long day ahead and the team would need sustenance; she could already sense the case wasn't going to be straightforward, soon sapping everyone's strength, and testing their resolve to the limit.

The morning had dawned bright and crisp, but the clear skies last night had meant it was a chilly start to the day for late May. She had decided to try out her new boots, but as she hadn't worn them before they were feeling stiff and had already started to rub.

"Whatever else you've got on at the moment, shelve it. We need to make this one our priority." Nicki deposited the greaseproof paper bags onto a central table. "Dig in."

"Definitely a suspicious death, then, boss?" DS Royston Carter, the team's newest recruit, got up from his seat to inspect the bags. Playing a key role in the Lucas Jackson investigation last year, which had earned him a fractured cheekbone, cracked ribs and a concussion in the process, he'd quickly become a loyal and trusted officer. "Not suicide?"

"That remains to be seen, Roy. Let's keep our options open." Nicki accepted the tall mug with BOSS emblazoned on the side, handed to her by DC Darcie Butler. Darcie was a promising young detective constable, quick-witted and smart, and Nicki had high hopes for her progression. She was the sister of one of Nicki's best friends, Amy, who worked in the emergency department at the West Suffolk Hospital. "But there's enough here to warrant us treating it as suspicious. Unexplained at the very least." She took a sip of the hot coffee, grateful for its warmth, before turning towards DS Fox. "Graham? You fancy giving us a round-up of what we know so far?"

Fox jumped to his feet, swiping up a pastry from the table as he approached the series of whiteboards fastened to the incident room walls. As well as being Nicki's most experienced officer in the team, Graham Fox was also the most respected — but it hadn't always been that way. The two of them had worked together as sergeants for many years before Nicki earned her promotion to detective inspector, and her rise up the ranks seemed to temporarily drive a wedge between them. Surly, impertinent and downright rude at times, Fox had developed an almost wilful disregard for following rules and instructions. At one point Nicki wondered how it all might end. But then they turned a corner — Fox admitting that his poor behaviour had been prompted by the breakdown of his marriage and separation from his children. It wasn't an excuse, but a reason nonetheless — and now that he was in a better head space, on a more even keel professionally and personally, the detective was back to his best.

It was something Nicki was grateful for.

"Although awaiting a formal ID, we believe our deceased to be a male by the name of Jacob Towers. Age forty, living out on Copse Close. Graphic designer by profession, he had a wife, Denise, and two children, Amber and Zeb." Fox paused to write the details up onto the first whiteboard, which already had the randomly generated name *Operation Jackdaw* scrawled across the top. "He was seen by a taxi driver shortly before he fell, up on the roof of a house on Crown Street, looking as though he was about to jump. The taxi driver was parked a little further up the road, close to the Dog and Partridge pub, and immediately called 999 on his mobile. When he looked back, our deceased jumped." Fox finished annotating the board. "Crime scene photos are being sent over but, believe me, it'll put you off your breakfast."

"Why do we think it's a suspicious death, if the man was seen to jump?" DC Matt Holland ripped into a warm sausage roll. A member of Nicki's team for the last five years, Matt was an avid Ipswich Town football fan — something his friend and colleague DC Duncan Jenkins often clashed with him over, Duncan being a stalwart Norwich City fan. The pair usually exchanged good-natured football banter, but tensions could sometimes fray when it was derby day.

Fox turned away from the whiteboard. "At the moment we only have the taxi driver's word for it. He seems to be our only eyewitness, which is surprising as it wasn't all that late at night and Crown Street can get quite busy. However, no one else has yet come forward. I guess as it was a Wednesday night, things were quiet. Suspicions were raised at the scene when the deceased's mobile phone was retrieved. The handset survived the fall intact and was locked to a parking reminder message. Towers had paid for three hours' parking at Ram Meadow which was due to expire at eight o'clock. In addition to this, our deceased booked a supermarket food delivery which arrived around ten thirty last night."

"And *those* are our suspicions?" DC Duncan Jenkins joined his colleague in picking out a sausage roll from the greaseproof paper bags, but his tone was more cautious. "A parking ticket and a food delivery? Doesn't sound like much to me. Surely this could still be explained by suicide? He *was* seen to jump, after all."

Nicki took a long sip from her coffee mug, grateful for the caffeine hit. "I hear what you're saying, but I'm not totally convinced yet. It's enough to raise a suspicion, at least." Rubbing her eyes, the lack of sleep threatening to catch up with her, she focused on the sparse details populating the whiteboard. "Let's see what CCTV there is in the area. Anything that shows him in the street outside and, crucially, if he was alone."

"How did he manage to get up there at that time of night anyway?" Matt brushed flakes of pastry from his shirt. "Surely the place would have been locked up?"

"That's definitely something we'll have to look into," confirmed Nicki. "We left Faye and her team at the scene last night, but initial reports suggest there was no obvious forced entry."

"Well, it all sounds suspicious to me." Darcie had opted for a warm croissant and was washing it down with a mug of tea. "If he was planning to kill himself, why would he bother to pay for parking beforehand? And book a food delivery? None of it makes any sense."

"Maybe he decided to kill himself *after* he'd paid for the car park — and the food delivery was ordered the day before anyway." Duncan rammed the last of his sausage roll into his mouth. "Maybe his wife put the order in. I think it's more than plausible that this could still be a suicide."

"Plausible, yes, but until it's definite, we investigate." Nicki placed her half-drunk mug down. "We certainly need to have a chat with the taxi driver, find out what he did or didn't see. And we also need to go and see the wife. Matt and Duncan, can you handle getting CCTV from surrounding streets and see if we can locate our deceased in the area beforehand? Check any car park cameras, too." She received nods in response. "And get in touch with the estate agents — we'll need to establish how he managed to gain access to the roof. And, obviously, get that phone looked at."

Walking over to the table, Nicki eyed the Danish pastries and felt her stomach grumble. She'd left home early without eating that morning, but her appetite was dampened by what she was about to say next. Pausing for a moment, she turned and faced her team.

"And then, of course, we have to consider the teeth."

\* \* \*

*Woodlands Camping and Caravan Site, Suffolk*

Slamming down the lid of his laptop, he felt the familiar frustration spark. How many times did someone need telling before they did what they were asked? The man was stalling. The last message he'd sent had sounded abrupt, he knew, maybe even verging on rude. But he had a timetable to keep to.

The man had come highly recommended — apparently, the only person suitable for such a high-risk job — but as the days ticked by, he questioned whether that was really the case. Not for the first time, he wondered if he could just go and do the job himself, stop wasting time. But caution always stopped him.

*Caution.*

Did he really need to be that cautious? Careful, he could understand, but cautious? There was a world of difference between the two.

He may not have done all that well at school, leaving with only a small handful of below-average grades that had served him poorly ever since, but he was a million miles away from stupid. Some of his teachers had called him "exceptionally bright" — one had even written on his school reports that he was "gifted" — but ultimately, everyone had agreed that he "refused to apply himself".

Well, he was applying himself now, wasn't he?

Turning his attention back to the laptop, he resisted the urge to send a follow-up message. It would only serve to infuriate him more if it went unanswered. Instead, he would give the man twenty-four hours; if he still hadn't received a reply with confirmation of when the deed would be done, then he would take matters into his own hands.

Satisfied for the moment, he willed his tense shoulders to relax and reached for his phone, pulling up the local news headlines. The elation he'd felt after last night's events had slowly evaporated as the hours passed, and now all he could find online was a brief mention of an "incident" overnight which had closed several town centre roads. He knew he had to be patient.

Pushing frustration from his mind, a taut smile flickered on his thin lips. As much as he wanted to savour Jacob Towers' demise, he had to move on.

It was time to turn his attention to the next one.

\* \* \*

*Bury St Edmunds Police Station*

"The teeth?" Darcie's hand hovered in front of her face, a second croissant about to brush her lips. "What about his teeth?"

Fox stepped in. "Probably the fact that most of them were inside his pockets, rather than inside his mouth."

Darcie dropped the pastry back onto her desk. "You're joking?"

The look on Fox's face told her that he wasn't. "Unfortunately not. Seven teeth were found in the deceased's trouser pockets — three in one, four in the other."

"*Seven teeth?*" Darcie's mouth hung agape. "Why on earth . . . ?"

Nicki resumed her position by the first whiteboard. "That's what we need to find out. It might not be connected, of course. There was evidence of blood around his face and inside his mouth, suggesting the loss of the teeth could well be recent. These details are understandably being withheld from the press for the time being."

"OK," conceded Duncan. "So maybe it does sound like it might not be a straightforward suicide." He swallowed the last of his sausage roll. "Or at the least it's suspicious."

Nicki nodded. "That's my thinking. Until we know for sure, let's see what we can uncover."

Fox caught Nicki's eye. "I'm told a family liaison officer will be heading over to the Towers' home this morning. I'm assuming we'll be joining them?" He received a nod in response.

"Definitely, and sooner rather than later. We need to build up a picture of our deceased as quickly as we can, try and find out how and why he fell."

"But it *still* could be a suicide, couldn't it?" Darcie tentatively picked the croissant back up. "Not something more sinister?"

"Could be suicide, could be an accident. Could be anything in between." Nicki started heading for the door. "I've got a few things to tidy up in my office. Graham — be ready to come and see the taxi driver with me. Then we'll call in on Mrs Towers. I'll give the mortuary a call and see when the post-mortem might happen, too. It would be useful if someone could head over."

Roy shot a hand in the air. "Happy to go when needed."

"Thanks, Roy. I'll let you know the timings before we leave." After agreeing with Fox to set out in half an hour, Nicki left the team to it. Hurrying towards her office, she prayed she didn't run into DCI Turner. She'd been doing her best to avoid him over the last few weeks, but not for any specific reason other than needing some space. Malcolm Turner was a family friend — her father and the DCI having worked together for many years in the past — and he always meant well. But her brother's reappearance had rocked her in ways she hadn't expected, and she needed time alone to process her thoughts.

Yet she knew she couldn't avoid the man forever. Their paths would cross again soon, especially with the new investigation up and running, so maybe she should just get it over with — put on her big-girl pants and go and see him herself.

*Maybe.*

Nicki closed the office door behind her.

Maybe another time — because right now, she had an investigation to run.

# CHAPTER THREE

*Severn Road, Bury St Edmunds*

"Thank you for seeing us, Mr Horner." Nicki slipped into an armchair by the window of the modest mid-terraced house. "It's very much appreciated."

"I'm not sure I can add much more to what I've said already." The taxi driver's tone was guarded.

"That may be so, but it's always useful to revisit things while they're still fresh in people's minds. It can be surprising how many additional details people remember second time around."

Dennis Horner gave a shrug, his expression telling Nicki the man wasn't convinced. "If you say so."

Nicki bit her tongue and maintained the forced smile on her face. "The sooner we get this done, the sooner you can get back to your busy day." She eyed the man sitting opposite her on a two-seater sofa, a small, squat coffee table between them. He was a short man, barely over five foot five in his socks, if Nicki cared to measure him — which she didn't. His grubby white vest barely covered the bulging belly that flopped over the waistband of his jogging bottoms, and he peered out from beneath pudgy, hooded eyelids.

The remnants of a full English breakfast decorated a chipped plate on the coffee table — some of which had also made its way onto the grubby vest — and on the arm of the sofa was a copy of the day's *Racing Post*, folded back to show the runners and riders at today's meeting at Nottingham. It appeared Dennis Horner had a busy day planned already.

Although he'd been at the scene last night, Nicki had barely acknowledged the taxi driver, having been too busy speaking to Faye and later Caz Mitchell, when the pathologist had eventually battled through the traffic. But in a thirteen-year career, she'd managed to pick up a thing or two along the way, and there was something about Dennis Horner that she didn't quite like — something that went beyond his dishevelled appearance and apparent disinterest in their visit that morning. Putting her prejudice to one side, she plastered a fresh smile onto her face and continued.

"If you could just take us through what happened yesterday evening, it would be most helpful." Nicki watched Fox take out his notebook. "What caused you to be in Crown Street at that time?"

Horner grunted as he shifted his weight on the sofa. "I'd had a call down Southgate Street, but when I turned up there was no answer. Another bloody waste of time. After a while, I gave up — drove off and pulled up outside the pub on Crown Street. Gave the office a call to let them know what had happened."

"And how long were you parked on Crown Street before you noticed someone standing on the roof?"

Horner puffed out his cheeks, his jowls wobbling as he did so. After rubbing his bulbous nose with a stubby finger, he shrugged. "I'm not sure, not long. Maybe five minutes or so? Maybe ten?"

"Five or ten minutes?" Nicki cast a pleasant, yet probing gaze towards the man opposite, her nerves starting to grate. "That's quite a long time to sit in a car, especially as I believe it might have been on a double yellow line. Were you doing anything in particular to pass the time?"

The taxi driver's blotchy cheeks reddened. "Well, when I say five or ten minutes, it could have been less. Maybe just a couple, you know how it is."

"I'm not sure that I do, Mr Horner." Nicki's tone sharpened. "These 'five or ten minutes' could be crucial. Especially for the person standing forty feet above the ground. Maybe you could think again and try to be a little more precise." She knew her words sounded harsh, but in the circumstances felt they were justified. Time was ticking; they still had Denise Towers to visit, and it wasn't something she was especially looking forward to. The investigation may only be twelve hours old, but her patience was already starting to wear thin. "*If* you would be so kind," she added, trying to inject some empathy into her voice.

Although the taxi driver's expression suggested otherwise, he seemed to give a conciliatory nod. "OK, so I might have looked at a couple of websites on my phone after I'd called the office. I was due a break, like, and I was pissed off at getting mucked around again. It happens all too often some nights — hoax calls. People think it's funny."

"What kind of websites?"

"Does it matter?"

Nicki found herself biting her tongue once again. "Probably not, but the whole point of asking these questions is to try and get as much information as possible. How long do you think you were looking at these 'websites' before you noticed someone on the top of the building?" She glanced sideways to DS Fox, who was busy scribbling in his notebook. "I could ask for your phone to be analysed, Mr Horner, but it would be a much simpler process if you just cooperated. Quite frankly, I couldn't care less what you were looking at, or the fact that you were parked illegally, but I do care about the poor man whose life was ended last night."

The taxi driver's already flushed face took on a sheepish look. Eventually he nodded. "I sat in my car for about ten minutes after ringing the office. I was looking at some online stuff — all above board and legit, you know. Nothin' illegal. It was just after quarter past ten, because I remember looking at my dashboard clock to see how much longer my shift was. It was then that I noticed him up on the roof."

"Go on." Nicki edged further towards the coffee table. "What in particular did you notice about him?"

The man shrugged. "Not a lot to begin with, like. I mean, people have rooftop gardens around here, don't they? They like to go up and enjoy the view."

"They do," agreed Nicki. *But what* is *unusual is having half your teeth in your pocket at the time.* She let it go. "Is there anything else about him that you can remember?"

There was another puff of the cheeks, followed by another shrug. "I watched him for a few seconds, like, and then I saw him climb up onto the ledge."

"He climbed up onto the ledge? You actually saw that?"

The taxi driver nodded, jowls wobbling. "I did."

"And did you see anyone else up there with him? Or someone outside the house, on the ground?"

A shake of the head followed, together with a fruity-sounding cough. "No. I never saw anyone else. Just him."

"I see. And what happened next?"

"I couldn't quite believe what I was seeing, to be honest. I thought it was maybe a prank, someone having a laugh." The taxi driver paused and took in a breath, his blotchy cheeks paling a little. "But then he straightened up, and it looked like he was moving closer to the edge. It was then that I knew he was gonna jump."

Nicki's eyebrows hitched. "What made you so certain?"

"Well, he wouldn't be standing up there otherwise, would he? Close to the edge and that?" Horner gave another shrug. "It just looked that way to me."

"OK, and what did you do next?"

"I called 999."

"Straight away?" Nicki already knew the time the call was made, and the taxi driver's account was stacking up so far.

Horner nodded. "Pretty much, yeah. I might have watched him for a couple more seconds, but then I called it in." The man paused, a haunted look crossing his puffy face. "For all the good it did. Didn't stop him jumping, did it?"

"Did you *see* him jump?"

More wobbling of the jowls followed as the taxi driver nodded. "Yeah, he fell right there in front of me, didn't he? Landed on one of them spikes. I won't ever forget seeing that, I can tell you."

"But the question I'm asking you, Mr Horner, is did you *see* him jump?" A frown formed on Nicki's brow. "I know you saw him falling, but did you actually see him *jump*?"

"Same thing, isn't it?"

Nicki shook her head. "No, Mr Horner, it's not the same thing at all. Think back — did you actually see the man jump off the roof?"

Silence filled the small front room as the taxi driver pondered the question. Eventually, he replied. "No, I suppose not."

\* \* \*

*4 Old Railway Cottages, Dullingham, Nr Newmarket*

Dean Webster rested his head against the back of the sofa and sighed. The restless night had soon turned into a restless morning, and he'd eventually risen before the sun. But now the lack of sleep was catching up with him.

*Dean Webster.*

It was taking some getting used to — his new name.

Although not exactly new as such, it was still new to him — as new as the driving licence and passport that had dropped through the letterbox that morning.

Dean Edward Webster.

His *real* name.

Seeing his birth certificate for himself had probably been the defining moment — the moment he realised everything was real, and not some far-fetched work of fiction or one of his crazy dreams.

He really was Dean Webster.

His parents had visited many times over the last few weeks, and he still found it odd calling them that. *Parents.* There had been a faint flicker of recognition when they'd first met, something stirring from deep within, but it had been nearly twenty-three years since they'd last been together as a family. When he looked in the mirror now, he could see that he looked like them — more so his father than his mother. They had the same square jaw, the same deep brown eyes. But he felt he had his mother's personality.

Taken from a November funfair by Annette and Larry Browning, he'd grown up believing his parents and sister were dead and spent the next two decades being brought up by his new family. The fact that his real family was still very much alive was a lot to digest, and he was still processing much of it.

Initially he'd felt elated at the reunion with his parents and Nicki, the next moment he'd felt heartbroken at the family that he'd lost. Annette and Larry had been good to him, there was no getting away from that; as a child, he'd wanted for nothing, and to start with he'd felt protective of them. But it didn't take long for his emotions to start shifting, heading towards anger instead — anger at a life taken away from him, at a life denied to him.

Annette and Larry had been remanded in custody, charged with abduction, preventing a lawful burial and failing to report a death, but Dean hadn't been to visit them. He didn't feel he could face them. What would he even say?

Nicki had immediately suggested he move in with her, but she lived in a one-bedroom townhouse and space was already tight. Dean knew she still felt awash with guilt over what had happened that cold November night — he could see it in her eyes every time they met. Maybe that was why she'd asked him to move in, to settle her conscience.

He'd also resisted the call to move down to Rye to live with their parents. That was a step he wasn't quite ready for yet. They would all get past the hurt one day, learn to live with what had happened, but it would have to be at a pace he was comfortable with.

So, he'd decided to stay exactly where he was — here in the Brownings' house in Dullingham, with Ade.

Adrian Browning had been his family for over twenty-two years and, although they were as different as chalk and cheese, with regular fallouts and spats, they rubbed along all right together. And, if the truth be known, Ade was the one constant that he needed right now — the one person to offer him stability and familiarity in what were otherwise choppy and unchartered waters. He knew it sounded strange, but it was a past that still held fond memories for him. He couldn't just turn his back on it all and pretend none of it had happened.

So, for now, Dean sought calm — and he sought quiet. Neither were attributes Ade particularly possessed to any great degree, but Dean felt that his brother — and he still found himself calling Ade his brother — needed him more than Annette and Larry did. Maybe even more than Nicki and their parents did.

So, here he would stay.

*For now.*

"Fancy a beer?" Adrian Browning stepped into Dean's sightline. "Looks like you could do with one."

"Cheers, Ade." Dean reached for the beer his brother was dangling in front of him, a beer he didn't really want. He wasn't a great drinker at the best of times, and it was only ten in the morning — but he also didn't want to appear unappreciative of the gesture. They'd had a fractured relationship over the years, Ade often voicing his displeasure at Dean landing into the Browning family so suddenly and then quickly becoming the favoured son. Ade had a quick temper and even quicker fists at times.

Now Adrian sank into one of the armchairs, gulping from his bottle. From the look in his eyes, Dean suspected it wasn't the first he'd had that morning. "You been to see Mum and Dad yet?"

Dean had been on the receiving end of the same question multiple times over the past few weeks, and he always gave the same answer. "No, not yet." He wondered if his brother was merely asking to get a degree of justification for his own refusal to see them.

"Me neither," came the expected response. "Don't know that I will."

"You working today?" Dean nodded towards the almost empty beer bottle in his brother's hand.

Adrian gave a quick shake of his head before sinking the rest of the beer. "Nope. Thought I might chill here today, do some gym work."

Dean had noticed the subtle transformation in his brother's physique over the last few weeks. Ade hadn't been a particularly large person to begin with, but he'd trimmed down, becoming leaner and fitter as the weeks had passed. Well-defined and sculpted muscles were now visible beneath his tight T-shirt.

"You should try it. Come into the garage for a session, I'll lend you some gear."

It wasn't the first time Ade had offered Dean a pair of boxing gloves and the use of his equipment, and each time Dean had politely declined. "Maybe another time, mate. I've got some work to finish today." Taking advantage of the excuse to escape, Dean hauled himself out of the sofa, taking his untouched beer with him. "Speaking of which, I'd best crack on."

* * *

*Copse Close, Bury St Edmunds*

Nicki and Fox were shown into the Towerscs' front room. Well furnished, the walls were decorated in pastel shades, the carpet was a soft cream. As they entered, a light and airy fragrance of orchids or lilies greeted them. But Nicki was all too aware of how appearances could be deceptive, for there was nothing light and airy about the Towers family home right now.

"Please take a seat." Denise Towers gestured towards a floral three-seater sofa below the main window. "Can I get you a tea or maybe some coffee?"

Nicki smiled sadly. "We're fine, Mrs Towers. Unless you would like one?" She caught the eye of DC Karen Gedge, the family liaison officer, who'd been the one to answer the door and let them into the three-bedroom link-detached house. DC Gedge started edging towards the hallway, but Denise Towers was already raising a trembling hand.

"Not for me. I think I'm all tea'd out." She tried a faint laugh. "Thank you, anyway."

Nicki and Fox sat down on the sofa while Mrs Towers took an armchair. Nicki noted how fragile the woman looked, as if she were made of brittle glass and could shatter at a moment's notice. Face devoid of make-up, her eyes brimmed with fresh tears. Nicki gave her as soft a smile as she could manage.

Judging by the dark circles beneath Denise Towers' eyes, Nicki suspected the woman hadn't slept since the news was delivered late last night — and was probably unlikely to do so for a good while to come. Grief manifested itself so differently from person to person, and Nicki had seen it all. Some would howl like wounded animals, while others stoically tried to hold it all together, keeping their true emotions locked inside. Others would resort to kicking and screaming as their pain deepened, taking their desperation out on the people closest to them. There was no right or wrong way to react, each was as individual as the way their loved one had been ripped from their lives.

Denise Towers simply oozed pain and heartache from every pore.

Nicki felt her own heart clench. She'd only been ten at the time of her brother's disappearance but could distinctly remember the police presence in the family home — it seemed to go on for days, maybe even weeks. And then came the inevitable stream of well-meaning visitors, neighbours calling by to offer their sympathies accompanied by a chicken casserole or pasta bake. Nicki could still recall her mother's grief-stricken screams bouncing off the walls. Not long after had come the arguments, as her parents tried to navigate their loss and find someone other than themselves to blame for what had happened. At ten years old, Nicki hadn't been emotionally mature enough to fully appreciate what her parents were going through, but she certainly could now.

And Denise Towers was displaying all the classic signs of a woman on the edge.

"Where are the children, Mrs Towers? Amber and Zeb, isn't it?" Nicki had noticed the family photographs on the sideboard as they'd entered — two blond-haired, blue-eyed children smiling into the camera lens. From the pictures, she assumed them to be twins.

"They've gone to stay with my parents — they don't live far away." Denise's voice quivered. "I just . . . I haven't told them yet. It's all so . . . all so . . ." The words seemed to stick in her throat as another sob escaped her lips. She dabbed at the tears streaming down her cheeks with the sleeve of her cardigan.

Nicki looked away. It was a part of the job that she disliked immensely. Although necessary, she couldn't help but feel they were trampling all over the woman's grief in their big size nines; shouldering themselves, uninvited, into the family's most private space. Were they making the heartache worse with their presence? Nicki wasn't sure they could make anything worse, but it made her feel uncomfortable all the same. Which was why she wasn't planning to stay long.

DC Gedge brought over a box of tissues, placing them on the side of Denise's armchair. The experienced family liaison officer provided a crucial link between the family of the deceased and the investigation team. Nicki and DS Fox would eventually take their intrusive questions with them, but Karen would remain behind for as long as necessary. The more they found out about the family, and about Jacob Towers in particular, the more likely they would stumble across the reason why the man had ended up on top of the house in Crown Street last night. And then what had caused him to fall.

"Is there any news?"

The question caught Nicki off guard. Close relatives often put off asking questions about the investigation, because asking questions made the whole thing real. If they didn't ask, then maybe they could convince themselves that none of it was happening and it was all just some terrible misunderstanding.

"Nothing yet, Mrs Towers, but it's very early on in the investigation. The reason we've come to see you this morning is to get as much background on your husband as we can. Do you think you'll be able to do that for us?"

Nicki watched the woman shudder, but it was quickly followed by a nod. "Of course, anything. Anything to help."

Fox slipped his notebook from his pocket while Nicki shifted in her seat. "How long have you been married, Mrs Towers?" Nicki wondered if her opening question would be too raw, but she needed to get a feel for the couple's relationship. If Jacob *had* jumped to his death, there would need to be a reason — and his wife could be the key to unlocking it.

"It was our twelfth wedding anniversary last year. We went to Athens." Nicki's heart clenched as she witnessed the raw pain on the woman's face deepen. "We've been together since we were fifteen — classic childhood sweethearts." Denise Towers choked back a sob. "He's my whole world."

"I'm so sorry, Mrs Towers. This must be so painful for you." Nicki watched the woman pull one of the tissues from the box, knowing her words were insufficient. She caught DC Gedge's eye. "Maybe that cup of tea would be a good idea after all, Karen?"

Nicki waited for the family liaison officer to leave the room before resuming her questioning. "Have you lived in the town long?"

"For the last nine years. We moved up from London. Jacob works . . ." Denise caught herself, seeming to visibly wince at talking about her husband in the present tense. "He worked from home as a graphic designer. It meant he could be here for the twins — while I picked up some part-time work with a cleaning agency. It suited us."

Nicki nodded. "I know this will be a tough question, Mrs Towers, but how was your husband's mental health recently?" She heard the woman draw in a sharp breath. "I'm sorry to have to ask, but it could be important."

Denise lowered her gaze to her lap, where she proceeded to pull apart the damp tissue in her trembling hands. "I know," she whispered. "I know."

A heavy silence filled the room, and it was a silence Nicki didn't want to break. Although time was ticking on, she didn't want to rush the woman. Karen quietly slipped back into the room, bringing a tray laden with mugs of tea that nobody wanted to drink.

With the unwanted tea distributed, eventually Denise took in a deep breath. "Jacob struggled sometimes, I won't lie. But it wasn't new. It was something he'd dealt with for many years. And he was coping — at least, I thought he was. He'd tried therapy some years ago — weekly meetings with a counsellor — and it seemed to help."

"Was he on any medication?"

Denise shook her head. "Not that I know of. And I'm sure he would have told me if he was." A fresh wave of tears started trickling down the woman's cheeks. "He was prescribed anti-depressants — I'm not sure exactly when, probably shortly after the therapy — but he said he didn't want to take them. He said he could cope without them." Denise held Nicki's inquisitive stare, her eyes starting to widen. "You're not saying that . . ." A hand flew to her mouth. "He *killed* himself?"

Nicki winced. Had Jacob Towers killed himself? She really didn't know. She tried an apologetic smile. "We don't know at this stage, I'm afraid. Which is why we need to find out all we can about him, about how he'd been feeling recently." She paused and cleared her throat. "Did he have a wide circle of friends?" Nicki knew the team would be trawling through Jacob's mobile phone and social media accounts, building up a picture of the man's social life and contacts, but there was sometimes nothing better than getting it straight from the horse's mouth. "Did you socialise much as a couple?"

Nicki saw the woman shudder. "No," came the response. "We don't . . . *didn't* . . . go out much at all. Not after we had the twins, anyway. And not really that much before then, either. We preferred to stay home, do family things together." Another shudder. "Jacob had a few friends, but I don't think he saw them very often."

"Anyone he might have fallen out with?"

Denise gave a strangled laugh. "Anyone that knew Jacob knew he was the most laid-back person you could ever wish to meet." A wistful look entered her eyes. "We didn't even argue. He was the easiest person to get along with. He didn't have an enemy in the world."

Nicki nodded but felt her lips start to thin. In her experience, no one was ever that perfect. Despite the sensitive nature of the conversation, she decided to probe further. "You said he'd struggled with his mental health in the past — can you identify what the trigger might have been? Was it work related? Personal problems?"

Nicki watched closely for the woman's reaction. Often it wasn't the question, or even the answer, that truly mattered — it was the *reaction* the person gave that could speak volumes. She didn't have to wait long.

A haunted look joined the pain in the woman's eyes. "The first time I noticed it was quite a few years ago now. We were still living in London, and I remember he went to a very dark place. It scared me for a while because it was so unlike him. He'd always been so level-headed, so steady. Nothing usually got on top of him. But all of a sudden, he just plunged down into the deepest, darkest depression."

Nicki found herself nodding. In the months that followed Deano's disappearance, although she was only ten, she had noticed the immediate change in her parents — especially her father. He seemed to spiral downwards, cutting himself off from everybody, including Nicki and her mother. She recognised it now as an acute reaction to the trauma of losing Deano, and the depression that followed quickly in its wake. She cleared her throat once more. "Did you ever find out what triggered that first episode?"

Denise paused then slowly shook her head. "Not really. We were having a few money worries at the time, but nothing out of the ordinary. He'd lost his job in the City a couple of years before and was trying to set himself up on his own. It was a difficult time for us, and I had to increase my hours at work for a while to compensate. We were also going through IVF, so it was a very stressful time. But after a while, things seemed to improve, so I didn't ask." A look of horror crossed her pale face. "Should I have?"

Nicki was quick to step in. "No, of course not. It's just useful background information for us, that's all. We'll be looking into any number of circumstances that might have contributed to what happened last night."

"He wouldn't have jumped, if that's what you're thinking." Denise's face remained pale, but her demeanour hardened. "He would never have chosen to leave us, to leave the twins; I know that for a fact."

Nicki had heard the same words countless times before when talking to bereaved families. She gave the woman another sad smile. "When the time comes, sometimes people aren't thinking straight. It's nobody's fault."

More shaking of the head followed, more insistent this time. "No. *Never.* He might have been in a bad place before, and maybe he was struggling again now, but there's no way he would jump off that roof. Just no way. I *know* him. He was my husband." Denise's voice cracked. "I've known him for twenty-five years — we talk to each other all the time and share everything. He would *never* do this."

"I have no reason to disbelieve you, Mrs Towers. All we are trying to do is build up enough of a case to prove that he didn't." Images of the graphic designer's teeth edged into Nicki's head, but she decided that was one detail Denise Towers could do without right now. "Did he tell you where he was going yesterday — why he was in the town? In particular, why he might have visited that address? Were you thinking of moving?"

The woman's shoulders sagged. "No, we weren't. I have no idea why he might have gone there." Another haunted look crossed her face as she toyed with the mug balanced in her lap. A sigh followed as she pulled another tissue from the box to dab on her cheeks. "He'd been very quiet all morning, a bit distracted." She held Nicki in a fixed stare. "But still nothing that would make him do something like . . . *this*. We'd had a few words, nothing serious, but then I noticed that he'd taken the car and gone out."

"When was this?"

"Just after lunch, early afternoon."

"And you don't know where he went?"

Sadness returned to Denise Towers' face. "No. I assumed it was something to do with work. I messaged him a couple of times during the afternoon, asking whether he would be back for dinner. We were due a supermarket delivery in the afternoon, but they'd messaged to say it was delayed until later in the evening. I asked him . . . I asked him if he wanted to pick up a takeaway on his way home instead."

Nicki knew she could get the answer to her next question from Jacob's phone but decided to ask it anyway. "Did he reply to your messages?"

Denise dabbed at her cheeks. "No."

Nicki and Fox exchanged a discreet look. For a couple who professed to share everything, Denise Towers seemed to know very little about what her husband was doing on the day he died.

"He was a family man," she continued. "Family was everything to him. There is no way he would have taken his own life. You *have* to believe me."

Nicki saw the desperation in the woman's eyes and felt her heart squeeze. "It's all right, Mrs Towers. We're not trying to suggest otherwise. We just have to cover all possible scenarios." She glanced sideways at Fox, giving him another discreet nod. "I think we'll leave you in peace now. Thank you for your time, it's much appreciated." Placing her untouched tea onto the coffee table, she got to her feet. "I'll leave you in the very capable hands of DC Gedge. If you need anything — and I mean *anything* — just let her know. We'll be in touch as soon as we have any further news."

"Was he murdered?" The question stopped Nicki in her tracks. "I need to know."

Nicki turned back towards Denise, unsure exactly what to say. Even now, certain questions still had the capacity to wrongfoot her, and this was one of them. She didn't want to lie to the woman, but at the same time she didn't want to give her false hope either, recognising the need to be cautious.

She continued heading towards the door. "Like I say, we're not sure at this stage. As soon as we know for definite, you'll be the first to be informed." That wasn't strictly true, but right now Denise Towers needed to hear it. Hesitating for a moment in the doorway, Nicki turned back. "All I can say is, if we do conclude there was foul play involved in your husband's death, I will move heaven and earth to find out what happened."

# CHAPTER FOUR

*Bury St Edmunds Police Station*

"I don't think you have anything to worry about, Hugh." DCI Malcolm Turner tapped his pen against his cheek. "It's probably all just routine." Taking a breath, he hoped he sounded convincing.

There was a sigh from the other end of the line. "I'm sure you're right, Malcolm. Maybe I'm making something out of nothing, but it's just . . . you know. After everything that's happened recently, I'm not sure poor Anne can take much more."

Turner nodded to no one in particular. "Of course, it's entirely understandable. What the pair of you have been through lately doesn't bear thinking about." And it was true. When Turner had learned that Dean Webster had been found — and not just found but found *alive* — his first thoughts had turned to Hugh and Anne. Friends of his for more years than he could remember, they'd had to live with the pain of losing a child for over twenty years. Turner admired their strength. When he enquired how they'd coped, Hugh Webster's response was always the same.

*"We just did what we had to do to survive."*

Turner had served in the same force as the now retired Detective Superintendent Webster, so he was well versed in the devastation that had hit the family when little Dean vanished into thin air. In among the devastation, he'd watched the young Nicola grow up, only to watch her disappear from her parents' lives in much the same way as her brother. Dispensing with the Webster surname, she'd forged a new life for herself as Nicki Hardcastle, trying to bury the memory of that fateful November day.

But guilt was a powerful emotion. Once it had its teeth into you, it rarely let go that easily.

Turner refocused his attention to his friend and former colleague. "How is Anne these days?"

For the next few minutes, the pair exchanged news of their respective families, and Turner ended with another promise to visit the Websters and have that long-overdue game of golf at Hugh's local club. With the phone now returned to its cradle, he pondered the main reason for the former detective's call.

No police officer, retired or otherwise, welcomed an investigation into their past cases, and the fact that someone seemed to be sniffing around Hugh Webster concerned him. Hugh was one of the most diligent officers Turner had ever met, and to think there might be something shady going on in one of his past cases — maybe more than one — didn't sit right with him. Hugh was straighter than an arrow. So why were his cases being reviewed — and by who?

An unwelcome gnawing sensation gripped his stomach. What if Hugh wasn't the man Turner had always thought him to be? Corrupt officers walked the same corridors as he did; it wasn't a pleasant thought, but it was the truth — their rank often giving them immunity. But the idea was absurd, and Turner dismissed the notion almost before it had fully formed.

Finishing the dregs of his coffee, he checked his watch. He knew he needed to catch up with Nicki — the new investigation that had landed on them overnight would need all the resources he could spare, and he hadn't seen that much of her lately. Just as he pushed himself up from his chair, the woman in question appeared in the doorway.

"Is now a good time?"

Turner waved her inside. "Perfect. I was just about to come and find you." He gestured towards a vacant chair and slipped back behind his cluttered desk. "Update me on the new case."

For the next fifteen minutes, Nicki outlined the facts of Operation Jackdaw, as sparse as they were, and then the visits to Dennis Horner and Denise Towers that morning.

"What's your gut feeling? That our guy *didn't* jump?" The DCI knew Nicki to be one of the sharpest detectives he'd ever met — easily a match for her father — so he respected and encouraged her opinion. He noted the brief hesitation before she replied.

"It's not a straightforward case, I'll say that much. I can't say for sure that he jumped, not yet. It's possible but there are too many unanswered questions and oddities surrounding it — too many variables."

"As I understand it, there was no one else seen at the location, or immediately before."

Nicki shook her head. "Our sole witness, the taxi driver, says he didn't see anyone else, but I'm not too sure he's the most reliable of witnesses. Seems to have been otherwise distracted with his nose in various porn sites at the time."

"Cameras?"

"Being checked as we speak."

"What are your next steps?"

"Well, like I say, we've been to see the deceased's wife. She's understandably devastated, but she also insisted he would never have jumped. We'll be digging into his background to find out all we can about him. We have his phone, so the team are analysing that right now. We'll also interview the staff at the estate agents. He had to have got up onto that roof somehow."

"All the resources are yours, take what you need. And, if I can help, let me know."

After Nicki left, Turner spent the next few minutes staring at the closed office door. Part of him felt he should have told her about Hugh's call, but another part of him urged caution. She could well want to hear what her father might potentially be facing, but it would be a major distraction from the case. And there was no need to worry her unduly — the whole thing might blow over within a week, without a word needing to be said.

Satisfied he'd made the right decision, for now at least, Turner put Hugh Webster and his problems to one side. They had a potential murder investigation on their hands which needed their full attention.

* * *

*Rye, East Sussex*

Hugh Webster rubbed his eyes as he replaced the telephone receiver. Malcolm was a good friend, an even better police officer, and he would trust the man with his life, no question about that. But no matter how many times Malcolm told him not to worry, that any investigation into Hugh's past cases would reveal nothing of substance and everything would then be returned to the dusty archives, Hugh had still sensed concern in his friend's voice. The man was worried — probably not quite as much as Hugh was right now, granted, but worried all the same.

"Everything OK?" Hugh glanced up to see Anne smiling around the door frame. "Coffee?"

Sitting back in his chair, Hugh tried his best smile in return. He didn't want to worry Anne — he was doing enough of that for them both.

"Coffee would be lovely, thanks." In reality, he fancied something a lot stronger than a cup of Maxwell House, but that would be a very long and slippery slope that he wasn't prepared to go down just yet.

"I'll pop a couple of crumpets in the toaster, too, if you have time. How does that sound?"

Hugh's smile widened. "Even better. I don't need to leave for an hour." He waited until Anne had disappeared before letting the smile slip. Coffee and crumpets wouldn't take long, even if she made it with those expensive beans that needed grinding first, so he knew he only had a limited amount of time at his disposal.

Pulling a notepad across the desk, he again scanned the list of cases that he'd heard were being investigated. "Investigated" wasn't the word they'd used, of course, but it was what it all boiled down to in the end.

*Investigated.*

On the face of it, there was no connection between them. He could remember each one, even though they spanned over a decade, the most recent being in 2005, the year he'd retired. But try as he might, he couldn't see why they'd been selected over and above the hundreds of others he'd been involved in during his career. The only connection he could see was himself as the senior investigating officer and his second in command, DI Mark Keeble.

Still wondering if it was the right step to take, Hugh pulled the phone back out of its cradle and dialled the number before he could change his mind.

\* \* \*

*Bury St Edmunds Police Station*

As Nicki re-entered the incident room, DS Roy Carter waved a hand in the air. "I think you might want to take a look at this, boss."

Nicki strode over to the detective's desk, wincing as her new boots continued to pinch her toes. She peered over his shoulder. "Is it news about the phone?"

Roy hesitated for a second before nodding. "In a way, yes." He brought up a series of images onto his computer screen. "First trawl through the messages and voicemails substantiates what we already know. From looking at his contact list, he doesn't have a particularly wide circle of friends — and there's only one who messaged him recently, someone called Harvey Mitcham. Mitcham sent four texts plus a voicemail to Jacob in the last seven days."

"What did the messages say?"

"The voicemail was just a standard 'call me back', but the text messages were a little more intriguing. One said, 'What do you want me to do with it?' and another said, 'I can't keep it hidden forever.'"

Nicki pursed her lips. "OK, we'll need to follow up on those. Anything else?"

"I also found two texts and a voicemail from the wife — all from yesterday — asking if he was coming home for dinner."

Nicki bit her lip, remembering what Denise Towers had told them earlier. "Yes, she mentioned that."

"The rest of the messages are quite mundane — a reminder for a routine optician's appointment and several notifications from Amazon for impending deliveries. All standard stuff really, and nothing unusual . . . except for one."

Nicki's expression changed. "Go on."

Roy tapped the keyboard, bringing the message up onto the screen. "Message received at eleven forty-five yesterday morning."

"*It's time to pay for what you did. 15.08.05.*"

"This was followed by a ten-second phone call."

Nicki's frown returned. "It's not a lot to go on, but it does suggest Jacob could have arranged to meet someone. It's feasible that ten-second call contained instructions of where to go. Denise Towers confirmed he went out just after lunch and seemed quiet all morning. I assume there's nothing useful from the number?"

Roy confirmed Nicki's fears with a sigh. "Nothing. It's no longer in use. Most likely a burner phone."

Nicki's mind started to churn. "It might not be much, but it's the only lead we have. Someone was in touch with Jacob Towers in the immediate hours before he died, and that same someone could have lured him up onto the roof of the Crown Street property. It's just the one message? Nothing before?"

Roy was shaking his head almost before Nicki had finished asking the question. "No other messages from that number. But it's a newish phone — only registered three weeks ago — so it's possible Jacob had a different one, maybe even a different number."

"We'll need to check that out with the wife. I'll give Karen a call, see if she can discreetly ask about another phone. I'll also get her to ask about Harvey Mitcham. Denise didn't seem to think her husband had a wide circle of friends, didn't really socialise — which is borne out by his contact list." As Nicki added the tasks to her mental to-do list, she noted the look on the detective sergeant's face. "Roy? What else is there?"

Roy pulled another image up onto the computer screen. "An encrypted file. Looks like a video, but I can't open it to see. The only thing we know is that it was created just after nine o'clock last night — approximately an hour or so before he fell . . . or jumped."

Nicki's interest piqued. "We need to see that video. Get the tech guys onto it. It could be something and nothing, but we need to check it out." She started heading for the door. "Our taxi driver, Dennis Horner, has confirmed that he didn't actually see Jacob jump — he only saw him fall. It's a fine distinction, but we work on the assumption this might not have been a voluntary act. In the meantime, I'll go and speak to Karen."

"I'll send the video file to Simon in the tech suite right now."

Nicki called back over her shoulder. "Let me know the minute you hear anything. And don't forget we also need to contact the estate agents."

"Already put in a call, boss." Roy tapped his notepad. "Just waiting for them to get back to me. I've asked for a list of current staff, and also anyone who had a viewing at the property in the last three weeks. Oh, and the mortuary rang — the post-mortem is at two o'clock."

"Excellent. Update me when you hear anything more."

# CHAPTER FIVE

*Islington, North London*

Mark Keeble stirred his now-cold coffee, the rhythmic clunking of the teaspoon the only sound disturbing the peace.

Hugh Webster's call had come out of the blue and he'd almost not picked up. He couldn't remember the last time the two of them had spoken, let alone physically seen each other. They'd worked together closely over the years, but since Webster's retirement in 2005 he could count on the fingers of one hand how many times they'd actually met. There had been a few calls a while back, something about meeting up for a game of golf with Malcolm Turner. Keeble knew he would never set foot on a golf course, with or without the retired detective superintendent, but had made the appropriate noises at the time. But although today's call had been a surprise, it wasn't entirely unexpected. He'd acted intrigued and was reasonably confident the ex-detective had swallowed it.

But rooting around in someone's past left a trail, no matter how hard you might try to cover your tracks; digital footprints were everywhere, and difficult to erase. Being off sick for the last four months had helped to a degree, giving Keeble the time he needed to poke about, but he knew it wouldn't last. Someone high up would soon notice and then his access would be blocked. He'd made enough ripples already to alert Hugh, so he needed this to be over. And soon.

Keeble had already come to terms with his own police career being over — he couldn't return now, not after what he'd done — but if he could stretch it out for a few more weeks, then the sick pay would come in handy, even if only to pay for his funeral.

Abandoning the coffee, he pushed himself up from the leather swivel chair and headed for the small window that looked out onto the street below. This was his world now — a poky one-bedroom flat that would be hard to swing a gnat in, never mind a cat. It was at times like these that he thought back to his life with Jennifer, and the three-bedroom house they'd shared in a much more salubrious part of the city. She'd been the keen gardener out of the two of them, joining any number of local horticultural groups and clubs. Keeble could take it or leave it when it came to the garden — and chose to leave it, mostly. His enjoyment was limited to sitting out on the patio to watch the sun go down, a large gin and tonic in hand. Which was probably why things had gone the way they did, their marriage slowly disintegrating until it couldn't be saved. He couldn't put his finger on exactly when the foundations had begun to crack, but he knew the drink had played a large part in it.

He felt he could do with a decent gin and tonic right now; it might go some way to settling the unease that had surfaced as soon as he'd ended the call.

Hugh Webster.

The man must be in turmoil, and part of Keeble felt guilty for that.

Turning away from the window, his gaze stretched to the wall opposite — and the list of names staring back out at him. He hadn't meant to use the wall as a pin cushion, but that was inevitably what had happened.

He remembered every name clearly, as if each was seared onto the surface of his brain by a red-hot poker.

And none more so than Wesley Barton.

Licking his increasingly dry lips, Keeble turned away from the wall and the list. It had been six days since his last drink and the cravings still hadn't subsided. Pulling out his wallet, he checked he had enough cash before grabbing the keys to the Jag. His self-imposed abstinence was at an end.

* * *

*Copse Close, Bury St Edmunds*

DC Gedge quickly climbed the stairs. With the children still at their grandparents', Denise Towers was having a lie down in the snug at the rear of the house. Karen had tried to get her to eat something for lunch, but she'd only nibbled at the cheese sandwich and managed just two mouthfuls of tomato soup.

Karen had suggested she might find it more comfortable upstairs, but Denise had refused. The snug was where she and Jacob would relax in the evenings after the children had gone to bed, watching TV or listening to music; sometimes they just talked. Understandably, it was the place she felt closest to him.

Karen had seen it all too often before. The spouse left behind struggling to comprehend what had just happened, why their world had just imploded. They would cling onto shards of broken memories as if they were life rafts from a sinking ship, anything to keep their loved one alive for that little bit longer and stop them from having to face the horrifying truth.

For Denise Towers, the snug was her life raft. The cushions probably still smelled of her husband's aftershave, the DVD boxes arranged just how he wanted, maybe even one of his jumpers discarded on a chair. In time, those things would fade away — but, for now, the snug was all she had.

The plush carpet beneath Karen's feet softened her footsteps as she made her way along the upstairs landing, and she was now thankful Denise hadn't taken her up on her suggestion of lying down in the bedroom. When Nicki had explained what it was she wanted her to look for, Karen knew the bedroom would need to be checked.

The compact box room contained nothing more than some empty packing crates and an exercise bike. She stealthily moved along, past the family bathroom and then onto the children's room.

Karen's heart gave a painful squeeze as she entered. Two single beds faced out from the far wall, separated in the middle by a single bedside table. Two lamps — one with a Batman shade and the other Barbie — were the only items on the table, except for two glasses of water, half drunk. The beds had been made, the duvets smoothed out and pillows plumped, ready for when the children came home. The left-hand bed had a teddy bear resting up against the pillow, the one on the right a plush green dinosaur. Karen could visualise the twins tucked up in bed, clutching their toys as they listened to a bedtime story.

But bedtimes here would never be the same again. The children had left the house oblivious to the turmoil the events of Wednesday night had caused, oblivious to the huge hole blasted through their lives in a matter of seconds. A quick Google search had established it took less than three seconds for someone of Jacob's height and weight to fall forty feet. Three seconds for life to change forever.

Karen didn't blame Denise one bit for sending the children away to their grandparents — better to let them have a few extra days of normality, a few extra days without the searing hot pain of losing a parent so young. Time would be upon them soon enough when their mother would have to tell them the brutal truth, tell them that their daddy wouldn't be coming home, wouldn't be helping them into their pyjamas and tucking them into bed, and wouldn't be reading them their favourite bedtime story.

Karen willed herself to refocus. She adored her job as a family liaison officer, and over the last eight years had built up a reputation of being one of the best. It wasn't a job for everyone. Immersing yourself inside another family wasn't easy — and it wasn't always welcome, either. All too often there was an underlying hostility at the intrusion, a natural reluctance to welcome a stranger into the house at a time of grief and pain. And why should they? The family had sometimes just been delivered the worst possible news — an unexpected death, a violent murder. Sometimes it was adults, sometimes it was children. Emotions ran high, tempers even higher. Anger was an expected reaction, and it would often be the family liaison officer in the firing line.

Despite all that, it was a job Karen loved. She had a natural ability that others didn't — an ability to see through people's pain, see through the heartache and loss. People lashed out when receiving devastating news, and Karen wanted to be the one to help them heal. So, she would soak up the hostility, absorb the harsh words and shouting, deal with the tirades of anger and frustration if and when they came hurtling her way.

For it never lasted long. No one could maintain that level of anger for any length of time; grief was exhausting and would soon drain even the most resilient. Then Karen would be there with her steadying hand and reassuring smile, ready for the next step of the journey.

Bending down, Karen checked beneath both beds and, apart from a collection of discarded toys and a random pair of socks, saw nothing of note. Certainly no phone. The wardrobe didn't contain anything other than clothes, either. A further check inside the stout wooden toy box at the end of one of the beds, and then through the contents of a small bookcase, also revealed nothing.

Leaving the children's room, she padded silently along the landing towards the main bedroom at the front of the house. A king-sized bed dominated the room, facing the bay window that looked out over the street below. A triple wardrobe on one wall, a dressing table on the other. In the corner, by the window, was a leather beanbag.

Evidence of Jacob Towers was all around. Shoes and trainers lined up in the bottom of the wardrobe, a variety of ties hanging from a rack just inside the door. Although the dressing table mostly contained items Karen presumed to belong to Denise, there was a can of Lynx deodorant, a bottle of Paul Smith aftershave, and a comb. As she neared, Karen saw a few strands of short hair trapped in the comb's teeth.

Jacob.

Karen wondered whether Denise would ever get rid of that comb. She suspected not.

A bedside table sat either side of the bed. One had a pot of night cream, a bottle of vitamins, and a chic-lit paperback book; the other sported a mug of cold coffee, a phone charger, and a hardback book featuring Lewis Hamilton's journey in Formula One.

His and hers.

Karen scanned the room once more, and bit her lip. Where would someone hide a mobile phone? When you shared your home with another person, true hiding places were very few and far between. She'd decided not to quiz Denise about Jacob having another phone just yet. The woman was exhausted. There would be time enough for that delicate conversation.

She pulled open the drawers on both bedside tables, but found nothing other than more books, more phone chargers, and some loose change. A cursory look under the bed revealed nothing but a pair of slippers, a stray pen, and a dog's squeaky toy bone.

Karen scrabbled back to her feet, the cartilage in her knees crunching as she did so.

Then she stopped and frowned.

* * *

Carolyn "Caz" Mitchell snapped the elasticated cap onto her head and faced the steel examination table. Opposite, she saw DS Roy Carter was also clad head to toe in a rubber apron, plastic cap, and rubber boots.

"Let's begin, shall we?" She felt a familiar flutter of anxiety as she turned on the digital recorder. Although she'd seen the victim at the scene yesterday evening, the sight of the body still managed to squeeze her heart. It was a life lost, a life cut short. It didn't matter how many times she'd picked up a scalpel, how many battered and mutilated bodies crossed her mortuary slab, each one touched her. She couldn't help asking herself what kind of life they'd left behind, and what sequence of events had brought that life to such an abrupt end.

*Jacob Towers.*

Most of the time, Caz didn't have a name to put to the body on the examination table. When she'd been a young and inexperienced pathologist, with only a handful of post-mortems under her belt, it seemed wrong somehow to be violating a person the way they did — cutting them open and removing their most vital organs — and to not even know the poor sod's name.

But the passing years had taught her a new perspective. Even without a name, each one was still an individual, a human being with a past. Caz thought the man before her on the table looked like a Jacob; it was a strong and dependable name.

The man had clearly suffered a devastating penetrative injury to the chest. Would he have lived if he'd missed the spike and hit the ground instead? It was impossible to tell, but he would have had a chance, at least.

Caz had seen plenty of impact injuries before — whether it be falls from a height like this one, or those struck by trains and buses — and it always surprised her how little evidence there was on the outside of the damage done. In the movies, there would be blood spilling and rapidly collecting in a pool beneath the body, before quickly spreading far and wide as the person's life ebbed away with it.

Reality was often very different.

"Today we have a forty-year-old Caucasian male, height 187 centimetres, weight ninety-six kilos. We will begin with an external examination." Caz edged closer, taking a small digital camera from the instrument trolley beside her and proceeding to take several close-up shots. She could, and probably should, delegate this part of the process — but she was always keen to be as hands-on as possible, be it dictating and typing up her own reports, or taking her own photographs. She'd been called a control freak, and much worse besides, on several occasions in the past — usually by a succession of boyfriends who'd never lasted the distance. She preferred to call it dedicated. Focused. *Invested.* She actually *cared* about the person gracing her mortuary table, so much so that she sometimes didn't entrust them to anyone else.

"Both lower limbs are free from external injury, other than some minor bruising to the anterior shins. Likewise both upper limbs — although there is one tattoo of a black heart on the right bicep area." Caz paused to take several more close-up shots. "Moving up to the pelvis, abdomen, and thorax. There is a large penetrating wound to the upper abdomen, consistent with the deceased landing on a metal spike, with surrounding superficial contusions and abrasions." Pausing again, she looked up. "You OK over there, Roy? Anything you want to ask so far?"

The detective sergeant seemed to hesitate before shaking his head, eyes still trained on the body. "Nothing so far. I'm just surprised that a fall from such a height hasn't caused more catastrophic injuries. I mean . . ." Roy's cheeks darkened. "Obviously, they were catastrophic enough — that's some wound there and the poor sod's dead — but, I don't know, I was expecting to see more."

Caz nodded. "Often, with a fall from a height such as this, the true damage is rarely seen on the outside." She paused

51

and flashed a sad look towards the table. "But you just wait until we open him up."

Nearing the top end of the table, the pathologist placed the camera on the side. A lot of what she saw on the mortuary table unnerved her, but nothing had quite prepared her for this. "Moving up to the head, again there is little by way of external injury. There is a slight discolouration to the neck, possibly due to a hyperextension injury from the fall." With a gloved hand, she parted Jacob's bloodied lips and directed a narrow torchlight inside. "Inside the deceased's mouth we have one, two, three, four, five, six, seven . . . seven cavities consistent with recent extractions. This corresponds with the seven teeth found in the front pockets of our deceased's jeans." The teeth in question now sat in a steel bowl, wrapped in a protective plastic bag. "The extraction sites look clean. There is evidence of bleeding inside the mouth, which would suggest the extractions were performed pre-mortem."

Caz could sense the detective sergeant shuddering from the opposite side of the table. She didn't blame him. As a form of torture, it had to be one of the worst imaginable. She reached for the camera once again, taking a final round of shots before straightening back up and catching Roy's eye. "Let's get him open, shall we?"

# CHAPTER SIX

*Copse Close, Bury St Edmunds*

Usually, the presence of an animal in a home — be it a cat, dog, hamster, or guinea pig — was relatively obvious. Food bowls on the kitchen floor, animal feed in the cupboards. Litter trays for cats, leads hanging on coat hooks for dogs. Baskets and cages, bedding and pet toys. Even that distinct animal smell was usually present somewhere.

But, in the Towers' family home there was nothing, nothing to suggest that a dog was resident there — apart from the squeaky toy bone beneath the bed. Karen made her way back downstairs to take another quick look through the kitchen cupboards, but it only told her what she already knew — no dog food, not even a biscuit. Another check of the floor confirmed it was free from food bowls, and the coat rack by the back door was devoid of leads.

Deciding the dog was turning into a distraction she didn't have time for, Karen wondered if there was time to return upstairs and continue looking through the wardrobe. But, before she reached the stairs, she heard the door to the snug creak open behind her. It didn't take long for Denise to appear in the doorway, hair tousled and her face showing the imprint of whatever it was she'd fallen asleep on. Her eyes had that just-woken-up look, her eyelids drooping with an unfocused watery gaze.

Karen afforded her a sad smile. "Feel any better?" The question was answered with a vague nod. "How about I make us some tea and toast, then?" Karen turned around and headed back towards the kitchen, making a mental note to recheck the main bedroom another time. As Denise followed her, the detective constable stopped. "Oh, and this might sound like a totally daft question, but do you have a dog?"

Denise floated in a dreamlike state over to the kettle, and for a moment Karen wondered if the woman had heard her. And then it dawned on her that maybe it was an insensitive question — perhaps the dog had died recently, and they just hadn't had time to get rid of the toy. Karen rapidly tried to think of a response in case Denise asked her why she was asking, a response that didn't involve saying, *Well, I was rooting around in your bedroom and found this dog's toy under the bed* . . .

Karen grabbed the loaf of bread next to the kettle and began to feed slices into the toaster. She was about to apologise for asking such an intrusive question, when Denise turned towards her and gave a weak smile.

"Yes, we do — Buster. He's gone to my parents with the twins. I thought . . ." Denise swallowed, her voice catching. "I thought it would be best. He's Jacob's dog, really." A single tear trickled down her wan cheek as she switched the kettle on. "He'll be pining for him — wanting to go out on his usual walks. I just don't have the energy, I can't . . ." Another swallow. "I just can't face it right now."

"Of course." Karen placed a hand on the woman's shoulder. "Why don't you sit down while I make the tea?"

Denise gave a grateful nod and lowered herself into one of the chairs around the kitchen table, while Karen found two mugs, two plates, and then filled the teapot with boiling water. A few minutes later, armed with plates of hot buttered toast and two steaming mugs of tea, she joined Denise at the table.

Deciding now might be a good time to try and tease more information out of Denise, she pushed one of the plates across the table. "Do you happen to know if Jacob might have another phone somewhere? Or maybe changed his number recently?"

"A phone?" Concern entered Denise's gaze. "Why, have you . . . have you found something?"

Karen was quick to respond. "No, no. Nothing like that. It's just that the phone we found on him . . . it doesn't look like he had it for very long, so we wondered if he had another."

"Oh, I see." Denise took in a deep breath, her voice shuddering. "Yes, I think so. He's had a few different phones recently. He changed his number a while ago . . . I could find it for you, if I remember where I left mine." The woman made a half-hearted effort of looking around her. "It'll be around here somewhere."

"No matter, Mrs Towers." Karen nudged the plate a little further towards Denise, deciding on a different approach. "My sister has a dog — a labrador — and there's muddy footprints and dog hair everywhere. You can't move in her kitchen for stepping into a dog bowl or tripping over a lead. Your house is spotless. No one would ever know you had a dog."

Denise managed a tired laugh. "Buster's a good dog. He doesn't seem to shed all that much, but I suppose I'm a bit of a clean freak — always dusting or vacuuming somewhere. His bed and food bowls have gone with him to my parents' house, to keep some kind of familiarity and routine. He's never stayed there overnight before — he's not much more than a puppy, really." A worried look crossed her face as she took a nibble from one of the slices of toast. "I do hope he's all right."

"I'm sure he'll be fine. Probably enjoying all the fuss." Karen spread a small amount of jam onto her toast. "My sister's dog enjoys a fuss. Every time I go there, he's all over me. *Plus*, he enjoys a bit of toast." She waved the slice in the air. "If he was here right now, he'd be whining for a titbit."

It wasn't a *complete* lie. Karen's sister did have a dog, and it was a labrador, and he did enjoy being fussed — although he wasn't all that enamoured with toast. But it was the best she could think of at short notice, and while the detective constable could swallow the fact that the dog's bed and bowls had gone with him to Denise's parents, it still didn't explain the lack of dog food in any of the cupboards. Not a single can, not a single box. Nothing. She decided to try a different angle.

"Does Buster pester you for food when you're eating?"

Denise wrapped her hands around her mug, eyes glassy. "He doesn't beg all that much, unless you're eating chicken. But he's a good eater."

Karen couldn't help her gaze flickering back towards the empty cupboards. "Would you like me to pop out to the shops for you? Just so Buster has some food when he gets back? I couldn't help but notice there doesn't seem to be any dog food anywhere."

*Subtle, Karen, subtle.*

Denise broke off a piece of toast and began to chew. "We keep Buster's food out in the garage. It's . . ." She paused, jaw tightening. "*Was* . . . Jacob's domain, walking and feeding the dog. He decided to keep everything out there. There's a door that leads in from the utility room."

Karen nodded, taking a sip of her tea. "Ah, that explains it, then. Mystery solved."

Once the toast had been eaten, and the teapot emptied, Karen suggested Denise take some time to herself and have a bath. They were due at the mortuary later to formally identify Jacob's body — a trip Karen wasn't particularly looking forward to. The woman didn't need too much persuasion and soon disappeared upstairs. As soon as Karen heard the bath water running and the bathroom door closing, she headed for the utility room and the door that led to the garage.

* * *

"I see what you mean." Roy's jaw tightened.

Caz stepped back from the table. "Sorry, but with a penetrating injury such as this, it's the internal organs that bear the brunt of the force. And it's always a lottery as to which organs are most affected." She slid a sad gaze back towards Jacob Towers' body. "Unfortunately for our man here, the metal spike has entered through his upper abdomen, puncturing the spleen and base of the left lung, before transecting the heart and coming out the other side. Our Mr Towers would have bled out very quickly."

Beads of sweat prickled beneath Roy's elasticated cap while another shiver shuddered up his spine. Although he'd attended a fair number of post-mortems since arriving on the team last November, he'd never seen anything quite like this before. And he wasn't sure he wanted to see it again.

Post-mortems usually intrigued him. It wasn't that he looked forward to them, exactly — that would be wrong — but he did appreciate the complexity of the human body. It fascinated him how disease and injury could so easily destroy it. On the outside, humans looked strong and robust, capable of withstanding and repelling any number of assaults — but there were times when something very small and insignificant could stop it in its tracks.

One such body had stuck firmly in Roy's memory. He'd been on Nicki's team a matter of weeks when there was a stabbing outside a school in the town. Knife crime was on the rise in many parts of the country — Suffolk was no more immune to it than anywhere else — and those involved seemed to be getting younger. The victim had been just thirteen years old, attacked by a gang of boys of the same age. Laid out on the mortuary slab, the boy looked to be merely asleep. His body, on first glance at least, appeared pristine — with not even a bruise to blemish his pale skin. It was only upon stepping closer, under the harsh overhead lighting, that Roy saw the thin three-centimetre puncture mark on the left side of the boy's chest.

The weapon had been a pocketknife — one single stab that had punctured the heart.

A life extinguished, just like that.

Game over.

"What killed him?" It seemed like a daft question to Roy and, as soon as it left his mouth, he wished he hadn't asked it.

But Caz didn't seem to mind. Pulling the elasticated cap from her head, she backed away towards the swing doors. "Catastrophic injuries like these, it could be any number of things. But a penetrating injury to the heart like that is unsurvivable. The stomach showed evidence of ingested blood, so I would say that the teeth were extracted fairly recently."

"Would he have been alive for any length of time — you know, after it happened? After he fell?" The thought began to turn Roy's usually cast-iron stomach. "Do you think he knew what was happening? That he was dying?"

Caz stopped in her tracks. "Difficult to say. There was a lot of internal bleeding, which would suggest the heart was still beating for some time after impact. But whether he was aware . . ." She could only give a faint shrug with an accompanying sigh. "It's possible he lost consciousness fairly quickly, if not from the blood loss itself then from the resulting shock." She gave Roy a sad smile. "Let's hope so, eh?"

* * *

*Bury St Edmunds Police Station*

Nicki had spent the last couple of hours tucked away inside her office. The incident room was a hive of activity but, until some results came in, the investigation was threatening to become stalled even though it had barely started. She'd asked Karen to broach the idea of a second phone to Denise Towers and was awaiting a call back. In the meantime, she'd left a message with Faye for an update on what was happening at the Crown Street property. She knew the crime scene manager was still at the scene but hoped they might be finished by the end of the day. They needed some good news, and some leads.

Crime scene photographs had now been sent through, and the images of Jacob Towers impaled on the railings wasn't a pretty sight. Nicki sighed as she printed them off ready for the whiteboard. While waiting for developments, she thought again about her visits to Dennis Horner and Denise Towers. The fact that the taxi driver hadn't seen anyone else with Jacob at the property niggled her. If they suspected this wasn't a straightforward suicide, then surely someone else had to have been there? But then she reminded herself that Dennis Horner may not have been all that attentive to his surroundings.

Denise Towers had oozed pain, as expected, but there was something about the Towers' relationship that had lodged in Nicki's brain. They seemed close, a loving couple, and Denise was quite insistent that they had the perfect marriage. But, in Nicki's experience, perfection was rare.

Before she could dissect the Towers' marriage any further, she received an urgent message from the incident room.

The video on Jacob's phone had been unlocked.

\* \* \*

Nicki felt her heart rate quicken. She'd only seen Jacob Towers' face once before, while the man was impaled on the metal spike on Crown Street, but there was no doubt that the face looking at her from DS Fox's computer screen was the forty-year-old graphic designer.

*Alive.*

"Whole thing lasts nine minutes and sixteen seconds." The detective sergeant broke off, the words seeming to catch in his throat. Nicki detected a slight quiver to his voice. "Well, I'll let you all see for yourselves — but maybe just the edited highlights for now."

Darcie, Matt, and Duncan had already pulled their chairs across the incident room to Fox's desk and, as the shortened recording started to play out, it didn't take long for their mouths to slacken and their eyes to widen.

"Like I said, the whole recording goes on for over nine minutes. I'll play the beginning, then fast forward through to the end for now." Fox tapped the keyboard. "If anyone wants to watch it in its entirety later, then be my guest."

Jacob Towers' phone may not have given the team much by way of clues from the meagre collection of text messages and phone calls saved on the handset, but the video file was explosive.

"*I'm sorry.*" Jacob's voice was barely louder than a whisper. "*I'm sorry for everything, Denise.*" The man's tear-stained face stared towards the camera, water-filled eyes blinking rapidly. His face was blotchy, lips quivering with every syllable they uttered. Snot dripped from his nose.

He was sitting on a simple wooden chair in the middle of an empty space, no bigger than a box room. The walls were bare plaster, no windows visible. From the camera angle, the door was presumably behind the person holding the phone.

Nicki recognised the clothes the man was wearing, no doubt the same clothing being cut from his body in the mortuary right about now.

"*I'm sorry!*" Jacob's voice was stronger now, his chin set, his moist eyes hardening. "*I know I did wrong, and I accept that now. I've accepted it for fourteen years.*" Breaking off, the man's jaw muscles tightened. "*Just as I accept everything that comes to me now and everything that I'm about to do. It's no less than what I deserve. I'm sorry, Denise.*"

Nicki detected the camera phone dip a little, the person holding it taking a step forward. She willed the phone to reveal the person's face but knew she would be disappointed. All they could see was a hand appearing in shot, passing something towards Jacob.

It wasn't apparent just what that something was, but it didn't take long for it to become sickeningly clear. Nicki sensed Darcie look away, the detective averting her eyes towards the incident room floor as Jacob brought the pair of pliers up towards his mouth. For the next few moments, everyone in the incident room held their breath.

*Who in their right mind pulled their own teeth out?*

The team watched Jacob open his mouth and place the pliers inside. He wrestled for some time before one bloodied tooth eventually appeared. The scream that followed tore through the room. Jacob then spat to the side, bloodied saliva dripping from his lips. Another tooth fell from the pliers before the man plunged the tool back into his mouth. The person holding the camera phone edged even closer, the picture refocusing.

Tooth number three came out soon after . . . then four . . . then five. Each extraction was accompanied by more splatters of blood, the heart-wrenching screams increasing in volume. After seven teeth had been pulled, the man slumped forward, his body shaking uncontrollably. Tears streamed down his cheeks, mixing with the blood before dripping from his chin, leaving his bloodied mouth yawning wide open in a perpetual silent scream.

Fox paused the video, then turned to catch Nicki's eye. "There's something else — at the end." Without another word, he resumed playback.

It didn't take long for them all to hear it.

*The sound of laughter.*

"What a sick fuck." Matt Holland blinked towards the empty screen. "What a seriously sick fuck."

Darcie slid her gaze back towards Fox's computer, her face a ghostly white. "I've seen a lot of things in this job, but I've never seen *that*. Who on earth would want to make someone pull their own teeth out and then stand back and record it?" Her voice was brittle, as if one wrong word could make it shatter. "Who *actually* does that . . . and then *laughs*?"

"Our killer," replied Matt, scooting his chair back towards his desk. "I think we can safely say that our man here didn't jump, don't you? If you were planning to kill yourself, you wouldn't go to the extreme of pulling your own teeth out first. My guess is this is the person that texted Jacob, then told him where to meet."

Nicki pursed her lips, still staring at the blank screen. "It certainly looks that way."

"What kind of a hold would someone have to have over someone else to make them do that?" Duncan, who'd been watching the video over Fox's right shoulder, caught Nicki's eye. "It's got to be something massive, right? Normal people don't do that."

Nicki nodded. "Agreed. So, we need to find out what that something was, because *that* will lead us to whoever *this* is."

"There is something we can take from all this, though." Fox turned in his seat. "We may not have got a look at his face, but at least we *heard* him."

Nicki stepped back from Fox's desk. "See what the tech suite can do with the recording. Maybe they can isolate that laugh. I'm not sure the technology is there right now, but let's ask anyway." Fully aware they were clutching at straws, she sighed heavily. Voice biometrics was an emerging science, not dissimilar to facial recognition. The latter had gathered extraordinary pace over the last few years, with techniques to identify people through facial characteristics now rolled out across the country. But the same couldn't yet be said for voices. "How are we getting on with the CCTV from around the scene, and the car park?"

"Not great news there, either, boss," replied Duncan. "Street cameras show our deceased walking alone along Crown Street at just before eight thirty yesterday evening. Unfortunately, there's no coverage that shows the building itself so, if he did meet someone there, they could easily have approached from the other direction undetected. I've made a list of vehicle registrations that pass close to the scene in the hours before, just following up on those now. We do see the taxi driver in his cab around the time he said, though — so it looks like he could be telling us the truth."

Nicki's heart dipped a little. Cameras could have provided them with the crucial lead they needed, so the absence of them was a setback. "What about the car park?"

Duncan flipped over a page of his notebook. "Jacob is seen to enter the car park at just after six o'clock. This tallies with the times recorded on the parking app on his phone. He parks his car — a Toyota — but remains inside the vehicle for some forty-two minutes. Seen to leave the car park on foot at six forty-five."

"Which means he then spent almost two hours doing something before he pops up on Crown Street." Nicki frowned. "Denise told us that he left home sometime after lunch — she couldn't be more specific than that — which means we need to find out where he went before entering that car park. Access the town centre CCTV and see if we can pick him up anywhere — and check his bank cards to see if he bought anything."

"Bank details requested, boss," confirmed Matt.

Sighing once more, Nicki turned towards the door. She needed to get out of these boots. "Although I'm sure no one really wants to look at that video footage again, we need to find out who the cameraman is. And where that footage was taken." She glanced around at the team's ashen faces. "It could well be that our video footage was shot at the Crown Street property. I'm expecting a call from Faye sometime this afternoon with an update, but whatever happens I'd like to go and have a look at it for myself. Have we heard back from the estate agents yet?"

"I don't think so," replied Fox. "Roy was speaking with them earlier. I'll chase them up."

"Yes, do that. And do the usual social media trawls, too."

# CHAPTER SEVEN

*Woodlands Camping and Caravan Site, Suffolk*

With his last two messages still unanswered, his irritation began to multiply. The twenty-four-hour deadline he'd imposed was more than twelve hours away but his patience, such as it was, was wearing thin. The next logical step was to take matters into his own hands. It was a thought that came with mixed feelings. The expected surge of excitement was tempered by a not insignificant element of trepidation. Doubt was rapidly starting to take seed, and it wasn't a feeling he was used to, or indeed enjoyed.

Turning to his phone, he refreshed the news feed. The carefully worded press release disclosed little more than it had before — still just an "incident" during the previous night which had closed a town centre road for several hours. He noted there was a mention of a man's death — the cause of which was being investigated — although no name was yet forthcoming. It made his mouth twitch.

Progress.

Putting the phone to one side, he picked up a silver-framed photograph bearing the image of his father. The man had been prematurely snatched from his life in the cruellest way possible, and even though fourteen years had passed, it still made his blood boil. He automatically reached for the bottle of whisky resting on the table, his usual coping mechanism.

Wrenching the lid from the bottle, he took a generous slug. What riled him the most was the injustice of it all. He was well aware his father wasn't a saint — no doubt guilty of many crimes that went unpunished — but he wasn't guilty of what eventually curtailed his freedom, and what eventually led to his untimely death.

After losing his father, various "uncles" came and went through the family's cramped mid-terraced house, but no one could ever replace Wesley Barton. As a succession of men crossed the threshold, his mother had spiralled down into repetitive bouts of deep depression — the black dog eventually taking her several years later. But he had little sympathy for her now. She'd never been whiter than white herself, knowing exactly what life with Wesley "Rocky" Barton entailed — but once the man was gone, she barely gave him or their children a second thought.

Then there were his sisters. A day didn't go by when he didn't think of Georgia and Grace. Too young at the time to understand what had happened to their family, the trauma doggedly followed them into adulthood, eventually catching up with both of them not long after their mother.

*They didn't deserve to die.*

Swallowing another mouthful of the fiery Macallan, he sensed the familiar flames ignite. Thinking about his sisters reminded him why he was doing this, why he was embarking on such a trail of destruction. He knew it wouldn't bring them back, nor would it do so his father; despite what people thought, he wasn't stupid. His actions sought to satisfy his inherent hunger for revenge — for revenge was all he had left.

Gripping the silver photo frame, he trained his eyes on the image of his father.

"*You know what to do.*"

His father's last words to him were imprinted on his memory. He could never forget them.

"*You know what to do.*"

And he had.

Sinking another generous mouthful of whisky, he placed the silver-framed photograph back on the camper van's table.

"Nearly there, Dad," he whispered. "I've nearly got them all."

\* \* \*

*Blackfriars Crown Court, London*
*Monday 15 August 2005*

Court Number One at Blackfriars Crown Court was packed, the media benches rammed with reporters squashed shoulder to shoulder. And the public gallery wasn't all that much better. Press coverage of the case so far had ensured it would be the best-attended court hearing on that hot and sultry Monday morning.

"All rise."

The weather outside was stifling — the hottest day of the year so far — but inside the courtroom it felt a hundred times worse. He'd been sitting on his hands for the last half an hour to try and keep them still, each nail already bitten to the quick, leaving them ragged and sore. The aged wooden bench creaked beneath his weight as he stood. With so many people packed so tightly together, the oxygen-depleted air made him feel light-headed and sick.

All five defendants were standing side by side in the dock, making it look uncomfortably cramped. He could easily see his father, the tallest of the group by more than a head, but they had rarely made eye contact throughout the seventeen-day trial and today was no different. The man stood up straight, his eyes trained directly and purposefully in front of him.

He knew why that was, of course. His father was preparing his boy for living life without him, preparing him for being the man of the house. It was something that made him feel anxious and sad. He didn't want to be the man of the house; he wanted his father back home.

On the last day of the trial three weeks before, just as the defendants were being led from the dock and back down to the cells, the word "guilty" still bouncing off the walls of the oak panelled courtroom, he'd finally caught his father's eye. The look on Wesley Barton's face had been one of weary resignation, and one of acceptance.

His father had remained stoic and strong throughout the trial — refusing to be tripped up no matter how hard the prosecution pummelled him repeatedly with question after question, attempting to tie him up in insufferable knots. Instead, the man had remained firm and resolute to the very end.

But everything had changed with that one, simple word. *Guilty.*

The robbery had been audacious at best — a word that had been used many times by the prosecution over the last few weeks. Alongside "bold" and "foolhardy". He hadn't known what audacious had meant before the trial, but he certainly did now.

The judge had taken up his usual position on the bench, after which everyone proceeded to sit down. Everyone, that was, except the defendants in the dock. As he sat, he felt the knots tighten in his stomach, threatening to force out the remnants of his hurried breakfast. The sweet taste of Coco Pops wasn't one he relished for the second time that morning.

Thinking about breakfast made him think about Georgia and Grace again. He'd left them with toast and orange juice that morning, before catching the bus to court. He fleetingly wondered if their mother was out of bed yet, but saw no reason to think that she would be. She hadn't been for the last week, maybe longer, so it was unlikely that today would be any different. It was the school holidays, which was a blessing, so he didn't need to get his sisters off to school. But he worried about them being home alone — for alone they might as well be, for all the good their mother was doing.

The man beside him in the public gallery smelled of toe-curling body odour, with visible damp patches beneath each armpit. Fanning himself with his hand only made the stench worse. Instead, he turned his head to the side and tried not to breathe in.

The shuffling and coughing in the courtroom suddenly hushed as the judge started to speak. As far as sentencing hearings went, it was short and sweet — the judge affording the courtroom only a brief resumé of the facts of the case before moving swiftly on to deal with each defendant in turn. Mitigation by their respective barristers was also rapidly dispatched.

His father was the last to hear his fate. The other four had all received lengthy prison terms, so there was no reason to expect anything different for Wesley Barton. That being so, his mouth and lips remained dry, his heart hammering so fiercely it seemed like it might burst from his chest.

"Wesley Barton, you have been convicted of the charge of conspiracy to commit robbery. You wilfully engaged in the joint plan to steal from commercial premises, in the full knowledge that force by firearms may be used. During the course of that robbery, a security officer was killed. I have heard detailed mitigation on your behalf by your defence counsel, but due to the serious nature of this offence I sentence you to life imprisonment — with a minimum term of twenty-two years. I have no doubt that removing you from the streets is a just way of dealing with your criminality. You have shown no remorse for your actions, no remorse for the loss of an innocent life." The judge paused and peered over the top of his half-moon spectacles. "Take them down."

* * *

It took a lot to make a man like Wesley Barton cry. He could count on the fingers of one hand how many times it had happened.

He'd fixed a neutral look to his face while the sentences were being handed down, not really listening to what was being said. It was all lies, anyway, so what was the point? Ten years? Fifteen? Twenty? Life? It made little difference in the end. Once that prison door was slammed shut behind you and the key turned in the lock, life on the outside was over.

As he'd turned to walk toward the steps leading to the cells below, he remembered seeing the mournful look on his son's face as their eyes finally locked. The boy had been crying, that was evident, but in among the fear and sadness he thought he also saw an element of hope.

But hope wasn't something Wesley Barton felt much of right now, and he didn't expect that to change much in the future.

*The future.*

That was at an end for him now — all he had was the present.

Inside the dock, he'd simply given the boy a nod and then ducked down the wooden steps and out of sight.

*Life.*

He'd been inside before; that was nothing new. But a life sentence certainly *was* new.

He'd been in plenty of cells before as well, but he knew this journey would be very different to those that came before, because this time he wasn't alone. The ones that had set him up, lied under oath to get him convicted, were mere feet away from him. And it didn't take long for them to start with their mocking.

"You better watch yourself, dickhead. Prison can be a dangerous place for people like you."

That had been the first one — but the others had soon joined in.

"Fucking loser."

"Your time will come, pal, you just wait."

"You can't fuckin' hide in here. We'll find you."

"Say your prayers while you can — you're done for."

Wesley knew that even if he secured himself a place in solitary, they would find a way to get to him — people like that always did. There was an outside chance they would all be sent to different prisons, which would give him some breathing space, but prisons were surprisingly small places — incestuous, even — and word would soon spread. The Broadacres gang had a long reach, and it wouldn't take long for word to get out.

How easily the gang had lied to get him in the dock alongside them, and then convicted, showed just how corrupt the English legal system could be at times. No doubt enough palms had been greased with enough cash to make the truth a distant ideal. And Wesley himself had crossed too many people in his time to be too surprised that his luck had run out.

Wesley Barton was a marked man, and he needed to get used to it.

Although the cell wasn't particularly cold — albeit cooler than the stuffy courtroom above, for sure — he found himself starting to shiver. He'd never looked death fully in the face before, but he was doing that now. Some would say he deserved everything he got — his life of crime finally catching up with him after all these years — and maybe they were right. He might be innocent of the charges put to him this time around, but did that really matter in the grand scheme of things?

*Innocent.*

The word felt somewhat alien.

Wesley ran a hand over his brow which felt cool and clammy to the touch. The Broadacres gang had got one over on him just because they could. But what if they weren't content with just him? What if they went after his family too? His wife had stayed away from the trial, just as he knew she would — everyone had their tipping point, and this was seemingly hers. But what about Georgia and Grace? What about the boy? His own demise he could just about come to terms with, but not that of his children. Blinking, he felt his eyes start to prick. Rubbing his palms into his eyes, he refused to cry. He couldn't — *wouldn't* — let them see him cry.

Georgia and Grace were still so young — what would happen to them now he wasn't around? Who would protect them? The boy would do his best, he knew that — but he was only sixteen. A boy thrust into a man's world. The thought made Wesley shiver again.

The jeers had subsided now but were quickly replaced with feet thudding against the metal doors, clenched fists hammering against the walls. He did his best to tune it out.

Maybe they wouldn't get to him inside like he feared; maybe he could actually come out the other end alive.

He closed his eyes and, for the first time in his life, he prayed.

\* \* \*

*Bury St Edmunds Police Station*

"It was found buried in the dog's biscuits." DS Fox pinned a copy of the photograph DC Gedge had taken with her phone inside the Towerses' garage. "A cheap Nokia pay-as-you-go. Goes without saying that it's untraceable."

Duncan gave a grin. "Except that up until about half an hour ago it was buried in a bag of Bonio."

Fox made a face before carrying on. "The phone is being analysed as we speak, but an initial check confirmed that Jacob — and I think we can assume the phone belonged to him and not the wife — was in contact with someone prior to his death. The phone shows a number of messages spanning the last eight weeks." Fox tacked a piece of A4 paper next to the photograph. "Full transcripts of the messages are being uploaded to the system, but these are the ones that instantly caught my eye. The messages aren't always from the same number — whoever was in contact with Jacob seems to have changed their phone regularly, too."

"More burners?" suggested Duncan.

"That would be my guess. There are three different numbers on here and all three are now out of service. Whoever this is, he — or she — doesn't want to be traced." Fox pointed towards the board. "One phrase is repeated several times. *'It's time to pay.'* Followed by the date — *15 August 2005*. The same as on Jacob's most recent handset. Whatever it means, it's significant for our killer — *if* we think we're looking for a killer."

"*'It's time to pay'* — could be referring to money?" suggested Darcie. "Maybe Jacob was in debt? What about a loan shark?"

Fox grimaced. "I know there are a few less-than-legitimate money lenders out there, but I'm not sure many resort to pushing people off tall buildings if they get behind on their repayments. It doesn't make a lot of sense."

Nicki nodded thoughtfully. "It's another line of enquiry." She remembered Denise telling them times had been tight before — maybe they still were. "Let's dig further into the family finances — see if there were any money worries over and above the usual. We also need to find out what relevance, if any, that date has. Matt and Duncan, can you dig into that? I want to know of anything significant that happened on 15 August 2005 — maybe even the insignificant, too."

Both detectives made affirmative murmurs and scooted their chairs back to their desks.

"What about this Harvey Mitcham?" asked Fox. "He's the only one we know who was definitely in touch with Jacob before he died. A brief background check hasn't thrown up much, other than him living over in Fornham All Saints. Maybe he's the one using the burner phones to contact Jacob?"

Nicki frowned. "We definitely need to speak to him. Give him a call — let him know about Jacob's death, but nothing more than what's already been disclosed in the press statement so far. Then fix a time to go and see him, the earlier the better. Have we had any joy with the estate agents?"

Darcie nodded. "They've supplied a list of current employees, plus a list of those who've been to view the property since it went on the market three weeks ago. The manager says he's happy to talk in person if it helps."

"Let's do that. Set something up for tomorrow morning." Nicki then gave the team a brief round-up of what Dennis Horner and Denise Towers had had to say for themselves, which didn't bring them much further forward. "Mrs Towers is going to ID her husband's body later today. We know it'll just be a formality, but it seems she wants to do it." Nicki took a look at her watch. "Faye and her team should be finishing up at the scene soon, so we should hear something before the end of the day."

Right on cue, Nicki's mobile burst into life.

\* \* \*

*Woodlands Camping and Caravan Site, Suffolk*

Whisky bottle now half empty, he stepped back from the camper van's table and the silver-framed photograph of his father, raising his gaze to the wall behind. His spine began to tingle.

*The list.*

It had been a part of him for the last fourteen years. To the spectator it appeared to be a series of random names, but to him it went far deeper than that. Each name he scored through brought him closer to the end of his quest, closer to justice for his father — with a not insignificant side order of revenge. It was a toxic mixture, but it was also addictive.

*Murder* was addictive.

And it all came down to the list.

Fifteen names.

Fifteen people who had contributed to his father's death. They may not have physically had their hands on him. They hadn't thrown boiling water in his eyes and then cut his throat with a kitchen knife.

But they were all culpable in their own way.

His hand twitched inside his pocket, his fingers curling around the black marker pen. Another twenty-four hours and two more would be dispatched. The end was within touching distance, he could feel it. It might have taken him fourteen years, but revenge aged like a fine wine; it tasted better the longer you waited. It had taken time to track everyone down, even in today's digital world, and then it had taken even more time to find everyone's Achilles' heel. Some were obviously weaker than others, but everyone had their price — all he'd needed to do was find out what that price was.

Just four left on the list.

Two tomorrow, then two soon after.

Revenge, and peace, would then finally be his.

# CHAPTER EIGHT

"Let's have a round-up of where we are, then call it a day." Nicki knew the team would stay on as long as required, but she could already see the weariness etched onto everyone's faces. Her father's words echoed inside her head — "*Investigations like these are marathons, Nicola, not sprints.*" She knew they would all need to conserve some energy for the coming days. Tired detectives made mistakes.

"I've spoken to the estate agents again," responded Darcie. "They've suggested tomorrow morning for a site visit. And I've made a start on contacting those that had viewings since it went on the market. Nothing suspicious so far. Shall I confirm with the agents for tomorrow?"

"Definitely. Members of the public can't just wander in off the street and climb up onto the roof — we still need to find out how Jacob managed to get up there." Nicki's gaze slid towards the crime scene photos now pinned to the first whiteboard. "And if anyone else really was with him at the time. Where are we with everything else? Social media?" Nicki knew how a person's online interactions could afford a useful window into their lives.

"Nothing further of note from his registered phone, or the new burner. His emails don't raise too many alarm bells, either. As for social media platforms—" Fox pulled his notebook closer — "Towers doesn't have much of an online presence. I've found a personal Facebook account, but it's been inactive for a while. Doesn't appear to have Instagram or Twitter accounts."

Nicki's heart sank a little as that particular dead end stared her full in the face. "OK, well if he isn't a social butterfly in his personal life, let's look more closely at his work. Having his own graphic design business, he's more than likely to have a website, or at least some online presence. Nothing we've seen so far has had much to do with his field."

Stepping closer to the whiteboard that bore a photograph of the forty-year-old graphic designer, she bit her lip. On the face of it, Jacob Towers appeared to be a regular man, someone who rarely went out, preferring to spend time at home with his wife and children. Was that who they were looking at here? Someone simple and uncomplicated who just made the wrong decision on the wrong night? But Denise was convinced he would never have jumped — *and then there were the teeth*.

Looking away from the whiteboard, she noticed DS Carter had settled himself back at his desk after returning from the mortuary. Staring at his computer screen, the detective had an uncharacteristically grave look on his face. Nicki had a suspicion that what he'd witnessed on the post-mortem table wasn't totally responsible for his paling complexion.

"First thoughts on the video, Roy?" Nicki made her way over, noting Darcie shudder as she passed by.

"I couldn't bear to watch that again." The detective constable wrapped her hands tightly around a warming mug of tea. "Once was definitely enough for me."

Although Nicki had watched the recording several times now, hoping to see something new to give them an edge, it certainly wasn't out of choice. It made for harrowing viewing, even more so when the whole team knew what was coming

— by the time the recording finished, Jacob Towers had approximately an hour left to live.

Roy rubbed his eyes, sitting back in his chair. "I can't say it was particularly pleasant."

Nicki arrived at his shoulder. "Did Dr Mitchell have anything more to say about the teeth at the PM?"

"Nothing other than they were most likely pulled out before Towers died. But . . ." Roy glanced back towards his computer screen, the video now frozen in the centre. "I guess we can see that for ourselves now, anyway. And there was blood still in his stomach."

"Whatever happened, whether Jacob jumped or not, it's clear someone else was with him not long before he died. I spoke to Faye earlier and they're processing a room at the scene that could possibly be the site of our video recording. Traces of blood have been found but it's too early to tell if it's Jacob's. We'll know more tomorrow." Nicki glanced up at the wall clock. "Unless anyone has anything new to share, I suggest that's it for today. It's been a long one, and I want us up and about early tomorrow. We've lots of leads to follow up. I'd like to go and see Harvey Mitcham first thing. Graham, be ready to leave here at nine. With any luck we can swing by the estate agents afterwards and head over to the Crown Street property, too."

"I think I'll just finish looking at the rest of this CCTV," replied Matt. "I've nothing else on tonight."

"And I'll start looking at Jacob's work interests," added Duncan. "See if I can't find a website for his business."

"Don't work too late, you two. Denise Towers has been to identify her husband's body, so we're releasing the name first thing in the morning. Be prepared for an influx of calls." Nicki grimaced. Sometimes the public could be an enormous help to an investigation — on occasion, some cases were solved purely on the information they supplied — but other times it just unearthed an avalanche of time wasters which the team would have to wade through, eating up valuable resources. "Let's reconvene bright and early tomorrow, yes?"

As Nicki left the incident room, intending to spend some time in her office before heading home, her phone chirped with an incoming message.

*Everything still OK for tonight? About 7?*

"Crap," she breathed.

* * *

*Copse Close, Bury St Edmunds*

DC Karen Gedge closed the front door behind them. "I'll just make sure everything's OK here and then I'll leave you to it." The trip to the mortuary had been as traumatic as she'd expected. Dr Mitchell and her staff had done everything in their power to make it go smoothly, but there was no getting away from the fact that Denise Towers would take the experience to her grave.

"Thank you. Most kind." Denise shuffled through to the kitchen and collapsed into one of the chairs around the table. "Don't let me keep you, though. I'm fine. You've been wonderful today. I couldn't have got through it without you."

Karen filled the kettle; whether tea was required or not she intended to make a cup before departing. While her back was turned, she heard a series of guttural moans coming from behind her.

Spinning around, she saw Denise with her head buried in her hands, sobs wracking her fragile body.

"Oh my goodness, Denise." Karen rushed to the woman's side. "You just let it all out. You'll feel much better if you do."

"No," wailed Denise, raising her head just enough to let the word out. "Nothing will ever make this feel right. It's all my fault. *Everything.* It's all my fault."

Karen abandoned the tea-making and instead let Denise sob on her shoulder. There was little she could do to make it better, other than simply being there — but sometimes that was all that was needed.

Eventually, Denise rubbed the sleeve of her cardigan across her tear-stained, blotchy face. "Sorry — I'm fine, really. I shouldn't take up any more of your time, you must have things to do."

"It's no trouble."

Denise started to push herself to her feet, shaking her head firmly. "I'm going to have an early night. I'm shattered."

Although not totally convinced, Karen bade the woman goodbye, with the express instruction to contact her if she needed to talk.

* * *

Once the front door was closed behind the family liaison officer, Denise Towers let out a shuddering sigh. Quite how she'd managed to hold it all together, she couldn't fathom.

Bypassing the kettle, she pulled open the fridge and took out the bottle of Sauvignon Blanc. She needed something much stronger than tea right now.

It hadn't been identifying Jacob's body that had thrown her, although that had been painful enough. Seeing him lying there, so peacefully, had ripped her heart to shreds. It would take a lifetime to heal, if it ever did.

Pouring herself a generous glass of the wine, she forced it down her throat. She wasn't a big drinker under normal circumstances — Jacob was the one who liked a glass of something in the evenings — but these weren't normal circumstances.

It had been the mention of the phone that had done it. When DC Gedge had asked if Jacob had a second phone in the house, her blood had instantly chilled, thinking that the police officer must have found it. Denise had tried her best to look confused, but deep down she'd felt the panic starting to bubble. Were all her lies about to unravel before her?

Shuddering, she took another mouthful of wine, wincing at the taste and knowing it would go straight to her head, having barely eaten all day. When the phone had been found in the garage, the relief she'd felt almost knocked her down. She wondered if DC Gedge had noticed.

"It's all my fault," she breathed, draining the glass and then stepping across to the cupboards on the far side of the kitchen. "All of it."

Hand shaking, she pulled down the box of granola from the top shelf. Jacob had shunned anything healthy, so she had thought the cereal was as good a hiding place as any; she was just fortunate that DC Gedge hadn't found it. Reaching inside, she pulled out the phone.

*How could I have been so stupid? How could I have done this to Jacob?*

Fresh tears starting to bubble, she switched it on and stabbed at the screen. Jacob must have found out, somehow. Maybe he'd found the phone after all, or maybe he'd followed her one day when she'd said she was going to the gym. It didn't matter, not now.

*I drove him to do this. It's all my fault.*

The call was answered on the second ring. She didn't give the recipient a chance to speak.

"We have to stop this — and we have to stop this now."

\* \* \*

*Rye, East Sussex*

Hugh Webster turned off the ignition and sat for a moment. Normally, he would have climbed out of the car without a second thought, visualising a generous glass of Merlot waiting for him inside. But tonight was different; something made him hesitate.

In the early days of his retirement, he'd struggled with the sudden change of pace — essentially going from a detective superintendent in charge of a busy department to nothing, overnight. He found himself with no real reason to get up in the morning, nothing to occupy his time. If there were jobs that needed doing around the house, he could always put them off until the next day — or the one after that. Days stretched out before him with nothing more taxing than deciding if he fancied a game of golf, or to take Anne out for lunch in a local pub. It had taken a while to adjust, but once he'd accepted his new life, his new position in the order of things, he'd adapted relatively easily.

And he wasn't a complete hermit. He frequented the local golf club most weeks, had monthly bridge nights with a couple of other retirees in the area, and spent a considerable amount of time tinkering with an old motorbike in the garage. But most of all, he enjoyed spending time with Anne. Over the years, she'd created a beautiful home for them, but he hadn't appreciated it when he was working sixty-hour weeks. But now, whenever he returned to their modest three-bedroom home, he couldn't wait to get inside and be enveloped in the comfortable cocoon she'd built for them.

Except for tonight.

Tonight, he lingered on the drive.

If he was being completely honest with himself, it wasn't the first time he'd felt like this in recent weeks. As an experienced police officer, he knew when he was being followed.

The first question that sprang to mind was, *why?*

Rapidly followed by, *who?*

There had been a period of time in the late seventies, early eighties, when an unspecified threat against all police officers in England and Wales was circulated to every force. It had been kept from the media — as a lot of things were around that time by necessity — but, for several months, Hugh could recall having to check beneath his car before driving to work each morning. It was never proven that the threat had been from the IRA, but he and his colleagues had been told not to take any chances. Car bombs were rife around that time, and not only in the capital.

Feeling his blood chill at the memory, he cranked open the car door and started heading towards the house, glancing over his shoulder as he did so. He'd been in Hastings all afternoon, and that was where the feeling had first started, that sense of not quite being alone. He might be being paranoid, of course — the unwelcome news that some of his old cases were being looked into was setting off all manner of unwarranted chain reactions inside his head. Maybe this was just one of them. As he slotted the key into the lock, he took another look at the car parked on the drive behind him.

Maybe he would check it over in the morning, just to be safe. And then perhaps next week he would tackle the garage — clearing it out so he could at least start parking the car inside for a change.

*Maybe.*

Turning back to the house, he began to wonder whether it was time to install some home security. Maybe some cameras. Or perhaps one of those new video doorbell things everyone was raving about. Twisting the key in the lock, he gave a muted half-laugh.

*Get a grip, Webbers. You're getting more and more paranoid by the second.*

Stepping over the threshold into the hallway, Hugh instantly began to relax. He thought he could smell roast beef cooking in the kitchen, his stomach growling as the aroma floated towards him. As he slipped off his coat, Anne appeared from the front room with a glass in her hand.

"Here. You look like you could do with this. How did it go?"

After hanging up his coat, Hugh took the glass and gave a grateful smile. "Thanks. Robert sends his regards. I think we managed to get everything sorted for now, after a fashion." Robert Goodchild was a chartered accountant and family friend. On retiring fourteen years ago, Hugh had taken the man's advice and invested his lump sum payment and other savings into a selection of stocks and shares. He didn't quite understand the mechanics of it all, trusting Robert to handle everything, but around this time every year came the dreaded task of starting to collate it all for the annual tax return. He gave another smile. "And is that beef I can smell cooking?"

The smile on Anne's lips made her eyes sparkle, even in the muted light of the hallway. "Nothing wrong with your spidey-senses, is there? It's nearly ready — I'll be dishing up in about twenty minutes, just waiting for the roast potatoes to crisp up. There's time for a quick shower if you want one?"

Hugh shook his head and instead headed into the front room. "Maybe later. Right now, all I want to do is crash on the sofa and drink this. I'm not built for town life these days."

Anne followed, closing the curtains before handing her husband the TV remote control. "I'll let you know when dinner's ready." With a light squeeze on his arm, she left.

Sighing, Hugh sank into the plush cushions on the three-seater sofa and took a mouthful of the red wine. The trip into Hastings had been tiring, even though it wasn't far, but that wasn't the real reason he felt so shattered. Knowing there was someone out there tailing him was draining.

As the wine warmed his blood, the trepidation he'd felt outside started to dissolve — the alcohol bringing him to his senses. In time, everything would work itself out. There would be some kind of explanation for both the investigation into his past cases, and the mystery stalker — and then life would get back to normal. The family had had a lot to deal with in recent weeks — the new-found elation at the reappearance of Dean had taken time to adjust to. You couldn't wipe out two decades of pain with just a hug and a handshake.

But they were getting there.

Some things were changing already. He could see a brightness in Anne's eyes that hadn't been there for many years, a lightness in her step that had nothing to do with the weekly yoga classes she attended. The pain was obviously still present for them both — it was so ingrained it would never leave them, not entirely — but it was no longer all-encompassing, no longer squeezing every ounce of joy from their lives. Instead, they now had something they'd never had before.

*Hope.*

Hugh took another large mouthful of wine and rubbed his tired eyes. He'd aged over the last two decades, looking older than the number of years that had actually passed. He knew the grey hairs had become more widespread, the lines on his brow that little bit deeper. Sadness had followed him around like a stubborn shadow. But life was, at last, offering them something to look forward to. *A future.* They were travelling up to Suffolk to visit Nicki and Dean at the weekend, which would take his mind off everything else.

Unable to stop himself, Hugh's gaze momentarily flickered over towards the closed curtains and the car parked outside.

Maybe he would check beneath it in the morning anyway. *Just to be sure.*

# CHAPTER NINE

*College Lane, Bury St Edmunds*

"This is nice." Dean Webster collapsed onto Nicki's sofa, a broad grin on his face. "Thanks for the invite."

Nicki returned the smile. Despite the long and busy day she'd had, and the infinite number of long and busy days that lay ahead, she couldn't help herself. Deano was here — sitting on her sofa, alive and well. Although it had been several weeks now, she still had to pinch herself that fate wasn't playing some cruel joke.

"My pleasure. But it's just a shop-bought takeaway, I'm afraid. I haven't the time or the energy to cook."

Dean gave a laugh. "I'm sure it'll be fine."

Nicki had often wondered how their relationship would be after all this time apart. Ten-year-old Nicola Webster was long gone, and in her place was thirty-three-year-old Nicki Hardcastle. Older for sure, maybe a little wiser, too; certainly more cautious. But what of five-year-old Dean Webster? Nicki knew her baby brother had been replaced by a newer, older version — *but who was he?* In the weeks since they'd met again, she felt she was no closer to finding out. He'd declined her invitation to sleep on the sofa while he sorted himself out, a decision she knew was both practical and wise. Her one-bedroom townhouse was cramped at the best of times. But she also detected an element of hesitation in him, which was understandable.

"Hardcastle suits you, by the way." Dean took a large mouthful from his wine glass, interrupting Nicki's thoughts. "What made you choose it?"

Nicki hovered in the doorway to the galley-style kitchen, realising there was still so much her brother didn't know about his family. "It was Mum's maiden name. It seemed like a good choice at the time."

Dean nodded. "Like I say, it suits you." A grin followed. "You weren't influenced by that song, then?"

"What song would that be?"

Swallowing another mouthful of wine, he grinned again. "That 'n-n-n-n-nineteen' song. Paul Hardcastle."

Nicki laughed as she returned to the kitchen to retrieve a bottle of Sauvignon Blanc. "That song must be way before your time!"

"Maybe, but it's still a classic!"

"More white?" Nicki returned to the living room, waving the wine bottle in the air. "Or would you prefer a beer?"

Dean raised his glass. "Wine's fine. Why don't you sit down and relax for a minute? You look done in."

Nicki didn't need asking twice, her feet still throbbing from the new pair of boots she'd put on that morning, topping up their glasses before she sat. "Sorry, it's been a long day. I'm still a bit wired — too much coffee, I expect."

"Anything I can do to help? I'm a whizz in the kitchen."

Nicki considered the question for a moment as she took another gulp of wine. Her brother, a whizz in the kitchen? There was still so much she didn't know about him, too — so much still to discover. It both excited and daunted her. "It's all in hand, thanks. Just warming everything through in the oven."

"You look stressed — is it work?"

Nicki squeezed her brother's hand. As much as she would love to offload, she knew she couldn't — not to Deano, anyway. Not to anyone, really, such were the constraints of the job. Many people believed that the reason so many relationships failed within the police service — and maybe others like the ambulance service, the health service and firefighters, too — was because there was no way to offload after a hard day. The person waiting for you at home may love you, may even claim to understand you, but they could never fully appreciate what you dealt with on a daily basis. And nor should they.

Nicki raised her glass and managed a smile. "Everything's fine. All I need is another glass of wine or two. Cheers."

A comfortable silence followed as they savoured the bargain bottle Nicki had picked up on her way home. Eventually, it was Dean who punctured the vacuum.

"Larry and Annette have asked me to visit them." He swallowed the rest of the sentence with a mouthful of wine.

Nicki's eyes widened. "And do you want to?"

Dean played with the glass in his hand, turning it around in circles before giving a small shrug. "I've not decided yet. I don't think so. I'm not exactly sure what I'd say to them. I can tell Ade doesn't want to go."

Nicki had met Adrian Browning on a few occasions in the past, and although he wasn't the most appealing of characters, she sometimes wondered how he must be feeling in the wake of what had happened. He was the forgotten victim in all this mess. He'd lost his parents *and* his brother, all in one go. Although it somewhat pained her to say it, she felt a degree of sympathy for the man.

"You know you don't have to meet them if you don't want to, right?" Nicki gave Dean's hand another squeeze. "You don't owe them anything."

"Maybe." Dean gave a quiet sigh, still toying with his glass. "But they looked after me for such a long time. I know it sounds weird, but they gave me a good life."

Nicki settled back against the sofa cushions and felt her eyes close. They'd touched on the subject a few times, whether Dean should forgive the Brownings for what they did to him — what they did to the whole Webster family. As the weeks passed, Nicki had found her position hardening rather than softening. Initially, she'd felt sorry for them — sorry for what they'd been through in losing their son Mason so tragically, and what had then driven them to snatch her brother from the fair. But as time went on, she found her opinion changing — and the sympathy soon began to disappear.

Dean was surprisingly accepting of what had happened, often talking about Larry and Annette in fond terms. Nicki struggled to understand but, then again, she hadn't been there; she hadn't lived the life he had. She was fully aware of the unusual impact of Stockholm Syndrome. It made her shudder.

Nicki dragged her eyelids open and stifled a yawn behind her wine glass. "Give it time. No need for hasty decisions. They won't be going anywhere for the foreseeable, I'm sure." She wasn't altogether appraised of the precise mechanics of the case against the Brownings but, from what she'd heard on the police grapevine, Larry and Annette would be staying in prison for a considerable time to come.

"The bloke that jumped from that house in the town—" Dean gulped down the rest of his wine, then reached for the bottle on the coffee table — "is that one of yours? It's all over the news."

Details had trickled into the media as the day progressed. After Denise Towers' positive ID only a few hours ago, Jacob's name was set to be released first thing in the morning, but the sparse information shared to date was still enough to get the town's tongues wagging.

"You know I can't really talk about it, Dean, but yes — it's one of ours. There's not too much to tell anyway. It's still early days." Needing to steer the conversation away from Jacob Towers, Nicki heaved herself up from the sofa. "The food should be ready now. I'll go and dish it up." As she made her way into the kitchen, she grabbed hold of the doorframe, feeling herself sway a little. Wine on an empty stomach wasn't the greatest idea she'd had that day.

The aroma that hit her as she opened the oven door made her stomach grumble, reminding her she'd had nothing to eat that day but a leftover Danish pastry halfway through the afternoon. Piling their plates with an assortment of curry dishes and rice, Nicki had only just deposited them on the coffee table when there was a sharp rap at the door.

Frowning, she checked her watch. It was after eight. She wasn't expecting anyone and those that knew her were aware she wasn't keen on unannounced visits. Leaving her brother to start digging into the food, she padded over to the door. The apprehensive look on her face transformed into a tired smile once it opened.

"Ben!" Stepping back, she waved a hand towards the living room, where Dean was already shovelling chicken madras into his mouth. "This is a nice surprise. Why don't you come in and join us? Dean's here — we're just having some food. Nothing fancy, just a takeaway, but there's plenty to go round."

"No, you're all right." Benedict Thatcher remained glued to the doorstep. "I can see you're busy. I'll catch up with you another time. I was just passing, really."

"Honestly, it's no bother." Nicki gestured once more towards the sofa. "You're more than welcome. We've got wine, too."

Benedict seemed to hesitate for a moment before taking a step back. "Nice offer but I've got a casserole in the slow cooker, so I'll pass. Thanks anyway. Although it does smell good. Maybe another time."

Nicki was about to reply but, before she knew it, Benedict had disappeared back into the night.

* * *

"You managing to get much from the CCTV?" Duncan placed two large pizza boxes onto the table between his and Matt's desks. "Found our man in the town yet?"

Matt exhaled noisily. "Nope, not a thing. Wherever he went, he didn't trouble the cameras — and from his bank details it doesn't look like he used his card anywhere." He reached over and flipped open the lid of the top pizza box. "Cheers for this, mate. I'm starving."

Duncan settled back into his chair and reactivated his computer screen. "No worries. You need to keep your strength up with this impending fatherhood of yours. Remind me when the little one's due?"

"Two weeks, but Danni's convinced it'll be sooner." Matt shrugged as he tore a slice of pizza in half and pushed it into his mouth. "I'm not sure how she can tell."

Duncan grinned, reaching for the meat feast pizza box. "Enjoy the peace and freedom while you can, mate. Life will never be the same again after it's born."

Matt made a face, wiping tomato sauce from his chin. "So everyone keeps telling me. How are you getting on with Towers' website?"

A quick call to DC Gedge had given them the web address for Jacob's graphic design business, Tower Graphics. It wasn't the most imaginative of company names.

"Just having a root around in it now. To be fair, it seems to be quite professionally done. Lots of pictures of work he's completed for clients. Quite impressive, if you like that kind of thing." Duncan tilted his computer screen in Matt's direction. "The 'About Me' section confirms what we already know about him — started the business in 2003 after a career in the City and now works mainly from home. Says here he'll travel to see clients where necessary. I did find something interesting, though." The detective constable clicked his mouse. "There's a secure messaging service where you can send him a direct message from a pop-up box. I've tried sending a message, but it doesn't seem to go through to the work email we've been given. It must go somewhere else. Maybe he's got a different email address we don't know about."

Matt slid his chair over. "You think there might be a glitch with the website?"

Duncan gave a half-shrug. "Not sure. Once the message is sent, you get a pop-up box saying thank you for your communication, we'll be in touch. Which makes me think it's all working fine. I just don't know where the message went."

Matt reached for the can of Coke that accompanied the takeaway. "Sounds like something for people far more technologically minded than us."

Duncan agreed, glancing at his watch. "The tech guys have probably left for home by now, but I'll flag it up for the morning."

"Good plan." Matt leaned back in his chair, plucking another slice of pepperoni as he did so. "What's your take on all this? Did our man jump — or was he pushed?"

Duncan's cheeks puffed as he ripped open his Coke can. "My gut tells me he didn't jump. I can't get past the teeth. If you were about to kill yourself, would you really go through all the pain and torture of pulling out your own teeth? It makes no sense, but then . . ." He gave a shrug. "Why the hell did he climb up onto the roof in the first place? That part must at least have been voluntary. Apparently, there was no sign of a struggle anywhere in the house and he's not exactly a small bloke, just over six foot. So, if he *did* go up there of his own volition, what was he intending to do? Stargaze?"

"I agree. And how did he even get inside? You think the estate agents were involved somehow?"

Before Duncan could reply, Matt's phone started to trill. "Shit, it's the wife." He dropped the half-eaten pizza slice back on his desk and stabbed the screen. "Danni, what's up?"

* * *

Benedict Thatcher sat behind the wheel of his BMW and swore under his breath. That was close. If Nicki's brother hadn't been there, he just might have told her everything. The temptation to come clean was almost overwhelming.

*Almost.*

But he wasn't stupid — he knew if he did tell her, then the whole precarious house of cards he'd been painstakingly building would come tumbling down around them. And the consequences would be catastrophic.

But he *had* been tempted — tempted enough to knock on her door, at least.

*What was he thinking?*

Hopefully, all he'd done was make himself look like an idiot, even more so than usual, and she wouldn't give it a moment's thought. But this was Nicki they were talking about; she was renowned for being sharper than the average copper. They may have met in rather unorthodox circumstances — with Benedict helping Nicki unravel the mystery of her brother's disappearance and eventually discovering what had happened to him, and then the fact that he was still alive — but there was something natural that had clicked between them. He valued her friendship more than anything in the world. Could he really keep lying to her?

He knew he was expected to follow through on his orders before long. Time was ticking, and he was fast running out of excuses. If he didn't do as they asked, he knew what the consequences would be. There were any number of new roads being built these days, plenty that wouldn't notice an extra addition to the foundations.

The thought made him shudder.

He didn't fancy propping up the latest local motorway extension if he could possibly avoid it.

Pulling the BMW away from the kerb, he headed for home. The urge to confess all would no doubt return, but he knew it wouldn't be tonight. Dean had given him the excuse he needed not to open his mouth — for which he was thankful.

But Dean couldn't be there all the time, could he?

Gripping the steering wheel, knuckles already turning white, he negotiated the roundabout and headed out of town. As he did so, his mobile rang. Glancing at the handsfree handset on the dashboard, he saw the withheld caller display.

He stabbed at the screen to decline the call.

# CHAPTER TEN

*Fornham All Saints, Bury St Edmunds*
*Friday 24 May 2019*

"Do come through." Eileen Mitcham led Nicki and DS Fox along the dimly lit, narrow hallway to a study at the rear of the house. "Sorry, we're having some work done at the moment and the front room looks like a bomb site." Giving a slightly nervous laugh, the birdlike woman stepped back to allow the detectives to walk in ahead of her. "I'll just let Harvey know you're here. Tea or coffee while you wait?"

Nicki was about to decline both offers but then had second thoughts. When they finished here, they were due to visit the estate agents and take a look at the house on Crown Street; after just half a cup of black coffee at home that morning, the refreshment would be welcome. She smiled. "Either would be lovely, thank you."

The study was small — in estate agent language it would probably be termed "compact" — with a grand-looking mahogany desk taking centre stage. Three of the four walls were flanked with deep-set bookcases, each shelf groaning under the weight of books and magazines.

As Nicki edged around the tight space, she noted there seemed to be little by way of organisation or order. Looking at the shelving, she spied a number of hardback atlases of the world stacked up next to an array of gardening books; then came a complete set of the works of William Shakespeare. On another shelf there was a collection charting the history of the Royal Navy, then a twelve-book series on the Impressionists. Below that was a shelf almost entirely devoted to World War I, with a small collection of self-help books ranging from meditation to yoga. Opposite that was an area specific to vegan cookery.

"What does he do, our Mr Mitcham?" Nicki cast a glance toward Fox. "Do we know?"

"I don't think we do." Fox gave the room a quick 360-degree scan, his gaze coming to rest on the cluttered desk. "But that's an expensive-looking MacBook he's got there." Fox nodded towards the laptop half buried beneath a stack of paper. "I guess he must work from home?"

Nicki gave a chuckle. "I'm not sure anyone could work in this chaos. Look at the state of it."

The desk offered barely an inch of free space between piles of paperwork and yet more books. It even surpassed the DCI's desk back at the station. Nicki spied more files and notepads stacked up on the captain-style chair tucked underneath the desk, and the floor fared no better, home to more towers of books that had yet to find their way to the overfilled bookcases.

After a few minutes, the door opened again and Eileen entered with a tray of coffee and biscuits, closely followed by her husband.

"Apologies, apologies," the man gushed. "I hope you haven't been waiting too long."

Harvey Mitcham wasn't quite what Nicki had expected. Admittedly, they hadn't had too much to go on when it came to Jacob Towers' best, and probably only, friend, but the man who now stood before them in the study doorway wasn't what she'd imagined at all. Although she tried not to judge on first impressions, Nicki couldn't help labelling the man as a mad professor — somewhere between Doc Brown in *Back to the Future* and Albert Einstein. Thin tufts of wayward hair curled up from his scalp, and a pair of wireframed spectacles balanced on the end of his nose.

"Not at all, Mr Mitcham. It's good of you to see us at such short notice — and in such sad circumstances, too." Nicki noticed a brief frown cross the man's lined forehead before realisation seemed to catch up.

"Of yes, of course. Jacob. Such a sorry business."

Nicki placed a well-practised smile on her face as she helped Eileen Mitcham clear a space on the cluttered desk for the tray. "Sorry business" wasn't exactly how she would describe it herself, but she decided to let it go for now. Moving a pile of papers to the floor, she took the tray from Eileen and perched it on top of a stack of chemistry textbooks.

"Thank you, Mrs Mitcham. This is very kind of you."

The woman gave a hesitant smile before departing, leaving her husband and the detectives alone.

"Shall I be mother?" Fox picked up one of the coffee cups and was already busy tipping a splash of milk into it from a chipped china jug. "Biscuit?" Handing the cup to Nicki, he waved the plate of digestives in her direction, receiving a shake of the head in response. Taking a cup for himself, together with the plate of biscuits, the detective sergeant leaned up against one of the crowded bookcases.

Harvey Mitcham made his way around the desk, unceremoniously dumping the notepads and files from the chair onto the already cluttered floor before eventually collapsing into it. "I was very shocked to hear about Jacob. When I saw the news headlines yesterday, I had no idea it was him. If I can help in any way, I will."

"That's very good to hear, Mr Mitcham." Nicki slipped her coffee cup back onto the tray. "At the moment, our enquiries are in the preliminary stages. We're trying to get a picture of Jacob and his life. We found your name in his contacts list. Anything you can tell us about your relationship with him would be greatly appreciated. Had you known each other long?"

Harvey leaned back in the captain's chair, which creaked beneath his weight. Nicki took another brief moment to take in his appearance. He was older than she'd imagined — with Jacob being forty, she'd assumed Mitcham would be around the same age, but the man before her had at least twenty years, if not more, on the graphic designer. He was dressed in an ill-fitting pale grey suit with an off-white shirt beneath, both of which looked to have had only a passing acquaintance with an iron; an old-fashioned fob watch tucked into his waistcoat pocket completed the look. The man peered out from behind a pair of half-moon spectacles.

"I would be hard pushed to put a timeframe on it, to be honest. Maybe about five years?" Harvey rubbed his whiskered chin with a bony finger. "Certainly before the twins were born. How old are they now?"

"I believe they're around seven," replied Fox, munching on a digestive. "Maybe eight."

"Gosh, seven." The man's bushy eyebrows shot up. "Doesn't time fly? In that case, it must be nearer eight or even nine years, then."

"And how did you meet?" Nicki flashed another look around the cramped study. "Was it work related, or more social?"

"Oh, it was definitely work related. I approached him, if I remember rightly. I needed a graphic designer and came across his name. I'm a bit of an entrepreneur, in case you were wondering. I think that's probably the best way to describe it. I have a lot of fingers in a lot of pies, always looking for that one invention that will change the world." The man gave what Nicki thought sounded like a forced laugh. "Or maybe save the planet."

"So, it was more of a professional relationship, then?" Nicki sensed a slight hesitation from the other side of the desk, the question appearing to catch Harvey off guard.

The man reached to pick up his coffee cup from the tray. "I think that would just about sum it up, yes. I mean, we got on, obviously — maybe shared a drink or two on occasion in the early days. Our wives were friendly, as I remember. But, as the years rolled by, we drifted." Harvey nudged his half-moon glasses further up onto his nose. "He was a pleasant young man, as I recall."

"And when was the last time you saw him?"

The man's brow creased as he took a sip from his cup. "I'm none too sure, to be honest. It must be some time ago now — probably early last year, at a guess."

"And what about speaking to Jacob? Did you have cause to speak to him recently? Maybe give him a call?" Nicki already had Jacob's phone records showing interaction between the pair in the week before he died, but she was still interested in the man's response. The best questions were often the ones you already knew the answers to.

"Speaking?" Harvey paused for a second, his eyes darting to the side to avoid Nicki's gaze, as faint colour flushed his cheeks. "Not recently, no. Not that I recall, anyway."

And there it was. The first lie. Alongside it came a slight tensing of the man's whiskered jaw.

Nicki heard Fox clear his throat, the detective munching his way through a second digestive biscuit. After enough time had passed, she edged a little closer, cutting down the distance between herself and the desk. And Harvey Mitcham. "You haven't had reason to contact him recently?"

Another few seconds of uncomfortable silence ticked by. Fox paused his biscuit crunching, while Nicki maintained her stance at the front of the desk.

Harvey continued to avoid her gaze, eventually shaking his head. "I could always check my phone, I suppose, assuming I can even find it." He gave what sounded to Nicki like another forced laugh, gesturing towards the carnage masquerading as his desk. "It's most probably under that lot somewhere. Eileen is always on at me to be more organised."

Returning the fixed smile to her face, Nicki took a step back. "No need, Mr Mitcham. At least, not yet. What is it that you do, by the way? You mentioned fingers and pies earlier."

With a more relaxed look about him, Harvey rubbed his chin and leaned forward on the desk. "Well, that's a question that could take some time, Inspector. Like I said a moment ago, I dabble in many things — but I suppose my main interest is robots and the use of artificial intelligence in the modern world."

Nicki's eyebrows twitched. "Artificial intelligence?"

"Oh, believe me, it's coming, Inspector. It'll be in all aspects of our lives before long, you mark my words." Harvey leaned closer, his voice turning grave. "And not all of it will be good, I can assure you of that."

"And Jacob, was he into this artificial intelligence thing as well?"

Harvey's eyes sparkled as another laugh quickly followed. "Not at all — at least, not in the same way as I was. He was helping me design a website, to showcase a few of my ideas. We were then going to work on some promotional material, if I ever got around to doing talks in the community about my inventions. I'm not really sure what he thought of the whole artificial intelligence thing, per se."

Nicki straightened up, reaching for her coffee and taking a mouthful. It was surprisingly good — smooth and strong. As she did so, her eyes strayed towards the bookshelf closest to her and the collection of written works that had missed her attention earlier. The first set of books she saw were on the moon landing of 1969, the title of one in particular catching her eye: *Were We Really There?*

Edging a little closer, she then saw books on the assassinations of JFK and Martin Luther King, the death of Princess Diana, the attacks on the Twin Towers, Roswell and even a couple of publications on Elvis Presley. "I see you have an interest in conspiracy theories, Mr Mitcham." She turned back towards the desk, noticing the man stiffen. "That's quite some collection you have there."

"I'm not a fantasist, Inspector, despite what it might look like. I'm a scientist by nature and I deal in facts." The man's gaze hardened alongside his tone. "Have you noticed how much information is fed to us these days? We're nothing but cattle being fed by machines. The media controls what we're told and when we're told it. We only ever see what they *want* us to see."

"Did they really land on the moon, then?" Fox took another digestive from the plate. "Armstong and the others?"

Harvey's gaze flickered back towards the bookcase, a haughty look crossing his face. "I suggest you read the articles and see for yourself, young man. Then maybe ask that question again."

"Let's get back to Jacob." Nicki didn't want the day to start disappearing down an unnecessary rabbit hole. "Were you aware of his state of mind recently? How he might have been feeling in the last few weeks?"

"I'm afraid not. Like I said, we weren't close, and it was some time ago that I last saw or heard from him." Harvey placed his coffee cup back on the tray. "Was it suicide?"

Instantly, images of Jacob Towers pulling out his own teeth flooded Nicki's head. She'd half expected the question, but that didn't mean it was any easier to hear — or indeed answer. "At this point in time, we're not sure. Hence our questions. Is there anything else you can tell us about his character? Anything at all?"

After a few moments' consideration, Harvey pushed himself up from the captain's chair. "I'm afraid not. Like I say, I didn't know him all that well — he was more of an acquaintance than a friend. I am truly sorry about his passing, but I'm not really sure I can be of much help to you."

Nicki was experienced enough to know when she was being dismissed. Maintaining the pleasant smile on her face, she returned her cup to the tray and caught Fox's eye. "In that case, we'll leave you in peace."

After the usual exchange of stilted pleasantries on the front doorstep, Nicki and Fox made their way back to where Nicki had parked the car. "First impressions, Graham?"

Fox hovered by the passenger door, glancing back towards the modest-sized detached house behind them. "Seems like a scatty, would-be scientist-stroke-inventor to me. Harmless enough, but . . ."

A smile crept onto Nicki's face. "But?"

"Well, two things, really. Firstly, he's blatantly lying about not being in touch with our deceased. We know that much just from the phone records. And although he gives a good impression of the archetypal nutty professor, he doesn't strike me as being all that forgetful. He's a smart one."

Nicki's smile widened, knowing what he was about to say. "And the second thing?"

"For someone who claims Jacob Towers wasn't a particularly close friend, there were a disturbing number of photographs lining the walls in the hallway that would suggest otherwise."

\* \* \*

*Hastings, East Sussex*

Detective Inspector Mark Keeble was grateful that breakfast at the Highcliffe Guest House was an all-morning affair. The place hadn't looked like much from the roadside, the windows in need of a clean, the paintwork peeling in places, but beggars most definitely couldn't be choosers when it came to finding a place to stay at the last minute.

Yesterday evening, he'd followed Webster back to the retired detective's home address in nearby Rye, hanging back as far into the shadows as he could. And as far as he knew, the man hadn't clocked him. Much of the afternoon had been spent waiting opposite the offices of R. Goodchild Accountancy Services, passing the time reading a selection of newspapers and trying his best to avoid the racing pages. He'd resisted the urge to place a bet, even though he'd seen a dead cert in the 3.30 at Goodwood, congratulating himself on his willpower. But such self-resolve hadn't extended to bypassing the off-licence three shop fronts down.

Unable to resist, he'd slipped inside on the pretence of buying a packet of crisps and a wizened-looking sandwich from the vending machine just inside the door — then two bottles of gin had somehow found their way into his basket. At least that had taken care of dinner last night.

Pouring himself a coffee, he was pleased to see it looked and smelled strong. Depositing three large teaspoons of sugar into the mug, he took a seat by the bay window. Bleary eyed, he consulted the laminated menu on the table.

The Highcliffe Guest House was different to the many others he'd frequented over the years — especially during the times he and Jennifer had been fighting. He'd often found himself in need of a place to stay at short notice while tempers calmed. With this one, however, there wasn't the usual breakfast buffet on offer, the series of stainless-steel platters and warming plates where guests would line up and help themselves. Instead, Mrs Briggs would make your chosen breakfast to order. The range might not be as extensive as other establishments, but the personal touch was a welcome change.

Keeble wasn't sure he could stomach all that much for breakfast, though. The bed had been comfortable enough, but he'd tossed and turned for much of the night, thoughts of Hugh Webster preventing him from sleep. This, despite the two bottles of gin.

After leaving Webster's house in Rye last night, the lure of the alcohol on the back seat of the car had been too overpowering. The sensible option would have been to drive straight home, but Keeble wasn't renowned for being sensible. He needed a drink and recognised that the only way to deal with the devil was to feed it. But he wasn't stupid enough to drink and drive. He'd witnessed enough of the carnage left behind on the roads when drivers thought themselves immune to the effect of alcohol in their system. So, he'd headed back into Hastings and stopped at the first guest house showing VACANCIES in the window. It wasn't as though he had anything, or anyone, to return home to. Not even a cat.

The coffee swirled in his stomach as Mrs Briggs waddled across the worn carpet towards him. The old-fashioned front room had been tastefully converted into a dining area, and with eight tables it was a rather snug fit. But, by almost ten thirty, Keeble was the only guest left.

"And what would you like from the menu, my dear?" Rosie Briggs was barely five feet tall but still managed to carry more than an extra few pounds — most of them collecting around her middle. A faded blue-and-white-striped apron was tied around her waist, a notepad peeking out from her breast pocket. "A full English to set you up for the day?"

Keeble felt his stomach shift. He smiled weakly. "I don't think I can quite manage that this morning, maybe just a round of toast and some scrambled eggs?"

Rosie plucked the notepad from her pocket and proceeded to write the order down with a stubby pencil. "White or brown toast, my dear? Or maybe a mixture?"

Hoping to douse the rumblings in his stomach with something strong and bitter, Keeble reached for his coffee. He couldn't tell if it was hunger or sickness he was feeling. "A mixture would be nice, thank you."

"Of course." More scribbling on the notepad. "And you're sure I can't get you anything else? How about some bacon to go with the eggs? It's locally sourced from a farm shop — none of this cheap supermarket stuff."

Bacon.

There was a faint aroma of it still in the air, and it was one smell that would normally get his mouth watering. But his head was still pounding, maybe not quite with the sledgehammer it had been earlier — perhaps merely a rubber mallet thumping against his temples instead — but it made him feel a little queasy, and he wondered if bacon might be a step too far.

Deciding it was kill or cure, he nodded. "Go on, then. Bacon as well."

Beaming, the woman swivelled round on her swollen feet and waddled back towards the kitchen. "Help yourself to cereal and fruit in the meantime."

Once she'd disappeared, Keeble finished the rest of his coffee and went for a refill. He was starting to feel a little stronger already — the painkillers he'd popped before coming downstairs were finally starting to take effect — so he decided to try a bowl of cornflakes. In for a penny . . .

Settling back at the table with his bowl, his thoughts invariably rewound to the day before. Hugh Webster was a creature of habit and Keeble had already followed him to the golf club and local DIY store in the last week, and the same the week before that. Yesterday had been the first time he'd left Rye and headed into Hastings, a half-hour drive away.

Keeble had had to sharpen his surveillance skills once they were out of familiar territory, but the biggest challenge had been following the retired detective back to his home. There had been little or no traffic heading in their direction and Keeble had worried the Jag might stand out like a sore thumb. Once they'd arrived in Rye, he'd lingered in the shadows while Webster went inside the house, watching for the curtains to close and the lights to go on. He'd then waited another thirty minutes, just to be sure.

Slipping the note under Webster's windscreen wipers had been a spur-of-the-moment decision. Time would tell whether it was a good one or not. It wasn't only that Webster might see him as he crept up the drive, or indeed the neighbours — it was more what the man might do when he found it. Would he make the connection Keeble wanted him to? The man had a reputation for being smart, and Keeble hoped retirement hadn't blunted his instincts.

Brushing away whatever misgivings still lurked in his fogged conscience — it was done now; he couldn't turn back the clock — he poured milk and a generous amount of sugar onto the cornflakes and started to eat. Hunger was now winning the race against the hangover.

Mrs Briggs soon reappeared with a plate of creamy scrambled eggs, topped with four rashers of thick-cut bacon, plus a toast rack containing three slices of white, three slices of brown.

Keeble made room on the small table, pushing his empty cereal bowl to the side. "Thank you — just what I need."

The woman beamed again. "You're more than welcome, my dear. If you don't mind me saying, you do look very tired. Hopefully this will perk you up."

Keeble plucked a slice of toast from the rack and started to butter it. He did feel tired, every bone in his body aching, every muscle as heavy as lead. He knew it was his own fault — a diet of gin was always going to catch up with him sooner or later — but what he really needed right now, after the eggs and bacon, was time to sleep it off. Instead, he had at least a two-hour journey back home, probably a lot more, knowing what London traffic was like even in the middle of the day.

"Are you sure you want to check out today, love? I don't have anyone else booked into your room — if it would help, you're more than welcome to stay another night." She collected the empty cereal bowl and started to turn. "No rush, my dear. You just let me know."

Taking a large mouthful of the freshly buttered toast, Keeble closed his eyes. Going back to sleep would feel like heaven right now. Maybe another night might be wise — perhaps he could even make it permanent. It wasn't as if he had much to return home to — not now, anyway. A job he no longer wanted to do. A job he was probably no longer any good at, either, if the truth be told. There was nothing else of substance in his life. No one would miss him, he was sure of that.

Maybe he could just disappear and never have to face up to what he'd done.

Just as he began to think that it might be an option, his mobile interrupted the calm. Swallowing a mouthful of eggs and bacon, he saw the message flash up onto the screen.

*It's time to pay for what you did.*
*15 August 2005*

* * *

Once the front door had closed, Harvey Mitcham made his way back to the sanctuary of his study. Although he'd been expecting them, having detectives in the house had unnerved him more than he'd thought it would. With his mind going blank, all the answers he'd rehearsed had evaporated from his head in seconds. He wondered if that was what it felt like to be interrogated.

Closing the study door, he went straight over to the desk and rummaged among the paperwork until he located his phone. Stabbing at the screen, he pulled up his contact list and deleted Jacob Towers from it. He then accessed the saved messages and did the same.

He repeated the same process for the MacBook. Any email correspondence, of which there was little anyway, was deleted and wiped from the system.

Satisfied, he then wrenched open the bottom drawer of the desk. Eileen was blissfully unaware of the bottle of Macallan he kept there, as far as he knew anyway. If she *did* know, then she was putting on a good act. It wasn't as if he drank all that much anymore — certainly not as much as he had done in his youth, but maybe somewhat more than he'd confessed to his doctor at his recent health check. But sometimes only a quick shot would do.

Such as now.

The fact that it was barely ten thirty in the morning was of no consequence and he quickly unscrewed the cap, chugging a generous measure into the remains of his cold coffee.

Jacob Towers.

The events of the last few days bounced around inside his mind like rusty old pinballs as he swallowed his first mouthful of the fiery liquid. The burn at the back of his throat sharpened his thoughts.

Jacob Towers was dead.

Whether by his own hand or not was largely immaterial to Harvey Mitcham. It sounded harsh, but Harvey wasn't renowned for his compassion. It was true, their wives had got along surprisingly well when they'd first met, despite the age gap, and slowly the professional relationship had morphed into something different. He'd gone along with it for Eileen's sake, but he could easily have dispensed with the whole "friendship" thing a long time ago.

But then the money had happened.

Harvey took another mouthful of the Macallan.

Bending down, he pulled the bottom drawer open once again, his gaze drawn to the bulging brown envelope hidden at the bottom.

# CHAPTER ELEVEN

*Crown Street, Bury St Edmunds*

"It could *never* happen again. I'm absolutely sure of that."
Grant Patterson's expression was grave, his cheeks flushed.
"And I'm still not entirely sure how it *did* happen. We take
security very seriously. There are only two sets of keys for any
property, and all keys are kept in a locked safe in the office."

Nicki followed the estate agent as they headed upstairs.
DS Fox had gone straight back to the station following their
visit to Harvey Mitcham, leaving Nicki to visit the potential
crime scene alone. "How it happened is largely immaterial to
us at this stage, although if you do find any explanation as to
how he got inside then we'd be interested to hear it."

Up on the roof, Nicki felt the breeze whip through her
hair. The rooftop garden was accessed in a similar way to her
own back in College Lane — from the top-floor landing, a
wooden ladder took them through a hatch to the roof above.
Nicki counted each step as she climbed, wondering what
might have been going through Jacob's mind at the time. Each
step made her shudder.

It was a clear day, with uninterrupted views of the whole town. With a rooftop garden of her own, Nicki welcomed the sensation of being up high. There was something inherently relaxing about being above all the commotion of the streets below, separated from the stress that modern life invariably brought with it. Up here you were free.

However, Nicki was starkly reminded — if she needed to be — that Jacob's last moments would have been anything but relaxing.

She knew the roof wasn't going to tell them much, certainly nothing in addition to whatever Faye and her team managed to glean, but she felt it was something she needed to do. She approached the edge and leaned up close to the wall. According to the position of the body on the metal spike, and the statement of the taxi driver, this was most likely the spot from which Jacob had jumped — or at least fallen — to his death.

Standing on tiptoes, Nicki leaned over the edge. She could see the metal railings below and shuddered again. Taking a breath, she stepped back from the ledge. "Thank you for supplying the contact details of your staff, and the people who'd had viewings over the last few weeks. We'll need to speak to everyone and take statements. Face to face will be best. Someone will call by later today, if that's convenient."

"Not a problem — anything we can do to help, just ask. This is all just so shocking."

As they descended from the rooftop, Nicki hovered on the top-floor landing. "May I take a look inside here?" She gestured towards an open doorway. The estate agent nodded, and Nicki stepped inside.

The room was small, no more than a box room, with bare walls and no furniture except for a solitary wooden chair. Nicki recognised it immediately, sending another shiver up her spine. It was undoubtedly the location of the gut-wrenching video they'd all watched the previous day, and the room

Faye had highlighted to her. She made a mental note to follow up on the bloodstains that had been found there.

Site visit complete, Nicki followed the estate agent back down to ground level. Inevitably, the man would be wondering if one of his staff had helped Jacob gain access to the building or at least made it possible by leaving doors or windows insecure, intentionally or otherwise. The fact it might be an inside job was something that had flashed into Nicki's head on Wednesday night and was a question that was still unanswered.

"We'll be in touch if we need anything further." She smiled as Grant Patterson held the door open for her. "Now the crime scene investigators have released the scene, you're free to open up this property for viewings as normal."

The estate agent gave a grimace. "Thank you. I'm not sure any of us much fancy returning to normal just yet, not after what's happened, but I still have a business to run."

"That's understandable." Nicki stepped out onto the pavement. "An officer will call by later today to speak to your staff. We would appreciate it if you could make as many staff members available as possible."

"Naturally. Anything to help."

As Nicki turned in the direction of the station, her mobile chirped.

\* \* \*

*Hastings, East Sussex*

Even after devouring the plate of scrambled eggs, with the bacon cooked just how he liked it, Keeble hadn't felt fit enough to drive home. Or maybe he was just putting off the inevitable. His head felt less foggy than it had been on waking, but the persistent headache seemed immune to further painkillers.

So, he'd taken Mrs Briggs up on her offer to book in for another night, but it wasn't as if he needed much persuasion;

the prospect of slipping back beneath the covers for a few more hours was too tempting to refuse. She hadn't wanted to take any money, saying he would be doing her a favour by staying on as all the other guests were checking out today, so it would just be the two of them alone in the eight-bedroom guest house. Feeling slightly awkward, he'd slipped a twenty-pound note under his toast rack when leaving the breakfast table.

Now he was lying here on the bed, he wondered if the woman had been flirting with him in some surreal way, letting him know they would be alone and uninterrupted. He immediately dismissed the idea as ludicrous. He was dishevelled, unshaven, had slept in his clothes, and stale alcohol was seeping out of his every pore. A catch he most definitely was not.

Intending to sleep for a few hours, he swallowed another couple of painkillers along with some more coffee. Hopefully they would work better on a full stomach.

An odd smile crossed his lips as he lay down and closed his eyes. As far as last meals went, it might not have been the steak and chips he would have ordered if he was on death row, but it hadn't been bad. It hadn't been bad at all. Just as he was about to drift off, his mobile chirped. Prising his heavy eyelids open, he saw the name of the caller.

Hugh Webster.

Sighing, Keeble silenced the call.

* * *

*The Bay Tree Café, St John's Street, Bury St Edmunds*

The text from Faye had been most welcome. Nicki had just left the house on Crown Street when it came through, immediately taking a detour to the Bay Tree Café.

"We ordered for you." Faye Armstrong pulled out a chair as Nicki approached the table. "Knowing how pressed for time you probably are right now, we thought it wise."

Nicki collapsed into the vacant seat. "Thanks, much appreciated. I don't have long, that's true."

"How's it all going?" Faye nudged the cappuccino across the wooden table. "Stupid question, I know."

Nicki took hold of the oversized cup and gave a grateful smile before taking a sip. "It's going. But I've a feeling there's more to it than we first thought. It's certainly not straightforward."

"I've finished the post-mortem report — just sent it through to your email." Caz Mitchell tapped her phone before nudging the remains of the carrot cake around her plate. "It's one that'll stay with me for some time, that's for sure."

Nicki wiped the froth from her upper lip. "It's looking that way for us, too." She hadn't told either Faye or Caz about the video of Jacob Towers pulling out his own teeth. An involuntary shudder swept through her as she took another welcome sip of the cappuccino. No one needed to hear about that over their mid-morning cake fix. "Anything in particular I should look out for in the report — over and above the usual?"

Caz stabbed the final chunk of cake with her fork. "It was an obvious fall from a height, body impaled on the metal spike. Naturally, there were the expected catastrophic internal injuries associated with that. Unfortunately, the spike sliced through his lung and then his heart — there's nothing anyone could have done to save him. Otherwise, he was relatively fit and healthy. Bloods and swabs have been sent off. I put a rush on them, so hopefully you'll hear something soon."

"I've just been up to the roof of the property." Nicki eyed the cake menu but decided the coffee would have to be her limit. "The only thing that really struck me was how much effort would have been needed to climb up onto the ledge. There's no way he could have just accidentally toppled over."

Faye nodded in agreement, pouring another cup of tea from the pot. "In my opinion, whether he jumped or was pushed, he would have needed to have got up onto that ledge first." She stirred a splash of milk into the cup. "We saw no evidence to suggest a struggle up there, or anywhere else in the house. As far as crime scenes go, it gave us very little."

Nicki had thought as much. Crime scenes could be rich in detail, or they could be as barren as the hottest desert. "I'm assuming there's no way to tell how many people were up there?" Already knowing the answer, she hid behind her mug.

"Afraid not," confirmed Faye. "The property stretches to four floors, and we've processed them all. I've already mentioned the blood we found in one of the upstairs rooms — it's definitely human and swabs have been sent to the lab for DNA testing. But there was something else as well."

"Oh?" Nicki eyed the crime scene manager over the rim of her coffee cup. "Anything pertinent?"

"I'll leave that up to you. It's on the question of potential entry points. The front and back doors were secure, no evidence of forced entry. But we did find a door wedge close to one of the downstairs windows at the back of the property, but nowhere near the door. The window itself was closed but not locked. I wondered if it might be a way in — the window wedged open. Again, we've taken samples and swabs."

"Thanks." Nicki's mind started to whirr. As far as potential ways into the property for Jacob and whoever may or may not have been with him, it sounded promising. "I'll chase that up."

"How's Dean?" Caz pushed her plate away, licking the last of the icing from her lips. "Adjusting OK?"

Finally telling two of her best friends about Dean had lifted a massive weight from Nicki's shoulders. "He's getting there, slowly. I caught up with him last night, and he's doing well, as far as I can tell. He seems happy enough, anyway — well, content at least." Nicki was unsure her brother would ever be truly happy, but contentment was certainly possible. "He showed me some of the illustration work he's been doing, so I think he's settling in and getting back into the swing of things." Nicki slipped her hand into her pocket, her fingers closing around the memory stick Dean had forgotten to take with him. When she had a spare moment, she'd have to drop it round in case it was important.

"You have time for another?" Caz finished the last of her coffee and gestured towards Nicki's almost empty cup.

Nicki's mobile answered for her. Glancing at the screen, she made a face. "Unfortunately not. Looks like I'm needed." Getting up from her seat, she reached for her bag. "Thanks for the heads-up about the door wedge. Let's get together again soon. It's been too long."

"Wine night," agreed Faye. "How about next weekend — Saturday? I'll text Amy."

# CHAPTER TWELVE

*Bury St Edmunds Police Station*

"We've had some preliminary results come in from the lab." Roy pulled his chair closer to his computer screen. "Jacob's blood results are in. Toxicology tells us that there were traces of painkillers and antidepressants in his system. Within therapeutic levels but . . ." He gave a shrug. "No alcohol."

Nicki frowned. "Denise seemed adamant when we spoke to her that her husband wasn't taking anything. I'll have a word with Karen, see if she can find out more. What about the medical records?"

"They've come in, too." Roy tugged a notepad across his desk. "He's been registered with the same GP since they moved to the town nine years ago. Rarely goes to the doctor, last time was in 2017 for an eye infection. He's been prescribed citalopram for the last twelve years, for depression, and has had annual medication reviews but that's about it."

"Something Mrs Towers seems unaware of." Nicki sighed, feeling the therapeutic effects of the recent cappuccino fading fast. "We might need to go and have another chat with her sometime soon, but let's see what Karen can find out for us first. In the meantime — Darcie, how are you getting on with the list from the estate agents? My trip to the scene wasn't all that enlightening — Grant Patterson can't offer an explanation as to how Jacob managed to get inside. He told me there are only two sets of keys, both kept in a locked safe when not in use. He also confirmed both sets of keys are accounted for."

Darcie pulled her notepad towards her. "Twenty-four people viewed the property over the last three weeks. Three viewed it more than once. I've managed to speak to six so far — none raise any suspicions and have alibis for Wednesday night. I'm working my way through the rest, leaving messages to call me back if they're unavailable, but I've noticed some of the phone numbers supplied aren't registered."

Nicki's brow creased. "That's odd. Do we have any further information on those?"

"I've called the estate agency back — someone's looking into it."

Nicki's mouth thinned a little. "I told Patterson that I think a personal visit might be best and that someone would drop by later today. Could you handle that, Darcie? See how many staff members you can speak to in person?"

"I can try. Something I did notice, however, was that Jacob's name wasn't on the list. Certainly doesn't look like he booked a viewing, not in his own name, at least."

"Well, we all know that some estate agents can be a little pushy at times — it's not inconceivable that someone might give a false number to stop future marketing calls. Apparently, there are people out there who make a thing of viewing houses without any serious intention of buying. But see what you can find out about those with unregistered numbers when you go and see them."

Nicki crossed over towards Roy's desk. "Anything interesting so far from Jacob's finances?"

The detective sergeant reactivated his computer screen. "A basic look at what we've got so far tells us the family is quite heavily in debt. Bank statements show they have a joint account which is in the red — and has been for some time. Three credit cards, all maxed out. They remortgaged the family home last summer in order to pay off another credit card. Jacob's business is just about breaking even, but not enough to make a significant dent in their debts. And looking at recent transactions, there's nothing on Wednesday afternoon or evening to suggest what he might have been doing in the hours before he fell."

Nicki felt her shoulders sag. Another dead end. "Thanks, Roy. Well, our visit to Harvey Mitcham earlier this morning told us one thing — that man is lying to us. And in my experience, when someone lies about one thing, other lies tend to follow. They're like buses."

"He certainly became very evasive when asked about the last time he'd been in contact with Towers." Fox was already adding Mitcham's name to the board. "We know for a fact that he's texted Jacob's phone and left a voicemail during the past week. He may not have physically spoken to the man, but he was certainly trying to contact him about something — something Mitcham seems to have conveniently forgotten."

"Let's do a full background check on him. He gives the impression he's a forgetful, hare-brained would-be scientist, but I'm not so sure. If he's creating a smokescreen for something else, I want to know what that something is." Nicki paused. "Then we need to bring him in."

Fox nodded. "He certainly tried to play down how well he knew Towers. Listening to him, you got the impression their paths rarely crossed, and it was nothing more than a casual yet professional relationship." He turned to catch Nicki's eye. "But we suspect something different, don't we, boss?"

Nicki smiled. "We do. The Mitchams had a surprising number of photographs in their hallway — and unless I'm very much mistaken, I saw Jacob Towers and his wife in a fair few of them. In particular, photographs that looked like a christening ceremony. I recognised Denise holding two young babies in her arms, which I suspect are the twins." Nicki turned to face Fox. "Can you get in touch with Karen again and see what the wife has to say about our friend Harvey Mitcham? How well they know him and whether I'm right about the christening?" Fox nodded. "And while you're at it, ask her about the medication, too. See if there's any evidence of Jacob's prescription in the family home."

"I'll get onto her this afternoon."

"Matt and Duncan." Nicki swung round to face the two detective constables sitting together at the back of the incident room. "As well as looking into that date, 15 August 2005, can you take a closer look at Mitcham? See what he's not telling us?"

The detectives nodded. "Boss," they chimed in unison.

"Everything all right last night, Matt?" Nicki had learned of the detective's hurried rush home the night before. "Danni OK?"

Matt grinned. "All good, boss. A false alarm."

Nicki smiled. "Good. Let me know if anything changes. Finally, I've just had an interesting chat with Faye on my way back from Crown Street. A wooden door wedge was found close to one of the downstairs windows at the property. It's plausible that someone wedged one of the windows open to get inside."

"You're thinking it might be one of the people who viewed the property?" Darcie flipped over a page in her notebook. "Maybe one of the ones who'd viewed it more than once?"

Nicki could only shrug. "It's possible. See what you can get out of the agency staff later."

* * *

*Rye, East Sussex*

Hugh closed the door that led back into the utility room. He'd told Anne he was going to spend the next couple of hours tinkering with the motorbike in the garage. He'd barely finished speaking when she'd started to shoo him out of the kitchen, telling him in no uncertain terms that she could do without him under her feet. She was planning to bake a Victoria sponge and preferred to cook in peace.

Now in the garage, Hugh eyed up the toolbox on the workbench but made no effort to pick up a wrench or a spanner.

He'd gone out soon after breakfast to check underneath the car. It had played on his mind all night, causing him to toss and turn for much of it. Luckily, Anne was quite a heavy sleeper these days, something new since Dean had come back into their lives. So, while she slept, he'd lain awake, staring at the ceiling, wondering if he was making a mountain out of the usual molehill.

Once he'd consumed his second coffee of the morning, and Anne had cleared away their breakfast things, he'd made an excuse to go out to the car. Lying down on his back on the driveway, he'd carefully checked the vehicle's underside. Every so often he would crane his neck to inspect the front window, hoping Anne didn't choose now to take a look outside. He wasn't quite sure what excuse he would be able to concoct that would explain what he was doing.

Seeing nothing of concern under the car, he'd scrambled to his feet and taken a quick look inside the boot.

Still nothing.

It was only when he turned to go back inside the house that he saw it — pinned beneath one of the windscreen wiper blades.

Now standing in the privacy of the garage, Hugh pulled the note out from his pocket.

*15 August 2005*

It hadn't meant much to him at nine o'clock this morning, and it still didn't now.

15 August 2005?

He'd wracked his brains, but nothing immediately sprang to mind. Frowning, he picked up a cloth and began to wipe down the seat of the motorbike, a bike that was still lying in various pieces across the garage floor. The dream was to finish the repairs and take it on a long road trip — maybe up to Scotland and do the North Coast 500, or maybe even across to Europe. But, right now, he couldn't think any further than the next few minutes.

And the note.

In 2005 he was in his last year serving as a detective superintendent, due to retire that October. It had been a busy year, with work taking up a lot of his time. Dean had been missing for nine years at that point, and the impending retirement had given him a new focus. But 15 August? *Should* it mean something to him?

The uneasiness he'd felt yesterday returned twofold. This surely was proof that he wasn't making it up, that this wasn't some figment of his overactive imagination getting the better of him — someone *had* been following him. Whether they'd followed him home last night, or came back this morning, it mattered not. The note proved it was real.

As soon as he'd found the note, Hugh's first thought had been to speak to Keeble — but the man hadn't answered. Pulling his phone from his pocket, he scrolled down to Keeble's number, noting the detective inspector still hadn't returned his call. The investigation into some of his old cases was already playing on his mind, but now he had the note, too. Not a lover of coincidence at the best of times, Hugh was convinced the two must be connected.

And if anyone knew what that date meant, maybe Keeble did. So he tried the man's number again.

\* \* \*

*Fornham All Saints, Bury St Edmunds*

Eileen picked her way carefully through the books stacked high on the study floor. She didn't come in here too often, which she was sure Harvey was thankful for, but she was a proud woman and disliked a build-up of dust. So, every once in a while, she took a duster and braved the onslaught.

She drew the line at tidying away her husband's clutter, though, of which there was plenty. Harvey would know if she'd moved anything — she'd only made that mistake once and could still remember the tirade that had followed. Gingerly, she straightened some of the teetering towers of papers on the desk and teased out two plates, one complete with the stale remains of a sandwich. Next, she plucked a coffee mug from beneath the desk lamp.

The window ledge was uncharacteristically free of clutter, so she simply gave that a quick wipe down. Next, she picked up the wastepaper basket from beneath the desk, intending to take it out to the recycling bin before the collection came the following day. As she bent down, she noticed the bottom drawer of the desk was pulled slightly open.

Harvey didn't realise she already knew what he kept in there, thinking it was his dark secret. Why he felt the need to keep it from her, she had no idea. They both enjoyed a small sherry from time to time, and often a glass of red wine with dinner. It wasn't as though it was a dry house.

A secretive smile danced on her lips as she recalled the occasional Pimm's and lemonade she would surreptitiously consume when doing her crocheting on a Sunday afternoon, Harvey firmly ensconced in his study or in the shed.

So, the presence of the secret whisky bottle made her confused more than anything. Why hide it away like that?

Instead of pushing the drawer shut, she tugged it open — intending to take a quick look and see just how much was left in the bottle, for she knew it had been new only a week ago.

Sure enough, there it was — a bottle of Macallan wedged beneath a handful of papers. Nudging the paperwork to one side, she saw that it was almost empty. Conscious Harvey could come in at any time, she went to close the drawer but found her eyes drawn to a large brown envelope instead. She couldn't say exactly why it caught her eye — it was just a plain, nondescript brown envelope, nothing unusual.

Whatever it was, curiosity quickly got the better of her and she pulled the envelope out from beneath the bottle. With a quick glance up at the study door, she felt a strange fluttering in the pit of her stomach. It was their anniversary in a couple of months — maybe it was a gift.

Pausing for a moment, she considered putting it back. If it *was* an anniversary present, then she was about to spoil the surprise. But just as children couldn't resist searching for hidden Christmas presents, she grinned and flicked open the gummed seal.

It took a while for the contents of the bulging envelope to register.

When it did, she thrust the envelope back where she'd found it and slammed the drawer shut.

# CHAPTER THIRTEEN

*Copse Close, Bury St Edmunds*

"Harvey?" Denise Towers accepted the plate of cheese and salad sandwiches. "Yes, of course I know him, why do you ask?"

DC Gedge took a seat next to Denise on the floral sofa. "We just noticed Jacob had been in contact with him over the last week or so, and we wondered what it might be about." She tried to keep her tone light, taking a small bite from her sandwich. "All part of the investigation."

Denise sighed. "It was probably to do with that bloody website. *Again.* Harvey asked Jacob to develop a website for him, even though Jacob isn't . . . wasn't . . . really a web designer. He did it as more of a favour, really, I think. But the man kept changing his mind about what he wanted. It's rumbled on for years. He must have called round here half a dozen times this year already, wanting Jacob to tweak it for him."

"Mr Mitcham's been here?" Karen paused mid-swallow. "Was that usual? For clients to call round to the house?"

Denise plucked a slice of tomato from her sandwich. "Oh, Harvey wasn't really a client. Not like the others, anyway. Jacob saw him as more of a friend in the end, I suppose."

"Oh?" Karen placed the sandwich back down on her plate. "How long had you known Mr Mitcham?"

"It must be getting on for eight or so years now. I'm sure Jacob first met him not long before we had the twins."

"And you've remained friends ever since?"

Denise gave a faint, sheepish smile. "Eileen and I both like needlepoint and crochet. So, we'd sometimes go to craft fairs and exhibitions together. The boys understandably weren't interested in that kind of thing, so they'd stay home. I think Harvey liked to show Jacob some of his latest inventions." A sad look entered the woman's eyes while her face fell. "I really should contact them and let them know what's happened — Harvey and Eileen. They both really liked Jacob."

Karen felt a tingle of excitement, knowing this was just what Nicki had wanted to hear. "Would you say you were close friends — you and the Mitchams?"

Denise gave a small laugh, her eyes moist. "I should say so — they're godparents to the twins."

* * *

*Rye, East Sussex*

The call still hadn't been picked up, so this time Hugh left a message on Keeble's landline instead. That had been over an hour ago now. The more he thought about it, the more he wondered if he was worrying unnecessarily. The note on the car might just be a prank or was meant for someone else. It was an idea that momentarily buoyed him, enabling him to get down to some of the jobs in the garage that he'd been putting off. But the more time that passed and Keeble still didn't call back, the more his nerves began to jangle.

Something didn't feel right. *None* of this felt right. Unable to concentrate on fixing the motorbike any longer, Hugh returned to the kitchen and was instantly met by an enticing aroma of home baking.

"Good timing," greeted Anne. "Sit yourself down and I'll pour you a nice cup of tea to go with this."

So here he was now — sitting at the kitchen table nursing a cup of cooling tea and trying to swallow the generous slice of Victoria sponge Anne had cut for him. Freshy baked, and still warm, it tasted divine — but Hugh couldn't stop it sticking in his throat.

After topping up his tea, Anne was called away — one of her yoga friends on the phone — and Hugh took the opportunity to check his mobile again.

Still nothing from Keeble.

Knowing it probably wouldn't help, he dialled the detective's number once more.

\* \* \*

*Bury St Edmunds Police Station*

"Found in the master bedroom, stuffed inside a pair of trainers in the wardrobe. Three packets of citalopram, two unopened. The prescription labels are current." DS Fox added a note to the whiteboard. "Once Karen had found them, she explained to Denise that low levels of antidepressant had been found in her husband's post-mortem bloods, and that his GP records also showed the prescription had been ongoing for the last twelve years."

"And what was her reaction?" Nicki joined Fox at the whiteboard.

"Understandably shocked, but maybe not altogether surprised."

"What else did Karen have to say?"

"Only that once they got back from the visit to the mortuary to ID Jacob's body, Denise kept saying how everything was her fault."

Nicki nodded. "It's not an uncommon reaction to grief. Did she say anything about Harvey Mitcham?"

Fox grinned. "We were right about Mitcham being less than honest with us. According to Denise Towers, he's much more than just a passing acquaintance. She classes him more as a family friend and also confirmed that Harvey has visited their house on numerous occasions over the years, for both work and pleasure. In fact, she told Karen that he called round only three weeks ago and stayed for dinner."

Nicki's eyebrows shot up. "Three weeks ago? Well, he certainly failed to mention that little detail, didn't he? Anything else?"

Fox's grin widened. "Just a bit. Mrs Towers *also* confirmed that Harvey and his wife are godparents to the twins, so you were right about the christening photos."

"Hmmm." Nicki's brow creased. "Harvey Mitcham is starting to bother me. I think we need to talk to him again."

"Have we thought about life insurance?" Roy gave a shrug. "Just a thought. If the family are up to their eyeballs in debt, like they seem to be, maybe Denise Towers is due a large payout now her husband's dead?"

Nicki bit her lip. She had to be honest, it hadn't been something that she'd thought about — but now the state of Towers' finances was known, it was a line of enquiry they would need to explore. "Good point, Roy. Let's dig deeper — we'll need to ask Denise if she knows of any insurance policy. It's a bit insensitive but needs to be done."

"So, he could have jumped after all?" Roy's eyebrows arched. "To help the family financially?"

Nicki considered the question but soon shook her head. "You're forgetting about the teeth. I might be able to swallow him jumping to his death if there was a big fat payout from an insurance policy at the end of it, but . . . it's the teeth that don't fit." She joined Roy at his desk. "It's a long shot, I know, but see if there are any other cases — solved or otherwise — that have some reference to recent tooth extraction in the victim."

Roy woke up his computer screen. "Will do."

"Karen also said she'd located a laptop in the snug." Fox turned away from the whiteboard. "Looks like Jacob used it for work. She's going to bring it in."

"Good. We need to dig into his work life just as much as his home life. Emails, contacts, that kind of thing. Duncan, anything more from the website?"

First thing that morning, Duncan had filled Nicki and the rest of the team in on the mysterious pop-up box on the Tower Graphics website — a messaging service that seemed to go nowhere. "I've sent the details down to Simon. He'll take a look and get back to us. He's still looking into the voice recognition thing, too. I'll give him a call in a bit and see how he's getting on."

Nicki glanced at her watch. "Good. Let's see what loose ends we can tie up today. Darcie is over at the estate agents' following up on the staff. While she's gone, I'll give Karen another call and ask her about the insurance policy angle — I'll also see if she can tease out of Denise why Harvey Mitcham came round for dinner three weeks ago."

\* \* \*

*Copse Close, Bury St Edmunds*
*Wednesday 1 May 2019*

"Come on through." Denise stepped back to let Harvey Mitcham across the threshold. "Jacob's in the kitchen, putting the finishing touches to dinner. Let me take your coat."

Harvey shrugged out of his overcoat and ran a hand over the tufts of white hair standing up from his scalp. "Most kind, Denise. And this is for you." He waved a bottle of port in the air.

Denise took the bottle, thanking him and then ushering him into the front room. "Make yourself at home and I'll go and fetch Jacob. Can I get you a glass of wine before dinner? Red or white?"

"Whatever you have open, my dear."

Denise scuttled back to the kitchen, where her husband was standing by the hob, stirring the homemade curry. She plucked the wooden spoon from his hand, her voice hushed. "I'll finish up here, you go and sit with him. You invited him — so you go and entertain him."

Jacob made a face as he dipped a finger into the bubbling liquid. "Ouch, that's hot!"

"Serves you right, now go on — scoot!" Denise flapped a tea towel in his direction and started to stir the curry. "And take him a glass of wine. We've a red open on the side."

Jacob poured two glasses of red and carried them through to the front room. "Harvey," he gushed, kicking the door closed behind him. "Good to see you again."

Harvey took hold of one of the wine glasses, eyes glinting behind his spectacles. "Most kind, young man. Most kind indeed."

Jacob slipped into a seat opposite, taking a large gulp of wine as he settled. He'd already drunk a glass, maybe more, while making the curry, and on an empty stomach it was making him feel a little light-headed. But he needed the alcohol — he needed something to give him the courage to do what he needed to do, to say what he needed to say.

The dinner invitation had been for Eileen, too, but Jacob was secretly pleased that the woman had declined, citing a migraine. It meant he only had to deal with Harvey. Knowing the curry wouldn't take long to finish off — all Denise had to do now was steam some rice — he decided it was now or never.

"Glad you could make it, Harvey. There's something I've been wanting to ask you." Jacob took another gulp of wine before placing his glass down on the coffee table. He then went across to a small bureau in the corner of the room, pulling out a key from his pocket to unlock the bottom drawer.

Jacob could feel the would-be inventor's inquisitive gaze boring into his back as he reached for the brown envelope, closing his shaking hand around it, just as a lump began to solidify in his throat.

*Just do it, Jacob. Stop pissing around and just do it.*

He returned to the coffee table, placing the envelope in front of Harvey. "Can you do me a favour and keep hold of something for me?"

Harvey's bushy eyebrows rose. "Sounds ominous." His gaze lowered to the table. "What's in there?"

Jacob reached for his wine glass, draining the rest of it. "It's a little delicate. Take a look."

Harvey hesitated for just a fraction of a second before lifting the envelope from the table. "The plot thickens . . ."

Jacob had left the envelope unsealed, so it was quickly and easily flicked open. He trained his gaze on the man's expression, watching it morph from intrigue to shock in a split second.

"Goodness!" Harvey looked up sharply. "That's an awful lot of money."

"Fifty thousand," nodded Jacob, his voice lowering a notch. "I wondered if you would keep hold of it for me — just until I know what I'm doing with it."

Harvey looked startled. "Look after it? Is there some reason why you can't pay it into the bank? That would be the sensible thing to do, unless . . . ?"

Jacob was already shaking his head vigorously. "No, nothing like that. It's not dirty money." The words stuck in his throat. Was that really the truth? It wasn't exactly whiter than white, was it? He brushed the thought from his mind, wishing he had more wine to help. "I just need to keep it under wraps for a while. Otherwise, it'll just get swallowed up by the bank to pay off the overdraft and credit cards." *And I'd have to explain to the tax man where it came from,* he thought. *And Denise.*

Harvey nodded, slowly, his hands still clutching the envelope. "I'm sure I can put this somewhere safe for you. If that's what you want."

Jacob felt immediate relief wash over him. "Thanks. And best not tell Eileen. Or Denise. I'm not sure either of them would understand. Keep it just between you and me, yes?" Jacob was aware his tone sounded pleading. He tried a half-smile. "If you don't mind."

A broad grin broke out on Harvey's face. "Of course not. What are friends for? I'll just go and pop this somewhere out of sight, shall I?"

Harvey rose from his armchair and headed back out into the hallway, spying where Denise had hung his overcoat.

Fifty thousand.

It was a handsome sum. More than handsome.

As he tucked the bulging envelope into the inside pocket of his coat, he thought about the look he'd seen on his friend's face. Jacob wasn't usually a worrier, but the man was concerned about something. More than that — *he looked scared.*

# CHAPTER FOURTEEN

"Just through here." Grant Patterson gestured towards the rear offices of Patterson's Sales and Lettings.

The agency was small, with space for just three desks in the main office, but it enjoyed a prime position on one of the streets close to the marketplace. As Darcie followed, she could feel two pairs of eyes boring into her back as she passed.

Stepping into a small windowless room, Patterson pointed to the back wall, where a large grey box was secured. "This is where we keep the key safe. Each staff member has a key to open it when needed, but when it's not in use we always keep it locked." The man proceeded to fish in his pockets for a key-ring, selecting one with a single brass key on it. He slipped it into the lock, and the metal door swung open to reveal a series of metal hooks.

Darcie stepped closer, noting that each hook had two keys — one with a red plastic covering, one with green. All hooks had their complement of two keys — except for one.

"The red key remains in the office," explained Patterson. "The green one we take with us on viewings."

"And do you keep a record of who has which key at any one time? Which members of staff are out on viewings?"

Patterson nodded. "Each time a key is taken, it's logged in the folder." He stepped to the side, pulling a lever-arch file from the top drawer of a battered metal filing cabinet. He handed it across to Darcie. "Each A4 page represents an individual day, rather like a diary. Whenever a key is taken, staff log the property it relates to, and the time it was removed. They then sign it back in when it's returned."

Darcie scanned the page that was presented to her — today's date. She quickly noticed there had been eleven viewings that day already, and ten keys returned. One was still outstanding.

"Is the property market good right now? Are you busy?" Darcie had no idea what the housing market was doing, but if a small outfit like Patterson's had had eleven viewings, she considered that to be a positive sign.

"Reasonably," conceded Patterson, receiving the folder back from the detective constable. "Things generally start to pick up at this time of year."

"And how long have you been here in the town? Do you find there's much rivalry with the other firms?" Like many market towns up and down the country, Darcie always thought there was an abundance of estate agents on the high street — that and charity shops.

"We've been here three years now. We have sister offices in Brentwood and Colchester. As for rivalry . . ." Patterson gave a sniff. "I think we rub along all right together. And any competition is healthy competition, right?"

Darcie held her hands up. "I've no idea." Taking a step back, she glanced around the compact back room, seeing nothing else of note. "Would it be possible to speak to the members of staff that are here today? I passed two on my way in."

Patterson returned the folder to the filing cabinet and proceeded to lock up the key safe. "Of course. Kellie and

Lynda are out front. Jon is out on a viewing at the moment, but he should be back soon."

"Hence the missing key," added Darcie, gesturing towards the locked key safe.

The estate agent hesitated for a split second before affording the detective constable a curt nod. "Indeed. Right, I'll take you through to see the staff."

Darcie followed Patterson back out into the main office, seating herself at a spare desk in the corner. She smiled as one member of staff slipped into the seat opposite.

"Hello. I'm Detective Constable Butler. I just need a few moments of your time to talk about what happened on Wednesday night." She saw the woman sit up straight in the uncomfortable-looking office chair, eyes wide, worry flooding her features. Darcie tried another smile. "Honestly, this is just routine. Nothing to be concerned about."

Over the next few minutes, Darcie asked her questions — but it was quite clear from an early stage that Kellie Meade was unable to tell her much about the house on Crown Street. She'd never been there herself and confirmed that she hadn't seen anyone acting suspiciously in the area. At just nineteen years of age, Darcie suspected the estate agency was the young woman's first real job and that being questioned by the police was a completely new experience.

The second member of staff to sit in front of Darcie was Lynda Brockman, and very quickly Darcie gleaned that the woman was the most experienced member of the team, with twenty years in the industry behind her.

"This is just so shocking." The woman seemed to shudder as she settled further back into her seat. "I can't quite believe it."

Darcie smiled. "It is. I'll try not to keep you long. Can I ask you about the property on Crown Street? Had you been inside yourself?"

Lynda seemed to hesitate, eventually giving a mixture of a nod and a shrug. "A couple of times, when it first came onto the market. But I tend to handle the lettings side of the business more than sales these days. The person you really need to speak to about the Crown Street property is Jon. He's our newest member of the team."

Jon turned out to be a young man called Jon Tierney, who walked through the door ten minutes later. Darcie immediately noticed a cautious look cross his features as her eyes caught his.

"Great timing, Jon. It's your turn now, my love." Lynda pulled herself out of the chair and waved towards the table.

Tierney remained rooted to the spot in the doorway. "That sounds ominous," he eventually replied, giving a nervous-sounding laugh.

Lynda gestured for him to take a seat. "It's about that awful business on Crown Street. I told the detective here that you'd be the best one to ask."

"I'm not sure about that." Another forced laugh as Tierney edged closer to the desk. "I don't think I'll be able to tell you much more than you know already."

Darcie smiled pleasantly. "Well, why don't you let me be the judge of that? Take a seat and we can get started."

Tierney appeared to hesitate once again but eventually slipped into the vacant chair. "Of course."

Darcie noticed the man was biting his lip as he still avoided her gaze. "Your colleague Lynda tells me that you knew the property on Crown Street the best. You'll be aware of what happened on Wednesday night?"

Tierney blinked rapidly, then nodded. "Yes, yes. Of course. Horrible business, just horrible."

Darcie noticed the man's hands knotted in his lap, and one of his legs jiggling beneath the tabletop. She knew enough about body language to be sure that Tierney was feeling distinctly uncomfortable. She pressed on.

"How many viewings have you handled for the Crown Street property since it went on the market?" Darcie knew she could get this information from Patterson — and the log kept in the folder in the back office — but there was something to be said for asking the question directly.

Once again, Tierney seemed to hesitate, with more rapid blinking. "I . . . I wouldn't like to say exactly. Quite a few. It's been a popular listing."

Darcie maintained her smile. "No matter — I'm sure there's a record somewhere should it become necessary." On leaving the back office, Patterson had confirmed that the property in question had been viewed by several potential buyers on more than one occasion, with one viewing it three times. She tried to catch Tierney's eye. "Do you recall if anyone went to view the property more than once?"

More hesitation followed Darcie's question. More rapid blinking. More lip biting. "I'm not sure that I do. We've had quite a lot of viewings for the property, as you can imagine, so one tends to merge into the next, if I'm honest."

Something Darcie always remembered was Nicki warning her about people who qualified their responses with "*if I'm honest*". Because invariably, they were being anything but. She filed it away and tried a different approach.

"Do you recall the name Samuel Drake?" The question was met with a blank look, so Darcie continued. "Mr Drake viewed the house on Crown Street three times. Once on Friday 17 May, and then twice the following Tuesday. I could get Mr Patterson to double-check, but I think the records will show that it was you that showed the man around?" Darcie knew she was heading out on a precarious limb here; Patterson hadn't yet confirmed it was Tierney who had handled the viewings, but she felt the need to risk it — another trait Nicki had passed on.

And the risk was worth it, hitting gold after a matter of seconds.

"Wait a minute, yes — now you mention it, perhaps I do remember that."

*Perhaps.*

"I would imagine it's quite rare for someone to ask to view a property twice in one day — wouldn't you, Mr Tierney?

That kind of thing would stick in your memory, would it not? And it was only a few days ago."

The man's cheeks coloured, and his leg started to jiggle even more. "I guess, yes. I do remember him now."

"Can you recall what he looked like? Anything memorable about him?"

Tierney took a few moments but ended up shaking his head. "No, not really. Like I said, one viewing tends to merge into another."

Darcie knew when she was beat and brought the informal chat to an end. There was something about Jon Tierney that didn't sit right — but she knew questioning him further in the comfort of the estate agent's office was unlikely to get to the bottom of it.

Leaving Patterson to follow up on the three phone numbers that seemed to be out of service — one of which belonged to Samuel Drake — Darcie headed back to the station.

\* \* \*

*Fornham All Saints, Bury St Edmunds*

Although it was all still there, somehow he knew it had been moved. He was sure he'd left the envelope face down in the drawer, beneath the whisky, but it now appeared to be the other way up.

Harvey checked the money once again.

Fifty thousand.

Still there.

He knew Eileen came into the study on occasion, just to dust and clear out his wastepaper bin, but she didn't usually go through his drawers. At least, he didn't think she did. He felt his stomach flip. If she *had* looked inside the drawer, then surely she would have seen the whisky? But she hadn't said anything during lunch, merely asking him how his latest invention was going and what did he fancy for dinner tonight.

Surely if she knew he had a secret whisky stash she would have confronted him about it?

The uneasiness began to spread. He wasn't sure what concerned him the most — her knowing about the whisky or the money. Both would need explaining.

Slipping into the captain's chair, he plucked the bottle from the drawer and poured a generous amount into a waiting tumbler. There wasn't much left. He could always tell her the truth, of course — that Jacob gave the money to him to look after. But that statement would almost certainly be followed by a question.

*Why?*

And Harvey didn't exactly know why. And he wasn't in a position to ask the man now, was he? Jacob was dead.

Harvey took a slug from the tumbler. No — if he was going to come up with an explanation, then he had to come up with something better than that.

Something better than the truth.

\* \* \*

*Bury St Edmunds Police Station*

Nicki replaced the telephone receiver and rubbed her eyes. The blood found at the Crown Street property was confirmed to belong to Jacob Towers. Operation Jackdaw was gathering pace and spinning off in any number of different directions. Karen had agreed to nudge Denise Towers a little more about Harvey Mitcham, in particular about why the man had come round for dinner three weeks ago. And she would also be discreetly asking about the possibility of a life insurance policy.

Harvey Mitcham.

Nicki stared down at her notepad where she'd jotted down the man's name.

She knew they were going to have to bring him in sooner or later and interview him properly, but she still wanted to find out more about the would-be scientist before they took that step. The more she knew, the deeper she could probe.

Taking a bite from the tuna sandwich she didn't really want, Nicki nudged her mouse to wake up the computer monitor. Images of the property on Crown Street were still populating the screen. They now knew that the room on the top floor was where the video recording had been made, just over an hour before Jacob fell from the roof. What they still didn't know was who was with him, and why.

A shiver travelled the length of her spine. As far as crime scenes went, it wasn't one of the worst she'd seen — far from it. The bloodstains Faye and her team had found had been miniscule, almost imperceptible to the human eye, and the house itself was empty and somewhat sterile. Some crime scenes would be thick with the heavy, metallic aroma of recently spilled blood, floors and walls covered in the victim's last attempts to cling onto life. The Crown Street property was nothing like that, but even without the stomach-churning, macabre display of a life lost, the house still chilled her to the bone.

And all because of the video.

Swallowing another mouthful of her sandwich in an increasingly dry throat, Nicki's thoughts were interrupted by a brief tap on the door. Roy's head appeared around the door frame.

"Darcie's back, boss. And you might want to hear this."

* * *

Darcie was already at her desk, sitting at her computer, when Nicki reached the incident room. Without taking her eyes off the screen, she recounted her visit to the estate agents. "Grant Patterson showed me the key safe, and it was just like you said. Two sets of keys per property, all kept in the safe unless someone is out doing a viewing. All keys are signed in and out, details kept in a folder."

"Whereabouts was the key safe? And the folder?" Nicki rubbed her eyes, tiredness starting to pinch. "Would a customer be able to access either of them?"

Darcie was already shaking her head. "No. Both are kept in one of the back offices. There's no way I can see that anyone but a member of staff would be able to get hold of them."

Nicki had already thought as much. "At least we know that's an unlikely means of how Jacob got inside the house. What about the staff? Were you able to speak to any of them?"

Darcie proceeded to tell Nicki and the team about Jon Tierney. "There was something about him that didn't quite sit right, boss. Nice enough fella, but just something shifty in his eyes. He certainly didn't feel comfortable talking to me." Darcie gestured towards her computer screen. "So, the first thing I did when I got back was run a check on him."

"And?"

Darcie grinned as she angled the screen towards her boss. "Two convictions, one in 2007 and the other in 2010 — both for theft. They're spent convictions now, so I'm guessing he passed the DBS check with the agency. Either that or they didn't bother to do one."

"That's interesting to know. It at least raises a question as to his honesty."

"He did eventually confirm that he handled most of the viewings for the house on Crown Street and remembered one man viewing it three times — a man that gave them the name Samuel Drake — although I had to prompt him. He seemed reluctant to say much and couldn't tell me anything about the man's appearance. Before leaving, I asked Tierney and Patterson about the false contact details the man gave them — but neither could offer me any explanation. Patterson did say he would follow up on the other unregistered numbers though. And there's no CCTV in the office that might have caught him on camera, either. I checked." Darcie paused and angled the screen back towards herself. "As for the other two members of staff I spoke to, I honestly don't think either had anything to do with this — they were both so shocked."

Nicki nodded and flashed a glance towards the whiteboards. "Well, we definitely need a further chat with this Jon Tierney. Add his name to the board and let's bring him in." She glanced at her watch. "And there's no time like the present — he should be about to finish work for the day."

# CHAPTER FIFTEEN

*Bury St Edmunds Police Station*

"Thank you for coming in, Mr Tierney. It's much appreciated." Nicki eyed the man sitting opposite them in the main interview room. Darcie had been right — Jon Tierney definitely wasn't comfortable in the presence of the police. With nervous jiggling of both legs beneath the table, and a wide-eyed, darting gaze about him, there was a thin sheen of sweat on the man's brow. For reasons that had yet to be determined, the estate agent was feeling under pressure. Nicki cleared her throat, intending to take full advantage.

People under pressure made mistakes.

"You spoke to my colleague, DC Butler, earlier today, and—"

"Am I under arrest?" Tierney had stopped jiggling his legs long enough to interrupt.

Nicki slid a sideways glance to Darcie next to her, then settled her gaze back onto the estate agent, where she noticed faint damp patches emerging beneath the man's armpits. "Not at all, Mr Tierney. This is just us having a chat about the property on Crown Street, in light of what happened on

Wednesday evening." She paused, holding the man firmly in her gaze. "You're free to leave at any point."

The news didn't seem to do much to relax the man, his legs resuming their incessant jiggling beneath the table.

"As I mentioned, you very helpfully spoke to my colleague DC Butler earlier today — we just have one or two further questions for you, seeing as you seem to be the one who took the most prospective buyers to view the property in question."

"Well, I suppose that's true. Yes, I did." Jon Tierney seemed to find his voice. "But I'm not sure I can add much to what I said before."

Nicki cast her eyes down to her notepad. "Tell me about Samuel Drake." On looking up again, she saw the estate agent appear to squirm in his seat. "You showed him around the property three times."

Face paling a little, Tierney eventually nodded. "I did. That's what I told the detective earlier."

"And twice in one day, no less. Is that usual? For someone to request to see a property more than once in the same day?"

Tierney's brow creased a little. "I guess. I don't think it's ever happened to me before."

"What reason did he give for wanting to see it again so soon?"

The estate agent's eyes widened. "I'm not so sure he did — give a reason, I mean. Not that I remember, anyway. I just arranged to meet him back at the property again."

"Have you had a chance to reconsider a description for this man?" Nicki raised an eyebrow. "You told DC Butler you couldn't recall what he looked like. But surely, something as unusual as someone wanting to see a property twice in one day would stick in your memory, would it not?" Nicki made a show of consulting her notepad. "You did just confirm how out of the ordinary it was — something that you couldn't remember happening before."

Tierney's pale complexion began to redden. "Well, when I say I can't recall what he looked like, what I meant was there was nothing distinctive about him. He just looked ordinary — normal."

"Describe normal to me, Mr Tierney. Height. Build. Ethnicity. Hair colour. Distinctive features."

The question was met with silence.

"Come on, Mr Tierney. I don't believe for a second that you can't recall *something* about him. You met him three times over the period of a few days." Nicki knew from experience that she was probably going to have to drag the information out of the man, bit by bit, and would need to work hard to keep the irritation from her tone. "Let's begin with his height, shall we? Was he taller than you? Shorter?"

Tierney swallowed. "I guess he was about my height — average."

"Average. And what about his ethnicity? His skin colour?"

"He was white."

"He was a white man — and what about his build? Was he bigger than you? Smaller? Looked like he worked out?" Tierney's mouth opened and closed like a goldfish, but no sound emerged. Nicki's lips thinned. "Let me guess — average." The estate agent nodded. "And what about his hair — short, long, dark, light?" Irritation was winning the race and Nicki felt her patience waning by the second. "Bald?"

"Short and dark," came the eventual response. "And he wore glasses, too — I just remembered."

Nicki gave a condescending smile. "A white man, average height, average build, with short, dark hair and glasses. Wonderful. Let's turn our attention back to the property. What was it this man was most interested in looking at?"

A blank look. "Looking at?"

Nicki swallowed her irritation and pressed on. "If this man had asked to see the property for the second time in the same day, surely it stands to reason that he had something specific he wanted to look at?" She watched the estate agent close his eyes and give an audible sigh. "Can you recall what that was?"

"I really don't know."

"You must have let the man in, Mr Tierney. So you must remember where he went, what he was interested in. Stands to reason, doesn't it?" Nicki flashed a look towards Darcie, the detective constable already making a series of notes in her notebook. "Did he want to go up and see the roof?"

More silence filled the interview room, the only sound being Darcie's pen scratching on the notepaper.

Tierney bit his lip again, his cheeks flushing darker by the second.

And then the penny dropped.

Nicki sighed, heavily. "How long was this man inside the property alone, Mr Tierney?"

\* \* \*

*Hastings, East Sussex*

Thrusting his hands into the pockets of his overcoat, Mark Keeble strode across the deserted car park to where he'd left the Jag. His headache had slowly melted away during the course of the afternoon, after he'd managed to sleep for a few more hours. He awoke, not exactly refreshed as such, but feeling better than he had that morning. After a quick shower, he'd dressed in yesterday's clothes once again and checked out.

Dinner had been an uninspiring plate of fish and chips in a town centre café, followed by a lengthy walk along the seafront. Time ticked by — walking and thinking.

The text message he'd received earlier had been followed by another.

*Tonight.*

There was a part of Keeble that was thankful he hadn't returned home last night — no one knew he was in Hastings, which gave him some breathing space. And more time to think. But time was marching on and he would have to return home at some point, which was why he'd started heading back to the Jag.

There was no parking along the narrow side street where the guest house was located, so he'd parked in a car park a few streets away. It was close to the bus station and what appeared to have once been a retail park — although most of the units were now deserted, many with faded CLOSING DOWN SALE! banners still in the windows. A ten-pin bowling alley looked to be clinging on by the skin of its teeth — but only just.

Yesterday, there had been a handful of cars parked up, but now the Jag was the only vehicle left. At least it was still there and appeared to have all four wheels intact, which was something. Some days he was tempted to leave it with the keys still in the ignition and the windows down, anything to get the car off his hands and some cash in his pocket. But he knew the insurance was unlikely to pay out if he did that, and he'd be in an even worse position than he was now — if that were possible.

Jennifer had virtually cleaned him out during their acrimonious eighteen-month divorce. Eighteen months of solicitors' letters bouncing backwards and forwards, achieving nothing more than racking up the bill each time one landed on the doormat. Eighteen months of arguing; eighteen months of mud-slinging. Eighteen months of anger. And now it was all done and dusted, agreement reached, court orders signed and sealed, he found himself living in a poky one-bedroom flat in a dodgy part of the city, three credit cards already maxed to their limit, and an overdraft the size of the debt of a small country.

But at least he still had the Jag.

She'd let him have that, at least.

The sun had almost sunk below the horizon now, with full darkness a matter of minutes away, and the car was illuminated by the one and only streetlight in the entire car park, reminding Keeble that he really ought to get it cleaned. There was a car wash not far from the flat, but he could save himself twenty quid and get the bucket and sponge out himself. Not the most exciting of tasks, but twenty quid was twenty quid.

Unlocking the driver's door, he slid behind the wheel and breathed in the familiar leathery smell from the upholstery. It was the only thing that kept him from selling it. The aroma normally took him back to the old times, the good times; times when he and Jennfer weren't constantly going for each other's throats like rabid dogs. He remembered he'd picked her up in it on their first official date — when their lives were full of wonder and possibilities. Now it just seemed to remind him of what a mess he'd made of everything.

He pressed the keys into the ignition and fired up the engine.

Not that it had been all his doing — it takes two to make a marriage work, and two to cause it to crash and burn on take-off. Sighing, he reached for the seatbelt — which was when he noticed it.

His shoulders sagged.

Bugger it. Another one?

Leaving the engine running, he creaked open the Jag's door and stepped back out, rounding the bonnet to grab the offending piece of unsolicited mail. It would no doubt be another one of those annoying adverts for some closing down sale, or one of those companies who wanted to buy all your gold jewellery. They seemed to be everywhere these days, peppering all the car parks, no matter where you went. He'd had three just yesterday, and four the day before. Wherever you parked, whatever town you found yourself in, there was always one stuffed under your windscreen wiper.

It was either that or the circus must be in town.

He could leave it where it was, of course, but the flapping would drive him insane all the way home. Plucking it from underneath the wiper blade, he almost didn't bother looking at it, intending to stuff it in his jacket pocket, but something made him flip the paper over. Turning his back on the Jag, he faced the dim streetlight for a better look.

And there it was again.

*It's time to pay for what you did.*

*15 August 2005*

Eyes sharpening, Keeble peered through the increasing gloom to see if the buggers who'd littered his car were still hanging around, but he quickly saw he was alone. The thought gave him goosebumps as he turned his attention back to the note.

*It's time to pay for what you did.*

*15 August 2005*

Slipping back behind the wheel, he crumpled the note in his hand, irritation multiplying. After tugging the door shut, he threw the scrap of paper to the floor.

As if he hadn't already had a shit enough day as it was.

Shoving the gearstick into first, he prepared to move off. But then the man spoke.

"Good evening, Detective Inspector Keeble. Such a good day to die, don't you think?"

* * *

*Sebert Road, Bury St Edmunds*

Aaron Nash killed the car's engine but remained behind the wheel. A large part of him didn't want to go inside, the other part knew it might be the last time he ever did. The thought chilled his blood.

*How had it come to this?*

Over the last fourteen years, he'd tried his best to put everything behind him — and he'd succeeded to some extent. It no longer occupied his thoughts day and night, not like it used to — although there were always times when he would think back to what had happened back in the summer of 2005.

Wesley Barton.

The man's name would pop into his head when he least expected it to.

It wasn't a name he would forget.

Sighing, he took the keys from the ignition and hauled himself out of the car. Rosalyn would have heard the car pull up on the drive, so would soon start to wonder why he hadn't come inside. The kitchen lights were on, so dinner preparations were no doubt already underway. Hovering half in, half out of the car, he wondered if they should splash out on a takeaway instead — maybe an Indian, Rosalyn's favourite. When the building business Aaron had founded slowly started to crumble into dust after the financial crash of 2008, treats like takeaways had become a thing of the past. He'd tried to keep the business afloat for as long as possible, but they'd had to face reality eventually. With mounting debts and unpaid bills, he'd wound the company up and instead spent the last eight years as a jobbing builder and handyman, going where the work took him — north, east, south, west. Rosalyn didn't like it when he worked away, and it soon created a tension between them.

Aaron trudged wearily towards the front door. He knew he could try and build as many new foundations for the future as he liked — but none of it would erase the past, none of it would eradicate what he'd done. Ever since that day, his life had been nothing but an ever-growing web of lies and deceit. Covering it all up was exhausting and he couldn't take it anymore. Hesitating with his key in the lock, he tried to plaster a suitable smile on his face. Rosalyn didn't need to see him like this; it would only spark another argument.

He knew they wouldn't get the takeaway. It had been a stupid idea. He had no appetite, and just the thought of food was making his stomach lurch.

Despite the warmth that hit him as he opened the door, he couldn't dislodge the ice forming in his veins.

He knew what he had to do.

And he had to do it tonight.

# CHAPTER SIXTEEN

*Hastings, East Sussex*

*Fear.*

It was a weird concept.

When someone asked, "What are you afraid of?" the usual answers would include things like spiders, heights, water, the dark, sometimes confined spaces. But Keeble wasn't afraid of any of those. You could lock him in a coffin-sized box full of water and slowly release the biggest and most venomous spiders known to man into it, and he still wouldn't be scared.

Just like he wasn't scared now.

If anything, he was irritated. Irritated with himself for being so stupid. He'd let his guard down and committed the cardinal error, an error that had let the enemy in. He was a detective, for God's sake — things like this shouldn't happen.

Keeble had been rejected by the army at eighteen, something he would later consider a blessing in disguise. But there were times when he wondered what kind of life he might have had if they'd taken a chance on him and not rejected him out of hand. He may not have made anything more than a private, but he would have pulled his weight and made a go of things.

And that way he might have died heroically in combat, maybe somewhere overseas and important — instead of here, in a rundown car park close to the A21. It wasn't exactly high up on anyone's list of places to meet their maker.

So, he was irritated more than scared.

At least he was divorced now, and all his worldly goods, such as they were, would go to the stray cat charity. It sounded bitter and twisted, but he'd rather the moggies got the lot than Jennifer saw a single penny.

A half-laugh strangled itself in his throat, sounding louder in the confines of the Jag. That was cruel of him. Jennifer wasn't that bad, really — and most of the blame for the disaster that became their twelve-year marriage was down to him. And he certainly couldn't lay his current predicament anywhere near her door.

He trained his gaze on the rear-view mirror, searching for the face of the man about to end his life. The offer of a gun with which to do the deed himself was quickly waved away. If the person behind him wanted him dead, then he would need to do it himself. That was the deal. Keeble wouldn't exactly stop him, but he wasn't about to do the man's dirty work for him, either.

As the seconds ticked by, Keeble knew he wasn't getting out of the Jag alive — but life as he knew it was over for him anyway, had been for a long time. He'd been treading water for the last few years until the dreaded day presented itself.

It wasn't that he was suicidal — he didn't actively *want* to end his life. It was more that he didn't have that much to live for anymore. And he was tired. As much as he and Jennifer grated on each other's nerves towards the end of their marriage, a life with her was the only life he'd ever known. Relationships had never been his forte, so he hadn't been fussed about finding someone to replace her after they went their separate ways, content instead to bowl along on his own, living day to day, week to week. And then there was the job — only just hanging onto it by the thinnest of thin threads.

With no children and no real friends to speak of, it wasn't all that much to lose in the grand scheme of things, was it?

Keeble wondered what was going through the man's mind. The eyes locked to his in the mirror were pale and empty, devoid of emotion, but it would be a particularly cold-hearted killer who felt nothing at all.

Keeble already knew the reason he was to die today; he'd been expecting it for the last fourteen years, so it wasn't exactly a shock. He'd done wrong — more than just wrong if he were being overly critical about it. He'd committed a crime — and not just any old crime, either; one of the worst crimes a police officer could ever commit. He'd been weak, and he'd been exploited. It wasn't an excuse, and he had no intention of pretending it was.

And here he was again.

Keeble wasn't sure if he believed in retribution or karma, but there was no escaping the fact that someone had died because of him because of what he did. Maybe not directly — there was no actual blood on his hands — but the man had died just the same. Guilt had an uncanny way of finding you, even when you didn't want to be found — and when it did, it clung to you like a leech. So, if he could accept his guilt, then he could accept his fate, too.

The summer of 2005 had been when life as he knew it changed, setting him on the rocky path that eventually led to the rundown car park in Hastings fourteen years later. If he'd made different choices back then, would it have ultimately made a difference? Or was he always destined to end up like this? His life snuffed out in front of an ageing bowling alley.

But maybe Keeble's choices were irrelevant. What if Colin Hedges had made a different choice that day, too?

\* \* \*

*Tuesday 19 July 2005*
*London*

Detective Inspector Mark Keeble hadn't been trained in covert surveillance, but it didn't strike him as being all that difficult.

All you needed to do was stay out of sight. And, let's face it, most people were inherently stupid and paid little attention to what was going on around them. He'd followed the man before, so knew exactly where he would be headed.

The envelope containing thirty-five thousand pounds felt thick and heavy in the pocket of his overcoat. To most people, it was a life-changing amount of money — and it had seemed that way to Keeble when he'd accepted it. Maybe it wasn't quite enough to make him give up his job, and the pension attached to it, but it enabled him to try and make Jennifer's life a little more comfortable. Not that he got much thanks for it.

He'd needed to embellish exactly where he'd got it from — she wasn't stupid. It wasn't as though the police usually handed out generous bonuses these days; and even if they did, Keeble was unlikely to be on the receiving end of one, especially if it was performance related. And he didn't have any long-lost wealthy relatives that he could invent a substantial inheritance from.

The best thing he could do was keep the whole thing under the radar. The less people that knew about it, the better.

So, in the end, he'd opted for the tried and tested lie — *a win on the horses*.

Jennifer had swallowed it without too much hesitation; Keeble had previous form in that regard, so it wasn't exactly an enormous stretch of the imagination. His betting addiction had almost ruined the early days of their blossoming relationship, when he'd blown the deposit they'd saved for a flat on the two thirty at Wetherby.

To give Jennifer some credit, she hadn't shown him the door immediately, but from then on had kept far stricter control of their finances. So, for him to suddenly come into thirty-five thousand pounds would take some explaining — or at least some hiding.

And he obviously couldn't tell her the truth.

So, a successful flutter on the horses had been all he was left with. Admittedly, he'd had to sleep in the spare room for a week and then endure many a frosty look across the cornflakes in the morning, but eventually she'd come around to the idea — especially as it meant she could book a luxury holiday, together with a new wardrobe of clothes to go with it, plus make plans for their future wedding.

Jennifer hadn't questioned the need to keep it quiet, for which Keeble was thankful. One lie was enough.

He saw Colin Hedges making a left turn up ahead, just as expected. Keeble could afford to hang back a little, knowing the man would cross the main road via the zebra crossing, and then head into the small corner shop to pick up his usual six-pack of lager. Keeble felt the familiar pangs of his other addiction — already knowing he would do the same on his way home later. The advantage of coming into so much cash meant he didn't have to go for the cheapest brand on the shelves anymore — he could push the boat out and get something decent instead. The thought buoyed him as he followed Hedges towards the crossing.

\* \* \*

*Hastings, East Sussex*

If silence could be deafening, then this was it. Apart from the sound of the Jag's engine still purring, all Keeble could hear was his own breathing. How was the man going to do it? Would he take the gun and just put a bullet in the back of Keeble's head? The handgun was still resting on the passenger seat where the detective had left it.

A gunshot would be short. Quick. Possibly even painless. But was that what Keeble deserved?

As the seconds dragged by, Keeble found himself thinking about Colin Hedges again. It was a name he hadn't had much cause to think about over the years — much less than Wesley Barton, anyway. On occasion, the man's face would creep into his thoughts, usually when he least expected it, finding its way through one alcoholic haze or another — but he always managed to banish it with another drink or two.

But Hedges had been different — different to the others, anyway.

Different because he'd stood his ground.

Different because he'd said *no*.

\* \* \*

Colin Hedges pushed open the door to the corner shop, the bell above announcing his arrival. The shopkeeper was in his usual position behind the till, and the pair exchanged a nod as Hedges made his way to the back of the shop.

Once out of sight of the shopkeeper, Hedges glanced over his shoulder. The man hadn't followed him inside, but he'd made little effort to keep himself hidden.

And it hadn't been the first time, either.

Quite what the detective wanted with him, Hedges wasn't sure, but he suspected it wasn't to monitor his drinking habits. Judging by the bloodshot eyes and crumpled clothes, the man looked like he enjoyed a drink or two himself.

Selecting two six-packs of the cheapest lager he could find, he made his way back to the till, picking up a large multi-bag of crisps on the way. That would be dinner sorted, at least. Standing by the counter, a sideways glance confirmed the detective was waiting by the traffic lights outside, pretending to light a cigarette.

Hedges paid for his purchases and, slipping the beer and crisps into his backpack, continued his journey home. Part of him wanted to confront the detective, ask him just what he thought he was doing. Fleetingly, he thought about trying to lose the man by cutting through the park. If he was quick enough, he could dodge through the traffic and hop over the park railings opposite. But at forty-four, Hedges was no David Soul, and this wasn't an episode of *Starsky and Hutch*.

Turning away from the traffic lights, he headed for home — thinking about the can of cheap, full-strength lager that he would crack open as soon as he got there. He hadn't quite sunk to the level of street drinking yet, but his lips and tongue felt dry at the thought.

With the main road stretching out in front of him, he lengthened his stride. As he walked, the shop fronts soon petered out, replaced by rows of tiny, terraced houses, squashed side by side. After a few more minutes, even the terraced houses would thin out, and Hedges would end his journey by crossing an expanse of wasteland, heading in the direction of the flats he called home on the other side of the river.

"River" was stretching it somewhat, however, as most of the time it was nothing but a dried-up trickle of water, revealing an assortment of abandoned supermarket trollies and old rusting bike wheels. It was possible to cross the river at the bridge ahead but, when it was dry enough, it was just as easy to scramble down one side and up the other. There was certainly zero chance of getting your feet wet.

With an ever-increasing urge to crack open one of his cans, Hedges intended to do just that. It would shave fifteen minutes off his journey time.

A dingy, greasy café on the corner marked the end of the row of terraced houses, the end of habitation as he knew it. Beyond that was the expanse of wasteland that would eventually morph into a disused industrial estate and motorway beyond. As he approached the café, he felt someone brush past him.

What happened next was over in a split second.

A hand grabbed Hedges roughly by the right upper arm, dragging him off the street and into the dingy café. Hedges stumbled over the threshold, banging into a cheap, plastic table.

"Over here." The voice sounded gruff.

Hedges had no choice but to be guided towards the back of the café, away from the window. The detective's grip wasn't tight, but Hedges got the message loud and clear that resistance was discouraged. Curiously, the café was empty — the staff behind the greasy counter choosing now to take a break. As Hedges slid into a chair, he took a glance back towards the door. The CLOSED sign was already showing.

"I'd get you a coffee, but we won't be here long." The detective sat down opposite, resting his elbows on the food-splattered Formica table. A heavy aroma of cooking oil and frying bacon still hung in the air, catching at the back of Hedge's throat. His stomach had been starting to grumble on the walk home, but any thought of food was now firmly banished from his mind. "You'll be wondering why we're meeting in here."

Sitting up close to the man, Hedges recognised the all too familiar signs of sleep deprivation, coupled with a generous degree of alcohol abuse. It was almost like looking into a mirror. Despite his predicament, Hedges dragged up a degree of bravery.

"I didn't exactly have much choice." Once the words escaped his mouth, Hedges clamped his lips shut, bravado evaporating just as quickly as it had arrived. His mouth had got him into hot water one too many times before — and he certainly didn't need to be doing it in front of the law.

"I'll give you that one." The detective's face broke into a hesitant smile. "Don't look so worried. I've just got a proposal for you — then you can be on your way."

# CHAPTER SEVENTEEN

*Hastings, East Sussex*

Colin Hedges had impressed him — and it took a lot to impress Mark Keeble. The man had barely flinched when Keeble had pushed the envelope across the table. Instead, he'd remained seated, back against the wall, staring the detective straight in the eyes.

"No."

The answer had been clear enough.

It was strange to think that of all the people he'd met in his forty-five years on this planet, Colin Hedges was the one he thought of now. Not Jennifer. Not his parents. Not even Smokey, the Siamese cat he and Jennifer had adopted before life had turned sour.

Just Colin bloody Hedges.

Once again, Keeble's gaze centred on the Jag's rear-view mirror. In the whole time they'd been in the car, the man hadn't moved, not even an inch. He'd barely even blinked.

A soft laugh began to bubble up inside Keeble's throat. He was done with it all now. "If you're going to do it — which

I assume you are — just go ahead and get it over with. I'm tired of this shit."

* * *

*Bury St Edmunds Police Station*

"Tierney left our prospective killer alone inside the Crown Street property for approximately twenty minutes." Nicki sighed as she approached the whiteboards. "Certainly long enough to suss out a way to get back into the house after it was locked up."

"The doorstop?" mused Roy. "Wedged in a downstairs window?"

Nicki added the extra detail to the first Operation Jackdaw board. "It seems the most likely explanation. Daring, but unless someone physically checked each window was secure before the property itself was secured, it's the best we've got. Tierney said the viewing was at around four p.m. on the Tuesday afternoon — the day before Jacob fell from the roof. There were no viewings at all on the Wednesday."

Nicki then took the team through Tierney's vague description of the mystery man. "If anyone fancies staying on tonight — and it's not obligatory as it's already getting late — then we need to reassess all the CCTV footage for Tuesday afternoon and see if anyone matching this description leaps out at us. Samuel Drake is obviously not his real name."

"I'll stay," volunteered Matt, crunching his way through a bag of Monster Munch. "I was going to carry on looking through Jacob's work accounts anyway, now that the laptop has arrived."

Nicki nodded. "Good. Thanks."

"And I'll keep him company," added Duncan. "I'm still gathering info on our Mr Mitcham."

"Excellent. And don't forget about that date, too." Nicki's gaze slid back to the first whiteboard. "The lab's confirmed that the blood found on the top floor of the Crown Street address belongs to Jacob Towers." She added the detail to the board. "I don't think there's any doubt now that the location of our video recording is that room."

"Grant Patterson left a message while we were interviewing Tierney," added Darcie, pulling her notepad towards her. "He's left contact emails for two of the three unregistered mobiles, but there's nothing for Samuel Drake."

Nicki nodded. "Get in touch with them, just to rule them out. Then we focus on this Samuel Drake."

"Why did Tierney feel the need to lie to us about him?" asked Darcie. "Drake, I mean. Things would have been much simpler for everybody if he'd just been straight with us from the beginning."

"I agree," conceded Nicki. "I think he must have just panicked when you started questioning him at the estate agents. We know he's got two spent convictions for theft, and he admitted during our little chat that he didn't mention either of them to his new employers. It's not inconceivable that he might have been concerned that talking to us could drag it all up again — the past he's worked hard to leave behind."

"Makes sense," commented Matt, scrunching up his empty crisp packet. "But all he succeeded in doing was to draw even more attention to himself. Do we really think he's telling the truth about leaving our potential killer alone inside the house? We don't think he was more involved than that? Maybe he was the one making the video recording?"

Nicki had considered the question before Tierney was allowed to go home. The man had been stupid to lie, that was evident, but there was a world of difference between a liar and a killer. "I'm inclined to believe him. He admitted to stepping outside the property to have a smoke, something he knew his employers would frown upon, while our man was left alone inside doing goodness knows what. I think his involvement begins and ends there, but we'll keep him up on the board for now."

Glancing up at the wall clock, Nicki turned away from the whiteboards. "Those not staying on, time to go home and get some rest. We've plenty to do tomorrow. And those that do stay — don't burn the midnight oil tonight. It's after nine already."

Heading towards her office, only intending to stop long enough to switch off the computer and grab her bag, Nicki winced as both her feet and head throbbed in time with each other. She knew she would end up going over the case in her head at home, but at least she could have a glass of wine in her hand as she did so.

As she reached her office door, she noticed Malcolm Turner heading in the same direction, head down and hands thrust into his trouser pockets. He brushed past as if he hadn't even seen her, despite their elbows nearly touching.

"Is everything all right, sir?" For a moment Nicki thought the DCI hadn't heard her, as the man continued towards the stairs, still appearing to be deep in thought. Abandoning her office, she hurried to catch up. "Sir?"

Turner flinched at the sound of his name, turning just as he started to descend the stairs. His face softened. "Everything's fine, Nicki. Just a long day, that's all."

Seeing the troubled look on the DCI's face, Nicki followed him to the ground floor. She knew him well enough by now, on both a personal and professional level, to know that all was not well. If anything, the grave look on his face deepened the further they descended.

"Anything I can help with?" she volunteered, as Turner held the main door open for her. "Take some of the strain?" For a moment Nicki thought he was going to say yes, but after a lengthy pause he merely shook his head and gave her an empty smile.

"Everything's fine, honestly. Nothing a good drop of whisky can't solve, anyway. You have any plans for tonight? I hope you're not working too late?"

Nicki followed the DCI out into the car park, even though home was in the opposite direction. "Nothing more complicated than a hot bath for me tonight. I've told the team not to make it a late one, too."

"Good." Turner stood next to his Lexus, fumbling for his keys. Nicki noticed the man hesitate slightly before catching her eye again. "How's your father doing these days? Have you seen him lately?"

Nicki's nerves immediately spiked. The DCI and her father spoke frequently, so why would he need to ask her how he was? Unless there was something wrong. She tried to look unconcerned. "He's fine, as far as I know. He and Mum are coming up tomorrow night for dinner."

After a minute or so of more chat, Turner made his excuses and slipped inside the Lexus. Nicki watched him pull away before heading back to the station to retrieve her bag. Malcolm Turner was as easy to read these days as an open book — the man was obviously worried about something. That wouldn't ordinarily trouble her too much — not with the case and her own life to think about — but she had a sneaking suspicion that the DCI's worries somehow involved her father.

\* \* \*

*Bury St Edmunds Bus Station*

Adrian Browning shoved his hands into the pockets of his tracksuit bottoms and strode away from the bus station. He still felt wired — despite an extra-long session in the garage that afternoon, pummelling the punching bag to within an inch of its life.

Usually such an intense workout, stretching his muscles to the limit, sweat pouring down his face, would dampen his irritation and calm his anger. The rush of adrenaline and the endorphins that kicked in afterwards would act like a protective blanket, smothering any flames before they fully ignited.

But not tonight. Tonight, he still felt wired.

The five bottles of beer probably hadn't helped.

But neither had the email.

He hated being told what to do.

Frustration multiplying by the second, Adrian had almost resorted to hurling the laptop through the window, but he wasn't stupid. He knew that wouldn't stop the messages. In the end, it would just be a waste of a perfectly good laptop — and one he hadn't finished paying for yet.

Instead, he'd bottled up his anger and hit the homemade gym for another hour, taking pleasure in visualising the man's face on the surface of the punching bag. He would reply to the message in time — when he was good and ready, and not before.

Leaving the bus station behind, he strode towards the town centre. It was Friday night and, with the weather pleasantly mild, the pubs were going to be busy. Feeling the way he did, the sensible option would have been to stay at home, watch a movie or play on the Xbox. He was bound to cross the path of someone who irritated him, someone who pushed all the wrong buttons; Adrian just hoped he could keep his hands in his pockets long enough to avoid trouble this time. He didn't need the police breathing down his neck again — not after what happened last year.

Needing another drink, he crossed the road and headed towards the Grapes.

\* \* \*

*Bury St Edmunds Police Station*

Leaning back in his chair, Matt sank his teeth into the Big Mac and sighed. "You don't know how good this feels, mate. Absolute bloody heaven."

Duncan laughed into his chicken burger. "You're easily pleased, I'll say that much. Pizza last night, burgers tonight. It's not exactly haute cuisine."

After another mouthful of his burger, Matt dragged his eyelids open. "Danni has had us on a health kick ever since she got pregnant. For the last nine months it's been nothing but kale, lentils and quinoa in our house. And filtered water. I don't remember the last time I saw a chip or slice of cake."

Duncan scrunched up his burger wrapper, tossing it into the bin by his side as he reached for his chocolate milkshake. "Ah well, not long to go now. Then we can have a pie and a pint to wet the baby's head."

"When we were at the hospital last night, they talked about inducing her if she goes too long overdue. Her blood pressure was a little bit up." Matt stuffed the rest of his Big Mac into his mouth. "I hope to God he or she puts in an appearance before then — I'm not sure how much more of this waiting around I can take."

"Fingers crossed, then." Duncan finished his milkshake then turned back to his computer screen. "In the meantime, did you find out much from Jacob's work accounts?"

Matt inched his chair closer to his desk, swallowing the remains of his burger and ripping open a can of Coke. "The main work email account is fairly standard. Various emails from satisfied customers, or quotes for potential ones. Invoices for work done, that kind of thing. Nothing jumped out at me as being all that unusual. But I did note that he hadn't had much work over the last six or seven months. Lord knows how he was paying the bills. Probably why their joint account was so heavily in the red. And not to mention the various maxed-out credit cards. From what I can see, they seemed to be living hand to mouth."

"What about our mystery man from the Crown Street property? You see him appearing in any of the CCTV recordings on Tuesday?"

Matt pulled a face behind his Coke can. "Not as yet. He either knows what he's doing, or he's been surprisingly lucky in avoiding the cameras."

"Well, I've pulled all I can find on this Harvey Mitcham bloke." Duncan tapped his screen. "He's penned quite a few online articles on conspiracy theories over the years, even getting a couple into some mainstream magazines."

"Conspiracy theories? Such as what?"

"Take this one, for example." Duncan angled his screen towards his colleague. "He reckons Lord Lucan was kidnapped — and was then framed for the murder of his children's nanny and the attempted murder of his wife."

"Kidnapped by who?"

"That's where it gets a little bit woolly. The gist of it seems to suggest it was an organised gang acting on the payroll of the wife. Then something went wrong, and the kidnappers disappeared without telling the wife where they'd hidden her husband."

Matt gulped down a mouthful of Coke and shrugged. "It's a theory, I guess."

"Not one that held much credence — there was quite a backlash afterwards and he had to retract a lot of it as unfounded speculation."

"Anything else about him?"

"Hasn't come to the attention of the police before. Seems fairly comfortable financially, although doesn't look to have had any paid employment for a good while. Been living in Fornham All Saints with his wife for the last twenty-five years."

"Once I finished looking at the CCTV, I started looking into that date — 15 August 2005 — and it's more difficult than it sounds." Matt pulled a notebook across his desk. "Seems to be quite an unimportant date all round. All I could find was it was the sixtieth anniversary of Victory in the Pacific; it was Independence Day in India, celebrating sixty-eight years since the country was liberated from British rule; Phil Mickelson won the PGA Golf championship; Israel began its disengagement plan to evict all Israelis from the Gaza Strip and four settlements in the West Bank; and James Blunt was at number one in the UK charts with 'You're Beautiful'." He looked up and pulled another face. "I don't see how any of it could be related to our case." Before he could say anything else, his mobile chirped. He stabbed the screen and brought the handset to his ear. "Yep — I'm still at work, babe. I won't be much . . ."

A split second later, the detective constable launched himself from his chair, grabbed his jacket and ran for the door.

\* \* \*

*Newmarket Road, Bury St Edmunds*

Aaron Nash tried to focus on the taillights in front of him but found his concentration wandering. Gripping the steering wheel, he dug his nails into the palms of his hands. The dinner he'd tried to force down earlier now churned uncomfortably in his stomach, threatening to reappear at any second.

They'd made small talk over the kitchen table, Rosalyn asking how his day had been. In response, he made the usual sugar-coated reply but without really answering the question. It had been this way for a while now, neither of them having the courage to ask what was really wrong. It pained him to think how much he was hurting her — she was the only person he'd ever truly loved — but he couldn't bear telling her the truth. How could he? That would be worse than the guilt he'd lived with for the last fourteen years.

But it was no life for either of them. They both deserved better than this — at least Rosalyn did. He, on the other hand, deserved everything that was coming to him. It was pointless to keep blaming the events of 2005, which were bad enough on their own. There was no escaping the fact that he'd continued to make mistake after mistake, tell lie after lie. And now everything was coming home to roost.

Squinting into the dark, he wondered why so many people were driving around the town at this time of night. Where were they all going? He'd made an excuse to Rosalyn that he needed to put petrol in the car ready for his trip north next week but instead had spent the best part of an hour driving aimlessly from street to street, trying to get his nerves under control.

As he slowed down for a set of traffic lights, he forced himself to bite back the tears threatening to spill. He was going to do this, he knew he was, but he didn't want to hurt anyone else; he'd hurt enough people already. The pragmatic part of him knew that it was more than possible others would suffer. Could he live with himself if he wilfully caused pain and injury to innocent people in some twisted attempt to ease his own conscience? Surely there were better ways?

A strangled laugh caught in his throat as he pulled away from the lights at speed. That was the whole point of this, wasn't it? *He wouldn't live.* Knowing what he had to do, and before he could change his mind, he thundered towards the roundabout, heading for the slip road. Stomach in knots and knuckles whitening even further, he stamped down hard on the accelerator.

As he reached the crest of the slip road, the A14 came into view. Tears were now flowing freely down his cheeks, dripping from his chin. Eyesight blurring, he pulled off the slip road and joined the carriageway.

Images of those he loved flooded his head as he nudged the speedometer up.

65 . . . 70 . . . 75 mph.

Deciding to kill yourself was a pastime few, thankfully, had direct experience of. But on this warm evening towards the end of May, it was all Aaron Nash could think about. Pushing thoughts of Rosalyn and everyone else aside, he found images of Wesley Barton soon replacing them.

*Wesley Barton.*

*That* was why he was doing this; why he *had* to do this.

He couldn't see another way out.

With another strangled sob, he closed his eyes and headed for the lights.

# CHAPTER EIGHTEEN

*College Lane, Bury St Edmunds*
*Saturday 25 May 2019*

Luna weaved her way around Nicki's ankles, the animal's purring increasing in volume.

"Nearly there, Luna, nearly there."

Nicki squeezed the salmon-flavour cat food from the sachet onto a clean saucer, feeling the cat's tail thumping rhythmically against her calves. Smiling, she bent down and placed the saucer onto the kitchen floor. "Don't eat too quickly, madam — I don't want to come home to a pile of sick on the carpet."

Seeming to ignore the instruction, the Russian Blue began devouring her breakfast at lightning speed. Nicki sighed and straightened up, wondering if she had time for one more coffee before setting out for work. Deciding that she did, she reached for the coffee jug.

Taking her mug through to the living room, she scrolled through the news headlines on her phone. Jacob Towers was still in the news, but precious little information had been released other than his name, and then a plea for any witnesses who might have seen him on Wednesday afternoon and evening.

On the local news page there was also a report of a serious accident on the A14 overnight, which had closed the road in both directions just outside the town. According to the latest update, the road was still closed. Nicki knew such a closure would mean diversions, sending swathes of morning traffic through the town centre. Aware of the carnage it would cause, she was again thankful that she lived close enough to the station to be able to walk to work.

Happy to see that Luna hadn't yet thrown up, Nicki drained her mug and placed it onto the draining board. Grabbing her bag and keys, she checked her face in the mirror to make sure she didn't look like she'd been awake half the night and then left the house.

As she headed towards Westgate Street, she could see the traffic already backing up, crawling along at a snail's pace. Passing the idling cars, Nicki crossed the road and made her way towards the station.

On entering the incident room, she could tell the team had been working for some time already. Immediately, Darcie made a beeline for her, thrusting the BOSS mug into her hands, full to the brim.

"The phones have been ringing off the hook, boss. People claiming to have seen Jacob on Wednesday afternoon."

"Oh? Anything useful?"

"Don't get too excited. We've got people convinced he was up in Bolton, or as far south as Exeter."

Nicki's shoulders sagged as she took a mouthful of the unsweetened coffee. "Great. But I suppose it's not necessarily a bad thing — one call could bring that valuable witness out of the woodwork. But let's still be prepared for an onslaught of time wasters." She headed over to Matt and Duncan. "How's Danni, Matt? I heard you had to rush off again last night."

Matt swung his chair around. "Another false alarm. We got sent home again in the early hours. Hence the slightly bleary eyes and intravenous coffee. Didn't get much sleep."

"Well, if you need to take some time this afternoon, just go. We can cope." She turned to Duncan. "What about Jacob's work laptop? Anything come out of his emails?"

Duncan proceeded to fill Nicki in on what he'd managed to find out so far — which wasn't much — and that Simon from the tech suite was still looking at the pop-up box messaging service. He then gave an update on what he'd managed to glean about Harvey Mitcham.

"Thanks, Duncan. Anything useful on the date?" Nicki's eyes slid towards the first whiteboard.

"I started looking into it before I had to leave last night." Matt stifled a yawn. "Like I told Dunc, I can't see anything even remotely connected to our case. Seems to have been a rather uninspiring date all round." Matt reeled off the key events that he'd managed to pick out.

Nicki pursed her lips. "I see what you mean. Let's put it all up on the board, though. The connection might come to us later. And Harvey Mitcham's details, too." She swallowed some more coffee. "I think it's high time we brought Mr Mitcham in and asked him about those text messages. He's lying about being in touch with Jacob, and I want to know why."

Just then, Darcie approached, armed with a packet of biscuits which were very quickly swiped out of her hands by Matt. Tutting, she said, "Karen rang a few minutes ago — she's had a good look around Jacob's home office but can't find anything to do with an insurance policy. Denise doesn't seem to know anything about one, either. Keeps saying that Jacob was the one who took care of the finances."

"Well, it was worth a shot. I know this was started last night but keep looking at any CCTV from Crown Street and further afield, especially for the dates our mystery man went for a viewing at the house — Tuesday last week, and also the previous Friday. We know he spent a considerable amount of time in the property on Tuesday — alone. Which was more than enough time to open one of the downstairs windows and wedge it open. Let me know if you find anything. In the meantime, I've asked for door-to-door along Crown Street, to see if anyone saw anything."

Nicki took her leave and started to head towards her office, intending to spend a few minutes wading through her emails before turning her attention to an interview strategy for Harvey Mitcham. Just as she neared the door, DS Fox caught up with her. "Just a heads-up. Your friend and mine, Adrian Browning, was arrested last night. Some punch-up in the town, outside the Grapes. He was kept in overnight but released early this morning, pending investigation." Fox held the office door open. "Although it was most probably the drink talking, I heard he kept asking for you."

"For me?" Nicki couldn't hide the surprise in her tone as she headed towards her desk. "Why would he ask for me? I'm not exactly his most favourite person in the world."

Fox shrugged. "No idea. Apparently, he just kept shouting your name. From what I can tell, he was quite drunk; they shoved him in a cell to sober up then decided it was probably better just to let him go."

"Thanks, Graham."

Just as Fox left her office, Malcolm Turner appeared. Nicki immediately noted the pensive look on the man's face. She recalled the worry and tiredness she'd seen the night before; this morning it looked more like exhaustion, as if he hadn't slept a wink. It was a look she recognised.

"Nicki. Just the person I was looking for."

"Sir?" Nicki frowned as she slipped behind her desk. "What's up?"

"I'll not keep you long — I've an urgent budget meeting to attend — but . . ." The man hesitated in the doorway. "No doubt you've heard about the crash on the A14 last night?"

Nicki nodded, picking up her desk diary. "Reports this morning say the road is still closed, so I expect the town's grinding to its usual standstill."

The DCI grimaced. "Indeed. And it could be that way for some time to come, so I hear — the accident investigators are still on scene."

"Oh?" Nicki's eyebrows shot up. "Investigators? I assumed it was vehicle recovery or road repairs that were delaying things. Something for us?"

Turner's pensive look deepened. "You could say that."

\* \* \*

*Woodlands Camping and Caravan Site, Suffolk*

He scored through the name of Aaron Nash. And then he did the same with Mark Keeble.

He'd been pleased to hear of the accident — knowing without needing to be told who had ploughed into the front of an oncoming lorry. The thought set off a delicious ripple of pleasure as a long sigh of relief escaped his lungs. He'd been worried about Nash the most, unsure how the man would react under stress — and, more importantly, whether he would go through with it.

But everyone had their price if you aimed high enough — and then turned the right screws.

However, Keeble had been different. He knew the detective was unlikely to make things easy and he'd been mildly amused by the man's apparent lack of concern for the situation he found himself in. Most people, when confronted with the person intent on ending their life, would display a modicum of fear. Maybe even panic. But Keeble had shown neither. Instead, the detective had worn a tired and almost accepting look on his face.

"*If you're going to do it . . . just go ahead and get it over with. I'm tired of this shit.*"

In an ideal world, Keeble would have taken his own life, just like Aaron Nash — the man seemingly only too prepared to ram his car into the front of an oncoming lorry. The thought made him smile again as he fleetingly considered what the police were making of *that* one.

It would have been a cruel but exquisite turn of events for the detective to have ended his own existence — for he was the one to blame for all of it. Without Keeble, his father would still be here — he had no doubt about that. So, to have driven the man to commit the ultimate act, to end his own life, would have been a just and fair outcome.

But it wasn't to be. Even when supplied with a loaded handgun to perform the job, the detective had merely laughed in his face.

*Laughed.*

That certainly hadn't been the reaction he'd been expecting and it had momentarily caught him off guard. *How dare the man laugh at him?* Anger soon replaced the confusion.

He could have put a bullet in the detective's head himself; all it would have taken would have been a quick squeeze of the trigger. He couldn't exactly miss from that range. It would have been swift, if not exactly clean.

But he didn't want the detective's death to be swift. He didn't particularly want *any* of them to go quickly or painlessly — but definitely not this one. Keeble had blood on his hands, more than the rest of them, and he would make the man pay right up until his dying breath.

So, he'd pocketed the handgun and brought out the wire instead.

It had been a while since he'd garrotted anyone, but it needed a surprisingly small amount of pressure when you got it right. Confined to the front seat of the Jaguar, the detective's room for manoeuvre had been severely limited, with little for him to grip onto other than the steering wheel, which wasn't going to save him. As he'd pulled the wire tighter, he heard the detective gurgling as the air was slowly expelled from his lungs, and — thanks to the rear-view mirror — he could also watch the life slip away.

Stepping back from the noticeboard pinned to the camper van's wall, he looked once again at his work.

There were thirteen names scored through now, and each brought with it an enormous sense of satisfaction. Every time one of them was snuffed out, he felt closer to his father's memory. And those of his sisters, too.

Next to the list was the only photo he had of Georgia and Grace. They were the true innocents in all of this, their lives snuffed out just as barbarically as their father's had been. So, he was doing this for them, just as much as he was doing it for his father.

He'd covered his tracks as best he could, but his own fate was inconsequential. He was confident he could outrun any manhunt, should it prove necessary — he'd successfully dispatched thirteen people so far, without so much as raising an eyebrow. With only two more to go, there was no reason to suspect he couldn't complete the list in the same fashion.

On the small pull-down bed that doubled as a settee during the day was a folded-up copy of the *Daily Mirror* from the summer of 2005. He hadn't kept it for any other reason than the head-and-shoulders photograph on page eight. Taking a pair of scissors, he began to carefully cut out the image.

A taut smile crossed his lips as he pinned the image next to the final name on the list. It was a name he'd added as an afterthought just a few months ago; the man hadn't featured on his original list of fourteen. But as he'd ticked off each one, after each of their lives were snuffed out, he felt a bigger scalp needed to pay for what had happened to his father. Time to go right to the very top of the whole stinking, corrupt pyramid.

And number fifteen would be the perfect finale.

Irritation made his nerves bristle as he considered how long it was taking to dispatch the man. Using a professional was meant to make it easier, more efficient. But it seemed to be having the opposite effect. Now the twenty-four-hour deadline had long since passed, he would be free to take matters into his own hands. The cruel smile on his lips widened.

He was sure he could do a better job with one hand tied behind his back.

\* \* \*

"Last night's crash victim has already been named as Aaron Nash — a local builder." Nicki resumed her seat in the incident room. "Age forty-nine, he lived on the Moreton Hall estate with his wife, Rosalyn. No children that we know of. At shortly before eleven o'clock last night, a number of witnesses saw him driving his car the wrong way along a stretch of the A14, where he then collided with an oncoming articulated lorry."

Darcie's hands tightened around her mug of tea. "Gosh, that sounds awful. Were there any other casualties?"

Nicki grimaced. "Thankfully, no one else lost their life. The lorry driver is in hospital, but his injuries are not thought to be life-threatening. Fortunately, at that time of night, traffic was light, and it was just those two vehicles involved."

"Well, that's something, at least." Darcie placed her mug down on her desk. "That poor lorry driver, though. He must be in total shock."

Nicki nodded. "I'm sure he is. Can you liaise with the hospital and find out how he's doing? Chap by the name of Gary Perkins. I'd like to go and have a chat with him when he's feeling up to it."

Darcie began to nod, then stopped as a frown peppered her brow. "Are we thinking this is more than just an accident, then? That this Aaron Nash purposefully drove into the lorry? Targeted the lorry driver on purpose, even?"

"The actual mechanics of the crash are still under investigation. The accident investigators are still on scene, but both vehicles have now been recovered."

"People do sometimes mistakenly drive the wrong way along a dual carriageway," added Duncan. "It's not particularly common, but it does happen from time to time. People get disorientated. Maybe he had some kind of medical episode at the wheel?"

Nicki let her gaze stray to the whiteboards. "Hopefully the post-mortem should tell us more about the deceased and whether he did, like you say, have some kind of catastrophic event behind the wheel. But we also have to consider that there was a note left behind at the family home."

"A note?" Darcie gripped her mug even tighter. "You mean like a suicide note?"

"It seems that way." Nicki's voice was grave. "Nash's wife found it when the officers called at the address late last night." She paused, turning back to face the team, eyes sombre. "But we also have something else. Something that explains why the investigation has been steered towards us." She took a breath. "There's every possibility that last night's crash could be linked to our investigation into Jacob Towers' death."

"Linked?" Duncan frowned. "Linked how exactly?"

Nicki looked each member of her team in the eye before replying. "Although all the evidence so far points to Nash's death being simply a tragic accident, the investigators found something after the body was removed from the remains of the car." Another pause. "In one of his pockets were seven teeth."

# CHAPTER NINETEEN

*Bury St Edmunds Police Station*

Details of the A14 crash were now populating a second white-board, the builder's name and a recent photograph pinned to the top. Beneath it were images taken from the crash site.

DS Fox stepped forward, pinning the last picture to the board. "CCTV first picks up his vehicle driving through the town at ten past ten last night. He's seen to circle the streets for a while before entering the multi-storey car park at ten thirty, staying until ten fifty-five. He then reappears and heads out along Newmarket Road to join the A14. After taking the wrong exit at the roundabout on Newmarket Road, he drives the wrong way up the slip road at junction forty-two. The crash happened twenty-two seconds later."

"Well, that doesn't make much sense for a start." Duncan's eyes narrowed towards the whiteboards. "If he lives on Moreton Hall and he was heading for the A14, he could easily have joined it at junction forty-four — why go all the way to the other side of town?"

"And it's not an easy thing to do, either," mused Roy, staring at the photographs pinned to the whiteboard. "Take the wrong exit at that roundabout, I mean. You'd need to take a pretty sharp left and then almost double back on yourself to manage it. Doesn't strike me as particularly plausible that it could be a mistake." He frowned at the boards. "As distasteful as it sounds, I think he knew exactly what he was doing."

"And we also have the note," agreed Duncan, gesturing towards a copy of the handwritten note that was now pinned to the board. "Looks intentional to me. As horrible as it sounds, and not wanting to appear callous, is it really something for us?"

Nicki sighed. "You've forgotten the teeth, Duncan. It's the teeth that makes it something for us. The teeth found in Aaron Nash's pocket means it *has* to be linked to our falling graphic designer. And if we're not convinced Jacob Towers jumped of his own volition, then it stands to reason that we're not convinced this was a simple RTC either. Remember—" Nicki turned towards her team — "the obvious is often there to trip you up, to guide you along a certain course — usually the less bumpy route, but it's often not the right one. Let's find out all we can about Nash — background, family, work history, social media. The usual. No phone found at the scene, but it may not have survived the impact. We'll need to go out and see the wife at some point, too. Caz has already confirmed that she'll schedule the post-mortem later this morning. That might tell us if anything happened to make him lose his concentration. Maybe he did have something like a stroke at the wheel, causing an episode of acute confusion — leading to him driving the way he did."

*But it still didn't explain the teeth.*

*Nothing explained the teeth.*

"But what about the teeth?" Darcie echoed Nicki's thoughts. "That makes no sense at all."

Nicki shuddered. "The teeth bother me, too. Roy, where are we on looking to see if there are other cases involving the extraction of teeth?"

"I've made some inroads." Roy tapped a notepad with the end of his pen. "I was looking at it some more this morning, before this came in. As you might imagine, it's not all that common a scenario."

Nicki nodded. "Good. Keep checking. And while you're at it, see what you can find out about the relevance of the number seven. Was it just a coincidence that both Jacob Towers and Aaron Nash had *seven* teeth removed? Or does it mean something? For the rest of us, let's carry on with the outstanding actions. Darcie, any luck tracing the customers who gave false mobile numbers from the emails Patterson gave us?"

"I've managed to get replies from both, and spoken to them this morning, too." Darcie flipped open her notebook. "Both have alibis for Wednesday, and both gave the same reason why they gave a fake mobile number — they didn't want to get harassed or spammed."

"OK, let's strike them off our list. We still need to bring in Harvey Mitcham and we'll need to go and see Mrs Nash. Darcie, how about you come with me to visit her later?"

The detective constable nodded. "Sure, just say the word."

Fox was still lingering by the whiteboards. "So, if we're thinking these cases might be connected because of the teeth, and that Towers may not have jumped voluntarily, what are we saying about Nash? I take it there's no suggestion there was anyone else in the car with him?"

Glancing at the crime scene photos, and the mangled wreck that was once the builder's car, Nicki shuddered again. "Just the one body was recovered from the vehicle. The car was completely crushed; there's no way someone walked away from it." Judging by the photos, crushed was an understatement, and Nicki wasn't exactly looking forward to the post-mortem later. Clearing her throat, she continued. "Do the usual checks, see if they knew each other — Towers and Nash — or if their wives did. It's a long shot, but see if there's anywhere their paths might have crossed. In the meantime, we'll go and see Nash's wife, and then on to the hospital to see the lorry driver, if he's up to it."

* * *

"Recently divorced, so I'm told." Detective Sergeant Nigel Brooke led Detective Constable Owen Thorpe into the first-floor flat's small living area. Old-fashioned dark wood furniture gave the room an overly cramped and claustrophobic feel. "Neighbours say he's lived here alone for the last year or so. No regular visitors. The chap who let us in — a Mr Rutherford from next door — says he can't remember the last time anyone dropped by."

DC Thorpe stood in the centre of the room. It didn't take long for the three empty gin bottles by the side of the only armchair to catch his eye. "Did he have a reputation as a drinker, by any chance?"

DS Brooke shrugged and made his way over to the room's only window. "No idea — I've never met him." The curtains were still drawn, so Brooke hooked them back with a gloved finger and peered outside. All that greeted him was a communal backyard housing an assortment of different-coloured wheelie bins and an old bike, minus a wheel. "Do we know where the ex-wife lives? Still local?"

Thorpe pulled out his notebook. "Only brief details so far. Looks like she lives over in Putney."

Brooke turned away from the window and re-scanned the room. Although Mark Keeble didn't seem to have much, what he did have was kept relatively clean and tidy. The room might feel cramped with the clunky furniture, but there were no piles of rubbish anywhere, no plates stacked up and stuck together with dried food, no mountains of bottles or cans. Admittedly there were the three gin bottles, but apart from that the room was well kept. The air smelled clean as if the place had been recently vacuumed.

"If our chap lived here, what do you think he was doing down with us in Hastings?" questioned Thorpe. "And using that car park in particular? It's not the most salubrious of places. I'm not sure I'd park a Jag there."

"Agreed. There's nothing much there anymore, most of the out-of-town shopping units have long since closed. As far as I know, all that's left is a discount electrical store, a ten-pin bowling alley and a sex shop." He glanced up at the detective constable, eyebrows hitched. "Which one of those do we think our detective inspector was frequenting?"

Before the detective constable could offer an answer, Brooke crossed over to a desk tucked away in the corner, noting a laptop stored on top and a rubbish bin beneath.

"Judging by the contents of this chap's bin, he's more than casually acquainted with online shopping." The bin was full of neatly collapsed and squashed Amazon packaging boxes. "So, I don't think he'd be in the market for the electrical store. That just leaves us the bowling alley or the sex shop."

"How old is he? Late forties? He doesn't strike me as your average ten-pin bowler demographic."

"Which leaves us the sex shop."

"Cameras?"

"Being requested as we speak — but don't hold your breath. The vehicle will be processed, but we're still looking for his mobile." The mobile phone bothered Brooke. What self-respecting detective went out without his phone? From the brief look around the flat so far, it wasn't there either. The only explanation was that the killer took it with them.

"What do you make of this?" Thorpe joined Brooke at the desk, gesturing towards the wall behind. "He was still working, right?"

Brooke gave a short shake of his head, peering at the list of names pinned to the wall. "Off sick for the last few months."

"Maybe it was one of his open cases and he carried on working on it while on sick leave?" Thorpe made a face. "On the quiet?"

"Maybe." Brooke's tone sounded unconvinced. "Take a note of the names and run them when we get back to the station. Let's check the bedroom before we leave."

The flat's only bedroom contained a single bed, small wardrobe, and a slim bedside table close to the door. Thorpe followed the detective sergeant inside and a quick search found no mobile phone, or anything else of significance. On turning around, Thorpe spied a landline phone on the bedside table, red light blinking.

He pressed the flashing red button, and the messaging system whirred into action. There was just the one message.

*Message received at 9.33 a.m. Friday 24 May.*
*"Mark? It's me, Hugh. Call me back when you get this, as soon as you can. There's a couple of things I need to discuss with you."*
*To delete the message, press 1. To listen to the message again, press 2. To save the message, press 3.*

"Let's take that with us, along with the laptop." Brooke headed out of the cramped bedroom, leaving Thorpe to disconnect the answerphone. "And the first thing we need to do is find out who this man Hugh is."

* * *

*Sebert Road, Bury St Edmunds*

"He was such an experienced driver." Rosalyn Nash shuddered as she sank back against the cushions of her armchair. "I really don't understand how . . ."

Nicki and Darcie took their seats on the sofa opposite. At the window behind them, the thick drape curtains were still drawn, plunging the room into a premature darkness. The air felt heavy with sadness and shock. Grief had yet to materialise, but Nicki knew it wouldn't be far behind.

"I know," she replied. "This must be very difficult for you. Is there anyone we can call?" Nicki raised her gaze to DC Gedge, who was standing in a doorway leading to another reception room beyond.

"Mrs Nash's sister is coming down from Hull. She's on her way as we speak."

Nicki nodded gratefully. "Well, Karen is here for you as long as you need. We want to help you as much as we can over the coming days." She paused, wondering if what she was about to say might be too soon. But she didn't feel they could delay much longer. "But we need your help, too."

Rosalyn Nash blinked through swollen, teary eyes. "H . . . help? How can I help?"

Nicki took a deep breath. "Despite the rawness of how you must be feeling right now, it would really assist our investigation if we could find out more about Aaron."

Rosalyn's voice was shaky, barely above a whisper. "What do you need to know?"

"You mentioned he was an experienced driver. Can you expand on that? How long had he been driving?"

"For as long as I can remember. I met him when I was seventeen, he was eighteen, and he had a car then. He's always driven; he needs to for work."

"And had he always been in the building trade?"

Rosalyn nodded. "Yes. In one way or another." Her gaze strayed towards the sideboard by the window, where a succession of silver-framed photographs was displayed. A wistful look entered her eyes. "He got his first job on a building site after leaving school. He eventually started his own building company, until the financial crash in 2008 changed things." A bitterness entered her tone. "We lost the business, and since then he's been working up and down the country, wherever the work takes him."

"Did he work away a lot?"

Nicki detected a guardedness cross Rosalyn's face. "He didn't have any choice."

"Of course. How far away did he travel? Did he have to stay away overnight?"

Rosalyn dabbed her eyes with a damp tissue and nodded. "The work was mainly up north, but he would go wherever the jobs were. He had a regular job that took him to the North East every fortnight. He's been doing that for the last seven or eight years, I think. He would be away for four to five days at a time, sometimes the whole week if he was busy." Rosalyn swallowed and her shoulders heaved. "We needed the money."

"I understand. And you've lived in the town for how long?"

"Eight years, give or take. Before that we were in Ipswich for a while. And before that we lived in London."

"And it's just the two of you living here?" Nicki had already checked the walls and shelves for photographs of children and had seen none.

The woman nodded. "We didn't have children — we did try, but it just never happened for us."

"Would you say your husband knew the area well?" Nicki knew where she was steering the conversation but was conscious of the sensitive nature of her questioning. She held her breath.

After a brief pause, Rosalyn started to nod. "Definitely. He certainly knew the A14 very well. There's no way he would . . ." The rest of the woman's words were swallowed in a torrent of sobs.

DC Gedge moved out of the doorway, handing Rosalyn a box of tissues.

"I realise how difficult this is for you, Mrs Nash. We won't trouble you for too much longer, just a couple more questions. Did your husband have any health problems at all?"

"Health problems?" Rosalyn frowned. "Such as what?"

"Did he suffer from epilepsy, or any other seizure disorder? Had he ever passed out or collapsed?"

The woman was already shaking her head before Nicki had finished the question. "No, definitely not. He was very healthy. He didn't even smoke."

Nicki shifted in her seat. She knew Rosalyn Nash was on a knife edge emotionally, and they should leave her to deal with her grief in private. But she still had one more question to ask.

"I'm really sorry, Mrs Nash, but I do need to ask you about the note."

When officers had called at the three-bedroom house on Sebert Road in the early hours of the morning, Rosalyn had taken some time to answer the door, having gone to bed with a migraine. After showing the officers in, she found the note propped up against the kettle in the kitchen.

The note itself was on its way to the lab for forensic testing, a photocopy gracing the incident room whiteboard. But each word was now indelibly imprinted on Nicki's memory.

*Sorry, Ros. I can't do this anymore. I need to pay for what I've done.*

"It's definitely his handwriting? Aaron's?" Nicki saw Rosalyn shudder before she nodded. "And you didn't hear him leave last night?"

The nod turned into a slow shake. "I went to bed early as I had a migraine brewing. Aaron said he would wash up for me, so I went upstairs and took some painkillers, and then a sleeping tablet. The next thing I remember is . . ." The woman's voice broke, sobs choking in her throat. "Two police officers telling me my husband was dead."

"I appreciate how hard this is for you, Mrs Nash. But can you tell me how Aaron's mental health was recently?"

The question made Rosalyn shudder. "He was fine."

"Fine" was a word frequently banded about, but Nicki was always suspicious when it was given in response to the "How are you?" question. More often than not, the person wasn't fine at all.

"Was he on any regular medication?"

Rosalyn shook her head again. "No, nothing."

Deciding they had imposed on Rosalyn Nash's grief for long enough, Nicki stood up from the sofa. "We'll leave you now, Mrs Nash. DC Gedge will stay behind to support you in any way you need. We'll be back in touch as soon as we have any further news."

"Can I see him?"

It was a question Nicki had been expecting. She gave the woman a sad smile as she made her way towards the door.

"The post-mortem will be taking place today. Once that's been completed, we can talk some more about visiting him."

Nicki and Darcie left the grieving woman to quietly sob into another damp tissue. Out on the doorstep, Nicki turned to Karen, who had followed them to the door.

"I know it's a little insensitive, but can you ask Mrs Nash about whether there might be a life insurance policy?"

Karen nodded. "Of course. I'll pick my moment, though. She's understandably still very fragile. The sister is due here soon."

"Good — and how is Denise Towers bearing up?"

"Her parents have arrived, bringing the twins back with them. They're staying for the foreseeable, so it made sense for me to leave them in peace and come here, instead." She handed Nicki a plastic evidence bag. "Rosalyn found Aaron's phone by the side of the bed. The passcode is inside."

Nicki smiled gratefully as she took hold of the bag. "See what you can find out about their relationship. He seems to have worked away from home fairly regularly — which can cause tension in even the most solid of marriages. Find out where he went and what he did when he was away." Before heading for the car, Nicki added one more task to the list. "And while you're at it — see if the date 15 August 2005 means anything to her. I didn't feel it appropriate to raise it just now, the poor woman looked fit to drop. But see if it rings any bells with her when you get a moment. And maybe see if there's another phone kicking about somewhere."

Just as Karen shut the door behind them, Nicki's mobile trilled. She grimaced when she read the message. "Looks like the post-mortem is starting soon."

# CHAPTER TWENTY

*West Suffolk Mortuary*

Nicki pulled on the elasticated cap while securing the rubber apron around her waist. She could have asked any one of the team to attend in her place. Roy, in particular, seemed to enjoy post-mortems — if "enjoy" was the correct word — but this was one she felt she needed to do herself. And Caz had been good enough to rearrange her list at short notice to accommodate it.

As she entered the examination room, she was met by a warm and welcoming smile.

"All set?" Caz Mitchell tucked a wayward strand of hair beneath her cap.

Nicki tried to return the smile, heading to her usual position on the opposite side of the table. She was careful not to stand too close — even after countless post-mortems over the years, she still wasn't comfortable with the process. It might be a necessary part of the job, but that didn't mean it was a welcome one. "Let's get it over with," she breathed, doing her best to put Aaron Nash and the suicide note from her mind. "Thanks for fitting it in so quickly."

Caz flicked on the voice recorder and switched her gaze back to the table. "Today is Saturday 25 May 2019 and the examination is of a male Caucasian, age forty-nine. Pre-post-mortem weight is ninety-seven kilograms, height is estimated to be 189 centimetres." Nicki heard the pathologist clear her throat before continuing. "Starting with the external examination."

Nicki placed a hand over her nose and mouth. Although the body had not yet had a chance to decay, there was still an underlying aroma circulating the post-mortem room. It was difficult to quantify and accurately describe — nothing quite did it justice. The cool air was crisp but had an unpleasant edge to it — an undercurrent of death and decay, which no number of air filters could entirely eradicate. She swallowed and willed her stomach to settle.

"The body shows extensive damage from the impact. Multiple open fractures of the tibia and fibula on both sides, plus a partial traumatic amputation of the right foot."

Nicki bit down on her lip, unable to drag her eyes away from the poor man's foot hanging from his ankle by a few exposed tendons and scraps of skin.

Caz edged slowly up the table. "The upper legs show further open fractures of both femoral shafts. Pre-examination X-rays have confirmed a fractured pelvis. Moving up, the chest shows significant impact injuries consistent with a high-speed collision. X-rays show multiple rib fractures and a fractured sternum consistent with crush injuries."

Nicki's gaze travelled towards the man's upper body. Aaron Nash looked to have been a relatively tall and well-built man, but his chest was flattened and concave. Nicki could only imagine the damage beneath.

"Moving to the upper limbs, both shoulders show fracture dislocations, with additional open fractures of both wrists. There is a large open wound to the frontal area of the head, with obvious crush injuries to the face. Pre-examination X-rays confirm bilateral orbital fractures, and fractures to the mandible and maxilla." The pathologist paused and caught Nicki's eye before reaching over to pull the man's lips apart. "Inside the mouth, there are seven teeth missing. Bleeding and damage is consistent with recent pre-mortem extraction."

Nicki felt herself shudder once more.

*Teeth.*

After the external examination was complete, with a number of close-up photographs taken to chart the external injuries, Caz reached for the instrument trolley, selecting a scalpel. "Ready?" She caught Nicki's eye once again, a cautious look crossing her features. "I'll warn you in advance, it won't be pretty."

\* \* \*

And it wasn't.

The external injuries caused by the collision had been bad enough, but they were nothing in comparison to those visible once the body was opened up. To Nicki's untrained eye, it seemed as though every organ had been turned to mush, each one indistinguishable from another. She had been grateful for Caz's running commentary.

Ruptured spleen, ruptured liver, both kidneys crushed, intestines ripped to shreds. The ribs had, indeed, been crushed in the impact, splinters of bone embedding themselves into the man's lungs. The only consolation Nicki could glean was that Aaron Nash was unlikely to have suffered for long. The injuries sustained were so incompatible with life that if death could ever be instantaneous, then surely this was it.

Even though the post-mortem was over, and she was now back in the changing room, what she'd seen refused to leave her. Even if the poor man had died on impact, she couldn't help but think about the seconds immediately before. That vital time between the car pulling onto the carriageway and then into the path of the oncoming lorry. *That* certainly wasn't instant. Those few seconds must have been full of nothing but terror.

*If*, of course, he was capable of feeling anything at all. Nicki had asked Caz whether they would be able to tell if the deceased had suffered something like a stroke at the wheel, some neurological problem that accounted for his bizarre behaviour. She'd left the pathologist examining Nash's brain and, with the various blood tests and swabs now on their way to the lab, there was the smallest glimmer of hope that they might find an answer.

Nicki had then wondered whether alcohol may have played a part in the night's events. Had the man been drunk at the wheel? So blind drunk that he didn't realise he was driving on the wrong side of the road? Part of her hoped he was, that he'd had some form of anaesthetic in his system at the crucial moment of impact. She knew, as a police officer, it was an odd viewpoint, and not one she planned to share with anyone else.

While they waited for the lab reports, everything pointed toward this being a wilful act. There was the note . . . and then there were the teeth. Nicki hadn't mentioned the teeth to the grieving Rosalyn Nash — there would be time soon enough for that particular bombshell to be dropped.

As she pulled on her jacket and slipped her feet back into her boots, she scrolled through the latest text from DS Fox telling her that the lorry driver was fit for interview. As she made her way to the door, she dashed off a reply to meet at the hospital. It wouldn't be a pleasant chat — the man would be traumatised on top of any injuries — but after witnessing the post-mortem Nicki didn't feel as though her day could get any worse.

* * *

*Rye, East Sussex*

Hugh Webster let the phone fall from his grasp, leaving it to clatter onto the desk.

Dead? How could he be dead?

He'd only spoken to the man three days ago.

The call had been short and to the point, but Hugh had been in the business long enough to know that it wasn't necessarily a compassionate one. Yes, they might have uttered the expected platitudes, the usual "Sorry for your loss" and "We know this must come as a shock" — but Hugh knew the real reason for the call. What they really wanted to know was why the retired detective superintendent had left a voice message on the recently deceased's answerphone.

*What was it you wanted to talk to him about, Mr Webster?*

Immediately, hairs had begun to prickle on the back of Hugh's neck. It was standard police procedure, he knew that — to find out who the victim had been communicating with in the time immediately prior to their death. For sometimes, that would lead to the perpetrator.

*The killer.*

The detective on the other end of the line hadn't said as much — hadn't used the word *murdered* — but Hugh knew the drill. They were looking for a killer. He could hear it in the inflection of the caller's tone, and sometimes it was what *wasn't* said that was important.

Rubbing his eyes, Hugh felt them sting beneath his touch. He could visualise his name being written on a whiteboard in an incident room somewhere, a room humming with the buzz of a new investigation. He'd answered the detective's questions adequately enough — or, at least, he thought he had.

"When was the last time you saw Detective Inspector Mark Keeble?"

"Did you speak often?"

And then the million-dollar question: "What was it you wanted to talk to him about, Mr Webster? Did he ever call you back?"

Hugh hadn't really lied — but he hadn't exactly told the truth, either. He concocted some story about keeping in touch with Keeble since his retirement, and their recent contact had been about Keeble wanting to meet up for a game of golf.

It was the best he could come up with when put on the spot like that.

And it wasn't entirely untrue — they *had* spoken about golf in the past, with Hugh offering to play a round with the detective at the local golf club one day. But that was as far as it went. And it had been some time ago now.

Hugh's eyes were again drawn to the note.

*15 August 2005*

He hadn't mentioned the note to the detective — he was still unsure what it all meant himself. Before Hugh could ponder just how much deep water he'd inadvertently landed himself in, the study door creaked open and Anne popped her head around the frame.

"Lunch? I've made a pasta salad."

Hugh did his best to raise a smile, swallowing the sigh on his lips. "Lovely." Eating was the last thing he felt like doing right now, but he didn't want to worry Anne any more than he had to. "I'll be through in a moment." He gestured towards the pile of receipts and other papers stacked neatly on the desk. "Just filing away last year's tax stuff after my meeting with Robert."

Anne smiled warmly. "I'll leave it in the kitchen for you, just grab it when you're ready." She turned to go, waving her mobile in the air as she went. "And I've just spoken to Nicki — about us going up to see her tonight. She's got a new case on but says it'll still be fine. I'm just going upstairs to pack a few bits — we should leave by three to miss the traffic."

Hugh tried to extend the smile on his lips. "Great." Once Anne had disappeared, he let out another sigh. "Just great."

* * *

*Sebert Road, Bury St Edmunds*

With Rosalyn Nash's sister having now arrived from Hull, the pair were ensconced in the front room, immersed in their evolving grief. DC Gedge had welcomed the time alone to think. She'd retired to the kitchen on the pretext of making a pot of coffee but, in reality, she was looking for a second phone.

She hadn't yet had a chance to ask Rosalyn about any possible life insurance policy, or the relevance of the date. Once Lesley had arrived, Karen decided the questions could wait a while.

Déjà vu soon started to prickle as she completed her search of the cupboards and drawers. Satisfied the kitchen wasn't providing any answers, she made her way towards the utility room. It was an unlikely hiding place, with limited places to conceal anything, but that could very well make it the *perfect* hiding place.

The Nash family didn't have a garage, for which Karen was thankful — but they did have a dilapidated shed at the bottom of the garden, which she didn't much fancy rooting around in. She imagined it full of dark, dusty cobwebs — and where there were cobwebs, there were usually spiders.

After two minutes, she decided her former view had been correct. The utility room was another dead end as far as hiding places went. Her thoughts fleetingly turned to upstairs, and she put it on her mental to-do list to check when she got the opportunity. But with Rosalyn's sister now in residence, that window of opportunity was somewhat smaller than before.

As Karen returned to the kitchen, she met Lesley making her way in from the front room. The woman's face was blotchy, and tear-stained, her eyes pinched and red raw.

"How's it going in there?" Karen knew it was a silly question on the face of it, but what else could she say? "Do you need me for anything?"

"I was just coming in to see if that pot of coffee was ready. Ros could do with something stronger, but I'm not sure that's wise just yet."

"Oh, gosh, yes — sorry." Karen's cheeks flushed pink. "I was meant to be making it, wasn't I? Apologies, I got distracted."

"It's fine, I can help. You've been brilliant today." Lesley tried a weak smile as she walked towards the sink. "Is there any news yet? From the investigation? I know it's still early days."

Karen joined the woman at the sink, plucking a freshly washed coffee pot from the draining board. "I'm sorry, nothing new as yet. You'll be the first to know if I hear anything. The post-mortem may well be finished now."

"And will . . . will Ros be able to go and see him? To go and see Aaron?"

Karen had been warned to expect the question. She gave a sad smile. "If that's what she really wants to do, then I'm sure something can be arranged — but you'll need to prepare her. It won't be a pleasant experience." Wanting to steer the conversation to calmer waters, she unscrewed the jar of instant coffee. "In the meantime, how about something to eat with the coffee? I could rustle up some sandwiches?"

Lesley's face relaxed a little. "Ros should eat something, I know. But maybe just some biscuits. Sandwiches might be a bit ambitious right now."

"Biscuits I can most definitely do." Karen gave Lesley another sad smile and turned towards the fridge, flicking on the kettle as she passed by. "I'll get the milk."

Reaching to pull open the fridge door, the family liaison officer froze.

# CHAPTER TWENTY-ONE

*West Suffolk Hospital*

"I couldn't believe it — he just kept on coming." Gary Perkins' face was a washed-out grey, matching the colour of his closely cropped hair. His right arm was strapped across his chest in a tight sling, his left wrist sporting a lightweight cast. Other than a few lacerations and bruises to his face, he'd escaped with surprisingly minor injuries and didn't look like someone who'd been involved in a head-on collision at high speed.

"You were lucky." Nicki pulled the curtain a little further around the lorry driver's bed, shielding them from the rest of the busy ward. It wasn't exactly private, but it would have to do. Nicki knew that "lucky" probably wasn't the first word that had sprung into the lorry driver's mind when he thought about the events of the previous evening, but it could easily have been so much worse. "It's fortunate your lorry had airbags."

Gary gave a weak nod. "I know," he breathed. "I could have died." The last word caught in the man's throat, and his eyes began to moisten.

Nicki knew it wouldn't have been the first time the lorry driver had questioned his own mortality since the crash, and it wouldn't be the last, either. He was likely to revisit the night's events multiple times in the coming days. She edged closer to the bed. "We're trying to build up a picture of what happened. Several cameras show us the vehicle's progress, the route it took before joining the A14, but it would really help if you could tell us in your own words what happened." Pausing, her face softened. "I realise it will be difficult."

Gary's eyes clouded over, losing their sheen. "Of course." Voice trembling, he gestured towards the plastic cup of water on the side table, just out of reach. "Would you mind?"

DS Fox stepped forward to lift the cup and hold it in front of the lorry driver's mouth. The man grasped the straw between his quivering lips. After a few mouthfuls, he turned his head to meet Nicki's waiting gaze.

"It all happened so quickly, yet each second seemed to last a lifetime." The lorry driver shivered beneath his hospital blanket. "I know that doesn't make much sense."

"When did you first notice it, the car?" Nicki and the team had watched the camera footage several times, showing Nash leaving the roundabout on Newmarket Road and travelling the wrong way along the slip road to join the eastbound A14. It made for heart-wrenching viewing.

Gary rested his head back against the pillows. "I was on a fairly long stretch of road, just past the Claas plant, heading east. I was the only one heading in that direction. I just remember . . ." The man took in a sharp breath and shuddered. "The first thing I saw was the headlights."

"From the car?"

The lorry driver nodded. "They were on the slip road, heading towards me, but I knew that couldn't be right because that would mean they were driving the wrong way. I . . ." He broke off, clearing his throat as his voice cracked. "In all my years of driving, I've never seen anything like it. It took a while for my brain to catch up with what was happening, with what I was seeing."

"Go on."

"I just . . . I didn't know what to do. Maybe I should have tried to pull over to the side more or maybe pulled into the outside lane." Once more, the man's voice cracked. "I just didn't know what to do. So, I . . . so I did nothing. I just froze. But if I hadn't . . . if I had just . . ."

Nicki had seen it a hundred times before — traumatised victims and witnesses frantically trying to piece together and make sense of what they'd seen or experienced, desperately grabbing at any reasoning that would explain it. In many cases, blame would follow swiftly afterwards — punishing their already fragile state of mind with statements like "Maybe I should have . . ." or "If only I hadn't . . ." Along with the blame would then come the guilt, eating away at them until it was all-consuming.

Nicki knew more than anyone how guilt could rip a family apart. "No." She fixed Perkins with a steady yet reassuring look. "Nothing you did or didn't do caused this to happen. If you'd somehow managed to avoid the collision, it would just have happened to someone else instead. Please don't lay any blame at your own doorstep."

The greyness of the man's skin tone seemed to intensify. "You mean, he did this on purpose? It wasn't . . . ?" The lorry driver's eyes started to blink rapidly, a frown creasing his brow. "I thought it was just an accident."

Nicki paused before replying. As unpalatable as it sounded, the investigation was taking them in that direction at breakneck speed. Eventually, all she could do was shrug. "To be honest, we don't know for definite — but my instincts tell me that, yes, it was a deliberate act."

The answer didn't seem to placate the lorry driver all that much, his unshaven chin starting to wobble as fresh tears began to sprout from his red-rimmed eyes. He tried to brush them away with his only free hand, but the plaster cast made it impossible.

Nicki reached forward and plucked a couple of tissues from the box on the side table, placing them in his trembling fingers. "Which is why anything you can tell us about the moments before the crash could really help."

The lorry driver dabbed his eyes with the tissues. "Of course."

"What did the vehicle do when it joined the carriageway?"

Gary closed his eyes, swallowing hard. "He just kept on coming, staying in the left-hand lane — *my* left-hand lane. He didn't move at all."

"He didn't swerve? Try and get out of your path?"

The question was met with a very definite shake of the head, and the lorry driver's eyes snapped open. "No. And I was all lit up like a Christmas tree — he can't not have seen me."

"And the outside lane was free of traffic? He could have swerved into that lane if he'd wanted to?" Nicki already knew the answer to the question, but felt it needed asking anyway. It got the response she expected — another shake of the head.

"No. I was the only vehicle on the carriageway. He could have avoided me." The lorry driver paused, crumpling the tissues in his free hand. "Did he have a heart attack or something? Pass out?"

"We're looking into whether there could have been a medical emergency at the time of the collision. But it could take some time for us to be sure." Nicki edged even closer to the bed, lowering her voice a notch. "Before we go, could I just ask whether you recognise the name Aaron Nash? Would this be someone you know?" She wasn't convinced the collision had been orchestrated — how could it be? There was no way Nash could have known Gary Perkins was on that exact stretch of road at that exact time, but it was a box they needed to tick, a line of enquiry they had to explore.

The lorry driver gave the expected reply. "No. I don't know the name at all. I'm from the Wirral. I only come down this way for work, to drive to the ports and back." He swallowed and then blinked rapidly. "Was that the guy's name?"

Nicki gave a sad smile. "It was." After exchanging contact details, Nicki and DS Fox left the lorry driver to the early afternoon ward round. As Fox held the door open for her, she felt her mobile vibrate in her pocket. Glancing at the screen, her stomach flipped.

"News?" Fox followed Nicki along the corridor. "We could do with a break."

Nicki started to jog down the stairs. "We're needed back at the station — there's a lead on the teeth."

\* \* \*

*Bury St Edmunds Police Station*

Roy jumped out of his chair the moment Nicki and Fox entered the incident room. "It just came in, boss."

Nicki hurried over to the detective sergeant's desk. "What can you tell us?"

"In July last year, the body of a man was found in a hotel room in Peckham." Nicki peered over Roy's shoulder as the detective pulled a series of images up onto his computer screen. "As you can see, he was found slumped in a chair, dressed only in a pair of underpants. His head was encased inside a clear polythene bag, secured with black masking tape at the neck. A large quantity of drugs and drug paraphernalia was found in the room, and the post-mortem bloods detected a high level of GHB in his system."

"Sex game gone wrong?" Fox joined Nicki at Roy's desk.

"That seems to be the conclusion the investigation team came to. The hotel in question — more of a seedy guest house, really — was known to be frequented by prostitutes and drug gangs, with numerous incidents reported over the years. Security is lax, people able to come and go as they please, guest records are patchy, to say the least. Cash payments only. The room was booked in the name of a Mr Smith." Roy rolled his eyes. "I know, you couldn't make it up. But what did prove interesting was that seven teeth were found in the pocket of the dead man's blazer, which was neatly folded up on the bed with his other clothes."

"Did the investigation team place any significance on the teeth?" Nicki watched Roy shrug a response.

"Hard to tell. They seemed to square it all away relatively quickly, putting it down to a game of auto-erotica gone wrong. No foul play suspected. But . . ."

"But what?"

Roy tapped his keyboard and brought up an image of the front of the door, taken from the corridor outside. "It might be nothing, but the room number caught my eye. 1508."

*There it was again.*

"1508," breathed Nicki, feeling her skin prickle. "Fifteenth of August."

By this time, the rest of the team had pulled their chairs over to join Nicki and Fox at Roy's desk. Nose wrinkling, Darcie shivered as she took in the images.

"So, he pulled out his own teeth, just like Jacob and Aaron? Then wrapped his head up in a plastic bag? Who on earth would do a thing like that?"

\* \* \*

*Blackfriars Gentlemen's Club, London*
*Wednesday 11 July 2018*

Ramsay O'Donoghue winced as he climbed the stone steps outside Blackfriars Gentlemen's Club. Every time he made this journey, it seemed to take a fresh toll on his ageing body.

Maeve had urged him to go back to the cardiac consultant at Harefield, concerned as to his declining health and stamina but, as always, he kept putting it off. It wasn't that he was stubbornly refusing to acknowledge the truth — he was fully aware of how the advancing years were catching up with him, and his lifestyle habits weren't exactly compatible with longevity — but increasingly he felt, "What's the point?"

He was exhausted, physically and mentally; living a lie was tiring.

The thick oak door of the gentlemen's club seemed heavier than before, making him grimace as he pulled it open. The concierge at the entrance greeted him with a nod, and the seventy-nine-year-old was led through to the Members' Lounge.

It was a route he'd taken many times in his thirty-nine years as a member, but the short journey felt more poignant today. For today he was going to set himself free from the past — rid himself of the guilt that he'd worn like a concrete shroud for the last thirteen years. It had been a long time coming.

As he made his way over to his usual table in the corner of the club's innermost chamber, an unwelcome thought crossed his mind.

What if the man didn't turn up?

Lowering himself into his usual armchair, he quickly scanned the room. He soon saw that every leather-backed chair and Chesterfield sofa was unoccupied — all except one, that was.

A mixture of relief and fear rippled through him.

O'Donoghue took in a deep breath. If he was going to do this, then he needed to do it now — before his resolve left him. Pushing himself up from the chair, he shuffled across the thick pile carpet, heart rate rocketing. The man was sitting in one of the wingback armchairs that flanked an ornate fireplace in the far corner of the room. An identical armchair sat opposite — a smooth, walnut table standing in between.

On the table was a glass tumbler — O'Donoghue recognising his own monogrammed lead crystal glass that was a perk given only to the most loyal of members. But his throat felt too dry to even contemplate a drink. After a brief moment's hesitation, he slipped into the vacant seat.

The man hadn't looked up as O'Donoghue approached, remaining seated with a copy of the *Financial Times* masking his face. After a few moments' silence, a hand appeared from behind the newspaper and took hold of a martini glass. O'Donoghue continued to watch as the man lowered the paper to his lap and took a slow sip from the glass.

"Have a drink, my friend." The man kept his voice low, despite there being no other guests in the lounge. He reached forward to nudge the glass tumbler a few inches across the table. "And help yourself to a cigar for later." A box of expensive Montecristo cigars was open next to the man's martini.

O'Donoghue could think of nothing he would like less and ignored the offering. Despite his throat constricting with every swallow, he took the glass tumbler and forced a mouthful of the fiery liquid down. He needed the alcohol to hit his bloodstream rapidly if this was going to go the way he wanted it to.

Another martini arrived on the table from a white-gloved waiter, who also wordlessly topped up O'Donoghue's brandy from a square crystal decanter. It was the seventy-nine-year-old's favourite brand, something the waiting staff at Blackfriars were more than aware of. Usually, he would while away several hours in the Members' Lounge, contentedly reading the day's papers and sipping his brandy — but today was different. The alcohol swilling in his stomach was making him feel agitated rather than relaxed.

The man sitting opposite seemed to sense O'Donoghue's disquiet, a taut smile stretching thinly across his face.

"Relax — enjoy the ambiance while you can."

O'Donoghue took hold of the glass tumbler once again and swallowed another generous mouthful of brandy. He felt his heart rate beginning to settle. Whether it was the alcohol having an effect or the relief at finally taking matters into his own hands, he couldn't quite tell. His fingers felt clammy as he returned the glass to the side table.

"I took the liberty of booking a room."

O'Donoghue felt a fresh lump constrict his throat. "Where?" Uttering that single word almost made him choke. With a hurried look behind him, he noticed the white-gloved waiter was nowhere to be seen. Renowned for their discretion, staff at the Blackfriars Club knew when to look the other way.

The man folded his newspaper into quarters, placing it on the arm of his chair before reaching into his pocket. Seconds later, a key card for the St Martin's Hotel slid across the side table.

"Three o'clock."

O'Donoghue felt his stomach tighten. Suddenly, images of Maeve at home, busy baking his favourite apple pie, flooded his head. He needed to be back home with her — not here, not with *him*. A renewed courage steeled his resolve.

"I'm not doing it." The words came out louder and far stronger than he imagined they would. Bolstered by the brandy, he felt his courage multiply. "I *won't* do it."

\* \* \*

*Bury St Edmunds Police Station*

"What is it with these teeth?" Leaning over Roy's desk to take a closer look at the computer screen, Matt echoed the rest of the team's thoughts. "No matter what anyone says, pulling your own teeth out is *not* normal — nor is getting somebody else to do it for you. And definitely not then sticking them in your own pockets."

"Agreed." Nicki straightened up. "Roy, can you pull everything there is on this case? See if anything else strikes a chord with our own investigation."

"Are we saying that Jacob Towers, Aaron Nash and now *this* case are all connected?" Darcie pulled her chair back to her desk. "All because of the teeth?"

"But it's not just the teeth, is it?" Nicki sighed. "We've got a potential link with the date now, too — from the door number at the St Martin's Hotel. I know it's a bit tenuous but . . ." She pulled her mobile from her pocket. "And I've had an update from Karen over at the Nash family home. She's found a note tacked to the Nash's fridge — a simple piece of paper just saying, *15 August 2005*."

Darcie raised an eyebrow. "Well, that can't be a coincidence, surely?"

"Unlikely, I would say." Nicki wasn't one for coincidences at the best of times and never had been. It was something she assumed she'd inherited from her father.

*There are no such things as coincidences, Nicola. Everything has a connection — it's just that you don't know what that connection is yet.*

And it was a theory that had stood her in good stead so far. The date seemed to mean something to their victims; it had been pinned to Aaron Nash's fridge door, and Jacob Towers had received it via text message.

And now there was the room number at the St Martin's Hotel.

"Although the circumstances of all three deaths are very different, I don't think we can ignore the similarities. Roy, keep looking for any more past cases involving the extraction of teeth — either found on the bodies or close by."

The detective sergeant nodded. "Will do, boss. I did manage to take a look at the number seven, though."

"Oh?" Nicki stepped closer. "Anything useful?"

Roy wrinkled his nose. "I'm not sure." He pulled his notepad towards him. "The number seven pops up a lot in everything from religion to the arts. We've all heard of the seven deadly sins and the seven gifts of the Holy Spirit. Then there's the seven ages of man, the seven wonders of the world and, of course, the seven days of the week. In the early days, people thought there were only seven planets." Roy flipped over a page and continued reading from his scribbled notes. "It's even been suggested that the short-term memory can only retain seven pieces of information at any one time — I'm not too sure how true that one is, though." He looked up and caught Nicki's eye. "I could go on . . . *Seven Brides for Seven Brothers*, the seven dwarves . . . but I'm not sure about the relevance to the case."

Nicki nodded in agreement. "Thanks, Roy. Let's park the number seven for now."

"Do we have any forensic detail from the London case?" DS Fox stepped closer to Roy's desk. "Anything to show that this Ramsay O'Donoghue wasn't in the hotel room alone?"

Roy shook his head. "Nothing particularly useful. The only DNA found in the room belonged to the deceased. His prints were also all over the drugs and drug paraphernalia they found."

"Well, that sounds suspicious straight away, don't you think?" continued Fox, glancing in Nicki's direction. "If I know the area like I think I do, those types of hotels aren't renowned for being the cleanest of places. No DNA or prints other than the deceased? Sounds unlikely to me."

Roy nodded in agreement. "Either the man cleaned the room himself, which seems like an odd thing to do, or there was someone else there who did it afterwards. My money's on the latter."

Nicki stepped away from Roy's desk. "Do we have any CCTV of the hotel?"

"Just the one camera at the end of the street, which doesn't really show much. Anyone could have approached from the other direction completely undetected. It's not really an area known for its camera coverage. The hotel staff were interviewed by the investigation team at the time, but they didn't get very far. No one seemed to recall seeing our victim, and they don't keep records." Roy consulted his notebook. "But the team did find a debit card transaction that same afternoon — from the Blackfriars Gentlemen's Club, close to the river. I'll take a closer look and see what stemmed from that."

Matt Holland tapped a biro on his notepad. "My money's still on a sex game gone wrong — wouldn't be the first."

Nicki's eyes gravitated towards the whiteboards. "You could be right, Matt, but only if you ignore the teeth. Our visit to Mrs Nash this morning has only served to convince me that the crash was a deliberate act on Aaron Nash's part. The only question is why he did it. We've got his mobile phone, which needs looking at." Nicki picked up the plastic evidence bag containing the handset and handed it to Matt. "See what you can find."

Just then, there was a brief knock at the door, and Simon Wilkins from the force's technical unit entered.

"Hey, Si," greeted Matt, as he resumed his seat at his desk. "Unusual to see you above ground during daylight hours."

Simon grinned as he headed over to Duncan's desk. "Thought I'd come and see what you slackers do for a change." In his hand he waved a sheaf of papers. "And while I was at it, I thought I'd bring you what I've managed to find out about Jacob Towers' website." He placed the papers down next to Duncan's keyboard. "You were questioning the contact form embedded into the website?"

Duncan nodded. "Each time I sent a message, it didn't seem to go anywhere. Certainly not into his regular work email inbox, anyway."

"That's because it went somewhere else." Simon selected one of the sheets of paper he'd brought in. "A second email address, linked to the website. It's quite common — most website hosting platforms offer any number of additional email addresses the site owner can use. And Towers had a dedicated one just for the contact form on the website." He tapped the rest of the pile of papers. "This is a printout of the most recent messages, stretching back over the last twelve weeks. I can go back further if you need."

By this time, everyone had crowded around Duncan's desk.

"A number of the messages are quite short," Simon continued. "Mostly just enquiries about the services the business provides and asking for a call back. They look legitimate as far as I can tell." The tech support officer paused, handing the sheet of paper he'd selected to Nicki. "But I took the liberty of highlighting a few that come from the same IP address. Ones I think you might want to follow up."

Nicki took the paper, her eyes quickly scanning the list of copied messages.

*I've found you.*

*You think you can hide — but you can't.*

*It's time to pay for what you did — 15 August 2005.*

Nicki passed the paper to Fox. "Is there a way of finding out who sent them? Who might be behind the email address?" Simon's expression told her the answer to that one. It wasn't unexpected.

"It's not all that easy. Whoever sent the messages has covered their tracks well. We might get something eventually, but it'll take a while."

After Simon had briefly updated the team on his enquiries into voice recognition — the short answer being it was another dead end — he left them to it. Nicki crossed back over to the whiteboards, her mental checklist whirring.

"We need to find a link between Aaron Nash and Jacob Towers. And now Ramsay O'Donoghue, too. Check Nash's social media presence, the usual. And get that phone looked at." She looked again at the whiteboards, which were filling up by the second. "And let's get O'Donoghue's details up on the board. Look more closely into him and his lifestyle and check out his visit to the Blackfriars Club on the day he died. See what the original investigation team made of it." With a final sigh she headed for the door. "I'll be in my office if anyone needs me."

# CHAPTER TWENTY-TWO

*Sussex Police, Hastings*

DS Nigel Brooke pulled his chair across the incident room floor, seating himself next to DC Thorpe. With Keeble's car now being analysed by forensics, and the detective's background from finances through to his work and personal lives picked apart, the team were at full stretch. For now, however, the incident room was empty except for the two of them. "What have the names from Keeble's wall given us? Anything?"

Thorpe tapped his pen against his notepad, the frown on his brow deepening. "I'm not really sure, to be honest. It's weird."

"Weird? How so?"

The detective constable pulled the photograph they'd taken of Keeble's wall up onto his computer screen. He pointed at the first three names. "Take these three, for example. Declan Hood, Sonia Parish and Grant Fielding. All three are now deceased. Declan Hood died in a road accident in 2009, his car leaving the road close to the A12. The investigation queried brake failure and possible tampering, but the inquest eventually concluded it was an accidental death.

Sonia Parish was found dead in her flat in Tooting in 2010, cause of death a suspected overdose. Parish was a habitual drug user, and the cause of death wasn't questioned at the time. Grant Fielding was killed after falling beneath a Tube train at Charing Cross in 2011. Camera footage shows a man bumping into him from behind, but the suspect was never traced — the case remains open."

Brooke peered at his colleague's screen. "And you think all three deaths could be suspicious? What about the rest of the names?"

Thorpe turned his attention back to his notepad. "The next six names are also all deceased. I'm still waiting on details for some, but they all seem to be accepted as accidents or suicides. There are a few that are more recent. This one — Ramsay O'Donoghue — was found dead in a London hotel last summer. And then we have these two." Thorpe pointed his biro at two more names in the centre of the computer screen. "Jacob Towers and Aaron Nash. I ran background checks to both names, and it transpires that both died in the last few days — and both in Suffolk."

"So, if my maths is correct, that accounts for twelve of the names. What about the last one?"

"Colin Hedges. Preliminary checks show no information as to his demise. Lives in Hampshire."

"We'd best put a welfare call in for him. Let's find out his current address and pay him a visit."

Thorpe made a note on his notepad. "What are we thinking about this Hugh Webster fella? He's a retired former detective superintendent, with a glittering career behind him. What did he sound like to you when you spoke with him?"

Brooke scratched the end of his nose. "The fact he was such a high-ranking officer means we'll need to tread carefully. But I'm not sure he told me everything about why he was trying to speak to Keeble. He was quite evasive. Phone records suggest he tried to get hold of Keeble several times — and all about a game of golf? I'm not so sure." Brooke got to his feet. "Although we don't have the handset, we know Webster called him on Thursday and the call lasted almost ten minutes. Dig a little deeper."

"As there are two open cases with Towers and Nash, should we pass what we have here onto the Suffolk investigation team?"

Brooke nodded. "Best to. Do we know who's heading up the team over there?"

"Seems to be a Detective Inspector Nicki Hardcastle."

"Well, I think we should give her a call, don't you?"

\* \* \*

*4 Old Railway Cottages, Dullingham, Nr Newmarket*

Gritting his teeth, Adrian Browning punched his way through the pain. He'd been called many names in his time, but "quitter" wasn't one of them. Spending last night in the cells hadn't been part of his grand plan, but the guy had had it coming. No one spoke to him like that and expected to walk away unscathed.

As the sweat poured down his face, he couldn't help a smile start to crack his features. Compared to the other fella, he'd got off lightly — that loser had needed a trip to the hospital. Adrian had refused medical treatment at the police station — preferring to fix his own cuts and bruises when he was eventually released that morning. History told him it was wise to keep a well-stocked first aid kit at home — steri-strips, antiseptic ointment, bandages and plasters. It was usually enough to dress his battle wounds and let him live to fight another day.

The punchbag swung fiercely beneath a flurry of sharp jabs, Adrian's face set hard with concentration. Closing his eyes to the discomfort, he delivered another deluge of punches to the bag. His knuckles felt like they were on fire, but he almost welcomed the pain now; it sharpened his senses. Pain focused the mind like nothing else.

Ripping off the boxing gloves, he reached for another can of energy drink. That would make three in the last hour already. He guzzled down the overly sweet, fizzy liquid, fully aware his heart rate was unlikely to settle if he drank much more, but his body needed the buzz. Crunching the empty can in his hand, he reached for his phone.

No new messages.

At least that was something.

If he was going to do this, he'd do it on his own terms, and in his own time. He didn't need chasing like he was a six-year-old.

After the taxi had dropped him off earlier, he'd taken his frustrations out on the laptop and sent back a fiery message — saying just that. *Leave me alone.* It remained to be seen what response it would earn him.

Flicking the volume switch on the sound system up to the max, he flooded the garage with pounding drum and bass and pulled the boxing gloves back on.

\* \* \*

*Bury St Edmunds Police Station*

"Cameras at the Blackfriars Gentlemen's Club clearly show our man entering the premises at 12.45 p.m. on the afternoon of 11 July last year." Roy angled the computer screen towards Nicki and Fox. "And crucially it shows he was alone when he entered."

The detectives watched the seventy-nine-year-old pull himself up the steps outside the club.

"And he's wearing the same blazer that was found in the hotel room in Peckham later that day. The one with the teeth in the pocket."

"Are there any more cameras inside?" Nicki peered closer to the screen. "Do we see where he goes?"

Roy grimaced. "Unfortunately not — they don't have any internal cameras at all. The staff on duty that day were interviewed by the original investigation team, but they were all a bit cagey and tight-lipped about whether they'd seen O'Donoghue that day — citing privacy and discretion for their members."

Nicki felt her lips thin. "Well, I don't give a monkey's about their privacy. I know it's ten months or so after the event, but get back onto the management at the club and ask to speak to the staff again. Threaten them with impeding a murder investigation if you have to. If anyone's hiding anything, then I want to know about it."

* * *

*2 Old Railway Cottages, Dullingham, Nr Newmarket*

Benedict Thatcher closed his eyes as the throbbing bass line thudded through the living room wall.

Not again.

It felt like it was all the man did sometimes — turn the music up and punch his way into oblivion.

But Benedict didn't really blame him. The Browning family had had a lot to deal with in recent months; it was bound to take its toll. When Larry and Annette Browning had moved in next door with their two grown-up sons, Benedict hadn't envisaged the drama that would then unfold. When he'd stumbled into their garden that windy day back in October, and then discovered their involvement in Dean Webster's disappearance, life had never been the same for anyone involved. And that included Adrian Browning.

On one of the rare occasions that they'd actually spoken to each other — Benedict drawing up outside the house just as Adrian stepped out of the taxi that morning — he'd learned of the man's unexpected night in the cells.

Benedict didn't need to ask what had happened to earn him a night behind bars — he could see the evidence on the man's face. After a few moments exchanging awkward pleasantries, they'd gone their separate ways. And then the pounding music had begun not long afterwards.

Sometimes, Benedict felt he could do with letting off some steam himself, and a boxing workout was just as good as anything else. He fleetingly thought about going for a run — anything to take him away from the house, and the laptop — and had got as far as pulling on a pair of trainers. But that was as far as it had got.

There were no new messages, no new instructions, but just the sight of the laptop reminded him of what still needed to be done. The wheels were so far in motion now that he was powerless to stop them, despite his best delaying tactics.

Jobs came and went in Benedict's world, and he barely gave them a second thought, usually carrying out his instructions without a conscience. He was a professional, and he wasn't the one ultimately pulling the strings; he wasn't the one in control.

*He just did what he was told.*

It was a feeble excuse, and he knew it — but he clung to it all the same. In his line of work, it was exactly what kept you safe. What kept you sane. *What kept you alive.* He couldn't recall a single job that he'd regretted, not a single instruction that had caused him to question the path he'd been asked to take.

Until now.

This one was different. It had been a freelance contract — something he rarely got involved in. He didn't ordinarily like dealing with people he wasn't familiar with — although sometimes the anonymity had its advantages. He should have trusted his instincts and declined the job.

But it was too late now.

He eyed the laptop again. Maybe he would go for that run, after all; it might help clear his mind. If he stayed here, then the relentless pulsating vibrations from next door might tip him over the edge.

\* \* \*

"I managed to find an employee willing to speak." Roy turned round in his seat. "Probably more to do with the fact that they're soon to be an *ex*-employee. But they're willing to say they remember O'Donoghue being in the Members' Lounge that day — and they remember it because O'Donoghue gave a large tip before leaving. I assume that's the card transaction the original team highlighted."

"Anything else about him they remember?" Nicki edged closer to Roy's desk. "Did he meet with anyone?"

Roy gave a wry smile and consulted his notebook. "Listen to this. They say O'Donoghue stayed about an hour and a half in the lounge, and for *some* of that time he was in the company of another gentleman."

"Another gentleman?" Nicki's eyebrows arched. "Who?"

"Unfortunately, that's where we hit a bit of a snag." Roy grimaced. "Our witness remembers the gentleman in question had been signed in as a day member and gave them the name of Mr A. Smith. But that's as far as the records go, I'm afraid. And he couldn't really give much of a description, either. The witness left O'Donoghue and this gentleman alone in the lounge — discretion again, you see. By the time he returned, O'Donoghue was on his own."

Nicki felt her shoulders sag. "That's a shame — but at least it's a lead, of sorts. Do we see anyone on the cameras outside that might be our mystery man?"

"Already ahead of you there, boss." Roy tapped his keyboard and brought up the CCTV recordings from outside the Blackfriars Club. "There's this image here which could possibly be him. He's seen leaving the premises at 1.33 p.m., which fits with what our witness is saying."

The detective sergeant played the recording which showed a man of average height and build, dressed in a smart suit, hurrying down the steps of the Blackfriars Club, head down and face turned away from the camera.

"Seems to be in a rush," commented Fox, who had come across to join them, peering more closely at the screen. "And seems to know where the camera is, too."

Nicki squinted at the monitor as Roy played the short recording once again. "See if you can get a still from that, and get the image made bigger. He could be our killer."

# CHAPTER TWENTY-THREE

With the mug of coffee now cold on her desk, Nicki placed the phone receiver back in its cradle, her eyes wide.

Another one?

The call from Detective Sergeant Nigel Brooke had caught her off guard, and the conversation that followed was completely unexpected.

Frowning, she turned back to her desktop computer, where the information the detective sergeant had sent through filled the screen. For the first few minutes of their conversation, Nicki had wondered why she was receiving a call about the death of a serving Metropolitan Police officer, and it had taken a while for her to get up to speed.

Detective Inspector Mark Keeble.

*Another victim.*

Another connection to Operation Jackdaw.

And *definitely* murder this time.

Once the initial shock had worn off, she questioned how DS Brooke had linked the case of the murdered detective to her own investigation — but then he had sent over a copy of the photograph of DI Keeble's wall.

Thirteen names. Twelve already dead, including Jacob Towers and Aaron Nash. And Ramsay O'Donoghue.

Mind racing into overdrive, Nicki sent the various email attachments to the small printer in the corner of her office and hurriedly made her way back to the incident room.

* * *

*Sussex Police, Hastings*

DS Brooke settled the phone receiver back into its cradle, brow creasing. His decision not to send everything across to the Suffolk team was already playing on his mind. But he didn't feel ready to divulge everything about former Detective Superintendent Webster just yet.

"What's your feeling on it all, Thorpe?" Brooke looked up at his colleague. "What's the connection between our retired detective superintendent and the recently deceased?"

Thorpe leaned back in his seat. "Initial enquiries show they were colleagues in the Met for many years. Worked a lot of cases together. But . . ."

"But what?" Brooke noticed the gleam in the detective constable's eyes. "You have more?"

Thorpe pulled his notebook into his lap. "Did you know Hugh Webster is the father of Dean Webster? The little lad who went missing from a fairground on the south coast back in 1996? Everyone thought he must be dead before he turned up about five months ago."

Brooke's eyebrows shot up. "*That* Webster?"

Thorpe nodded. "The same. I get the feeling it was hushed up in the media, the fact that Hugh Webster was the father — as far as it could be, anyway. But the whole story came tumbling out — sounds like something from a Hollywood movie. The boy was snatched at a fair then raised by another family as their own. Larry and Annette Browning — currently on remand charged with abduction, among other things."

"Jesus. I had no idea."

"Webster's had many commendations over the years, very highly regarded. Retired from the force in 2005."

"But the man's lying to us, Thorpe. I can't ignore it." He caught his colleague's eye. "I don't buy the answers he gave us about wanting to get in touch with Keeble over a game of golf. You don't ring someone that number of times to discuss a tee-off. He's hiding something."

"Connected to Keeble's murder?"

Brooke could only shrug. "Who knows. It's certainly interesting timing."

"There's something else that ties in with Webster, too." Thorpe turned back to his computer screen. "Some initial results from the examination of Keeble's car."

"Oh? Such as what?"

"In the boot, where the spare wheel is." Thorpe pulled the lab report up onto his monitor while Brooke came to stand at his shoulder.

"What exactly am I looking at?" Brooke bent down and peered more closely at the screen.

"It's a brown envelope, containing fifty thousand pounds in cash. Buried under the spare wheel."

"Fifty grand?" Brooke's eyes widened as he puffed out his cheeks. "You're serious?"

Thorpe nodded. "All in fifties."

"What's Keeble doing with that kind of cash in his boot? That's not a DI's wage, I know that much."

"And that's not all, boss." Thorpe clicked the mouse and brought up another image. "This note was found wrapped around the envelope. It's addressed to Hugh Webster — signed from Keeble himself."

"And what does it say, this note?"

Thorpe gave a non-committal shrug. "Not a lot that makes sense, to be honest. It merely says, *If this finds you, you've worked it out.* Then finishes with the date 15 August 2005 before his signature."

"OK, keep digging in Keeble and Webster's backgrounds. Apart from working together, do they have any other connection?"

Thorpe closed the lab reports down on his screen. "Have you mentioned it to the Suffolk team? Webster and his calls to Keeble?"

Brooke returned to his own desk. "Not yet. I want to see if we can dig a little deeper into Webster first. This could be sensitive stuff, bearing in mind who he is, and I don't want to put the cat among the pigeons, unless I really have to."

"There is something else, of course." Thorpe leaned forward in his chair, the gleam in his eyes still evident. "Related to the DI in charge of the Suffolk cases."

"DI Hardcastle? What about her?"

Thorpe paused, the gleam intensifying. "She just so happens to be Webster's daughter."

\* \* \*

*Bury St Edmunds Police Station*

"*It's time to pay for what you did — 15 August 2005.*" Nicki tacked a series of crime scene photographs to yet another whiteboard. "This note was found on the floor of the victim's car, in the driver's footwell. Deceased has been positively identified as Detective Inspector Mark Keeble, still serving with the Metropolitan Police but on sick leave at the time of his death. Lived alone in a flat in Islington. The vehicle was found shortly before midnight on Friday night, with our victim still in the driver's seat." A photograph of Mark Keeble joined the others on the board. "Local detectives in East Sussex have opened a murder investigation and the post-mortem is being held today. But I don't think anyone is in any doubt as to the cause of death here." One of the photographs showed the thin garrotting wire still embedded in the detective's neck, his head pulled back against the headrest. Wide, bulging eyes stared straight ahead.

"Killer must have been seated behind," volunteered Roy, "to have choked him like that. Which suggests they were in the car already — perhaps our guy left the car insecure?"

Darcie gave a visible shudder. "You see it in the movies, don't you? Killer on the back seat, attacks the driver from behind."

Nicki made her way back to her seat. "Seems most likely but, from what I hear, Keeble was a very experienced detective. It's a big ask to suggest he left his car unlocked, especially in that part of the town. I'm told it's not the nicest place in the world, even in daylight, with numerous incidents of vandalism, drug use and vehicle theft. DS Brooke said that the whole area is something akin to a racetrack after dark, and as for cameras . . ." She gave a tired shrug. "They've been vandalised so often in the past that the council have refused to replace them."

"Something the killer knew?" Roy's eyebrows hitched a notch. "Did his homework and chose this location on purpose?"

"It's certainly possible," mused Nicki. "But it still doesn't explain what our victim was doing in a car park in Hastings. He's a long way from home. The investigation team lifted a laptop from his home address, but so far there's nothing to explain his actions. They've also checked his bank records, and it shows a card payment for the Highcliffe Guest House in Hastings on Thursday night, plus a purchase in an off-licence earlier in the day."

"That Jag's quite a collector's piece." DS Fox stepped up to the whiteboard and peered closely at one of the crime scene images. "If you own something like that, I'd think you'd look after it. You certainly wouldn't leave it unlocked — not intentionally, anyway. Maybe he was drunk? Bearing in mind the off-licence?"

"Toxicology will tell us in time, but let's assume he was stone cold sober." Nicki let her gaze slide towards the crime scene photos once again, feeling herself flinch. "How would a killer get into the back seat of a car without the driver noticing? Detectives are usually quite observant creatures."

"Maybe he knew them?" volunteered Matt. "Maybe he was about to give them a lift home, then . . ." He made a slicing gesture across his throat.

Nicki's brow creased. "Maybe. But surely if it *was* someone he knew, then that person would get in the *front* of the car, wouldn't they? Not the back?"

"What if the note was under the windscreen?" suggested Darcie. "It's dark, you get into your car and start the engine, only to then see the flyer. Your first instinct is to get out and see what it is, but I was always told not to. It gives a potential attacker an opportunity to get inside your car while your back's turned."

Fox nodded. "It's certainly plausible. I have to ask the obvious. I know we have the connection with the date — but why do East Sussex think this is connected to our cases?"

Nicki returned to the whiteboard to pin up another image, this one showing seven human teeth, blood still clinging to the roots. "That will be the teeth found in the victim's left hand."

Darcie gave another shudder. "What is it with these teeth? Is this killer a dentist or something?"

"Well, it's not a dentist I fancy visiting anytime soon," Fox commented darkly. "I'm partial to keeping my teeth in my mouth."

"Odontophilia." Roy gestured towards his computer screen. "I just googled it. It's a fetish involving teeth — ranging from licking your partner's teeth during sex to actually removing them."

Darice made another horrified face. "People really do that?"

Nicki took a step back, arms folded. "I'm not sure any of the deaths so far have been sexually motivated. There's certainly no suggestion of sexual assault in any of the post-mortem reports — but I'll check again and give Caz a call if necessary. The report on DI Keeble confirms that his teeth were extracted *after* death, whereas with Jacob Towers and Aaron Nash it was before. I'm not sure about Ramsay O'Donoghue."

"Well, at least we know this one is clearly murder," added Fox, turning away from the board. "You don't exactly garrotte yourself very easily."

"The East Sussex team are going to send through more details when they have them. What we do have, though, is this." Nicki tacked a sheet of paper to the whiteboard. "A list of thirteen names found pinned to the wall in Keeble's flat. You'll see it includes our two victims, Jacob Towers and Aaron Nash. Ramsay O'Donoghue is on there, too. Twelve are known to be deceased. As I said, they're sending more details over, but let's see what we can find out about Mark Keeble in the meantime."

"I've just had word from the mortuary, boss," added Duncan. "Aaron Nash's ID has been confirmed from dental records. So, there's no need for a formal identification from the wife."

Nicki shuddered. "I'm not so sure that's going to stop her, I'm afraid. Karen seemed to think she was quite intent on going to see her husband. But I'll let her know and see if we can persuade her that it might not be wise. Now the ID has been confirmed, we'll need to release the name to the press."

After telling the team to wrap up what they were working on and go home, as it was nearly six o'clock, Nicki made her way to her office. Back at her desk, she brought up the post-mortem reports for both Jacob Towers and Aaron Nash. As expected, there were no signs of any sexual assault and Nicki was sure that particular avenue of investigation was a dead end. Whatever Ramsay O'Donoghue had been doing at the St Martin's Hotel, she had her doubts that it was of a sexual nature — despite the conclusion the original investigating team had reached.

Rubbing her eyes, she was about to shut her computer down when she spied her desk diary poking out from beneath a set of files.

"Damn," she muttered, pulling the diary out and flicking it over to today's date. With everything that had happened that day, she'd completely forgotten her parents were coming up from the south coast for dinner tonight. She checked her watch and knew that they would already be on their way by now, and most probably already arrived. She could hardly call them to cancel at this late stage.

Instead, she grabbed her mobile and stabbed at Ben's number.

"Ben? You've remembered about tonight, right?"

# CHAPTER TWENTY-FOUR

*College Lane, Bury St Edmunds*

"Here." Hugh Webster handed over two bottles of Prosecco. "Our contribution to the evening."

Nicki took the bottles and spun back towards the gal-ley-style kitchen. "Perfect. I'll just get us some glasses." Returning with three tall wine glasses and one of the bot-tles, she placed everything down on the coffee table. "Dinner should be about twenty minutes, so I'm told. Let's open one now."

"Don't mind me. I'll just slave away in here on my own, shall I?" Benedict Thatcher raised his voice over the sound of the popping cork while transferring two thick-cut ribeye steaks to the frying pan, the meat sizzling on contact. "You just carry on enjoying yourselves. Never mind me sweating over a hot stove." He wiped his brow with a tea towel then slung it over his shoulder.

"You hate Prosecco," countered Nicki, pouring three glasses and handing them round. Leaving the bottle on the coffee table, she headed back to the kitchen, giving Ben a good-natured peck on the cheek as she passed. "Which is why

I got you some beers in." Pulling a bottle of Budweiser from the fridge, she ripped the cap off and placed it next to the frying pan. "For the chef."

"Does he need a hand?" Taking a sip of her fizzing drink, Anne Webster glanced anxiously towards the kitchen as she took a seat on the sofa next to the fireplace. "I don't mind helping."

Returning to the living room, Nicki flapped the gesture away and collapsed into the single armchair. "He's fine. Don't fall for any of this 'woe is me' performance — he loves to cook, *and* he offered. Ben's very territorial when it comes to the kitchen, especially when cooking steaks. So, trust me, we're best off staying out here."

"I heard that." Ben raised his voice over the sound of the sizzling meat. "Just because you cremate everything as soon as look at it . . ."

Anne glanced around the living room as she sipped her drink. "I like what you've done in here — that colour by the fireplace is lovely. Are you planning on doing the rest of the house?"

Nicki sighed and felt herself shudder. "Not if I can help it." She tried a smile, aware of how tired she must look. After getting in from work, she'd barely had time to pull a brush through her hair and change before her parents had knocked at the door. "It seemed like a good idea at the time, but it just takes so long to do."

"Well, I think it looks lovely."

For the next ten minutes, the three of them exchanged news while emptying the first bottle of Prosecco.

"We're seeing Dean tomorrow." Anne accepted a top-up to her glass. "For lunch."

Nicki nodded, finishing off the bottle. "He mentioned it when he came over for dinner on Thursday." Dean had been invited to join them for tonight's meal, but he'd politely declined. Nicki knew he was still struggling with everything, so it was probably the right decision. It was too much to expect everyone to just slip back into family life as if the last two decades hadn't happened. They all needed time and space to pick up the fragments of their lives and try to slot them back together again.

After the second bottle of Prosecco had been opened, Ben announced that the steaks were ready. Nicki brought through the bowls of salad she'd hastily prepared after getting in, Ben content to let her loose with those as, apparently, she couldn't cremate a cucumber. She'd also made her mother's favourite potato salad — something Nicki fondly remembered from her childhood. She waited with bated breath to see if anyone noticed.

She didn't have long to wait.

Anne's eyes sparkled as she slid the wooden spoon into the bowl. "Gosh, I haven't had this in many a year!" She placed a large serving on her plate, next to the perfectly cooked ribeye steak. "I'm surprised you remembered after all this time."

Nicki tried not to react — she knew it wasn't meant to be a dig. Her mother didn't blame Nicki for the disintegration of the family unit, but that didn't mean she didn't blame herself. It would take more than a bowl of the family's favourite potato salad to persuade the guilt to finally leave her.

She took another slug of Prosecco before helping herself to the second salad bowl, spooning a mixture of lettuce leaves, cherry tomatoes and cucumber onto her plate. "Yours is the best potato salad recipe I've ever come across — I just hope it tastes as good as it should."

"I'm sure it will," replied her mother, handing the bowl across the coffee table and then picking up her wine glass. "This all looks fabulous. Thank you, both of you." She raised the glass, smothering a small hiccup as she did so. "I'd like to propose a toast before I drink too much of this and can't string a sentence together properly!"

Hugh balanced his plate on his knees and gave his daughter a fatherly wink. "Gosh, a speech, lucky us."

Anne shushed her husband and continued. "I just want to thank my beautiful daughter for putting on such a wonderful spread for us." Benedict gave a small cough as he raised his beer bottle to his lips. Anne flashed him a wide smile. "And not forgetting this young man here for the wonderful steaks, cooked to perfection." She paused to take another sip from her glass. "Just a few months ago I would never have thought any of this was possible — us all sitting here together like this." She glanced from Nicki to Hugh, and then back to her daughter once more. "What you did, how you managed to find our beloved Dean again, words cannot express how that makes me feel." Anne gave another small hiccup, her eyes glistening. "It's such an incredible feeling to have the whole family back together again — it's a day I thought would never come." Another hiccup and a fortifying mouthful of Prosecco followed. "Just thank you — both of you. From the bottom of mine and your father's hearts." She raised her almost empty glass. "To Nicki and Benedict."

"To Nicki and Benedict," echoed Hugh, getting to his feet. "And on that note, I'll fetch us another bottle of something."

Nicki felt an unexpected lump forming in her throat and her cheeks beginning to warm. She wasn't one for speeches, either giving or receiving, and didn't have herself down as a particularly emotional person, but even she could feel the tears welling. Maybe it was the Prosecco. Clearing her throat, she drained her glass and called after her father.

"There should be a bottle of white in the fridge, or there's red in the cupboard."

After Hugh had topped up everyone's glass with a crisp white Pinot, and brought through another beer for Benedict, everyone continued tucking into the steaks around the cramped coffee table.

"How's work, Ben?" Hugh helped himself to another serving of potato salad. "I think you said it was shipping, didn't you? The last time we met?"

Benedict darted a quick sideways glance towards Nicki, maintaining the smile on his lips. After taking a long gulp from his beer, he nodded. "That's right, shipping. There's not a lot to tell, really. It's not exactly the most exciting of jobs."

Nicki busied herself in spooning another helping of salad onto her plate, giving it a liberal dressing of mayonnaise. They had agreed in advance to maintain the shipping angle if the question ever arose. It seemed to have gone down well enough the first time around. To create a new back story now would just over complicate matters, and with the alcohol flowing, such as it was, there was every possibility she might inadvertently let something slip. So, the less lies and falsehoods to trip them up the better.

In reality, she knew very little about Ben's work, which was probably just as well. All she did know for sure was that it didn't involve selling shipping routes.

Nicki's father seemed to swallow the reply and moved on. "Mum tells me you've got a new investigation on the go?"

Nicki chased a cherry tomato around her plate with a fork. "We have, yes. It's already quite complex. We've got four deaths that we think are linked, but it's not as straightforward as it sounds. The manner of each one is very different, and only two occurred in or around the town — one a fall from a height and another in a road traffic collision."

"Would it be the ones I saw in the news?" Hugh gestured towards his phone. "I was catching up with the local headlines in the hotel before we came over."

Nicki nodded. "Yes, and we believe both deaths are suspicious." *Because of the teeth*, she wanted to add but knew she probably shouldn't. Her father might be ex-force, but she still had to abide by the rules, so instead she merely disclosed what had already been released to the media so far, which wasn't much. "The third death occurred in a hotel in London last summer, and only this afternoon I was informed of a fourth — this one was a serving Met Police detective, found dead in his car in Hastings last night. He lived in North London, so no one's quite sure what he was doing there."

"Gosh, you were only in Hastings on Thursday, weren't you, Hugh?" Anne speared a potato from the pile on her plate. "When you went to see Robert to do the accounts?"

Hugh gently placed his knife and fork down and wiped his mouth with a serviette. "I was, yes. If he's a London boy, like you say, that's a bit out of the area. What makes you think his death is connected to your others?"

Nicki returned her plate to the coffee table and finished her wine. What with the Prosecco earlier, she was starting to feel a little light-headed. Clearing her throat, she reminded herself not to say anything about the teeth. Or the list found pinned to Keeble's wall. "Nothing is very clear at the moment, but there's a date that keeps cropping up in relation to them all."

"A date?" Hugh's hand hovered over his wine glass. "What kind of date?"

Nicki smothered a hiccup, wondering if she'd already said too much. But she considered mentioning the date wasn't breaking any rules. "Just a date — 15 August 2005. We're not sure of the significance but it seems to be a common denominator with them all for some reason."

"Enough of the shop talk, Hugh." Anne began collecting up the plates. "Nicki doesn't need to be quizzed about work after such a long day. She'll be shattered enough as it is. Let me clear these things away and I'll pop the kettle on."

* * *

*Gosport, Hampshire*

Colin Hedges bent down to kiss his sleeping grandson, breathing in the boy's intoxicating scent. It was a mixture of baby shampoo, bubble bath and that inexplicable aroma unique to each child.

The boy didn't stir, and Colin silently padded out of the small box room and headed downstairs.

The letter sat on the kitchen table, although "letter" was pushing it somewhat; note was more apt. It had arrived several days before, and Colin had instinctively known who it would be from, despite there being no signature. It matched the other four that resided in the glove box of the car outside.

He knew he should come clean to Alice about the letters — the notes. But where would he start? July 2005 was where he would need to begin, but it was a period of his life that he tried hard not to think about these days.

*It wasn't my fault.*

It was a statement he'd repeated many times over the years. But no matter how many times he said it, it never quite absolved him from the feeling of guilt, the feeling of responsibility.

*It wasn't my fault.*

How the man had managed to track him down, Colin could only imagine. Even through three house moves, one divorce, and a near mental breakdown, the notes had still managed to find him. But he supposed it wasn't so hard — lives were led in the public domain so much these days; it was difficult to keep anything private. You may as well give everyone your home address and be done with it. So, it wasn't so much that the man had found him, more what he was asking Colin to do next.

No, not *asking*.

*Commanding*.

Alice had gone to bed with the aid of a herbal sleeping tablet, her arthritis getting progressively worse as each day passed. A new hip was on the horizon, which would alleviate her discomfort and give her a new lease of life — they just needed to wait. For now, she would sleep through until morning, as would little Archie.

Gathering up the latest note, he slipped it into his pocket and swiped up the keys to the Astra. If he was going do this, then he needed to do it now. Hesitating at the front door, he shot a glance over his shoulder at the slumbering house behind him, wiping an unbidden tear from his eye. Things couldn't carry on the way they had been, he knew that much. Fourteen years was enough. He couldn't be sorrier for what had happened, couldn't be sorrier for how things had turned out.

*But it wasn't my fault.*

\* \* \*

*College Lane, Bury St Edmunds*

The dinner had gone as well as could be expected. The Websters were decent people, which hurt Benedict all the more when he thought about what he'd been tasked to do. Nicki had been the one constant in his life over the last few months, so he hated lying to her — and she deserved so much better from him. But was it really lying? He wasn't telling her the truth, he knew that much, but he wasn't exactly lying to her, either. It was a fine line to be treading, and it didn't sit comfortably with him whichever way he tried to spin it.

Hugh and Anne had made it quite clear during the evening that they thought their daughter's relationship with him was more than it was — but he and Nicki had both agreed that it was friendship only. When they'd met towards the end of last year, it had seemed like an odd pairing. The straight-down-the-middle detective up against the man operating on the fringes of legality. But, for some reason, it had worked. For some reason they connected. Neither wanted nor was in the right frame of mind for anything more, and in Ben's line of work relationships were actively discouraged. The fewer ties you had, the less likely you were to be distracted. And distractions could be deadly.

While they were eating, he'd managed several surreptitious glances towards the retired detective, and the man had looked troubled on occasion. No one else seemed to notice — maybe it was the alcohol dulling everyone's senses.

Placing the rest of the dishes into the dishwasher, Benedict pulled another beer from the fridge. Not wanting to drive home now he'd had a couple of bottles, he knew Nicki wouldn't mind him stopping on the sofa tonight. After feeding Luna a few more scraps of the leftover steak, he made his way back to the living room.

He could hear the bath taps running upstairs, having persuaded Nicki that a long hot bath was in order while he tidied the kitchen. She hadn't needed asking twice and had disappeared upstairs with a cup of tea fifteen minutes ago. With the bathroom door now closed, he was alone — and if he knew Nicki as well as he thought he did, she would be occupied for the next hour at least.

Which gave him ample time for one last-ditch attempt to put off what was coming; if he had more time, he might be able to untangle himself from it completely.

Pulling his laptop from the backpack he'd brought with him, he opened up the secure messaging service and logged on.

# CHAPTER TWENTY-FIVE

*4 Old Railway Cottages, Dullingham, Nr Newmarket*
*Sunday 26 May 2019*

Nicki drew up outside number four, immediately noticing that Benedict's car wasn't on the drive next door as she'd expected. He'd left early that morning, after making her a round of tea and toast, saying he was going straight home. So where was he? Then again, he didn't have to tell her his every movement, did he? She wasn't his keeper. They were friends — nothing more, nothing less.

Benedict had been his usual cheeky, chatty self last night, cracking jokes and interacting with her parents, but there was something about his demeanour that made her feel like he was keeping something from her. The man was an enigma, no question about that. She'd never met anyone quite like him before. They were quite similar in a lot of ways, which was probably why they got on so well, but she wasn't exactly the queen of transparency herself. Look how long it had taken her to tell her closest friends, and even her colleagues, about Deano. Amy, Faye and Caz had all taken it quite well, once the initial shock had worn off. She'd opened up to them during one of their customary wine nights soon after Dean was found, and she could still recall the incredulity on their faces. But there'd been none of the recriminations that she'd been fearing. No blame, no judgement, no reprimands. Instead, there had just been a lot of hugging, plenty of tears — and then more wine.

Putting aside thoughts of Benedict and where he might possibly be at this time on a Sunday morning, she got out of the car and hurried up the garden path to number four, rapping hard on the front door. She noticed the curtains were still closed, both upstairs and down, but with two twenty-something men living inside, it was of no real surprise. Adrian Browning's van was parked on the drive, so she assumed he and her brother would be home.

About to knock again, maybe a little louder this time, Nicki's hand froze in mid-air as the door was pulled open, Dean's sheepish smile greeting her.

"Morning, sis," he yawned, stepping back to let her inside. "I've got some coffee on already."

He showed Nicki through to the kitchen at the back of the house, where the comforting aroma of percolating coffee reached her nostrils. Another, sweeter aroma made her stomach growl.

"Croissants warming in the oven," explained Dean, reaching for a pair of floral oven gloves. "They're just the cheap supermarket ones, but they taste nice enough when you heat them up. Help yourself to some coffee." He gestured towards the coffee pot and the fresh mug next to it before tugging open the oven door. A rush of warm air flooded the kitchen.

Nicki grinned to herself as she poured some coffee. "This is all very domesticated." On the way in, she'd spied the egg basket full of eggs, the fresh loaf sitting on top of the bread bin, the sink curiously free of dirty dishes. The air had a sweet, citrusy smell over and above the aroma of baking pastries, and the worktops of the country-style kitchen were clean and tidy. "I'm impressed."

"You sound surprised." Dean deposited the tray of warm croissants onto the kitchen table, pulling off his oven gloves.

Nicki almost said that she was — but then realised that she hadn't seen Dean since he was five years old. He'd done a lot of growing up in the time they'd been apart. He was a man now, and not the little brother she remembered.

Dean slid the croissants onto two plates. "I used to do a lot of the cooking back . . ." Nicki watched her brother swallow the rest of the sentence, assuming the word "home" featured in it. She saw a slight flush enter his cheeks. "Back with Annette and Larry," he finished, handing her a plate as she took a seat at the table.

Nicki gave him a reassuring smile. "Glad to hear some-one inherited Mum's baking genes, because I certainly didn't. Anyway, here's your memory stick. The reason for my drop-ping in on you, after all." She placed it on the table.

"Thanks, you needn't have made a special trip, though. I could have picked it up myself. You must have more impor-tant things to be getting on with this morning."

Nicki broke apart one of the croissants. She did have things she needed to be doing, but found the early morn-ing drive over to Dullingham served an additional purpose. Driving helped her to think. All night the case of the mur-dered detective had plagued her thoughts — how was Mark Keeble connected to Operation Jackdaw? For connected he most certainly had to be because of the date. And the teeth. And then there was Ramsay O'Donoghue. What did they all have in common?

The thirty-minute drive hadn't enlightened her much, with no eureka moment behind the wheel of her Toyota, but it had sharpened her mind from what had been a somewhat groggy start to the day. She silently chastised herself for drink-ing so much Prosecco last night when she had work the next day.

For the next ten minutes they sat around the kitchen table eating the warm, crumbly croissants and drinking strong cof-fee. Nicki welcomed the caffeine hit. Trying to push thoughts of the case out of her head for the short time she would be here, she positioned herself with her back to the kitchen window. She could feel the early morning sun warming her shoulders through the glass as she resisted the urge to turn around and look out into the garden.

The brief glance she'd taken before sitting down had been enough to reveal that the tangled mass of brambles and bushes at the very bottom had been cut back, giving an unrestricted view of the exact spot where Nicki had learned only a few months ago that her baby brother was still alive.

An involuntary shudder shot up her spine as she took another mouthful of the caffeine-laden coffee. "How's work going?" She brushed the remains of her second croissant from her lips. "You finding enough around here? The stuff you showed me on the memory stick the other night was really good."

Dean drained his mug and reached for the percolator to pour another. He then gestured towards a pile of sketchbooks at the side of the table.

"I'm working on some illustrations for a local author at the moment. They seem pleased enough with my work, so hopefully they might recommend me to others. We'll just have to see how it goes."

"That sounds fantastic." Nicki smiled a genuine smile, her gaze sliding towards the sketchbooks. "Can I see?"

Dean took another gulp from his mug before selecting one of the books and sliding it across the wooden table. "These are the latest ones. They're still a work in progress but you'll get the general idea. This author writes children's fantasy books, so there's lots of dragons, goblins and wizards."

Nicki wiped her hands before opening the sketchbook. The pen-and-ink drawings were incredible, and her eyes widened with every turn of the page. "These are amazing, Dean. Really outstanding."

Her brother's cheeks flushed again. "There's still a lot to do, but I'm pleased with how they're coming along." He plucked another pastry from the tray. "It's so quiet out here

— Ade goes to work most days, so I have the place to myself. It's perfect."

Nicki turned the final page of the sketchbook and, as she did so, a loose piece of paper fell to the floor. As she bent to scoop it back up, the image she saw squeezed her heart. The drawing was in charcoal pencil and depicted a children's fairground ride, the same ride that had been firmly stamped in Nicki's memory for the last two decades.

The caterpillar ride — the ride Deano had been on immediately before he disappeared.

Nicki's heart squeezed again. Clearing her throat, she slotted the loose paper back inside the sketchbook, but not before she caught her brother's eye. She'd half expected to see a fearful, maybe even tormented look on his face, but instead he seemed to find it amusing, a grin teasing his lips, familiar dimples popping out on either side.

"It's OK," he breathed, his face soft. "I can look back on it now and accept it for what it was. Drawing actually helps."

Just at that moment, the kitchen door creaked open and Adrian Browning shuffled in, still dressed in his pyjamas.

"Sorry, didn't know we had company." Adrian's gruff tone suggested he wasn't sorry at all, a scowl darkening his features. He headed straight for the fridge. "We got any bacon?"

Nicki felt herself stiffen. Adrian Browning was no stranger to the inside of a police cell and made no secret of his loathing and contempt for the local force. Bacon? Was he trying to make a not-so-subtle dig at the "pig" currently sat at his kitchen table? Nicki plastered a plastic smile to her face.

"Good morning, Adrian. How's life treating you these days?" She knew it was a risky opening gambit, but the words escaped her mouth before she could stop them. Evidence of the fight he was alleged to have been involved in on Friday night was all over his face, with three steri-strips holding a cut to his forehead tightly shut. There were a multitude of purple bruises visible around his left eye and across both cheekbones.

She watched Adrian's expression morph from a darkening frown to one of indifference.

"OK, I s'pose." The man wrenched open the fridge and pulled out a packet of bacon. "I'm making a sandwich if anyone wants one?"

"I'm all right thanks, Ade." Dean got up to refill his coffee mug. "Not sure about my sister here, though."

Nicki's heart gave a little jolt at the word "sister". It would still take some getting used to. "I'm OK, too, thanks." Draining her coffee mug, she got to her feet, eyeing Adrian as he slapped several bacon rashers into a frying pan. She turned away and caught Dean's eye. "I'd best be getting on. But let's catch up again soon, yes? I hear you're seeing Mum and Dad later? They were at mine for dinner last night."

Dean nodded as he followed his sister to the front door, leaving behind the smell of sizzling bacon. "Yeah, I'm meeting them for lunch. I think Mum wants to walk around the Abbey Gardens and the cathedral."

After saying their goodbyes on the doorstep, Nicki made her way back to the Toyota, just as her mobile chirped in her pocket.

* * *

*A143 lay-by, Bury St Edmunds, Suffolk*

Colin Hedges killed the engine of the Astra. He'd never been to Bury St Edmunds before, and certainly didn't know his way around. The closest he'd come was passing signs on the main road en route to the coast sometime in the long and distant past. The drive up from Hampshire had taken three hours but seemed far longer. He'd parked up in a lay-by just outside the town not long after midnight and tried to get some sleep. Tried and failed. His eyes now felt raw with exhaustion, the lids gritty beneath his touch.

Once the sun was up, he found a petrol station for a morning coffee, picking up a sausage roll and a copy of the *Sunday Express* at the same time. The coffee had been surprisingly good, but the sausage roll still rested on the dashboard. He'd returned to the lay-by to drink his coffee and read the newspaper — and then to consider his next move.

As soon as he'd read the front-page headlines, and the more detailed articles inside, he was glad he hadn't decided to try the sausage roll. His stomach clenched as all manner of jumbled-up memories started to tumble through his head.

Jacob Towers and Aaron Nash were dead.

And so too was Mark Keeble.

And then there was Ramsay O'Donoghue.

It couldn't be a coincidence.

Fourteen years may have passed — which seemed like a lifetime. But it felt like yesterday.

He hadn't expected an officer of the law to attempt to bribe him. Many things had crossed his mind as he'd sat at the sticky Formica table all those years ago, the air thick with burnt onions and cooking oil, but that certainly hadn't been one of them.

Thirty-five thousand pounds — in cash.

Colin remembered almost falling off his chair with shock — although with the generous amount of grease and muck on it, falling anywhere was virtually impossible.

But thirty-five thousand pounds? It had been a large sum back then, and still would be today.

The money, in fifty-pound notes, had been stuffed inside a simple brown envelope and nudged across the table towards him. Not for the first time, Colin wondered what would have happened if he'd decided to say yes. Would the direction of his life have changed? Would he have been able to buy a bigger house, send the kids to a better school? Maybe he could have made his first wife happy, enough so she would stay. Colin wasn't so naive to believe money was the route to success and happiness, but it might have made a difference.

Although he hadn't accepted the bribe, it hadn't stopped it following him around like a black shadow for the next fourteen years, the guilt weighing him down like a ship's anchor. Taking a stance hadn't changed anything in the end — what happened had still happened, with or without his morals.

Colin stared out of the car's windscreen. Now he was here, he wasn't really sure what to do or where to go. He let his eyes stray to the burner phone on the passenger seat. The simple Nokia handset had arrived through his letterbox with the last note. He didn't need an explanation to accompany it. Almost as soon as he'd opened the box and switched it on, a message had chirped through.

*It's time to pay for what you did* — *15 August 2005.*

Another message followed, giving an address and a time.

Which was how Colin had ended up travelling through the night to where he was now — parked up in a lay-by just outside Bury St Edmunds.

Not for the first time, Colin asked himself what he was doing. He could easily fire up the engine, turn around and be home in time for lunch — maybe take Alice and Archie out for the afternoon. But although his fingers hovered over the ignition, he knew he wouldn't.

He had to finish this — and now.

It was time to stop running.

\* \* \*

*4 Old Railway Cottages, Dullingham, Nr Newmarket*

It felt unnerving and distinctly unnatural to have a copper in the house. And to think his brother was actually related to the woman, too. It made him shiver. Did that make *him* related to her as well, in some kind of convoluted way? Adrian Browning gave the punchbag another swift jab with his right hand. She might have said she was off duty, but her sort never were, were they? He suspected every copper even slept with one eye open.

He'd made the bacon sandwich, even though his appetite left him the minute he saw they had company at the kitchen table. *His* kitchen table. It currently sat, half eaten, on top of the workbench, a mug of stewing tea by its side.

A round of upper cuts landed on the bag. He'd been trying to keep his nose clean for the last few months, Mr Arnold at the butchers telling him in no uncertain terms that he either cleaned up his act or hung up his meat cleaver. Butchery wasn't exactly Adrian's chosen profession, but it was a job — and not a bad one at that. He could think of a lot worse and, with his track record, employers weren't exactly tripping over themselves to have him on their books. So he was trying to toe the line. It wasn't easy and certainly didn't come naturally — Friday night being a case in point. The cut on his forehead still stung, the bruises more tender as time went on.

Adrian had always had issues with his temper, ever since primary school. Maybe even before that. He likened himself to a coiled spring, poised to unleash himself on anyone who happened to cross his path. It could be something as innocuous as an inadvertent knock of his elbow in a pub, making him spill an inch of his beer. Or maybe someone accidentally bumping into him in the bus queue. No number of apologies would be able to quell the flames already flaring inside.

Attacking the punchbag with several more quick, hard jabs, he felt the impact ripple through his body. He spent a lot of time in the garage these days — it was a good way to let off steam. Sweat started to trickle down his back as he quickened his punches, jabs to the left rapidly followed by jabs to the right. Sometimes, he imagined faces pinned to the bag, giving him that extra motivation to beat the living daylights out of it, and right now those faces were Larry and Annette. He struggled to call them his parents anymore.

Boxing helped him think. It helped him focus. His brother — and he still called him that, despite what had happened — had dealt with a lot over the last few months. Discovering your real family weren't dead as you'd been led to believe must seriously mess with your head. But Adrian had suffered too — what had happened had affected him just as much as it had his brother. And most people forgot about that.

More punches pummelled against the punchbag, more sweat trickled down his back. With each workout he tried to push himself that little bit further, otherwise what was the point? And he was getting results now, too — his muscles were more defined, his stamina improved. He'd even managed to give up the fags.

As he subjected the bag to another flurry of thunderous upper cuts, he heard his mobile chirp with the sound of an incoming email. He initially chose to ignore it, wanting to finish his routine, but the longer he left it, the more trepidation began to seep in. He knew it would be a response to his own terse message sent yesterday. He didn't like the feeling it gave him. He was used to being in control, calling the shots — he didn't like being told what to do.

After another round of quick punches, he wiped his brow and went to pick up his phone. As expected, the message was short and sweet. Well, maybe not so sweet this time.

*I'll do it myself. You can't be trusted.*

# CHAPTER TWENTY-SIX

*Premier Inn, Bury St Edmunds*

Hugh Webster paced up and down outside the front of the hotel. He hadn't slept particularly well, lying awake for most of the night, listening to Anne's rhythmic breathing and faint snoring. He couldn't, not after Nicki had mentioned the date.

15 August 2005

And Mark Keeble.

Nicki might not have mentioned the man by name, but he knew it was Keeble she was referring to. It couldn't be anyone else. How many other serving Metropolitan Police detectives had been killed in the last few days? Especially those found in their car in a car park in Hastings.

The date couldn't be a coincidence, either.

The moment he'd pulled the small scrap of paper from underneath the windscreen wipers on Friday morning, the feeling he was being watched had intensified. The date didn't spark any immediate recollection for him, which was one of the reasons he'd tried to call Keeble.

If only the man had answered.

And the fact that the date was now linked to his daughter's murder investigation made his skin crawl.

Hugh checked his watch. He didn't have long.

Nicki's small townhouse wasn't big enough to swing a cat, a fact her Russian Blue Luna was no doubt eternally grateful for, which meant he and Anne always checked into a hotel each time they came to visit. It wasn't far from the station, so a quick call had secured a meeting before his daughter had to get back to work.

It seemed to take an age for Nicki to appear, but when she did he tried his best to shed the pensive look on his unshaven face. He knew he looked like he hadn't slept — the telltale dark shadows around the eyes, the heavy eyelids. It was a look he knew she recognised, so he didn't bother trying to disguise it.

"I've left your mother having a coffee inside." Hugh gestured for Nicki to follow him around the side of the hotel, away from the entrance. "She thinks I've popped back up to the room for something, so I can't be long."

Nicki frowned as she followed. "What is it, Dad? Why all the cloak and dagger?"

Hugh Webster's shoulders sagged as he eventually stopped and turned around. Satisfied they were suitably far enough down the side of the hotel not to be seen, he took in a deep breath and just came out with it. "It's the date — the one you mentioned last night."

"Oh?" Nicki's eyebrows sprang up. "What about it?"

Hugh hesitated, running a hand over the bristles on his chin. "It's a bit of a long story, and I'm not entirely sure what it all means, but . . ." He paused again, the worried look on his face redoubling. "A few of my old cases are being looked into — I don't think it really means anything, and I've been told not to worry, but . . ."

"Looked into?" Nicki edged closer, concern in her voice. "What do you mean, looked into?"

Hugh gave a tired shrug. "I'm really not sure, but when you mentioned that date last night, it got me thinking. Especially when you mentioned Keeble."

"Keeble? I'm not sure I mentioned him by name." Hugh detected a sharpness to his daughter's tone. "What aren't you telling me, Dad?"

243

"It might be nothing . . ."

"Tell me anyway." The sharpness intensified.

Hugh sighed. "Mark Keeble was someone I used to work with — I knew it was him when you mentioned a detective being murdered in a car park in Hastings."

"How did you know that?" Nicki's tone retained its edge. "The name wasn't released to the press until this morning."

Hugh glanced over his shoulder again to ensure they were still alone. "I got a call — from one of the investigating officers down in East Sussex. They knew I'd been in touch with Keeble recently. They have a record of a message I left on his answerphone. They wanted to ask me what I knew."

"And what did you tell them?"

Hugh stopped short. "Well, the truth, obviously."

He saw his daughter's eyebrows arch. "Really? I've been speaking to the detectives down in Sussex, and they haven't mentioned you to me at all."

Hugh sighed heavily. "Keeble was my second in command before I retired. We worked many cases together over the years, but we haven't really kept in touch since my retirement beyond the odd Christmas card and promise to play golf sometime. But I spoke to him when I heard some of my cases — our cases — were being looked into, to see what his take on it was."

"And what did he say?"

Hugh could only shrug. "He didn't think I needed to worry."

"Was he the one doing the investigating, this Mark Keeble?"

Hugh shook his head. "When I told him about it, he seemed surprised. Malcolm tells me I don't need to worry, too, but . . ."

"Hang on — *DCI Turner* knows about this?" Hugh could hear the incredulity in his daughter's tone. "How long has he known?"

"Not long. But I'm not sure that's the most concerning thing . . ."

"And what *is* the most concerning thing, Dad?" Nicki edged closer to her father. "What's really going on?"

Hugh felt his stomach shift. He hadn't managed anything more than a coffee at breakfast that morning, managing to convince Anne that he'd just eaten too much at their daughter's the night before. "Friday morning, the day after I got home from Hastings after visiting my accountant, I found a note under my windscreen." Hugh saw his daughter frown.

"A note? What kind of note?"

"Just a small scrap of paper." Hugh pulled his phone from his pocket and scrolled to the image he'd taken. "Here."

He watched as Nicki took the phone and studied the photograph.

*15 August 2005.*

She looked up at him, confusion building on her brow. "I don't understand, Dad. This is the date involved in my investigation."

Hugh let out a pent-up breath. "I really don't know what it means, Nicki. But when you mentioned it last night, as well as Keeble, it made me think. I tried to ring him as soon as I found the note, to ask him who might have sent it — and also whether the date meant anything to him. But I never got to speak to him. He didn't answer his mobile or his landline. That was the message I left on his answerphone — the one the detectives found." Hugh's face greyed. "They told me he'd been murdered. They didn't beat about the bush. So, when you said last night about the victims in your case all being linked by that date . . ." He broke off and slipped the phone back in his pocket. "I thought you should know."

"What have you said to the investigating officers?"

Hugh sighed again. "There wasn't much I could tell them, to be fair. I didn't tell them about the note, if that's what you mean. And I didn't tell them we'd been speaking recently — Keeble and me. I'm not sure why, but I'm sure they'll have found out by now. They'll have looked into his phone records."

"And you have no idea what it means? This date — 15 August 2005?"

Hugh rubbed his eyes and then checked his watch. "I really need to get back inside. Your mother will wonder where I am."

"But does it *mean* anything to you, Dad? 15 August 2005?" Hugh could hear the desperation in his daughter's voice. He wished he could help her. "Who put that note under your windscreen wiper? Do you think it was Keeble?"

"I don't think so. I don't know. I was just about to retire, that's all I remember."

"Look, Dad, I . . ."

Hugh stepped forward and enveloped his daughter in a bear hug. "I know. You need to go — and your mother will be wondering where I've got to. This is all I can tell you so far. I'll try and think where this date comes from. I'll do some digging. As soon as I get anything, I promise I'll let you know."

\* \* \*

*2 Old Railway Cottages, Dullingham, Nr Newmarket*

*I've waited long enough. I'll do it myself.*

Benedict Thatcher stabbed the screen and erased the message from his laptop. His head was still pounding after the restless night's sleep on Nicki's sofa. After making her breakfast that morning, he'd made his excuses and left, but he didn't go straight home. Instead, he went for a drive in an effort to clear his head.

It hadn't worked.

Arriving back home, it hadn't taken long before he heard the familiar ping of a new email.

He knew he was going to have to do it, one way or another. His delaying tactics and attempts at finding a different solution had all fallen at the first hurdle. All he'd succeeded in doing was passing the job to someone far less experienced than he was.

*It was going to happen.*

*The man was going to die.*

All Benedict could do now was make sure it was done properly.

Once again, Benedict questioned his choice of career, if you could call it a career. It didn't come with sick pay or a pension, but it did pay handsomely. And it *had* been his choice; no one had forced him to take this path. As a "fixer", he fixed things — things and people. Mostly people these days. Operating below the radar, on the fringes of a dark and dangerous world, Benedict had lost count of the number of jobs he'd completed. Jobs which gave him no qualms, or crises of conscience.

Except for this one.

This one was always going to be different.

With another sigh, he resigned himself to the knowledge that it would be done — and it would be done tonight.

* * *

*Bury St Edmunds Police Station*

The team were already hard at work when Nicki made it back to the station. Matt had called in — Danni went into labour in the early hours, so he wouldn't be in. After checking in briefly, she made her excuses and headed for her office. She needed time to think. What her father had just disclosed about Mark Keeble had unnerved her and was an entirely unexpected connection. Even though he'd been trying to hide it, repeatedly telling her that everything would be fine, she could tell he was worried. She could see the concern scored deeply into his eyes.

And it was a concern she shared.

She didn't want to come right out and say it, but everyone who had received a note or text quoting 15 August 2005 had ended up dead not long afterwards.

*Dead.*

Another chill rippled through her. Why had he lied to the detectives about his contact with Keeble? Was it something more than being caught off guard? Nicki didn't have her father down as one who panicked under pressure.

Even though the walk from the hotel to the station was short, it was long enough for her worries to treble with every step. She noticed the mug of coffee on her desk, still warm. One of the team, most probably Darcie, had been thinking of her that morning. She took a grateful sip.

Although they hadn't come up with much so far regarding the date, Nicki increasingly felt it was the key to it all. It had to be. It was the only thing linking the deaths — that and the teeth. Thinking about the teeth made her shiver, despite the warm mug in her hand.

When she'd checked the news headlines that morning, she was irritated to find that Ramsay O'Donoghue's name had been leaked. An unnamed source had confirmed that questions were being asked about the link between the elderly gentleman's death and the recent cases in Suffolk. No mention had been made of the teeth, but she still wasn't impressed. The release of the name wouldn't do them any favours, putting them instantly on the backfoot. She didn't suspect any of her team were behind the leak, but that didn't narrow the field by much.

Nicki turned her thoughts to Mark Keeble. The screwed-up note in the footwell mentioned 15 August 2005 — had it been left there on purpose? Had the detective, in his last moments of life, been trying to tell them something?

Headache building, Nicki reached for the packet of painkillers she kept in her desk drawer and swallowed a couple with another glug of the coffee. Discovering the relevance of the date had to be their priority.

Just as she reached forward to switch on her computer, a breathless DS Carter knocked and poked his head around the door frame. "Sorry, boss. But Harvey Mitcham's here. He's in an interview room downstairs."

# CHAPTER TWENTY-SEVEN

*The Bury Gazette*

Jeremy Frost didn't usually look a gift horse in the mouth. For the last few months, if not longer, he'd thought his time with the *Gazette* could well be coming to an end. He had ambitions — ambitions that went far beyond what the town and local area could offer him. He'd researched and reported on a case earlier in the year, thinking it could be his golden ticket to the big time, and although it had made positive waves in certain literary circles and caught the eye of some of the major players in the reporting industry, the job offers hadn't come flooding in as he'd secretly hoped.

Even after nearly two decades in the business, he was still classed as a relative unknown. The series of articles he'd penned had opened up a national debate on the age of criminal responsibility in England and Wales, and whether it was still fit for purpose. It had even made national TV, making it onto some of the more popular daytime and even the evening schedules.

But the big time had never beckoned, and here he was nearly three months later, still reporting on local road closures, potholes and graffiti.

Sighing, he leaned back in his chair and balanced his feet on the edge of the desk. The message taken by Alan, the receptionist downstairs, had only been as detailed as the visitor had allowed — and Jeremy defaulted to Alan's usual resumé at the bottom.

*This one has something to hide. And he's scared. Petrified, I would say.*

Alan was surprisingly perceptive, with an uncanny ability to read people in a heartbeat. It was a skill Jeremy had yet to acquire and often coveted.

Reaching for the mug containing the dregs of his morning coffee, Jeremy kicked his feet back to the floor and woke up his desktop monitor. The death of Detective Inspector Keeble from the Met was the lead story on just about every news channel there was, and the man who'd left the message at reception had mentioned the detective's name alongside three others — Jacob Towers, Aaron Nash and Ramsay O'Donoghue.

Jeremy's investigative instincts were immediately spiked. The deaths of Jacob Towers and Aaron Nash were big news in the town, although very little detail was being released by the police. Although he and Nicki were very good friends, Jeremy was still part of the media and he understood her reluctance sometimes to divulge anything of pertinence, off the record or otherwise. It was a dance all participants were well versed in.

Sighing again, he reread the online news article one more time. The death of Mark Keeble sounded horrific — even from the sparse details the media had been given. Killed in his car, garrotted by a piece of wire. An involuntary shudder travelled along his spine, causing the hairs on the back of his neck and head to prickle.

And then he reread Alan's message.

*This one has something to hide. And he's scared. Petrified, I would say.*

Mind made up, Jeremy pushed himself out of his chair and grabbed his jacket. He would give the man five minutes — not a minute more.

\* \* \*

In the end, it had only taken four.

Jeremy had managed to secure them one of the basement rooms that no one else ever used. Colin Hedges had been reluctant to show his face beyond the reception desk, so a compromise was found in the shape of a storeroom — well, more of a cupboard, really.

With a small recording device in the centre of the rickety table that separated them, Jeremy sat back, not taking his eyes from the man that had shown up less than thirty minutes ago. He may not have the same powers of evaluation as Alan, but even Jeremy recognised when someone was frightened — and frightened for their life. It didn't take a genius.

When informants or witnesses were being interviewed, Jeremy would often lay on tea or coffee, maybe even some posh biscuits from M&S; on occasion they would even stretch to sandwiches, depending on the information they were hoping to extract. But there hadn't been time for any such niceties today. Hedges had agreed to talk to Jeremy, but it had to be done *now*.

With his journalist nose twitching, Jeremy had readily agreed.

Hedges sat ramrod straight in the uncomfortable wooden chair, eyes wide and staring. Jeremy noted one of the man's legs was already trembling.

"In your own time." Jeremy used the most encouraging tone he could muster. "Tell me everything again — in your own words."

A minute or so went by before Hedges took a deep breath and began to speak once again. "In the summer of 2005 I was called to be on a jury at Blackfriars Crown Court. It was three weeks that would change the course of my life, forever."

\* \* \*

*Bury St Edmunds Police Station*

"Thank you for coming in, Mr Mitcham. It's very much appreciated." Nicki took a seat at the small wooden table.

With all that had already happened that morning, she'd toyed with the idea of requesting he come back later, unsure if the eccentric old man would have anything useful to add to the investigation.

But then she remembered.

*The man had lied to her.*

Mitcham sat up straight, an expectant yet wary look on his face. It was hard to see behind the whiskers gracing his chin, and the half-moon spectacles perched on his nose, but Nicki thought a part of him looked troubled. Pale blue eyes peered out from behind the lenses, eyes that she guessed would usually sparkle with good humour — no doubt fuelled by a decent whisky or two. But today they seemed dull, and the man's brow creased with concern.

"Do you mind if I record this, Mr Mitcham?" It wasn't really a question. Nicki gestured toward the recording system, already activated. "It saves me having to make notes."

Mitcham's bushy eyebrows arched, his eyes darting towards the tape decks. Mouth open, he seemed to struggle to find his voice. "Well, I guess so . . ."

"Good." Nicki beamed and settled into her seat. "I just wanted to follow up on a few things — after our earlier chat about your friend, Jacob Towers."

Rubbing a finger over his whiskered chin, Mitcham nodded. "Of course. Anything to help. Am I . . ." The man glanced again towards the recording system. "Am I in trouble?" The question was followed by a nervous laugh.

Nicki maintained her smile. "I don't think I would go that far, Mr Mitcham. You're here voluntarily, and if you wish to leave at any moment, then you're free to do so. There are just a few questions I'd like to ask, clarification on a few points, if you would be so kind as to indulge me." Nicki saw the man's shoulders relax a little, so she pressed on. "I wanted to return to Jacob Towers and how well you knew him."

"Oh?" Trepidation entered Mitcham's tone.

"When we spoke last, you seemed to infer that you didn't know Mr Towers all that well — and that it was more of a professional relationship between the two of you."

"Yes?"

"So, I was wondering how that fitted with being a godfather to his twins?" Nicki held her breath and eyed the would-be scientist over the table. The man's immediate reaction was one of confusion, rapidly followed by a widening of the eyes and a colouring of his cheeks. "Or am I mistaken and you're *not* a godparent to Zeb and Amber?"

Harvey swallowed and tried another nervous-sounding chuckle. "Well, no — I mean, yes, of course I am. *We* are — Eileen and I. Godparents, that is. But it was more something for Eileen to be involved in rather than me."

"I see," replied Nicki, even though she didn't. "And there was something else I wanted to clarify. You told us that you hadn't been in contact with Mr Towers for . . ." She made a point of glancing sideways towards Graham Fox at her side. "What was it Mr Mitcham said before, DS Fox?"

Fox pulled out his notebook, flipping over a few pages before nodding. "When asked about the last time Mr Mitcham had seen Mr Towers, the response was, 'It must be some time ago now — probably early last year, at a guess.' And then in answer to the question whether Mr Mitcham had spoken to Mr Towers recently, given him a call, the response was, 'Not recently, no. Not that I recall, anyway.'" Fox closed the notebook, a fixed smile on his face.

"Indeed," added Nicki, turning her attention back to Mitcham. "Would you care to expand on that, Mr Mitcham? Especially when Mr Towers' mobile phone records show several texts sent by you in the week before his death — and even a voicemail."

Nicki watched the man's face drop as he pulled a handkerchief from his pocket and dabbed his sweating brow. After rubbing his eyes from beneath his half-moon spectacles, he eventually nodded. "Yes, well — I see what you mean." He locked his gaze to Nicki's. "I may not have been entirely honest with you when we spoke before. Not intentionally, I hasten to add. But I now realise that was remiss of me. I *had* been in touch with Jacob prior to . . ." The man's voice hitched. "Prior to his unfortunate demise, and it was wrong of me to lead you to believe otherwise. I fully appreciate phone calls and messages are easily checked, what with technology the way it is these days." Another nervous laugh followed, but this time it was accompanied by a heavy sigh and a grim expression. "However — before we proceed any further, Inspector, I need to tell you about the money. And the affair."

* * *

"Fifty thousand pounds." Nicki wrote the sum up onto one of the whiteboards, her brow furrowing. "Harvey Mitcham confirmed that he went to the Towers' home for dinner three weeks ago at the specific request of Jacob. And that, not long after arriving, Jacob asked him to look after a sum of money for him."

"Fifty grand?" Duncan's eyebrows arched. "Where the hell did he get that kind of cash? According to their bank statements, the family were broke."

Nicki turned away from the whiteboards. "That I don't know. Mitcham was unable to say — Jacob didn't give him a reason."

"And he didn't *ask*?" Duncan's eyebrows arched even higher. "I find that hard to believe."

Nicki could only shrug. "Mitcham said Jacob was quite cagey that night. Agitated. As if he had something on his mind. He didn't feel like he could push it."

"And he's just chosen to tell us about it now?" Duncan puffed out his cheeks and gave a snort. "Sounds suss to me. Why didn't he think to mention it before?"

"I asked him that very question, Duncan, I can assure you. He was already holding back on us — primarily about his relationship with Jacob and the Towers family. Once we brought him into the station and he realised we had access to Jacob's phone records, he knew he'd need to start telling us the truth. But as for why he kept quiet in the first place?" Nicki felt her shoulders sag and gave an exasperated sigh. "The only explanation he gave was that he panicked. He thought keeping quiet about the money was the right thing to do at the time, and that it wouldn't have had anything to do with Jacob's death."

"Wanted the money for himself, more like," scoffed Duncan. "He only came clean once he knew we were onto him — otherwise he'd have kept it, and no one would be any the wiser."

Roy gave an encouraging nod. "I'm with you. Jacob gives him fifty thousand pounds in cash, then three weeks later falls to his death from a four-storey building. And Mitcham doesn't think the two are connected? I don't buy it for a second."

"It's unusual, I'll grant you that." Nicki rubbed her temples, the late night and too much Prosecco still clouding her head. That, and her father's revelations about Mark Keeble. "But what connection it has to Jacob's death . . ." She left the rest of the sentence unsaid.

"Surely, if the family were in financial difficulties, which by the look of it they were — or at least only just keeping their heads above water — and then they come into a potentially life-changing sum of money . . ." Duncan stood his ground. "You wouldn't go and throw yourself off a tall building, now, would you?"

"More evidence, as if we needed it, that this wasn't anything even remotely like a suicide," confirmed Roy. "Do you think the wife knew about the money?"

Nicki frowned. "My guess is not. Otherwise, why would Jacob need to give it to Harvey to look after? It sounds like he wanted to keep it hidden, for whatever reason. I'll ring Karen and see if she can ask Denise — but I suspect the woman was kept in the dark. Just as she was about the affair."

"The *affair*?" Darcie's eyebrows shot up. "What affair was this?"

Nicki turned back to the whiteboards, adding the word to the first board. "It seems that some years ago, Jacob had an affair with a woman he met online. It was around the time the two families were spending more time together, just after the twins' christening. Jacob confided in Mitcham but, as far as Mitcham knows, it fizzled out after a while and Denise never knew."

"Wives always know," sighed Fox. "Do we know who she is?"

"Mitcham said he never knew her name — and I'm inclined to believe him this time."

"Do we think the two are related?" questioned Roy. "The money and the mistress?"

"Ordinarily I would say yes — sex and money often go hand in hand. But Mitcham thinks it was about six years ago that the affair ended, so it's hard to see how they can be linked. I think the affair is just another dead end. What we really need to focus on is how Jacob came into fifty thousand pounds just a few weeks before his death."

"What about a loan shark?" suggested Darcie. "Jacob could have been trying to dig the family out of the financial hole they were in and maybe borrowed from the wrong people?"

Nicki wrinkled her nose. "It's possible but doesn't quite feel right. If Jacob defaulted on his payment terms, pushing him off a four-storey building isn't going to help any loan shark get their money back. Let's keep thinking but don't let it sidetrack us too much. Anything else from today so far?"

With her temples still thudding, Nicki could feel the headache spreading — despite the painkillers she'd swallowed on getting back to the station. What her father had revealed to her outside the Premier Inn was still occupying her thoughts, and despite her best efforts to quell it, fear was starting to churn and build.

The date still concerned her, and someone had now taken steps to seek her father out, drawing him into Operation

Jackdaw whether he liked it or not. She needed to know why. Was her father next on the killer's list? But they had the list from Mark Keeble's wall and former Detective Superintendent Webster didn't feature on it. She'd seen the evidence for herself, a copy of which was up on the whiteboard in front of her, which should be reassuring.

*Should* be but wasn't.

Biting her lip, she tried to refocus her thoughts. Thinking about her father was a distraction she didn't need on top of everything else.

Darcie stirred Nicki from her troubled thoughts. "I've taken a look into the other names from the list on Keeble's wall. There isn't an awful lot to go on, but this is what I've managed to get so far." Darcie got to her feet and crossed over to the whiteboards, taking a marker pen with her.

"The first one on the list, Declan Hood, died in a car accident in 2009. A year later in 2010, Sonia Parish died from a suspected overdose, and Grant Fielding a year after that in an accident at Charing Cross Tube." Darcie wrote all three names onto a fresh board. "Heidi Butcher died in 2012 of a suspected allergic reaction causing anaphylaxis, and in the same year, Glenn Palmer died of carbon monoxide poisoning at his home, a faulty boiler suspected to be the cause. In 2013, Scott Hayward took his own life by hanging." She added those names to the board. "In 2014, Danielle Stannard died in a motorbike accident. The following year, Victor O'Neill died after an accidental overdose of prescribed medication, undiagnosed dementia said to be a contributing factor. Then in 2017, Grayson Burrows died of smoke inhalation and burns after a fire at his home." Darcie added the final names. "In each of these cases, the deaths were put down to accidental causes — apart from Grant Fielding, where the investigation is still open." Snapping the lid back on the marker pen, she turned towards Nicki. "But I can't find any mention of tooth extraction in any of the cases, either before or after death. And no mention of the 15 August date, either. The only ones that have those are Towers, Nash, O'Donoghue and now Keeble."

"So, those earlier deaths might *not* be connected to our cases, after all?" Roy voiced the question on everyone else's lips.

Nicki grimaced. "But we still have the list. They must all be on Keeble's wall for a reason, teeth or no teeth, so it must follow that they're all connected somehow. We just don't know the reason why yet."

"I could dig deeper?" Darcie pulled her keyboard closer. "We certainly don't have all the details and maybe the original investigation teams overlooked something?"

"Good idea. Get everything you can about each one."

"Could *he* be our killer?" Duncan gestured towards the third whiteboard. "Keeble? He's got all the names on his wall, after all."

Nicki made another face. "That may be so, but he didn't kill himself in that car park. I still think the date is the key, even though that hasn't given us a breakthrough yet."

"Maybe we're looking at this too widely?" Roy pulled himself back towards his computer screen. "Nothing of note might have happened globally on 15 August 2015, but what about closer to home?"

Nicki's eyes skimmed the names on the whiteboards. "You might have something there, Roy. Let's see where all our victims were on 15 August 2005. Everyone on Keeble's list, including Keeble himself."

Just as Nicki was about to pick up a marker pen, one of the desk phones trilled. Roy jumped up from his seat to snatch up the receiver. After a few moments, he caught Nicki's eye, his gaze widening by the second.

"Boss? We've just had a call in about Aaron Nash." Roy waved the phone receiver in Nicki's direction. "From someone in Sunderland claiming to be his wife."

# CHAPTER TWENTY-EIGHT

"I killed him, didn't I?" Denise Towers buried her face in her hands. "I killed him — Jacob. It's all my fault."

DC Karen Gedge edged closer, handing the woman a box of tissues. "No, Denise. None of this is your fault."

"How can you say that?" Denise dragged her gaze out from beneath her hands, her face red and blotchy. "You don't know. You don't know what I did."

Karen watched the woman bury her face again, her shoulders heaving with grief-ridden sobs. Edging even closer, she placed a comforting hand on Denise's arm. "What is it that I don't know, Denise? You can tell me anything, you do know that, don't you? I'm here to help."

Denise's shoulders gave another shudder, more anguished sobs escaping her throat. She gripped the box of tissues so tightly, the cardboard collapsed in her hand.

"Why don't you start at the beginning?"

Another thirty seconds or more silence followed, which made Karen wonder if she needed a slightly different approach to get the woman talking. It had been Denise's parents who had called her, worried about their daughter's change in mental state, concerned that she was deteriorating. When Karen called at the house, she saw exactly what they meant.

The woman didn't look as though she had slept, and maybe not eaten much either. Her skin looked pale and washed-out, her eyes sunken.

"Surely it can't be that bad?" offered Karen, giving Denise's arm a squeeze. "Nothing ever is."

Denise's head snapped up, her eyes wide and her lips trembling. "Oh, but it can be! And it is! I can't keep it a secret any longer, it's eating me up inside."

"What is it, Denise?" Karen's brow creased, her concern for the woman growing. "What is it that you think you've done?"

Denise sucked in a shuddering breath. "I killed him. I know I did." Karen saw a defiant look in the woman's eyes, mixing with the pain. "His death is all my fault."

Karen maintained her reassuring grip on the woman's arm, acutely aware that Denise Towers was a woman on the edge. Before she could say anything, Denise reached into her cardigan pocket and brought out a phone.

"The only reason Jacob jumped from that building was because of me. I put him there. I drove him to do it." She paused again, raking in another trembling breath. Colour began to flood her pallid cheeks as she held the mobile out towards the family liaison officer. "I was having an affair — and Jacob found out."

\* \* \*

*Bury St Edmunds Police Station*

"Why is everyone either lying to us or keeping secrets?" Nicki slumped down into her chair. She'd left the team in the incident room following up on the new actions — in particular, where each victim was on 15 August 2005. It was a long shot, but Matt was right — they needed to cast the net as wide as possible. Karen had called before making her way back to the station, imparting the bombshell Denise Towers had just dropped, and the family liaison officer was now sitting opposite her.

"Before we talk about Denise, you have something else on Aaron Nash, Graham? Before I ring this Abbie Carpenter back."

DS Fox slipped into a vacant chair. "I thought it prudent to take another look at the Nash family finances — in light of the cash Jacob Towers came into before he died — and everything isn't quite as it seems."

"Why am I not surprised?" Nicki groaned. "Give it to me, good or bad."

Fox pulled out his notebook. "We already knew the family were on a tight budget, ever since Nash lost his business after the financial crash of 2008 and never seemed to fully recover. Like the Towers' family, they seem to live week to week, month to month. Then I found some red flags."

"Flags?" Nicki's eyebrows shot skywards. "What kind of flags?"

"Such as the fact that twenty-five thousand pounds was deposited into the pair's joint account the day before he died. It's only just cleared, so didn't show up before. With the family struggling like they were—" Fox pulled a loose piece of paper from his notebook — "I took the liberty of going back through the couple's bank statements for the last few years. Remember Rosalyn Nash told us that Aaron worked away every fortnight? Would go up to the North East for anything up to a week at a time?"

Nicki nodded.

"Well, something didn't sit right. The money paid into the joint account didn't quite seem enough for the time spent away. The whole reason for doing it was to earn extra cash, right? So, I dug around and found a second bank account in just Aaron Nash's name. Regular deposits are made, tying in with his time working away. But while he's away I noticed he seems to spend a considerable amount of money — money, according to Rosalyn, they don't have. Eating out, clothes shopping, grocery shopping. It's a regular pattern, every fortnight. All centred in the same part of the country. But weirdly, there's no hotel or guest house booking to cover the time he's away."

"You're going to tell me he goes to Sunderland, aren't you?" Nicki's eyes strayed to the note with Abbie Carpenter's details on.

Fox grinned as he handed the paper across the desk. "Every time. All the shops, restaurants, supermarkets — all in Sunderland."

Nicki pursed her lips as she took hold of the bank statement. "Do we believe her, this Abbie Carpenter?" She skimmed the statement, seeing a number of transactions from Sunderland-based shops. "Could Aaron Nash really have a second wife tucked away?"

Fox exhaled and shrugged at the same time. Nicki saw the exhaustion on his face, which she knew mirrored her own. "We get crank calls, you know that as well as I do, but . . . There's so much about this case that doesn't ring true — I don't think we can discount anything."

"OK, I'll ring this Abbie woman back, see what I can get out of her. In the meantime, keep digging into their finances. If she knew about this twenty-five grand, then that could be reason enough to claim to be his wife." Nicki handed the bank statement across to Karen. "I take it Rosalyn has never mentioned any suspicions about Aaron?"

Karen took the piece of paper, already shaking her head. "Do you want me to go and have a word? See if I can discreetly tease something out of her?"

Nicki pondered the idea for a moment. "Maybe, but not right now. Let's see if this woman's claim has any foundation first, shall we? Before we bring Rosalyn's world crashing down."

"What about Denise? Shall I go back to her and see if she'll give me more details about this other man she's meant to be having an affair with?"

"What other man?" Fox's eyes widened.

Nicki rolled her eyes before filling the detective sergeant in on Denise Towers' revelation about her private life.

"Well, I'll be buggered," he breathed, getting to his feet. "They're all at it. Can't anyone keep their pants on these days?"

"Quite."

After Fox had left to go back to the incident room, Nicki walked Karen to the door.

"Good idea to check back in with Denise Towers, though. See that she's OK. She'll be feeling all manner of emotions right now, but there's no need to add a hefty dose of guilt in there, too. Whatever she's done, I feel it unlikely it contributed to Jacob's death."

"Should I fill her in on where we are with the investigation?" Karen shrugged into her jacket. "I've been holding back up to now, so as not to alarm her."

"I think we'll have to," agreed Nicki. "She needs to know that whatever's going on in her private life, Jacob didn't kill himself. Give her as much information as you think she needs."

Once Karen left and Nicki was on her own, she slipped back behind her desk and reached for the phone. It was time to find out what Abbie Carpenter had to say for herself.

# CHAPTER TWENTY-NINE

*Premier Inn Hotel, Bury St Edmunds*

"Why do you keep staring out of the window, Hugh?" Anne Webster looked up at her husband while patting the mattress next to her. She placed the paperback she'd been reading face down on the bed. "Come and sit down. Let's have a drink before we think about what to do for dinner."

Hugh turned away from the window, plastering what he hoped was a reassuring smile on his face. The room was decent, a surprising amount of space for what was such a budget price. He wondered if they'd been upgraded without their knowledge — having stayed at the hotel several times over the last few months, maybe they were honoured guests.

Anne swung her legs off the bed and crossed over to the small desk in the corner. She'd picked up a bottle of Merlot on her way back from the town that afternoon and started to pour them generous servings into two china mugs, sniggering as she did so. "I feel a bit like a naughty teenager here, Hugh — drinking out of mugs!"

Hugh kept the smile fixed to his face the best he could as he accepted one of the drinks and settled down on his side of the bed. He didn't really feel like alcohol right now, his head still scrambled by the day's events, but he knew he had to at least try to act normally, whatever that may be. "Cheers." He held up the mug. "Here's to us."

Anne chinked her mug against her husband's as she climbed back onto the bed. "I'm so glad we made the trip up here again. I really do feel like we're starting to heal, as a family."

"I feel the same," replied Hugh. And he really did. The family had been through a trauma that most psychologists could only imagine, but they were managing to crawl out the other side relatively unscathed, which was no mean feat. He took a sip of the Merlot and closed his eyes, unable to think of anything else but the date.

Anne had dragged him around the town before meeting Dean for lunch, choosing to eat at the Pilgrims' Kitchen, the café inside the cathedral. Once they'd finished, Hugh had given the excuse of needing to look at something for Robert before the tax return was filed, and Anne had quite happily taken herself and Dean off for a tour of the cathedral and the Abbey Gardens.

This had allowed Hugh to return to the hotel and spend the next few hours researching 15 August 2005. The downstairs bar area had several secluded booths affording privacy, so even if Anne did come back unexpectedly, she was unlikely to see him — not straightaway, at least. He thought he was good for at least a couple of hours.

The results of his initial internet searches had been disappointing — nothing of note seeming to have happened on that date, much less involving Hugh. Feeling somewhat deflated, he'd found his thoughts turning back to Mark Keeble.

Fuelled by a swift double whisky from the bar, it didn't take much longer for the penny to finally drop — it had been staring him in the face all this time. Pulling out his pocket diary, he quickly located the scrap of paper containing the scribbled list of cases Keeble had tipped him off about.

And there it was.

Hugh and Keeble's last case together.

*15 August 2005.*

The deaths *were* all linked, just as Nicki had suspected. Jacob Towers. Aaron Nash. Hugh had seen the names in the paper that morning, alongside Keeble's. And then he'd seen an additional mention of Ramsay O'Donoghue; the old man had died the previous summer, but it sounded like the case was being re-opened.

The inclusion of O'Donoghue's name had clinched it for Hugh. *Why didn't I see it before?* he'd chastised himself, downing the remains of his whisky in one. *It's so bloody obvious.*

And then there was Keeble himself. Hugh felt more convinced than ever that the detective was behind the note left under his windscreen wiper. *The man had been trying to give me a clue.*

As he sat there in the hotel bar, another chilling thought edged into his head.

*Am I going to be next?*

"Hugh?"

Hugh dragged his eyes back open and his thoughts back to the present, taking another mouthful of wine from the china mug. "Sorry, love, I must have just zoned out there for a moment. What were you saying?"

Anne giggled, the sound she usually made when wine had made its way to her head. "I said we should think about where we want to go for dinner tonight. We could eat here in the hotel restaurant, or venture back out into the town if you prefer?"

*The town.*

Hugh felt a coldness start to spread. He hadn't said any-thing to Anne at the time, but while they'd been out with Dean earlier in the day, the feeling that he was being followed had returned. He just couldn't shake it. But no matter how many times he stopped to look behind him, there was nothing and no one to be seen.

Whoever it was, they were good at this. And with Keeble dead, it certainly wasn't him.

So, who was it?

Unless, of course, it was just his own fertile imagination.

He tried a smile. "Whatever you wish, my dear. Maybe we could stay here tonight? I'm feeling a bit tired, to be honest. Either down in the restaurant, or perhaps we could even order room service? I'm sure there's a film or two we could watch with dinner."

Anne seemed to like the idea. "Room service sounds perfect."

\* \* \*

*Copse Close, Bury St Edmunds*

"You didn't kill Jacob, Denise. I can assure you of that." Karen brought two mugs of strong tea over to the coffee table. She'd considered the need for something stronger, but decided what needed to be said would be better with a clear head.

When she'd left Denise earlier to return to the station and speak to Nicki, the woman had been a quivering wreck. And during the intervening hours, nothing much had changed. On Karen's reappearance Denise was still whimpering like a wounded animal, inconsolable sobs making her shake from top to toe.

"Take some tea, it'll do you good. There's sugar in it."

Denise made a face but did as she was told, clasping the hot mug in her hands before taking a sip. After another shudder, she shook her head firmly.

"No, you're wrong. You have to be. I killed him — or as good as." She took another sip of tea, but it almost made her choke as it coincided with another painful sob. "I was having an affair, and he must have found out. That's what drove him to jump off that building . . ." She swallowed another mournful sob. "That's what made him do what he did."

Karen leaned forward and held Denise's hand in her own, a reassuring expression on her face. "He really didn't, Denise. You've got this so wrong. Jacob didn't jump because of you."

"He didn't?" Denise shot Karen a look that told the family liaison officer that she didn't necessarily believe her. "What do you mean?"

Karen drew in a deep a breath and renewed her grip on the woman's hand. "Denise, Jacob didn't jump to his death."

"He . . . he didn't?" Denise's tear-ridden eyes widened, her bottom lip quivering. "Why do you say that?"

"Because," replied Karen, steeling herself for the response. "Because we believe Jacob was murdered."

\* \* \*

*Bury St Edmunds Police Station*

"Abbie Carpenter." Nicki sat back in her seat, legs stretched out before her. She'd kicked off her boots a while ago, her feet relishing the freedom. "A pleasant-sounding woman, clearly distraught to hear what had happened to Aaron."

"Not a timewaster, then?" queried Duncan, arms folded and an unconvinced look on his face.

"I didn't get that vibe from her, no. She sounded genuine. Once I managed to calm her down, she confirmed she'd seen Aaron's name in the paper, which was why she'd called. She then recounted her relationship with him, telling me that they met eight years ago when he was up working in Sunderland. They have two children, aged six and four. They married five years ago — again, in Sunderland. She then told me exactly what Rosalyn did, that he works away a lot, but Abbie thinks Aaron works on the oil rigs. With only four or five days at home per month."

Roy's eyebrows shot up. "Really?"

Nicki's shoulders sagged. "I suppose if that's all you've ever known, then you accept it. He sends regular money home — spends his four or five days 'leave' with her. It's either that or she refuses to accept what the real truth might be.

Some people are like that. I asked her if she knew of the name Rosalyn, but she claimed not to. I didn't push it further. She did mention that she's never been to Suffolk."

"Did you ask her about the money?" queried Roy. "Does she know about the twenty-five grand?"

Nicki sat forward in her seat, a smile on her lips. "In a roundabout way, yes. And this is where it gets interesting. I felt that if she truly didn't know about Rosalyn, then she would be unlikely to know about the twenty-five thousand deposited the day before Aaron died. But . . ." Nicki paused, ensuring she had everyone's attention. "When I mentioned unusual cash deposits, she volunteered that twenty-five thousand had been deposited unexpectedly in *her* account last week, which matches with the last time Aaron had visited. She assumed it was from him, some work bonus or something, and planned to ask him about it next week when he was due to come home."

"*Another* twenty-five K?" Roy's eyebrows arched. "Someone's rich."

"Indeed." Nicki's smile slipped a little. "Although I don't think this case is really about money, we can't ignore the fact that we've got Jacob Towers coming into fifty thousand shortly before he died, and now Aaron Nash, too."

"Are you going to tell Rosalyn? About Abbie? And vice versa?" Darcie's tone was guarded. "If I was either of them, I'm not sure I'd want to know — not on top of everything else."

Nicki sighed. "I don't really see how I can avoid it. Abbie was asking about funeral arrangements and although I've put her off for now, it's not something we can bury for long. I don't look forward to that particular conversation with either of them, to be honest. How do you tell someone that the man they've been married to for the last goodness knows how long has another secret family? And, as far as Rosalyn is concerned, they couldn't have kids. But here Aaron is with two kids living up in Sunderland."

"It's going to be messy, whichever way you spin it," agreed Roy. "Do we think Nash might have thought his secret was about to be revealed, so killed himself?"

"Unlikely," voiced Duncan. "We've still got the teeth, remember?"

"But it could have been a contributing factor, could it not?" continued Roy. "Another motivating factor?"

"What if Rosalyn knew?" volunteered Darcie. "About Abbie?"

"If she knew, then she's hiding it well." Nicki sighed again and checked her watch. "Time's marching on, everyone. We can continue with most of this in the morning. Anything further before we call it a night?"

"I might have something more on the date." Roy pulled his notebook towards him. "I've managed to find out that all victims were living in London in August 2005 — all twelve from the wall and Keeble, too. Maybe the connection is more about something that happened in the capital on that date? Maybe I could try the teeth angle again, but restrict it to London and the surrounding area?"

"Good idea, Roy. And let's keep trying to find this Colin Hedges. He's the only name on the list that hasn't shown up dead. We need to find him." Nicki made to get up from her chair, glancing at her phone screen as she did so. Two missed calls — one from her father, and one from Jeremy Frost, both leaving voicemails. "Thanks, everyone, I'll just finish up in my office, but I'll see you all first thing in the morning."

Nicki made her way back to her office, pulling out her phone to play the two voicemails. The first one, from her father, merely asked her to call him back. She checked the time and wondered how urgent it was. Surely if he'd found something out about the date, then he would have said so? While she thought about it, she played the second message from Jeremy.

"*Nicki?*" The reporter's voice sounded breathless. "*I need to talk to you. I've had the most bizarre story land in my lap this today, and I've spent all afternoon following it up. A chap called in to see me, Colin Hedges, with some insane story about jury tampering and murder. Call me.*"

# CHAPTER THIRTY

*Woodlands Camping and Caravan Site, Suffolk*

Riley Barton expected to feel more euphoria from the act of killing. Instead, he felt a little deflated; disappointed, even. Revenge was an emotion that had, up to now, fed his soul — but it seemed that each time he took a life it satisfied him for increasingly shorter periods of time. Was it an addiction? Would he ever get to the point where death meant nothing to him anymore?

Once again, he picked up his father's picture and held it up against the list of names. His father had agreed to see him just the once after the sentencing hearing, one visit to the maximum-security prison he was being held in. After that there had been the occasional letter — but neither of them was particularly great at writing, so the communications had eventually petered out.

Although he hadn't said it out loud, he was sure his father had wanted him to seek revenge. Surely it was a natural reaction — to want revenge against those that had signed your death warrant. During their one and only meeting, his father had told him about the money — the stash of cash and jewellery he'd accumulated from his criminality. He knew his father had been behind the country's second-biggest robbery in history, only behind the Brink's-Mat heist of 1983. The multi-million-pound robbery in South East London in 2003 had involved vast sums of cash and jewels, and Wesley Barton had told his son where to find it all.

"You know what to do."

Those had been his final words.

"You know what to do."

And he had.

It was only now that he questioned what that instruction had really meant, now that he was getting towards the end of his list — the end of his revenge.

He took a slug of whisky as he stared into his father's eyes. The instruction — *you know what to do* — had been followed with a statement — *look after Georgia and Grace.*

He knocked back another mouthful of whisky, wincing at the burn. Surely getting revenge for their father *was* looking after his sisters, wasn't it? Looking after their memory at least? Sorrow and pain sent ice flooding into his veins that not even a half-bottle of the finest single malt could temper.

All he had left now were the names on the list.

The killings had been precise, targeted; he'd done his homework over the years to make sure of that. The hidden stash of money and jewels had made things easier, of course. Money was a great incentive; it focused the mind like nothing else.

As he delved deeper into each of their histories, he quickly found out that each one had an Achilles heel. Most people did, after all; no one was perfect. Money and mental health were the motivating factors for Towers and Nash. Both in debt up to their eyeballs, they'd spiralled down into depression following the verdict, and deeper still when his father had been murdered in prison. His father's death had made the national news, but he'd made sure the message got home by posting newspaper clippings to each and every one of them — taking every opportunity he could to twist the knife. He wouldn't let them forget what they did, not for a second.

Consequently, it had been easy to tap into their consciences and feed them the necessary lies to cultivate their growing sense of guilt. Nash had caved in quite quickly, especially when he was told that his secret family in Sunderland might be something his current wife would want to know about, but Towers had needed some additional persuasion, *physical* persuasion in the end.

Topping up his whisky tumbler, he smiled at the recollection of pushing the man to his death from the top of the house on Crown Street. Killing did have its bonuses.

The detective had been different, however. Even at sixteen, he could see the telltale signs in the man — the dishevelled clothing, the unshaven face, the smell of stale alcohol. The man also had an inherent inability to keep control of his finances, and an inexplicable draw towards the delights of the betting shop; it created a heady mixture that was ripe for exploitation.

Ramsay O'Donoghue had been another difficult one. With a predilection for young men — nothing wrong with that, as everyone the man engaged with was above the age of consent — the seventy-nine-year-old had concerns that his activities would be made public, and so did his wife.

In the end, it didn't take much to lure him to the hotel and finish the job.

When he'd started out on his campaign, revenge had been enough for him; the deaths had been enough to sustain him. It was only when the act of killing started to bring him less and less satisfaction that he introduced the teeth. And it became an essential part of the killing process — feeding his desire for retribution, and pain.

Watching someone pull their own teeth out was harder than he'd expected, but it rewarded him with intense satisfaction. With each pull, each scream of agony, he felt his father's pain start to ease.

Sighing, he swallowed another mouthful of whisky and placed the photograph back down on the table. He needed to get ready for tonight. For tonight it would all be over, the final two names crossed of the list. The thought made his lip curl.

Colin Hedges was in town, he already knew that. He'd followed the man to the newspaper offices that morning and waited outside. Initially he'd been concerned that Hedges was spilling the beans on Riley and his activities, but his concern soon dissolved into indifference. He didn't really care. After tonight it would all be over; they could lock him up and leave him to rot.

It didn't matter, not anymore.

Alongside Hedges, he was looking forward to the end of retired Detective Superintendent Webster — something that was long overdue. He'd added Webster to the list almost as an afterthought, but people were in charge for a reason. And when things went wrong, the people at the top had to pay the price just like everyone else.

Barton took one last look at the list, then left the camper van and went on his way.

\* \* \*

*Premier Inn, Bury St Edmunds*

Anne had taken herself off into the bathroom to change for dinner — even though they weren't going out, she still wanted to make the effort.

"We don't get out much, Hugh. Let's make the most of being away from home."

While she was gone, room service had arrived, and Hugh couldn't resist the urge to peer through the drawn curtains while he waited for her to reappear. Surely, if someone *was* following him, they'd be waiting outside now, wouldn't they? But no matter how hard he looked, he couldn't see anything or anyone.

"This is nice, isn't it?" Anne settled back against the pillows, plate in hand. They'd both opted for a pasta dish — Anne the tagliatelle and Hugh a traditional lasagne — and the aroma of parmesan cheese and garlic bread soon filled the hotel room.

Ordinarily, Hugh's stomach would be growling — lasagne was his favourite dish, especially when accompanied by a thick slice of garlic bread — but tonight he had no appetite. The bottle of red wine that accompanied the meal was the only thing Hugh felt he could stomach, already on his second glass. And that was on top of the bottle they'd opened earlier.

He made the appropriate noises as he pushed the lasagne around his plate. "It's lovely."

"There's a new drama series on the BBC tonight." Anne wound several strands of pasta around her fork before popping it into her mouth. "We could watch that, if you fancy. Or there's a film on later."

Hugh broke apart one of the garlic bread slices and did his best to swallow some. "Both sound fine to me, my dear. I'll let you choose."

For the next twenty minutes Hugh only managed to eat half of his lasagne, making an excuse as to how large a portion it had been — which wasn't entirely a lie. After another glass of wine, he plastered a smile to his face and got to his feet, brushing stray garlic breadcrumbs onto the floor. "As lovely as that was, I feel it's given me a touch of heartburn." He patted the front of his chest and made a face. "If you don't mind, I'll just pop out for a walk and see if some exercise might help settle it."

Anne placed her plate back onto the food tray. "Oh? Are you sure? I've probably got some Rennies in my bag somewhere, if you need them?"

Hugh was already pulling on his overcoat and slipping his feet back into his shoes. "Maybe when I get back," he replied, edging towards the door. "Some fresh air will probably do the trick. Do you want me to bring anything back? Maybe another bottle of wine?"

Anne plucked her wine glass from the bedside table. "Not for me. I'll just finish this and maybe have a bath while you're out."

Once outside in the hotel corridor, Hugh let the smile slip. He didn't like lying to Anne, but it wasn't a complete untruth. He did have some discomfort, akin to indigestion, but he knew it was more to do with the anxiety that had crippled him over the last few days than anything he'd eaten. Stomach tying itself in knots, he took the lift down to the ground floor.

The main reason he'd wanted to get outside was to call Nicki. *Again*. He'd already left a message on her voicemail that afternoon — once he'd discovered the truth about the date — but she had yet to call him back. He hadn't gone into any detail in the message, wanting to tell her face to face, fully conscious that their discussion earlier about Keeble and the note on his windscreen would have worried her enough. The last thing he wanted to do was cause her any further anxiety, but he needed to tell her what he'd managed to find out — the relevance of it, or at least his connection to it.

As he walked, his earlier concern for his own safety had lessened a little — which, of course, could also be the effects of the red wine. Who in their right mind would want to kill him? It might have been his investigation, but he had no control over what happened in the courtroom, much less the jury room. Once they were locked away to consider their verdict, the jury were on their own.

*They* were the ones who had convicted Wesley Barton, not Hugh Webster.

Buoyed with the feeling that he was being overdramatic, he turned towards the town. If there *was* anyone following him — anyone out here right now, watching him — then let them show themselves and be done with it. His patience was wearing thin. Pulling his phone out, he scrolled down to Nicki's number and tapped the screen. The call went once again to voicemail — so this time he left a longer message, detailing exactly what he'd managed to find out.

If Hugh had taken the time to look over his shoulder as he walked, looking into the dark recesses of the street behind, he might have noticed a movement in the shadows.

He wasn't alone.

\* \* \*

*Bury St Edmunds Police Station*

"I know it sounds incredible — but I'm inclined to believe him." Jeremy Frost's tone was urgent but to the point. "What do you think?"

Nicki cast her eyes back to her computer screen, where a copy of the list from Mark Keeble's wall was still centre stage. *The list.*

"Colin Hedges is the only name on the list that's still alive — as far as we know," she replied. Nicki had had to divulge the existence of the list once Jeremy had told her about Hedges' visit that morning. She'd sworn him to secrecy but was fully aware how the media operated — friend or no friend.

"I wasn't aware of the list until you told me, but Hedges was quite insistent that several members of a jury he sat on in 2005 had died in suspicious circumstances."

"Well, it's more than several," grimaced Nicki. "Do you know where he is now?"

"He told me he was staying in the area but was quite cagey about his exact whereabouts, understandably. He gave me his mobile number, but it's been switched off."

"Can you give it to me, and I'll keep trying? We really do need to locate him." Nicki reached for a pen and quickly jotted the number down as Jeremy reeled it off. "And he definitely mentioned Jacob Towers, Aaron Nash and Ramsay O'Donoghue?"

"He did. And Mark Keeble, too — the detective found down in Hastings on Friday night. He saw them all in the news; he's understandably worried for his own safety."

"And so he should be. I'll keep calling him. Thanks, Jeremy — I owe you."

Nicki hung up and immediately dialled Colin Hedges' number. Frustratingly, it went straight to voicemail. After leaving a brief message to ring her back urgently, she then returned her father's call. His first brief message hadn't told her much, but she noted that he'd since left another, much longer message.

She bit her lip as the call connected, and her father's deep tone filled her ear.

"Nicki — I need to speak to you. Call me back when you get the chance." There was a lengthy pause, and Nicki could imagine her father wrestling with what to say next. Then it all came out at once. "I found the date — it's one of my cases. My last ever case, to be precise. Man by the name of Wesley Barton. Convicted of conspiracy to commit robbery. The two men in the news — Jacob Towers and Aaron Nash — they're both connected to Barton's court case. Ramsay O'Donoghue and Mark Keeble, too. O'Donoghue was the judge, and Keeble was my second in command. Your two men were on the jury. On 15 August 2005, Wesley Barton was sentenced to life. Call me back."

The call ended and Nicki sat, open-mouthed, at what she'd just heard. Her office door flew open, and DS Carter blustered in. "Sorry for barging in, boss, but you need to hear this."

Nicki pushed thoughts of Colin Hedges and her father to one side. "What's happened?"

"I've been looking into that date again, and although nothing particularly notable happened in the capital on that day, something a bit later on did catch my eye."

Interest piqued, her heart rate began to gather pace. "Tell me."

"In November 2005, an inmate at HMP Westland was murdered in the prison kitchen. And seven teeth were removed."

"Do we know the name of this inmate?" Nicki was already halfway out of her seat, having a feeling she knew what was coming.

"Wesley. Wesley Barton."

# CHAPTER THIRTY-ONE

*West Suffolk Hospital, Bury St Edmunds*

Leaving the hospital through the ED entrance, Matt felt the cool air hit his face. Hospitals were always warm, and the maternity ward had been no different, so to finally breathe in something fresher was extremely welcome. As he took in a gulp, he couldn't help but grin.

*I'm a dad.*

Little baby Louis had eventually put in an appearance that afternoon. If pushed, Matt would describe the experience as one of the most terrifying of his life — but at the same time exhilarating, something akin to a rollercoaster.

Danni had clung to his hand so tightly towards the end that he still bore the marks where her nails had broken the skin. And then had come the screaming. He hadn't been prepared for quite how vocal she could be.

And then there was the language she'd used.

But when it was finally over, he'd watched her face transform from bone-shaking pain to one of unadulterated love in a split second. Mother nature was truly amazing.

Taking another deep breath, he crossed the road towards the hospital car park. He had no idea how much the parking was going to cost him, but neither did he care. Nothing could possibly dampen how he felt right now.

*I'm a dad. I'm really a dad!*

Danni had told him to go home and get some sleep, and Matt hadn't needed telling twice. He was well aware it was likely to be the last good night's sleep he got for a while, certainly if the stories he'd heard were true. But now he was outside in the fresh air, he didn't feel like going home and going to bed just yet.

Just as he reached the pay station, he had a change of heart. What he wanted right now, more than falling into bed and getting an uninterrupted night's sleep, was a pint.

Just the one.

Or maybe two.

Mind made up, he carried on walking through the car park and out the other side, pulling out his phone as he crossed the main road heading into town.

"Dunc? You fancy a pint?"

\* \* \*

*Bury St Edmunds Town Centre*

Benedict Thatcher was well practised in becoming invisible. You didn't operate in the murky depths of the underworld without knowing how to blend in. And it was easier than most people thought.

On the whole, the general public weren't very observant. Take witnesses to a crime, for example — there could be five witnesses, and each would remember something different. Hair colour changed from blonde to brown, eyes from blue to grey, height from tall to short. Eyewitness testimony often wasn't all it was cracked up to be.

Although he knew his footsteps were soundless, already swallowed whole by the dark, he kept out of earshot as best he could. He didn't want to make a rookie mistake at this late stage of the game, scuffing his shoes on some wayward gravel, or stepping onto a scattering of broken glass. The air was warm and still, meaning sound would travel. And tonight needed to go like clockwork — for it was now or never; the deed *had* to be done.

The town was busy with the Spring fair in the Abbey Gardens. He weighed up the need to keep away from the crowds with the knowledge that more densely populated areas sometimes offered more of a smokescreen than a deserted street ever could. It was a fine line.

Leaving the hotel behind, he noted that the man in front seemed unconcerned as to his personal safety. Not once did he look over his shoulder, not once did he check his stride. Benedict swallowed the dry laugh in his throat as he thrust his hands inside his pockets, feeling the cool handle of the knife in his grasp. An unsuspecting target would make it all the easier.

\* \* \*

*Bury St Edmunds Town Centre*

Colin Hedges jogged across the road, unsure of where he was heading. It was too late to drive home now, even if he'd wanted to. It was dark and he was shattered — with only a few fitful hours' sleep in the lay-by last night, he felt dead on his feet. The man wasn't going to give up, he'd proved that already. The problem would only follow Colin home, and then maybe put Alice at risk — perhaps even Archie.

No, he needed to face it — and end it.

And it had to be ended *tonight*.

After visiting the newspaper offices that morning, he'd found himself wandering aimlessly through the unfamiliar streets, wasting a few hours in the middle of the day in a pub, picking at a plate of chicken and chips. He'd periodically switched his phone on during the afternoon, hoping to have heard back from the journalist — but there were no messages.

The reporter had seemed genuinely interested in the story, but Colin wondered if that was all the man saw it as — *a story*. It sounded so far-fetched. When he explained how Keeble, a serving Metropolitan Police officer, had attempted to bribe him that hot summer's afternoon back in the summer of 2005, he'd watched the reporter's eyebrows hitch higher and higher as the story progressed.

The reporter had then asked the question Colin had been expecting.

"Why didn't you say anything at the time, Mr Hedges? Report what this man Keeble had attempted to do? He was committing a crime, after all."

It was a question Colin had asked himself multiple times over the years. Why hadn't he done just that? Bribery by a police officer had to be up there with the most serious of offences, undermining the very cornerstone of the English legal system.

*So why didn't I?*

Colin buried his hands in his pockets and carried on up the street. He knew exactly why he hadn't said anything: Colin Hedges was a spineless runt of a man and always had been. He hadn't wanted to do jury service in the first place but had been unable to get himself out of it. His marriage had been falling apart for a while, his job as an electrician rapidly going the same way, and his debts were rising with very little prospect of improving. The easy option would have been to take the detective's money, but Colin Hedges wasn't renowned for taking the easy option.

It didn't help that he'd had enough weed on him to attract a possession charge, maybe even an intent to supply. Keeble had somehow known this and targeted him accordingly. Before leaving the café, Keeble had told him in no uncertain terms that his drug use would be common knowledge by the end of the week. Goodbye, marriage. And goodbye, job.

So, Colin Hedges had done what Colin Hedges did best — he stuck his head in the sand and pretended it wasn't happening.

It was a decision that had plagued him for the next fourteen years — and now it had come back to bite him.

He'd recognised the names instantly. There was something about being cooped up with eleven other people in a small, stuffy jury room for three weeks — you saw more of them than your own family. By the end of the trial, they were all on first-name terms and had a detailed account of everyone's work history, the names of their children, favourite holiday destinations, and even knew the way they preferred their coffee in the morning.

He'd gelled with Jacob Towers from the very first day; they'd spoken about graphic design and their mutual love of motorbikes. Aaron Nash had sat next to him on the jury panel, but it had taken a little longer for the man to open up. He was a quiet man, secretive even, but he was likeable enough and Colin eventually learned he was a builder by trade and, like Colin, supported Chelsea Football Club.

And everyone remembered Ramsay O'Donoghue.

With the internet the way it was, it didn't take long for Colin to find out the fates of the others.

He knew how incredible it all sounded, watching as the reporter methodically wrote down the pertinent details in almost total silence. Things like this didn't happen outside Hollywood.

Except they did.

And it had.

Without the need for Bruce Willis or Jason Statham to drop in.

When he'd mentioned Jacob Towers and Aaron Nash, the reporter's eyes had sparked with a degree of interest — but was it enough? The man had simply said he would need to do his own research, check out the story and get back in touch for a follow-up interview. And that had been that.

Colin didn't hold out much hope of getting a call back tonight. And certainly not in time.

If he was right, and he had no reason to suspect he wasn't, then he was the only surviving member of the 2005 jury. A shiver ran up the length of his spine as realisation hit. The killer was here in the town — the note and subsequent text messages had been explicit enough. Back in the comfort and safety of his own front room, Colin had welcomed the chance to come face to face with the man who'd tormented him for fourteen years, to finally stop this whole surreal pantomime once and for all.

But now he was here, all such bravado dissolved into the deepening night.

\* \* \*

*Bury St Edmunds Town Centre*

After spending much of the day in the garage, repeatedly thumping the punching bag until his hands had gone numb, Adrian Browning had hopped on the early evening bus into town. Knowing he had to do the task tonight had put him on edge, although the energy drinks and two joints wouldn't have helped either.

He didn't much fancy spending another night in the cells, so he'd avoided the pubs, which were full of drinkers enjoying the good weather. He'd circled the town on foot, buying a couple of cans of cheap lager from the shop and downing them in the Abbey Gardens as the light began to fade. Several people had thrown him disapproving looks, but a snarl followed by a string of expletives had soon sent them on their way.

The evening was warm, so he didn't really need the over-coat he'd pulled on, and he was already starting to feel the sweat build up beneath it as he lengthened his stride. But the coat was necessary tonight.

Hands thrust into his pockets, he felt his fingers close around the handle of the blade. He wasn't usually one for carrying a knife; only a special kind of idiot tooled up with a blade these days — it was nothing less than a sure-fire ticket to a stretch inside. But tonight, he had no choice. He wasn't one for firearms, that was a whole new level of stupidity.

Pulling his hands from his pockets just long enough to light up a hand-rolled cigarette, he swung a sharp left, heading down a side street. He needed to keep away from people tonight; he couldn't afford to get into another fight and be lifted by the coppers, not before he managed to take the man out, anyway.

What happened afterwards was fair game.

Fingers circling the knife once more, he put his head down and continued walking.

# CHAPTER THIRTY-TWO

*Bury St Edmunds Police Station*

"On 15 August 2005, at Blackfriars Crown Court, Wesley Barton was sentenced to life for conspiracy to commit robbery." Roy tapped the screen of his computer monitor. "His Honour Judge Ramsay O'Donoghue was presiding. Then, some three months later, Barton is killed in the prison kitchen at HMP Westland. Two inmates were charged and later convicted of his murder."

"Did anything come out at trial?" queried Nicki, her mind racing. "Why they did it? Why was Barton targeted?"

"They never said," replied Roy, sighing. "Pleaded guilty, so there was never a trial."

Nicki had played her father's voicemail three times now and played it again for Roy and DS Fox to hear.

"So, we have four victims connected to that original case — Wesley Barton." Fox went to stand by the first whiteboard. "Towers and Nash were on the jury. O'Donoghue was the trial judge. And Keeble was one of the SIOs. So, what's the betting these other names are connected too?" Fox gestured towards the whiteboard containing the nine additional names from Mark Keeble's list.

"More jury members?" volunteered Roy.

"Could be." Nicki then recounted her conversation with Jeremy Frost. "Colin Hedges was definitely a jury member, but he appears to be the only one from the list still alive. We need to find him." She crossed to the bank of whiteboards and tacked Hedges' mobile number up. "Keep trying him. In the meantime, I need to get some bodies on the streets to locate my dad."

"You think he's in trouble?" Fox flashed across a look of concern.

Nicki swallowed, her mouth curiously dry. "I honestly don't know. But he received a note with the date 15 August 2005 on it — pinned beneath his windscreen wiper the day before Mark Keeble was killed. And now . . ." She swallowed again, feeling the panic start to rise. "And now he's gone missing."

Fox immediately sprang into action. "Roy, you concentrate on getting hold of Colin Hedges. Nicki, go back to your office and get yourself a cup of something strong, the stronger the better. I'll go make a few calls and see if we can't flood the streets with bodies." As he was about to dash from the room, he stopped and gave Nicki a reassuring look. "We've got this, OK? We'll find him."

* * *

*Bury St Edmunds Town Centre*

Heart rate increasing, Colin Hedges rounded a corner and was faced with another darkened street. He had no idea where he was going, but equally knew he needed to be around people. No one would kill another person in front of witnesses, would they?

Glancing back over his shoulder, he briefly wondered who might be lurking in the shadows already. He'd had the feeling of being followed all day but there was never anyone there when he checked.

Making his way towards what he hoped was the town centre, he considered going directly to the police. If the reporter couldn't, or wouldn't, help him — and the lack of contact that afternoon suggested just that — maybe the police would? After switching his phone on again, he noted a brief message from a Detective Inspector Hardcastle. The temptation to return the call was almost too much to resist — but a split second later a scornful laugh choked in his throat.

Keeble had been a police officer, hadn't he? A detective inspector, no less. That hadn't stopped him attempting to bribe him and the rest of the jury — for Colin was sure that he wasn't the only one Keeble had approached with his brown envelope. So who could say how far up the tree the rot went? For all Colin knew, it went all the way up to the very top. He couldn't very well start making accusations about bent coppers and then expect them to fall over backwards to protect him.

He wasn't daft — he knew how the world worked.

Just as he was considering his options, thinking maybe another pub or a guest house for the night would be a better idea than the lay-by again — he heard a sound coming from behind him.

He wasn't alone.

* * *

*Crown Street, Bury St Edmunds*

"Congratulations, mate." Duncan slapped Matt on the back as they headed along Crown Street. "Welcome to fatherhood. Otherwise known as sleep deprivation and bankruptcy."

"Cheers — I think." Matt gestured ahead of them. "You have any preference as to where we go? I'm knackered, so the closer the better."

"How about the Dog and Partridge? Although it's after ten, you might be lucky — they might rustle up some food for you, if you ask nicely."

"Suits me."

As they headed along the pavement, Matt already thinking about a pint of beer and maybe a serving of shepherd's pie if one was still on offer, they found themselves looking up at the four-storey building that had sparked Operation Jackdaw.

Duncan checked his stride. "Doesn't bear thinking about, does it? Falling all that way and ending up on one of those spikes?" He gestured towards the railings as they approached. "And to look at it now, you'd never know anything had happened."

Matt slowed a little as he passed the building's front door. "I wonder if they'll struggle to sell it now, given what went on? Or maybe it adds to the attraction in some macabre way?"

"No idea, mate, but it's well out of my price range, I know that much."

They carried on walking, and as the pub came into view, Matt tapped his colleague on the arm as his gaze narrowed. "Dunc? You see what I see?"

Duncan followed his fellow detective's line of sight. "Well, well, well. What do we have here, then?"

Matt sped up a little, not taking his eyes off the back of Adrian Browning, who was some distance ahead of them. "Correct me if I'm wrong, but it's not often our friend Mr Browning walks straight past a pub, is it?"

"Indeed it's not," agreed Duncan, as they watched Adrian shoot past the door of the Dog and Partridge. "And it's a warm night to be wearing that overcoat, don't you think? Where the hell do you think he's off to?"

"Wherever it is, I doubt it's a knitting club. Bloke was only released from the cells yesterday morning, expressly told to keep his nose out of trouble. And he's not hanging about, either."

Duncan's eyebrows arched as he matched his colleague's stride. "You think he might be looking for trouble?"

"When isn't he?" Matt cast a longing look inside the windows of the Dog and Partridge as they passed it by. "There's something about him that's making me twitch. Let's see where he goes."

Before Duncan could argue otherwise, Matt strode after the rapidly disappearing figure of Adrian Browning.

\* \* \*

*Bury St Edmunds Town Centre*

Despite the bravado with which he'd left the hotel room, and the warming red wine still circulating his bloodstream, Hugh felt the hairs on the back of his neck prickle.

Someone was following him.

In his haste to get away from the hotel, he'd inadvertently turned the wrong way down a small side street and was now heading away from the town centre.

While sitting down for a pleasant lunch with Anne and Dean in the cathedral café, they'd noticed the Spring fair in the Abbey Gardens, the sound of children's laughter and delightful screams carrying on the breeze as they twirled around in the waltzer or whizzed down the helter-skelter.

Hugh had initially wondered if it would resurrect too many painful memories for them all, but Anne and Dean had taken it in their stride. Dean had even remarked on how good it was for the town to put on such a large event for the public to enjoy. But Hugh also noted that his son didn't seem to want to hang around for too long.

The more he walked, the more Hugh heard the sound of the children's laughter waning, and it didn't take long for him to be completely alone with just his overactive imagination for company, although he was sure he wasn't imagining the second set of footsteps behind him.

Although desk bound for the final few years of his career — the reward for hard work and promotion — he knew when someone was close by. He contemplated his next move.

He could obviously start running, although it was unlikely to take him far. The only form of exercise he undertook these days was an occasional round of golf, and nine holes at the local course didn't usually require anything quicker than a slow stroll.

Maybe he should call out, shout at the top of his voice to attract attention. But what would that achieve? In today's modern world, the public didn't generally want to get involved, preferring to shut themselves away behind their net curtains where it was safe.

The other remaining choice was to turn around and fight — get the first punch in, so to speak.

But that wasn't the most enticing option, either. Although Hugh was more than six feet tall and still had a degree of bulk behind him, he was no street fighter.

Out of attractive options, he did the only thing left open to him and quickened his stride. As he did so, he thought about Anne back at the hotel, hoping she was relaxing in the bath surrounded by bubbles with that final glass of wine. Not for the first time, he wondered whether he should have left her at all. Pulling out his phone, he noticed there were two missed calls from Nicki. He hadn't heard it ring, so assumed the signal must have dropped and sent to calls to voicemail.

Before he could ring her back, he felt something blunt jab him in the small of his back.

"Keep walking," the voice said. "Don't turn around, don't make a sound. And put the phone away."

# CHAPTER THIRTY-THREE

*Friars Lane, Bury St Edmunds*

Colin Hedges made a spur-of-the-moment decision and headed down a side street. He knew he was still heading in the wrong direction, away from the town centre rather than towards it — and crucially away from safety — but he didn't want to turn back.

The street he found himself on didn't have the usual lines of parked cars, something that momentarily buoyed him. Surely it would make it more difficult for whoever was following to keep out of sight without vehicles to dodge behind. It was a strange logic, and not one that Colin was totally convinced he wouldn't live to regret.

Or maybe that was the point — he *wouldn't* live. Not for much longer, anyway.

The thought chilled his blood, and he hurried on.

A snatched glance over his shoulder told him that whoever was behind him was easily matching his stride, maybe even making up ground. Another few seconds and he could be on top of him. With his breath catching in his throat, he focused on the road ahead, searching for a way out.

And then he saw it — a dark figure stepping out of the shadows ahead.

"You're a difficult person to track down, Mr Hedges."

Colin almost tripped over his own feet, his legs turning to jelly as ice flooded his veins. His panicked gaze travelled to the man's hands, one containing the unmistakable glint of a knife.

"But you know why I'm here, don't you?"

Colin came to an abrupt halt, knees threatening to buckle. He transferred some of his weight to the balls of his feet, ready to run if needed — although he knew running would be impossible. He wasn't familiar with the streets, so would be on the back foot before he even moved a muscle.

"I'm not sure that I do." Colin figured playing for time was as good a plan as any. He hadn't come prepared, not in the slightest. What had he been thinking? Coming to confront a serial killer with nothing in his pockets other than a lolly stick and a bunch of keys. What had he hoped to achieve with that? Images of Alice and Archie flooded his head once more.

If he could just string the encounter out long enough, someone might see them.

Someone.

*Anyone.*

He was clutching at straws, but it was all he had.

The statement earned a scornful laugh as the man took two steps forward, the knife still visible in his right hand. "Oh, I find that very hard to believe. You're a smart man, Mr Hedges. You must know why I'm here, why I tracked you down. Why I tracked you all down. You must have known that day would come back to haunt you."

"I didn't do anything that day." Colin found confidence from somewhere and stood a little straighter. "What happened wasn't my fault."

"So, you *do* know why I'm here, then?" The man's tone sharpened. "I don't like people who lie to me, Colin."

Colin's stomach tightened, his eyes still trained on the blade in the man's hand. "I might know why you're here, but you're mistaken. It had nothing to do with me. I voted not guilty."

The darkness around them seemed to deepen as the figure took a step forward. He was so close now that Colin could hear the man's ragged breathing and smell his stale breath. He bit his tongue; he had nothing further to say — nothing that might save his life, anyway.

Silence ensued for what seemed like an eternity, but eventually the man continued. "You knew what Keeble was trying to do, what he *did* do. Your sudden moral high ground doesn't absolve you from anything. You knew. You could have reported it. You could have stopped it. But you chose to do nothing. You *chose* to let my father die."

\* \* \*

*HMP Westland*
*November 2005*

Wesley Barton didn't mind working in the prison kitchen. Aside from the library, which many considered to be the most coveted job for an inmate, the kitchen was top of many a prisoner's list.

Westland was a maximum-security establishment that cooked food for the prison from scratch, or near enough. There was talk of prisons in England and Wales adopting a more commercially based food supply, buying in ready-made food for inmates, but the sheer numbers in the prison system was eye-watering. And it was only ever likely to get worse as the years went by. Many a catering company had begun eyeing up the lucrative contracts that might be on offer, but the service had pulled back from the brink before crucially stepping over the edge. The huge number of meals needing to be shipped in to serve the prison population made the whole proposal unworkable. The idea had died a death quicker than a one-hit wonder.

Instead, inmates in HMP Westland were paid to work in the kitchens, providing meals for the rest of the prison. It was a much more cost-effective use of resources, which pleased the pen-pushers. There were some prisons, like Westland, that had their own vegetable gardens, greenhouses and allotments. Some even kept chickens and pigs.

The main reason Wesley liked working in the kitchens, however, was that it made the day go faster. Inside, time often felt like it was going backwards, not forwards, with very little to do to pass the hours. Days merged into each other — then days into weeks, weeks into months. The monotony of prison life could send you mad if you weren't careful.

And Wesley Barton had a lot of time to fill.

*Life.*

The sentence itself wasn't too much of a shock in the end, but Wesley wasn't guilty of the charges that had put him behind bars. Wesley Barton was one of those rare entities inside the prison walls — *he was an innocent man.*

Of course, *everyone* in prison was innocent these days. One of Wesley's favourite films was *The Shawshank Redemption*, and Red — played by Morgan Freeman — summed up prison life perfectly.

"You're gonna fit right in — everyone in here's innocent."

But in Wesley's case it was true. He wasn't responsible for the shitshow that had landed him in here. Other things, yes — he was no angel — but not this.

This was something else entirely.

The Broadacres gang had set him up perfectly. Broadacres was an area of London renowned for organised crime, and Wesley Barton had strayed into their territory one too many times. And then the Hinckley Road heist had happened. It was 2003 and Wesley's finest hour. Said to be the biggest haul since the Brink's-Mat robbery twenty years earlier, Wesley had managed to orchestrate the ransacking of a series of warehouses in a South East London industrial estate.

And he'd got away with it, too.

Once he'd paid off the others involved, his share had been a cool twelve million — mostly in cash, the rest in jewellery. The robbery had put a lot of people's noses out of joint in the criminal underworld, not least those of the Broadacres gang. Hinckley Road was *their* territory, and Wesley had encroached too far over the wrong side of the water.

And gangs like the Broadacres were like elephants — they didn't forget.

So this was their retribution. Dragging Wesley into a crime he had nothing to do with, and then into prison. Each member of the dock knew full well what was happening, but kept their mouths shut and played the game.

The Broadacres robbery had gone wrong from the very outset and had cost a security guard his life. Wesley remembered laughing out loud when his solicitor had given him the details — the whole thing was embarrassing from start to finish. Poorly planned and even more poorly executed, the gang deserved to get caught in the act, every last one of them.

But he hadn't expected to be caught in the crossfire.

Wesley took his punishment on the chin. His legal team repeatedly told him he had grounds for appeal — both on the conviction and the sentence — but he wasn't interested in fighting, and his response probably surprised them as being lukewarm at best. He knew his days were numbered; even if he did manage to get released on appeal, the rest of the gang would be waiting for him. Disrespect needed to be punished, and it needed to be *seen* to be punished. He wouldn't be allowed to just melt back into society, carry on like nothing had happened. There was a bounty on his head now, and his demise wouldn't be pretty.

As silly as it sounded, he was more at risk on the outside than he was locked up in here.

And he had Claire and the kids to think about. Maybe not so much Claire — she'd declared her allegiance elsewhere some time ago — but the kids were something different. Wesley had never classed himself as a family man, for obvious reasons, but his kids meant the world to him — Grace, Georgia and Riley. They were the true innocents in all of this, and if him being on the outside put them in danger, then he would rather spend the rest of his days behind bars, never to see daylight again, if it meant they could be safe.

Riley was a good son. He was fiercely loyal, which at times made him feel both proud and frightened. He was the mirror image of Wesley, something Wesley had recognised early on. He didn't want his son to follow in his footsteps along the path to criminality; he wanted something better for the lad.

Wesley smiled as he made his way towards the kitchens. The stash of cash and jewellery from the Hinckley Road job would see the family right while he was inside, and far beyond. It was an eye-watering sum, and Wesley had worked hard to keep it hidden.

He'd given Riley enough clues as to where to find it; it was now up to the boy to put it to good use.

The prison kitchen was already a hive of activity by the time Wesley arrived. Hot steam filled the air and caught in his throat as he entered.

"Over here, Barton — look lively. You're on spuds this morning."

The instructions came from Leon Fletcher — Fletch to his mates. He was someone Wesley respected. The man was a seasoned prisoner and no longer had an axe to grind. Each inmate's journey was different, completely unique to themselves — but there came a time, to most at least, when they accepted where they were and what they had done and decided to work *with* the system rather than against it. It was especially true of those serving a long sentence; there was little point in continually butting up against those in charge when they weren't going to give you an inch. When that particular reality hit home, acceptance began to take root.

And it made for a much less bumpy ride.

Wesley merely nodded and took his place at the vegetable station. Pulling a plastic cap over his head, he slipped on a pair of disposable gloves and tied an apron around his waist. Those that worked the kitchens were given a level of trust that many others didn't have. Inside the drawers and cupboards were all manner of implements that could be used as weapons. It was a balance of risk for any prison.

Most of the time they got it right — only very occasionally would they get it wrong.

In front of him was a stack of potatoes that needed peeling and then chopping. Picking up a vegetable peeler, Wesley reached for the first potato. It was a mind-numbing job, monotonous and repetitive, but he didn't mind so much. He liked the process, seeing the finished product — be it simple mashed potato or chips. Occasionally, the potatoes would go into something more creative like a casserole, or maybe a Spanish omelette. Given his time again, Wesley often thought he would like to work as a chef, or at least in a restaurant kitchen somewhere. He enjoyed creating things, and he enjoyed food.

The mood in the kitchen was relaxed, but it often depended on the prison officers assigned that day. Wesley had noted that Rutterford and Dunne had kitchen duty that day, and both had a reputation for not taking any nonsense — but if you showed them respect, they would show it back to you. He liked that. You knew where you stood. Consequently, if you behaved yourself and did as you were told, the kitchen was a pleasant place to work.

And today, like most mornings, it didn't take long for the banter to start.

"Your missus been in to see you again lately, Clarkey?" Kevin Rutterford leaned up against one of the kitchen counters.

"Depends on what you mean by his missus," barked another inmate. "He's a right Casanova, that one. Got a whole list on the go." A series of jeers erupted, and Wesley smiled as he carried on peeling the large stack of potatoes. "His wife only makes it in every other month, so he's got to fill his time somehow."

An inmate busy chopping a pile of carrots started chortling to himself. "Let's hope none of them turn up on the same day then, eh? I'd pay to watch that, though."

Paddy Clarke made a face. "Just because you can't get anyone other than your old aunt Ethel to visit you, O'Malley. We can smell the mothballs on you for hours after she's been."

Wesley grinned as he chopped. He'd worked with Paddy and the others many times before, although there were a couple of faces today that he didn't recognise. New blood. They were keeping themselves to themselves on the far side of the kitchen.

Wesley tipped a pile of peeled and chopped potatoes into an industrial-sized saucepan. The kitchen was warm and already a light sheen was forming on his brow. He was doing an honest day's work, and it felt good. He could do his time in here; if this was all he had to contend with, he could adapt and get by.

Picking up the short-edged knife once more, he started peeling another pile of potatoes. The knife felt good in his hand, comfortable. He'd handled many a weapon over the years and was renowned for being an expert in their use — but he always preferred using his fists. He wasn't called Wesley "Rocky" Barton for nothing.

Tipping another pile of peeled and chopped potatoes into the pot, he chuckled at how circumstances had changed him. At home with Claire and the kids, he never lifted a finger in the kitchen, not even to wash up.

"Something funny, Barton?" Rutterford locked eyes with Wesley.

Pulling another bag of potatoes onto the counter, Wesley shook his head. "Not in the slightest. Just enjoying my job."

The next twenty minutes passed by in a haze of steam and good-natured banter. Today's menu of cottage pie was a prison favourite, and once Wesley had finished with the potatoes, he found himself moving across to help the two inmates he was unfamiliar with prepare the mince.

But before the meat hit the frying pan, life changed forever for Wesley Barton.

It was very simple in the end — and maybe not as prolonged or painful as the perpetrator had intended. Rutterford and Dunne had been called away — not an unusual occurrence in itself, HMP Westland was understaffed like so many others up and down the country — but whether it had been orchestrated that way, no one would ever be able to say for sure. But in the time both prison officers were away from the kitchen, one of the inmates at Wesley's workstation had taken a knife and plunged it into Wesley's side, followed by a pan of near-boiling water to the face.

For several seconds, Wesley had remained on his feet, wooden spoon still in hand. Shock subsiding, his legs then crumpled beneath him and sent him crashing to the tiled floor. He'd been stabbed before, and a quick check of his abdomen told him that the knife wound didn't look bad enough to kill him, not yet anyway. Blood had started to seep out into his prison-issue T-shirt, but it wasn't spurting — which had to be a good sign. His face throbbed and was starting to sting.

Not long after hitting the cold floor tiles, he felt two pairs of hands pin him down. Blood was starting to spread around the small of his back, a warm sticky feeling beneath his clothes. But what was more concerning were the two faces now bearing down on him from above.

And the set of rusting pliers.

Before he could wonder how a set of pliers had managed to be smuggled into the prison, another pair of hands wrenched open his mouth. The scream in his throat was smothered as the pliers plunged inside.

Seven teeth were ripped from his gums before reinforcements reached the prison kitchen — but by then it was too late. Before the prison officers could pull Wesley's attackers off him, the knife appeared again and slit his throat.

* * *

With panic threatening to overwhelm him, Colin took a step closer. It was an odd decision to make, stepping closer to a man wielding a knife, but Colin's legs moved independently to the rest of his body. After several shuddering breaths, he finally found his voice.

"What happened to your father couldn't have been foreseen. The jury had nothing to do with that."

Barton paused, as if considering Colin's words. "If you were so sure of my father's innocence, why didn't you try to convince any of your fellow jurors of that? Ten voted guilty. Two not guilty. Just *one* more would have meant a hung jury. It would have made all the difference. My father would never have died."

Colin's legs threatened to buckle, but he planted his feet as wide as he could for stability. This was hardly the place for a discussion on the vagaries of the English legal system, but what else could he say? He couldn't very well tell the man half the jury had been bribed — what would that do to a crazed knifeman hell bent on seeking revenge? Whatever it was, the end wouldn't be pretty.

*I just need to keep him talking.*
*I need time.*
*Time to figure this out.*

# CHAPTER THIRTY-FOUR

*Bury St Edmunds Town Centre*

Despite the warm evening, Hugh had left the hotel wearing an overcoat with a jumper beneath, and even through the thickness of his clothing, he knew a blade when he felt one. During his thirty-year career as a police officer, he'd been fortunate enough never to have been stabbed — not everyone could say that these days — but the feeling was unmistakable, nonetheless.

Ice flooded his veins as his heart rate rocketed.

Maybe he should have run after all.

Somehow, he managed to continue putting one foot in front of the other without tripping over himself in the process. He noted the street he found himself on was home to terraced-style housing, doors opening directly onto the pavement. As the pair of them walked, Hugh willed one of the doors to open, or one of the curtains to twitch. Just some kind of movement. Anything.

But all the doors on the street remained shut, the curtains firmly closed.

Blood pulsated in his ears, as Hugh recalled his assailant's words.

*"Keep walking. Don't turn around. Don't make a sound."*

Despite the panic rising, he focused on the voice itself. There was something about it that resonated with him. He was good at voices, faces not so much. He could walk past someone in the street and have no idea they'd met merely minutes before. But voices? Voices he could do.

Confusion overtook him as realisation suddenly began to dawn.

It couldn't be, *could it?*

"I know you, don't I?" Hugh knew it might be a risk to speak but couldn't help himself. The words had escaped his mouth before common sense had a chance to catch up.

The response was curt and to the point. "I said, don't speak."

And it was then that he knew — knew *exactly* who it was frogmarching him along the street, a sharp blade digging into his back.

"Why?" Given the situation, Hugh's voice was surprisingly calm. "All I want to know is why. I deserve that at least, surely? Why are you doing this to me?"

The man pressed the knife a little harder into Hugh's back. "I *said*," replied Benedict Thatcher, a cold edge to his tone, "*don't speak.*"

\* \* \*

*Friars Lane, Bury St Edmunds*

With his eyes trained on the blade, Colin held his breath. Riley Barton continued to talk, but Colin tuned out the words, his concentration fully focused on the man's right hand. Throat dry, he clenched his teeth while images of Alice and Archie remained fixed in his head. This couldn't be the end, could it? He had so much life still to live. At fifty-eight, life had only just begun — especially as he was now intent on severing all ties with the past, a past that housed Wesley and Riley Barton.

He'd paid his dues many times over, guilt steadily eating away at him as the years passed.

But no more.

Today it stopped.

Hands balled into fists at his side, Colin crouched down lower, in readiness for what was coming. Barton lunged forward, a blood-curdling yell escaping the man's lungs as he did so.

Colin saw the blade coming towards him, but his legs had already turned to stone. Horrified, he watched Barton fly through the air, knocking him from his feet — the weight of the man's body dragging Colin down to the pavement beneath. As they landed, the force squeezed the air from his lungs and his whole world went black.

\* \* \*

*Friars Lane, Bury St Edmunds*

After leaving the Dog and Partridge behind, Matt and Duncan had made up some ground on Adrian Browning. After completely bypassing the pub, Browning had walked to the end of Crown Street, taken a right, and then headed the short distance along Westgate Street until its junction with Friars Lane. All the while, he'd remained focused on the road ahead, not once looking behind him to notice the two police officers on his tail.

"He's up to something, Dunc, I can feel it." Matt kept his voice low. "Shall we call it in?"

Feeling increasingly out of puff with the change in pace, Duncan tried to keep his breath sounds to a minimum — as well as his footsteps. The still night air wasn't making it easy to follow Browning unnoticed. "You think he's following someone?"

"Has to be. Either that or he's meeting someone somewhere. I don't like the way he's kept his hands in his pockets all this time. Makes you wonder what he's got in there."

Browning had momentarily disappeared from view when he'd turned the corner into Friars Lane and, silently, Matt and Duncan broke into a jog, rounding the corner themselves twenty seconds later.

"What the fuck?" Matt sprang forward, breaking into a sprint as soon as he saw Adrian Browning lunging, arm extended. "I think the bastard's got a knife!"

Duncan matched his colleague's speed as the detectives hurtled towards the commotion. The failing light made it difficult to work out exactly what was happening — but there was no mistaking Adrian Browning. And the glint of a knife blade.

"Drop it, Browning!" yelled Matt. "Police!"

Within a split second, Matt and Duncan were onto Browning, each grabbing an arm and pulling him backwards, away from the figure sprawled on the ground.

"Get off me!" roared Browning, twisting beneath the officers' grip. "It's not me, it's him!" With a final, concerted effort to break free, he shoved the detectives far enough away to regain his balance. "He's fucking killing the bloke!"

Matt and Duncan froze, watching as Browning launched himself back towards where the victim of the assault was lying on the ground.

Except there were *two* figures wrestling on the pavement, not one; and the glint of the knife they'd seen earlier wasn't in Adrian Browning's hand at all.

"Fucking hell!" shouted Matt, springing back into action. "He's bloody right!" Before the detective managed to get to Colin Hedges' side, Adrian Browning had already wrenched the man's attacker to his feet and delivered the sweetest, swiftest upper cut to the man's chin.

Riley Barton spun on his feet, knife clattering to the ground from his outstretched hand. With a well-aimed kick, Browning sent the knife skimming across the pavement and into the kerb. A second later, Barton slammed down onto the concrete, out cold.

\* \* \*

Benedict jabbed the blade once more into the small of Hugh Webster's back. "Don't look round, keep walking." His BMW was parked at the end of a no-through road, beneath a bank of trees and out of sight of prying eyes. With no streetlights, they were in near-total darkness.

Hugh Webster did as he was told, barely checking his stride.

Arriving at the car, with one hand still brandishing the knife, Benedict clicked open the boot and gestured towards the cavernous interior.

"In."

Hugh froze and half turned. "You've got to be kidding me."

Benedict held the knife up in front of Hugh's face. "Do I look like I'm joking?" He gestured once more towards the open boot. "Don't make me have to force you."

Hugh took a hurried look around him — even if he shouted, the sound wouldn't carry far. Certainly not enough to reach the nearest house. And running was clearly out of the question; the knife was too close.

Heart thudding, Hugh sat on the edge of the boot. He had no choice — this was really happening. Unless he wanted to die out here on the pavement, he would have to comply. Swinging his legs up and over the side, he slipped his six-foot frame into the cramped space.

Just then, Hugh's mobile began to ring. He knew it would be Nicki. Why didn't he think to turn it onto silent mode? That way he could ring her from the boot of the car. Instead, he froze, his body curled up in the foetal position.

"Give me the phone." Benedict leaned into the boot, jabbing Hugh's overcoat with the knife. "Now."

Hugh reluctantly reached into his pocket and extracted the handset, which Benedict snatched from his hand. Before

Hugh had a chance to say anything more, the lid of the boot came crashing down and secured him in darkness.

* * *

The BMW roared into life and Hugh felt it pull away from the kerb. The boot smelled of petrol and leather and, as Hugh tried to turn in the confined space, his face came up against a plastic fuel can. It made him feel sick.

The car took a sharp turn and then accelerated, Hugh hearing the pitch of the engine change. As he blinked, he tried to peer through the darkness, but there was nothing to see. If only he still had his phone. He mentally kicked himself again for being so naive. Retirement must have dulled his senses more than he'd realised.

He thought of Anne, back at the hotel. She would be wondering where he was. Fear gripped his insides as the car lurched around another corner.

*Anne.*

They had so much life left together to enjoy, this couldn't be the end. He didn't want his life to be snuffed out in the back of a BMW.

It wasn't so much the why that clogged Hugh's thoughts as the BMW hurtled its way to whatever destination they were heading for — it was the *who.*

*Benedict?*

Hugh prided himself in being able to read people, but Benedict Thatcher had managed to outsmart him. The handful of times he'd met the man, he'd been impressed with his quiet and thoughtful demeanour, his ability to keep Nicki on an even keel.

*Nicki.*

Another painful squeeze tore through his heart. This would destroy her, destroy them as a family. And when they had worked so hard to repair the damage after Dean's disappearance — here they were, having it ripped to shreds once again.

Just how much more heartache could his family cope with?

And then there was Dean. The boy had only been back in Hugh's life a matter of weeks, and now it would be over.

As the minutes dragged by, Hugh explored his tiny, dark prison as much as he could, but it only served to confirm that there was no way out. He'd rammed his fists up against the lid of the boot but only succeeded in making his knuckles bleed. And there was no way to punch his foot through the rear light casings — that was something you only saw in movies, not real life.

He was stuck in here.

Until Benedict decided it was time.

Time came sooner than Hugh wanted, feeling the BMW skid to a stop. Several heart-stopping minutes ticked by before the boot was prised open. Hugh peered out of the opening, seeing they were parked beneath a bank of trees. Benedict Thatcher's face loomed closer.

Eyes wide in horror, Hugh watched as Benedict dangled something in front of him. Convinced it was the knife, the man taunting him before lunging forward to slice his throat, Hugh recoiled as far as he could into the depths of the boot.

But then he saw that it wasn't a knife at all.

It was a phone.

# CHAPTER THIRTY-FIVE

*Bury St Edmunds Police Station*
*Tuesday 28 May 2019*

The events of the last thirty-six hours were still sinking in. When Nicki had received the call from Ben, calling on her father's mobile, she hadn't quite known what to believe — or *who* to believe.

"I've got your dad here," had been his opening words. Rapidly followed by, "He needs to speak to you."

When her father's voice had come haltingly onto the line, fear instantly gripped her. She'd already had a call from her mother wondering if Nicki had heard from him — he'd gone out for a walk to settle a bout of indigestion but had failed to return.

*Failed to return.*

Nicki had tried to brush off her mother's concerns, assuring her that Dad would be fine — maybe he'd just bumped into someone, somewhere, and lost track of time. She didn't go on to say that it was the *someone, somewhere* that worried her. Hoping her mother swallowed the lie with the good intent that was behind it, she'd hung up and immediately started to panic.

Was her father going to be the killer's next victim?

So, to hear his voice, even though it was shaky, gave her a rush of emotion that threatened to send her crashing to the floor. She'd had to steady herself before gently lowering into her office chair. Despite the lateness of the hour, she'd refused any suggestion from the team to go home.

"I'm fine," he'd eventually said, sounding anything but. "Benedict has got me. I'm fine."

Ben had then come back on the line to explain.

And what a story it had been.

"I needed to make it look convincing," he'd begun, after explaining that he'd basically abducted the retired detective at knifepoint from the street, then forced him into the boot of the BMW. What he hadn't told Hugh Webster, or his daughter, was that he had actually done the same thing on more than one occasion in the past — but the outcomes had been very different. "You can never tell who might be watching."

After the initial shock had subsided, Nicki discovered that her father was, indeed, fine. Just like he said. Ben had staged the whole thing to save his life.

"Riley Barton was coming after him, Nicki. Because I was dragging my heels and refusing to commit to the job. I had to step in."

Thirty-six hours on, the shock was only just starting to recede. Riley Barton had been taken to hospital with a suspected fractured jaw but discharged less than twenty-four hours later into police custody. He was now in a cell awaiting interview. He'd had two short introductory interviews already that morning and had been surprisingly compliant.

Further details of the murders of thirteen people were slowly making their way to the whiteboards in the incident room. It was clear that each of the twelve jurors had been targeted by Wesley Barton's son in an act of twisted revenge for what he considered to be a miscarriage of justice. Mark Keeble's involvement was less clear, but with Colin Hedges alive and well — due to an unexpected act of bravery on the part of Adrian Browning — the man was helping to fill in the gaps to an extraordinary story.

Bribery.

Corruption.

Murder.

It was a heady combination.

Riley Barton had already insinuated that Keeble had bribed some, if not all, of the 2005 jury. But with only Colin Hedges left alive, this would be difficult, if not impossible, to prove.

Unless they got a confession.

Riley had already admitted giving large sums of cash to Keeble, Jacob Towers and Aaron Nash before they died — fifty thousand pounds each — in a bizarrely twisted attempt to persuade them to take their own lives. Whether he had done the same with the other nine jurors who had died, only time would tell — and maybe they would never know for sure.

Nicki approached the whiteboards in her socks, having kicked off her boots as soon as she'd arrived at the station, where the twelve jurors' names were all printed.

*Declan Hood — RTA 2009*

*Sonia Parish — overdose 2010*

*Grant Fielding — Charing Cross Tube 2011*

*Heidi Butcher — allergic reaction 2012*

*Glenn Palmer — carbon monoxide poisoning 2012*

*Scott Hayward — hanging 2013*

*Danielle Stannard — motorbike accident 2014*

*Victor O'Neill — accidental overdose 2015*

*Grayson Burrows — smoke inhalation and burns 2017*

It would take time to unpick everything, link all the deaths together, but in her heart of hearts Nicki knew that Riley Barton was telling the truth. They were all murdered. And all by his hand. She just needed him to say so on tape.

The reason why he did it was immaterial.

Revenge?

It was a potent emotion, but rarely had Nicki seen it taken to such extremes.

They had yet to question Riley about the teeth. Nicki didn't relish listening to him recounting the whys and wherefores of what led to such barbarity. *If* he chose to talk. She suspected that the extraction of seven teeth from Jacob Towers, Aaron Nash, Mark Keeble and Ramsay O'Donoghue had little relevance beyond the fact that Riley's father had seven teeth pulled out during the prison attack.

Nicki had had a brief conversation with Maeve O'Donoghue — the late judge's wife — who turned out to be a pleasant woman, if a little hard of hearing, which made the phone call all the more difficult. A local family liaison officer would be calling by to offer support and ensure she'd understood the purpose of Nicki's call.

"Adrian Browning was a turn-up." DS Fox's voice dragged Nicki from her thoughts, as he handed around mugs of morning coffee. "I never had him down for a have-a-go hero."

"Me neither," agreed Duncan. "Me and Matt were as surprised as anyone when we saw what he was doing."

Browning had hung around long enough to give an account of his actions that night, but eventually he'd been allowed to go on his way. The punch that had floored Riley Barton and knocked him out must have hurt, but Adrian refused to be checked out by any medical personnel. Edgy and cagey, Matt and Duncan had suspected he hadn't been out that night to perform his Good Samaritan act. Were they really convinced they hadn't seen a knife in his hand?

Matt could have sworn he saw the blade, but by the time the detectives got close enough it seemed to have vanished — the only visible knife being now in Barton's grip. And the only weapon retrieved from the scene was the one Browning then kicked into the gutter — a blade with only Barton's prints on it.

"You think we should have searched him?" Duncan had asked, as Browning slipped away into the night and Riley

Barton was being loaded into the back of an ambulance. "See if he was carrying after all?"

Matt had trained his gaze on the departing Adrian Browning before giving a shrug. "I could have been mistaken. I hate to say it, but we were lucky he was here. We should probably give him the benefit of the doubt."

"But only for tonight, right?"

"Yes, just for tonight."

Browning had given an explanation of sorts — he was meant to be "meeting someone" when he stumbled across Barton setting about Colin Hedges. Neither Matt nor Duncan had wanted to press the man further, and it was unlikely they would get the truth anyway. Whoever Browning was meant to be meeting could very well have had a lucky escape.

Nicki continued hovering by the whiteboards, clutching her steaming mug. "Colin Hedges has been discharged from hospital. Just cuts and bruises and a bang to the head which required observation overnight. He's back at home with his wife, but he's already given us a lot of background on the Wesley Barton trial and Mark Keeble's involvement in it."

"You believe him when he says it was Keeble bribing the jury?" asked Roy, tipping a large quantity of sugar into his drink. "A bent copper behind all this?"

"Initially, no. But a search of Keeble's car has revealed another envelope containing cash — and this time there's an explanatory note along with it." Early yesterday morning, after the events of Sunday night were just starting to become clear, Nicki had taken another call from DS Nigel Brooke from Sussex Police. He'd revealed what they'd found in the boot of Keeble's Jag — the money, and the letter addressed to her father.

The letter had gone some way to explain Keeble's actions.

Nicki faced her team. "Keeble was blackmailed back in 2005 to bribe the jury on behalf of the Broadacres gang. They wanted Wesley Barton convicted at trial and would go to any lengths to make sure it happened. Keeble was on their payroll.

After Barton was convicted, and then murdered in prison, his son — Riley — took it upon himself to exact revenge against those he held responsible, which included Keeble. Keeble's note confirmed what we'd already suspected — that Riley tracked down every member of the jury and either blackmailed them into killing themselves or murdered them himself."

"Why didn't Keeble just report what Barton was doing?" Duncan's face sported a deepening frown. "Or at least tell your dad, boss? Why all the cloak and dagger? Messages and notes?"

It was a question Nicki had asked herself several times but was no nearer to an answer. "I really don't know. And I suspect we'll never know."

"Where did he get the cash from?" enquired Roy. "If he's going around throwing fifty grand at people, that's some serious money."

Nicki tapped the whiteboard bearing Wesley Barton's name. "Barton was the main suspect in a high-value robbery in South East London back in 2003, but no charges were ever brought. Although the final sum was never made public, it is thought that some twenty million pounds might have been stolen. My guess is that he left his ill-gotten gains to his son — and his son put them to use. It's all conjecture, obviously, but the timing fits. We'll have to see what Riley says when he's interviewed again."

"Jon Tierney from the estate agents says he'll come by and identify whether Riley Barton was the man who viewed the Crown Street property multiple times, if needed," added Darcie. "Whether he was the mysterious Samuel Drake. Although I don't think there's much doubt about that now."

Nicki nodded. "Get him in anyway. Just so we can tick that box and place Barton at the crime scene. He might be playing nicely with us at the moment, but there's no telling how long that will last. Especially if a half-decent defence solicitor gets hold of him. Now we have Riley's fingerprints and DNA, these are being checked against samples taken at Crown Street — we should hear more later today."

"Initial reports from the search of Barton's camper van have thrown up some interesting finds." Fox gestured towards his computer screen. "A list, similar to the one found at Mark Keeble's flat, was pinned to the wall. Fifteen names — all twelve jurors plus the judge, Keeble and Detective Superintendent Webster." Fox flashed a concerned look towards Nicki. "Glad your dad's all right. Must have been a hell of an experience."

"You could say that," breathed Nicki. "What else do we have from Barton's van?"

"A significant quantity of burner phones which are all being analysed right now. At least three have already been linked to our victims — I wouldn't be surprised if that increased once they've all been looked at. One of them matches the number given to Patterson's Estate Agents — contact details for Samuel Drake. Another link in the chain. It's thought that Barton has been living in the camper van for some considerable time — touring the country tracking down his victims. The teams re-opening the cases of the other deaths will be looking to see if they can place his van near any of the murder scenes."

"Do you think he's going to cooperate, boss?" Darcie blew across the rim of her mug. "Tell us what happened to each of the victims, I mean. I know we can guess, but is he going to do the decent thing and tell the families what they need to know?"

"I'm not sure. Our line of questioning will mostly be centring on Jacob Towers and Aaron Nash. Plus, the assault on Colin Hedges. Investigations into the deaths of everyone else will be re-opened, but it'll take a while for all that to come together." Nicki paused and sipped her coffee. "But I hope he does the decent thing."

"I'm thinking about poor Denise Towers," continued Darcie. "Even though we believe Jacob didn't jump, and that someone else — Riley Barton — was there with him on the roof, we can't really be sure, can we?"

\* \* \*

Jacob Towers stood as close to the edge as he dared, heart continuing to race. His mind was once again flooded with thoughts of Amber and Zeb, their faces battering his brain incessantly on fast forward, a kaleidoscope of bittersweet memories assaulting him from every angle. He'd tried to do his best by them over the years, or at least he hoped he had. And he prayed they wouldn't think badly of him, of the decisions he'd made. No one was perfect, least of all Jacob Towers.

It all came down to a simple balance between his own life and the lives of those he loved. When it came down to it, there was no choice. He always said he would die for his family — the moment he first set eyes on Denise, the time he first held his children in his arms. His life was nothing in comparison to theirs.

Standing here, some forty feet above the ground, he knew none of that was about to change. His family would be rec-ompensed in the event of his demise; Harvey Mitcham would give them the money and eventually they would all move on with their lives. They wouldn't mourn him for long, not when they learned what he'd done.

His mind flickered away from his family and back to 15 August 2005.

And Wesley Barton.

If he could turn the clock back just for a moment, to the fateful day when he accepted the envelope from DI Keeble, then none of this would be happening. If he'd had the strength of character to stand up to the man, fight for what was right, stick to his principles, then the outcome would have been very different.

It was his own fault — his and everyone else's on that bloody jury.

He took another step closer to the edge.

Although he'd known the end was coming, he hadn't expected it to be today. He glanced up at the clear night sky above, the stars still winking. Was it his imagination or were they shining brighter than usual? A shudder rippled over his skin. It wasn't cold, but there was a keen edge to the air, everything suddenly fresh and crisp. Spring was a time for new birth and new beginnings — but instead he was confronting his own death.

As he stood there, contemplating the end of forty years on this earth, he found all the soul-searching and recriminations that had been racing around inside his head simply melting away. It was as though someone had lifted the burden from his shoulders and made peace with his soul.

Feeling his heart hammering inside his chest, his breath catching in his throat, he realised he couldn't do this; he *wouldn't* do this.

*He didn't want to die.*

"No." The single word came out strong and even. "I won't do it." Jacob took a step back from the edge and jumped down. "I won't do it," he repeated, his jaw set firm while his legs began to shake. "I won't. And you can't make me."

The words sounded different, as if it wasn't really his voice uttering them — but that would be the teeth, or rather, the lack of them. Determination began to multiply as he thrust his shaking hands into his pockets, feeling the sharp edges of his fractured incisors and molars catching his skin. His jaw ached, his gums throbbed, the metallic taste of blood coated his tongue, but all he could think about now was Denise and the children — and how he didn't want to leave them, not like this. What was he thinking? How had he let the man get inside his head like this?

"I think you'll find you have no choice." Riley Barton's voice was steady, but not much more than a whisper. The keen breeze blowing across the roof garden almost snatched the words away as soon as they'd left his mouth. "We've been through this. You have to."

Confidence mounting, Jacob held his ground. "You can't make me do this. I'll take whatever punishment you think I deserve. I'll go to the police myself, confess what I did. I'll own up to the affair to Denise, I'll give you all the money back. Anything. But you can't make me do this."

The man acted quickly, much quicker than Jacob had expected, crossing the distance between them in a split second. With a hand as strong as steel, he grabbed Jacob by the wrist. "I can, and I will," he snarled.

Jacob opened his mouth to reply, trying to twist out of the man's vice-like grip. As he did so, he stumbled backwards and found himself trapped up against the brickwork. The man pounced forward like a wild animal, pushing Jacob further over the edge.

With his back arching, Jacob felt his feet lift high off the ground. Before he could formulate the word "no" once more, his legs rolled over the side, and he was gone.

\* \* \*

*Bury St Edmunds Police Station*
*Tuesday 28 May 2019*

Evidence had begun to trickle in all day. Riley Barton's DNA and fingerprints had been found inside the Crown Street property, crucially on the door wedge found by a downstairs window, and burner phones inside his camper van were proven to have been in touch with Jacob Towers, Aaron Nash and Colin Hedges in recent weeks. Further tests were being undertaken by Sussex Police to try and put him inside Mark Keeble's car — as every contact leaves a trace, the team were hopeful.

A confession from Barton would be great, but she was hopeful that the evidence now stacking up against him would be enough for the CPS to authorise some charges at least.

Contact had been made with the other police forces involved in the investigations into the deaths of the other nine jurors — and Ramsay O'Donoghue, too — and the case seemed to be snowballing by the second. Another unsolved murder investigation was also being linked to Riley Barton — this time a member of the notorious Broadacres gang who was found brutally murdered in 2006. The post-mortem at the time revealed extensive injuries, akin to torture, on almost every inch of his body — and the man's head almost separated from the rest of him with the force of the garrotte around his throat. Could Riley Barton really be behind that, too? The thought made Nicki shudder — the man would have been just a teenager at the time. But it could explain how he managed to get hold of the details of each juror; the Broadacres gang had contacts in useful places, and it wouldn't have been difficult. Again, Nicki suspected they would never truly know.

She'd spoken to Denise Towers and found the woman slowly coming to terms with the realisation that she may not have driven her husband to his death after all. The guilt she felt at her affair — something she assured Nicki was now over — would stay with her for some time, if not the rest of her life, relief and grief irrevocably intertwined.

The detectives interviewing Barton were giving Nicki regular updates. She'd stepped back from conducting the interview herself, content to monitor from the sidelines. The fact that her father could have been another one of Barton's victims still chilled her — if Ben hadn't done what he did, then maybe the outcome could have been very different.

Entering the incident room, she noted that the team were regularly updating the whiteboards as the evidence came in.

"Have you spoken to Rosalyn Nash again, boss?" Darcie turned, marker pen in hand. "She left a message earlier."

Nicki sighed and nodded. "I did. She's doing remarkably well, considering. I had to tell her about Abbie Carpenter — and, similarly, I had to tell Abbie about Rosalyn. As you might expect, they were difficult conversations."

"How did they take it?"

"Surprisingly well. I was expecting fireworks, a lot of shouting and screaming, but what I actually got was quiet acceptance. It could, of course, be the shock talking. Once it all starts to sink in, things might be different." Nicki slipped into a spare chair. "Rosalyn has asked if she can meet them — Abbie and the children. A meeting might be some way off, but it's encouraging."

"I guess they've both lost someone they loved. It might give them some common ground, something to share. It's an odd situation, I grant you, but they could end up becoming friends."

"I think friends might be pushing it, Darcie," commented Fox, adding the latest report from the lab onto the last whiteboard. "I'd settle for them not wanting to scratch each other's eyes out."

Nicki yawned and stretched. "While we wait for more news, who fancies a drink? I'm buying."

# CHAPTER THIRTY-SIX

*The Beer Café, Bury St Edmunds*

"I've never been in here before." Roy accepted his second pint of ale. "It's nice."

Nicki slipped back onto her seat opposite and smiled. "You need to get out more, Roy."

The rest of the team had stayed for just the one drink, each wanting to head back to the station and find out what was happening with Riley Barton before they clocked off for the day. With the custody clock counting down, a decision would need to be made soon. Nicki placed her phone next to her drink, having requested a call the minute the CPS got in touch.

"They do good food here, too, if you're hungry." She glanced at her watch. "Although I think we might be too late for that. And the bar will be closing soon, too. But I can get you a packet of crisps if you want?"

Roy took a long sip of his drink, shaking his head. "No, you're fine. This is just right, thanks."

Nicki cradled her orange and lemonade in her hands, the ice clinking against the side of the glass. She caught the detective sergeant's eye. "How are you doing, Roy? It's been a bit of a baptism of fire since you joined us. And the case up on Hardwick Heath must have been painful for you."

Nicki was all too aware that on Roy's first day joining the team back in November, they'd been flung into the search for Lucas Jackson. There was no gentle introduction to the town or its crimes for the new recruit. Then, not long after that case had come to a conclusion, a body found on Hardwick Heath had had particular poignancy for the young detective sergeant.

Roy placed his pint glass back down on the table. "I'm good, thanks."

"Well, if you ever need to talk about anything, I'm a good sounding board — so I'm told, anyway." She took a sip of her drink. "And anything you say will be strictly between us, of course."

Roy's gaze dropped to the table, a pensive look entering his eyes. "I'm going to meet him, Ellis's dad." The detective sergeant paused and looked up. "He wants to get involved in a suicide prevention charity, and I've said I'll help him."

Nicki found herself nodding. During the Hardwick Heath investigation, Roy had disclosed to her that his childhood friend, Ellis, had killed himself — and Roy had been the one to find him, hanging from a belt in his bedroom.

"I think that's a very brave step," she replied. "Something positive to come out of such a tragedy. I'm sure Ellis's dad will appreciate your input. Have you spoken much?"

Roy picked up his glass again. "A little. I took the plunge and rang him — I knew they still lived in the same house, so I rang the landline. He answered and, well . . ." Roy sipped his beer. "I wasn't sure what to say at first, but we chatted for a while — about this and that — mostly about Ellis, and then he told me about the charity. Strangely, I had been thinking about something like that for a while. And it'll be a good way to remember Ellis."

Nicki clinked her glass against Roy's. "I completely agree. Good for you — good for you both."

They finished their drinks, and Nicki was contemplating whether they had time for another before the café closed, when her mobile sprang into action. Heart in her mouth, she snatched up the handset.

"DI Hardcastle," she replied, getting to her feet. "Any news?" As she stood, empty glass in hand, a broad smile crept onto her face. "That's fantastic. I'll head back and let the team know."

"Good news, I take it?" Roy stood up, already reaching for his jacket. "Riley Barton?"

Nicki nodded as they made their way to the door. "CPS have authorised charges — the murder of Jacob Towers and Mark Keeble. Sussex have confirmed that the lab has found traces of Barton's DNA inside Keeble's car, and on the wire used to garrotte him. We can also charge him with the attempted murder of Colin Hedges. That's enough to get him remanded while the investigation into the other deaths continues."

"Anything that sounds like a confession?"

"He's been talking, yes. The interviewing officers have described him as almost revelling in his actions. There's no doubt in my mind that he killed the whole jury panel — apart from Hedges."

"How on earth did he find out who they were?"

"I guess that might be a question he gets asked once the deaths of the other jurors are fully investigated. Jurors' names are read out in open court at the beginning of the trial, so it's not a huge stretch of the imagination that someone, somewhere might have written them down. If we think the Broadacres gang were behind the initial bribing of the jury, then it's not inconceivable that they kept the details." Nicki thought back to the post-mortem report for the unsolved murder of a Broadacres gang member. "And Barton then extracted that information from one of the gang using the only method he knows — violence."

"And what about the seven teeth?" Roy held the door open, and they both stepped outside. "That still puzzles me."

"And me," concurred Nicki, crossing the road and heading for the station. "But from what Barton has been saying during interview, and some more digging on Graham's part, the Broadacres gang were well-known for using the number seven in their killings and tortures. Seven bullets in the head. Seven fingernails ripped out. Seven stab wounds. It's a bit of a reach but, with Barton's father having seven teeth ripped out in prison when he was murdered, Riley has stuck with it and incorporated it into his killing spree. Or at least some of it — there's no evidence of teeth being extracted in some of the earlier murders. It might be something he takes to prison with him and we never quite learn the truth."

The station was only a short walk away from the café, and while they made their way along Honey Hill, Nicki's phone trilled again. Thinking it would be the CPS again or one of the interviewing detectives, she answered it without looking at the screen.

"DI Hardcastle . . ."

But it wasn't the CPS, or one of the interviewing detectives. It was Dean, and he sounded anxious. Knowing her brother rarely made phone calls, preferring texting, her stomach tightened.

"Dean, what's wrong?"

After a lengthy pause, Dean replied. "I'm going to see them — Larry and Annette. With Ade."

Nicki's eyebrows arched as she continued towards the station. "Oh, I see. When are you going?"

She noted her brother's hesitation on the other end of the line. "First thing tomorrow," he eventually breathed. "Ade's driving."

## THE END

## MESSAGE FROM THE AUTHOR

There are many people I need to thank for helping get the latest DI Nicki Hardcastle book onto the shelves.

First, I must thank Detective Inspector Steve Duncan and Police Sergeant Rebecca McCarthy for once again being on the end of my often weird and vague-sounding questions. Your help is much appreciated, and if there are any remaining procedural inaccuracies, then I can assure you that they are mine and mine alone!

Once again, I have included many real locations in my hometown of Bury St Edmunds — two of which are the Bay Tree Café on St John's Street (well worth a visit!) and the Beer Café at the Greene King brewery. They also do a brilliant tour!

I must also thank my good friend Karen Gedge for lending me her name for inclusion in this book.

Sarah Bezant always deserves a special mention — you have the most amazing hawk eye when it comes to plot holes, typos and missing words. I really appreciate everything you do for me and the books.

And, of course, I must thank everyone involved at my publishers, Joffe Books — and especially Kate Lyall Grant for believing in me and making my writing the best it can be.

And, finally, to you — the readers! Without you, none of these books would ever see the light of day. I thank each and every one of you.

To keep up to date, there are various ways to get in touch:

www.michellekiddauthor.com — join my author newsletter for information on future releases and special offers. I also give away free downloads, content not available anywhere else!

www.facebook.com/michellekiddauthor
X @AuthorKidd
Instagram @michellekiddauthor

# THE JOFFE BOOKS STORY

We began in 2014 when Jasper agreed to publish his mum's much-rejected romance novel and it became a bestseller.

Since then we've grown into the largest independent publisher in the UK. We're extremely proud to publish some of the very best writers in the world, including Joy Ellis, Faith Martin, Caro Ramsay, Helen Forrester, Simon Brett and Robert Goddard. Everyone at Joffe Books loves reading and we never forget that it all begins with the magic of an author telling a story.

We are proud to publish talented first-time authors, as well as established writers whose books we love introducing to a new generation of readers.

We won Trade Publisher of the Year at the Independent Publishing Awards in 2023 and Best Publisher Award in 2024 at the People's Book Prize. We have been shortlisted for Independent Publisher of the Year at the British Book Awards for the last five years, and were shortlisted for the Diversity and Inclusivity Award at the 2022 Independent Publishing Awards. In 2023 we were shortlisted for Publisher of the Year at the RNA Industry Awards, and in 2024 we were shortlisted at the CWA Daggers for the Best Crime and Mystery Publisher.

We built this company with your help, and we love to hear from you, so please email us about absolutely anything bookish at feedback@joffebooks.com.

If you want to receive free books every Friday and hear about all our new releases, join our mailing list here: www.joffebooks.com/freebooks.

And when you tell your friends about us, just remember: it's pronounced Joffe as in coffee or toffee!

www.ingramcontent.com/pod-product-compliance
Ingram Content Group UK Ltd.
Pitfield, Milton Keynes, MK11 3LW, UK
UKHW041051171125
9002UKWH00031B/173